ALSO BY ROSALIND KILKENNY MCLYMONT

Middle Ground

Africa Strictly Business:
The Steady March to Prosperity

The GUYANA Contract

ROSALIND KILKENNY MCLYMONT

The Network Journal Communications Inc.
New York

THE GUYANA CONTRACT

This book is a work of fiction. The characters portrayed are the products of the author's imagination and any resemblance to anyone living or dead is purely coincidental. Actual places and events are used fictitiously.

First printing: June 2015

ISBN: 978-0-578-15916-451995

Published in the United States by
The Network Journal Communications Inc.
39 Broadway, Suite 2430
New York, NY 10006
www.tnj.com

Cover design by:
Brian P. Walker of BW Designs

Printed in the United States of America

To the entering class of 1961
at The Bishops' High School, Georgetown, Guyana.
I will eternally cherish your warm embrace.

If ail ah float watah deh ah batam
(A Guyanese proverb)

Translation: If oil is floating, there's water below
(A little evidence can tell the whole story)

PROLOGUE

Marseille, France
August 1985

Terror tore through the woman's body as the man with ink-black eyes and boil-infested skin dug his thumbs into her shoulders and slammed her into the wall.

The back of her head struck the rough stone wall with a sharp *thwack*. A tornado of white-hot pain swirled behind her eyes.

Blood ran from her head in warm rivulets that tickled her neck and spread across the back of her white blouse.

She was going to die.

She knew it now, just as she knew her name.

For a few moments she tried to determine which was the worse terror.

The certainty of death.

So dark.

So final.

Or a slow torture at the hands of the man whose hot breath scorched her face with a fury not unlike the tornado behind her eyes.

All of a sudden she wanted to laugh.

Imagine! A sliding scale of terror. How droll!

The man saw the flash of amusement in her eyes. Wrathfully, he whipped his forearm across her throat and held it there, trapping her against the wall. His thick brown lips curled back from his teeth in a malevolent sneer as the woman fought for air.

She struggled wildly, instinct her only defense. Her fingers found the soft flesh of the man's forearm and she sank her nails into it. Deep, until they would sink no further. Then, with all the strength she could muster, her frantic gasping suddenly transformed into an angry growl that began in the depths of her throat, she clenched her fists, ripping the flesh apart.

The man felt the fiery bite of the wound. He looked down and saw the blood. He stared at his mutilated flesh, eyes wide, disbelieving, unable to accept what they saw.

Silently, he eased the arm away from the woman's throat and brought it toward his mouth. His movements were slow. Lethargic. To the woman, it was like watching a heroin addict on a high trying to feed himself.

The man seemed transfixed by the crater of hair and flesh and blood on his arm. He slid out his tongue and licked the wound, making a slow trail from one end of the gash to the other, pausing every now and then as if to savor the taste of his blood.

He raised his eyes to the woman's, hooded obsidian orbs that, for the first time since he had caught her, said nothing.

The woman stared back at him, her own eyes mirroring the emptiness of his. She could breathe without a struggle now, and she sucked greedily at the air, all the while recording the glaze in his eyes and the trancelike way he drew his tongue along his bloody wound. Instinctively, she knew. He would kill her when he reached the end of his trail.

That's when the thought crept into her head.

The thought moved cautiously, stealthily, as if it dared not startle her and make her betray its presence.

Run! Now! Right now!

It would take a few seconds for him to react, the thought said. Precious seconds. Enough to get you out into the street. Among people. To freedom.

The woman blinked, but she willed her eyes to remain empty.

2

Someone will come to my assistance, she told herself. Surely my screaming and all the blood on my blouse will draw someone's attention. Surely someone will notice and come to my aid.

Her heart slammed harder and faster against the walls of her chest. Her skin seemed to contract. Every nerve in her body screamed.

Go!

A bloodcurdling scream pierced the air. At that very moment, in that infinitesimal breath of time, when her mind and her body became one in rebellion against death in a nameless, fetid alley, the murderous sound tore through the air.

It was a primal sound that sprang from the man's throat.

He had seen the faint clench of muscles at the base of her throat, the telltale twitch that gave advance warning of movement of some sort.

The man was trained to read such signs.

The woman froze. Before her mind could register what was happening, the man was slamming her against the wall again.

Again her head exploded.

The man brought up his knee with every ounce of force he could summon and jammed it into her groin.

Once.

Twice.

She cried out. Her legs gave way, but she willed her strength to stay. To stand her upright.

She would die with the dignity of resistance.

She stared at him, wanting him to see the scorn in her eyes.

She thought she laughed. She could not tell.

She was beginning to feel light, as though death's imminence were filling her with air, liberating her body from its torturous bondage in the dark, foul-smelling alley into which she had fled, believing it a refuge.

She was drifting now, toward a place beyond all fear, beyond all pain.

She thought she laughed. She could not tell.

She was becoming nothing. She was breaking up and floating away in tiny, formless wisps.

Up, up and awaaaay.

3

From way up high, she heard it.

The sharp click of a blade snapping to attention.

How well she knew that sound. The metallic carnivore made ready to sink its teeth into its prey.

Behind her eyes she saw the knife. It was the defining weapon of the man's ancient clan. Its ivory handle, golden amber from the passage of time, was rubbed smooth and shiny by generations of loving hands.

She saw the feline upcurve of the gray-black steel.

Makes it easy to cut the heart out, the man had breathed into her ear when they had brought her back from her first escape.

He had caressed the knife as if it were a woman.

The second time he had started to show her how easy it was. She could not even remember the pain.

Third will be final, he had whispered then.

She was nothing now.

Again she thought she laughed.

This was third now. Her third and final escape.

A bittersweet victory for the ones she had left behind.

She was almost with the wind, now. Soon she would be free.

The blade would encounter nothing.

"Tabatha!"

I am with the wind.

"Tabatha!"

It was a whisper among the wisps.

"Tabatha! Tabatha!"

The sound of her name.

A voice she knew. Voices she knew. Trying to pull her from the wind.

"It's okay, Tabatha. They can't hurt you any more. We're here now."

"Stay with us, Tabatha. Dear God, please make her stay with us."

"It's over, Tabatha. They've gone. We're here now."

She thought she smiled. She could not tell.

1

August 20, 1986

The train from Rome pulled into Gare de Marseille Saint-Charles just after eight in the morning.

"Reveilles-toi, Mademoiselle. Nous sommes arrivées." *Wake up, Miss. We've arrived.*

Dru felt the insistent tug on her sleeve and opened her eyes. The old woman's face, wrinkled and smiling, was just a few inches from hers.

"Allons-y. On est là." The woman's voice was gentle. She peered into Dru's eyes with amusement. *Let's go. We're here.*

Dru blinked, smiled back, and squinted into the daylight beyond the window. They had shared the compartment all the way from Rome. The woman had spent a month in a small town just outside the city with her daughter and grandchildren, and she had talked about the visit for most of the journey.

"A whole month in beautiful Italy with my beautiful grandchildren," she sighed.

She had been visiting them every year for the past ten years, ever since her first grandchild was born. There were four of them now. Her daughter had married a rich Italian, a man twenty years older than she was.

The woman laughed. It was a full laugh that gathered itself from the bottom of her belly. "And my daughter was not that young when she married, mind you. Yes, he was old. But I had no problem with that at all. Her own father was twenty-five years older than I was. A man like that is comfortable with himself and so he can give more of himself to a woman, much more than someone your age would give."

Of course, they wanted her to live with them. But she wouldn't hear of it. After forty years in the shadow of her husband, now that he was gone she was having the time of her life. She owned the land on which she lived and she grew most of the food she needed. She was in excellent health. Strong, she said with pride. And she pulled up her sleeves and lifted her skirt to show off the firmness of her arms and legs.

Her friends, "those who are still on this earth," were a short walk away from where she lived. And her other children and grandchildren came often to see her.

"Being alone is not the same as being lonely. I am very happy, mademoiselle, because I love and because I know love in return. I hope you will be happy like me in your America when you reach my age." Her eyes shone.

Dru had listened with genuine interest, intrigued as much by the woman's stories as by the way she moved her hands and cocked her head when she spoke, how she puckered her thin lips when her tongue kissed the roof of her mouth and made that tut-tutting sound Europeans made. Her infectious giggles.

And the shadows that scampered between the wrinkles every now and then.

Dru gazed at her, enthralled. *Now there's a woman who has lived!* Then she told the woman about her own life in America, and about the journey she was making across Europe by train. The woman had reacted in a strange way, speaking in a troubled, faraway voice.

"Traveling across Europe, that is a very worthy and exciting thing to do. But I must warn you to be careful. There have always been bad people in the world, but the bad people today are so much more evil."

She had grown silent after that, her face closed, the light in her eyes gone. Dru didn't press her, realizing that the woman was in a private place in her past, where some awful thing refused to die, refused to stop hurting her.

Neither knew when the other fell asleep.

"Merci. Merci beaucoup. J'étais en plein sommeil," Dru said to the woman now, as she stood up and stretched. *I was sound asleep.*

"Pas de quoi, mademoiselle. Tu fais un long trajet. Bonne chance!" *You're welcome, Miss. Your journey is long. Good luck.*

They parted company, embracing tenderly, the way two people do when they know they will never see each other again, but know, also, that at times they will recall this moment when their lives intersected.

It didn't matter that they would not remember each other's name. They would still see each other's face. Still feel the delight of their time together.

⁂

Dru stepped onto the platform and deftly moved aside so as not to block the passengers alighting behind her. She stood still for a long moment, looking around.

Her eyes seemed to pierce every person and every object they fell on.

A smile played at the corners of her mouth, the spillover of an excitement that bubbled up from deep down inside her.

No one was there to meet her. She knew no one in Marseille. She was in a new place at a time in her life when the world was boundless and she was like a bird on a breeze with no destination.

She closed her eyes and inhaled deeply, filling her lungs, expanding the breath until it billowed inside her, all the way up under her shoulder blades. Then she exhaled slowly. She, Drucilla Durane, native of East Flatbush, Caribbean capital of Brooklyn, New York, was now standing on a railway platform in one of Europe's oldest and most famous port cities.

History books tell that Greeks founded Marseille in the sixth century B.C.; that the city had flourished since then as a center of trade. It still is a city where races collide and passions boil.

There had been times when war and destruction were as common as the sunshine in Marseille. No other city in France, Dru thought as she reflected on the city's history, could have produced the fighting song that became the national anthem of France.

She imagined the five hundred volunteers during the French Revolution setting out from Marseille to Paris to bring down the monarchy. She could almost hear their voices, deep and resonant, rousing their compatriots along the way to revolutionary glory with the song known today as "La Marseillaise."

Americans call Marseille "the New Orleans of France." Never having been to New Orleans, Dru could not draw all the parallels. She knew that both were port cities, that both were steeped in French history, and that in both blazed the red-hot soul of the Creole.

And here *she* was now, in this very city.

She yearned to know what it was like, being here. She wanted each of her senses to communicate to her the differences between here and Brooklyn. And between here and Madrid. And Cádiz, and Rome, and Florence, and Venice.

She wanted to distinguish its scents and its sounds. The timbre of its voices. The fall of its feet. The touch of its air on her skin. The taste of its spices.

She recalled the words of the writer Alexandre Dumas, scion of a French marquis and an African slave from Haiti. Dumas had written that Marseille was "the meeting place of the entire world." And indeed, here, at this port on the Mediterranean Sea—"the sea in the middle of the earth"; the dividing line between the north world and the south world and the east world and the west world—was where Europe, Africa, and the Middle East converged.

Opening her eyes, Dru could see that convergence in the people around her. No matter what the Greeks, Italians, Portuguese, and Spanish thought of themselves, this was where the stroke of the tar brush began, she thought.

Or ended, depending on which way you were traveling.

Dru giggled as she stared boldly into the faces of the men, women, and children rushing past her.

Hey, cousin! she said to each of them under her breath.

Chuckling, she picked up her bags and fell in with the crowd as it made its way to the station.

She was twenty-two, traveling alone across Europe on a one-hundred-dollar Eurail Pass, armed with instincts to which she paid serious attention, and a fourth-hand copy of Arthur Frommer's *Europe On 5 Dollars A Day* that she had found in a musty corner of an old musty bookstore in Greenwich Village in New York.

From 1957 when it was first published up until the 1970s, *Europe On 5 Dollars A Day* was the bible of low-budget travelers. Dru had bought a copy on the advice of Susan Palermo, an Italian girl in one of her French classes who crisscrossed Europe every summer. "My mother turned me on to it," Susan had said. "She used to be a hippie and did Europe on the cheap every summer with my dad, right up to the year I was born. Prices have gone up since then, of course—the latest edition is *Europe on $25 a Day*—but the advice and tips in that first edition are still good and many of the places to stay and places to eat are still around, run by the same families even. Europe isn't like America, you know. They build things to last over there."

Susan's mother was now a big-shot executive on Wall Street.

This was Dru's first trip to Europe.

Why Europe?

She must have answered that question a thousand times, it seemed, to skeptical family and friends who had genuinely wished her well once she explained that it would help her get into graduate school. When she had explained it to two of her favorite professors, not only had they cheered her decision but they had also voiced their envy of her courage. And one Thursday, during club hours, she had bumped into the president of the Black Students Organization and told him about the trip.

She remembered that day well, talking to Chalmers Freeman, all excited but still a little guilty about going off to Europe instead of to a Third World country.

She was going to the University of Madrid to bone up on her Spanish so she could follow the courses on Latin America that she planned to take in graduate school, she had told him. And after that she would travel across the continent "just for the experience," she had added, barely able to control her excitement.

But Chalmers, who was entering Yale in the fall on a full scholarship, refused to share her excitement. Instead, he accused her of betraying The Cause.

His words of rebuke were hurtful enough. But it was his tone and his body language that made Dru feel as if she had been slapped.

"If you've got all that money to burn, bourgeois girl, what's wrong with going to Latin America to study Spanish? Better yet, why not major in something that will take you to Africa?" He had spoken in that nasal, aloof tone he reserved for white people. He had drawn himself up to the full measure of his six-foot-eleven frame and looked down at her as if she were a dirty old rag. His chin jutted out, and the corners of his mouth angled down, causing his bottom lip to push up. This was his signature scowl of contempt. It cowed those who were in awe of him.

Chalmers was a good ten years older than she was. She respected his age and his legendary intelligence. She'd even had a stupid crush on him when she was a freshman.

He was an evening student and had a full-time day job for five of the six years he was in college. He finally managed to arrange his working hours so that he could spend his final year as a daytime student. He wanted to take advantage of the wider choice of electives offered in the day, he claimed, and to get to know the tenured professors who knew where all the grant money was and how to get it.

Dru explained to him, her voice cracking with apology, that she was a student of Latin American affairs, and that by being in Spain she could experience for herself the nature of the people who did what they had done to the people of Africa, Latin America, and the Caribbean. She could learn firsthand what it was about Europe that drove its people to subjugate other races and plunder their land and their treasures.

"And, yeah! I also want to see what they built with all that loot from Africa, and what imprint our people may have left on their character," she said, her voice growing more confident. There was also something about Europe that had attracted all those black American writers and singers and political thinkers. She needed to see what that was all about, too, she explained. "You can understand all that, can't you, Chalmers? Our people, our history, they're as much tied up with Europe as with America."

She so wanted his approval.

But he continued to torment her, alternating between berating her and treating her as though she did not exist, until it suddenly dawned on her that his quarrel was not with her going to Europe at all. Rather, bogged down by the responsibilities of a wife, two kids, and the need to find a new job in Connecticut to support them, scholarship or no scholarship, Chalmers was jealous of her freedom.

It was as simple as that. Even if she were going off to Mexico, Chalmers Freeman would have found fault with that, too.

The moment she realized what was going on in Chalmers' mind, she stopped shuffling her feet and avoiding his eyes. One day, as he ranted and raved to her in the Black Students Organization office in the Student Center, she jerked her head up—out of its hang of hurt and shame—looked him straight in the eye for one full minute, and burst out laughing. She spoke no words to him. She just laughed and laughed while he looked at her slack-mouthed, as if he were staring at someone suddenly gone mad.

A few other people were in the office at the time, and all during Chalmers' tirade against her they kept giving her the evil eye, shaking their heads, curling their lips, and making those *unh-unh-unh* sounds to let Chalmers know they were on his side.

One of them had even volunteered that Dru was behaving like a "Negress," like an "Aunt Jemima" who had taken too many "white people" courses and had lost her sense of priorities.

Dru refused to look at any of them. Her eyes remained glued to Chalmers' face as she laughed. Still laughing, she had stalked out of the office and slammed the door.

Walking along the corridors of the Student Center, she felt light, totally in control, as though she had defeated an old and formidable enemy at long last. Never mind that she might have made an enemy for life in the person of Chalmers Freeman. As smart as he was, it wouldn't take him long to figure out—if he hadn't done so already—that she was laughing because she had seen through him, and not because she was high on weed, as he had suggested to his adoring lackeys.

She didn't care what he told them. She comforted herself with her mother's frequent pronouncement that "even the Good Lord had enemies."

Packing her suitcase the night before she left for Europe, she told her anxious parents that plain human instinct was the best protection a person could have in an unknown environment.

"Plain, ordinary instinct is like an eternal state-of-the-art radar system. No technology in the world can match it, neither in speed nor in accuracy," she had declared with the superiority of a brand-new college graduate addressing her high school-educated parents.

Her father had simply given her that poor-fool look and walked out of the room, shaking his head and muttering that he had gotten a raw deal for all the money he had doled out for his only girl-child's college education.

Her mother, on the other hand, was not one for the silent treatment. At Dru's words, she had *hmmphed* with the know-it-allness of a graduate of the school of commonsense and hard knocks, and fired back that instinct might do the warning but that it was God in heaven who did the protecting and Dru had better remember to say her prayers while she was a lone young woman—black at that—riding around in trains in "strange white people's countries."

"Not that you'd be any safer traveling around in America, mind you," her mother had added quickly. "But at least these are *our* white folks. We know them and they know us. We may not get along, but we know what tricks we each got up our sleeves. But over *there*! It's like, you're like..." She had broken off and flung both arms up to the heavens, turning her head from side to side, her mouth hanging open, her eyes wide with dread as she imagined the unspeakable things that could happen to her daughter.

It was the first time in all her twenty-two years under her parents' roof that Dru had seen her mother at a loss for words. Softened, she had climbed down, grudgingly, from her high horse and put her arms around her mother. "I'll be all right, Mom. Don't worry. Not a thing is going to happen to me. Not with you praying for me."

Her mother had sighed and held her tight. "I know, baby, I know. I always knew you'd be traveling off one day. The way you carry on speaking all that French and Spanish." There was pride in her voice. The moment stretched out, then she pushed Dru away, dug into her pocket, and pulled out a fifty-dollar bill. "Here. Your father wants you to have this," she said gruffly, stuffing the money into Dru's hand and looking around to make sure her husband was out of earshot. Not trusting her eyes, she leaned into Dru and whispered, "You know how he gets when he doesn't want you to know how pleased and proud he is."

Even now, in Marseille, Dru still had that fifty-dollar bill. It was folded in four, just as her mother had given it to her, and tucked away in one of the countless slits in her wallet. She had thought of putting it toward her Eurail Pass, but she had changed her mind. She would keep it for the rainy day everyone talked about. It was desperation money.

Italy had been her first stop after Spain. The Eurail Pass would take her through twelve countries in just over two weeks—as far east as Austria, all the way up north to Norway, Sweden, and Denmark, then back down to France, where she would catch a plane in Paris for New York.

Aside from all she had told Chalmers Freeman, she had decided that the trip across Europe was a present to herself for sweating through the three-month certificate course in Spanish language and literature at the University of Madrid.

She had paid for everything herself. All of it. The airfare, the cost of the course, books, rent for the tiny studio on Calle Ayala in New Madrid, and the Eurail Pass itself. She had used the money she had saved from four years of tutoring other undergrads in French and Spanish, and from summer jobs as a counselor in the day camp that City College had set up for the children attending the neighborhood elementary school. The camp was part of the community outreach program black students had demanded, along with open admissions, back in 1969 when they had shut down the campus and forced the president to resign.

Thank God Spain was so cheap.

She absolutely *had* to strengthen her Spanish before she could dream of taking graduate courses in Latin American studies, New York University had told her. They were even giving her a scholarship, but they wanted proof, on paper and verbally, that she was conversant in the language.

The course was tough. Conducted in Spanish. And not New York Spanish. *Castilian.* The difference was like the difference between American English and British English.

Daily, Dru blessed the Spaniards for being smart enough to put the sexiest white man she had ever laid eyes on to teach the first class in the mornings. Had it not been for her mammoth crush on *el profesor* Oricain—which, she regretted, had gotten her nowhere beyond her own lustful dreams—she probably would have flunked out of the course for failing to show up after nights of swilling sangría with a raucous bunch of American students in the *mesones* on and off the Gran Via.

Someone jostled her, yanking her out of her reverie. She had stopped walking and was standing in the middle of the platform.

Self-consciously, she looked around. A few people were staring at her, their faces pinched with curiosity. A few of them looked downright annoyed.

When had she stopped walking and put down her bags? She had been so engrossed in her thoughts that she did not realize she had done so.

They must think I'm crazy.

She entered the station, wrinkling her nose at the pervasive stench of European tobacco. *Does every friggin' one in Europe smoke? Phew!* The odor of their cigarettes hung somewhere between a cigar and an American cigarette. Dru doubted she would ever get used to it.

The penny-pinching wisdom of *Europe on 5 Dollars a Day* was kicking in. Dru found an empty locker, stored her bags—two smart pieces of American Tourister that her parents had given her that year for her twenty-first birthday—and headed out into *Place Victor Hugo*.

She would grab a bite to eat—that café across the street didn't look too bad—do some sightseeing and come back to catch an early afternoon train to Paris.

Standing on the sidewalk, she dug into her shoulder bag, pulled out a small map of Marseille and began to study it.

"Excuse me. Are you lost? May I help you find where you want to go?"

English. A native French speaker with an American accent.

Dru frowned. Barely lifting her head, she followed the trail of the long, lean body standing before her, all the way up to the head of a black man with a low haircut, so short it said "establishment."

I guess black people in France don't wear Afros.

Wordlessly, she dropped her eyes and continued to study the map.

The man did not go away as she hoped he would. He repeated, "Excuse me, Miss. May I help you?"

Dru slowly lifted her head and settled a hooded gaze on the stranger. His skin was a shade or two darker than her own café au lait complexion. He might be in his late twenties. Not too bad-looking.

No Denzel, but no slouch either.

He had a strongish square jaw; deep-set small eyes; full lips; and a hint of a dimple in his chin. There was a birthmark on his left cheek—a raised, jet-black patch of skin the size and shape of a black-eyed pea. The cut of his clothing was definitely European—chocolate brown, snug-on-the-hips, wide-legged trousers; fitted white shirt, open at the neck, belted neatly into the trousers; expensive-looking laced leather shoes. Brown.

The man folded his arms and waited for Dru to speak. The corners of his mouth twitched with amusement under her aloof appraisal.

Dru was not impressed. She had seen good-looking, smartly dressed men before. "No, thank you. I'm not really lost," she replied coolly, her guard firmly in place. She was, after all, in a place no different from the Port Authority Bus Station, Grand Central Terminal, or Penn Station in New York. All types of con artists—of every color and from any country you could name—drifted in and out of port cities. They swarmed around bus and train stations, on the hunt for innocence and starry eyes. They were maggots who could do you in and fade away before you even suspected what was happening.

"What does 'not really' mean? Either you're lost or you aren't," the stranger persisted with a pleasant laugh.

Dru's chin snapped forward. *This guy clearly can't take a hint.*

She deadpanned him, and then she let her face go slack gradually, until it was drained of expression. Still staring at him, she crossed her eyes, and rolled her neck ever so slightly from side to side. This was the graceful, snakelike movement of a belly dancer with attitude. Only hers was no intent to tantalize. No come-hither. This was the Brooklyn visage. Blank. Silent. Eloquent. The signature gesture of that borough's peppery black and Hispanic females who knew they were right even when they were dead wrong.

Oh, sure. Women and girls all across America rolled their necks and crossed their eyes. It meant the same thing everywhere: bored, but downright dangerous if touched. But no one did it quite like the women of Brooklyn—slow, with the wisp of a pout.

The stranger seemed to understand Brooklynese.

His smile collapsed. He held up his hands and took a step back. When he spoke, his voice had a slight edge and his English was more formal. "I am sorry. I mean you no harm. But if you don't mind my saying so, you are a sitting duck for the miscreants around here if you continue to stand with your head in a map. But if you know where you're going, and you're okay, then again, my apologies for the intrusion. Good day."

He stared at her for an instant, inclined his head slightly, then turned and walked away.

Dru stared at his back, her mouth open. *Can you believe this? He's got the nerve to be offended!*

She rolled her neck again, rolling her eyes at the same time. "And a good day to you, too! Thank you for asking!" she called after the stranger with a flick of her wrist. *Yeah! And just keep stepping, Mr. French Slickeroo,* she added under her breath.

She resumed her study of the map, tracing the route to La Canebière, the bustling main street of Marseille that took its name from the hemp that grew there. The locals used the hemp to make rope.

La Canebière—"can of beer," American World War II GIs called it—led to the Vieux Port, where there were supposed to be two huge forts and all sorts of buildings dating back to neoclassical times.

There would be lots to see along the way, Dru was sure. A city's main street was a window to that city's soul. She was confident she would find a restaurant where she could get some bouillabaisse at a reasonable price. The *bouillabaisse* in Marseille was supposed to be the best in France. She had read all about it when she studied French.

A shadow fell across the map and she looked up. He was back. The same man was standing in front of her again.

Dru's eyes narrowed and she opened her mouth to hurl her iciest "get lost." But before she could form the words, the stranger started to speak. The words seemed to tumble from him, his accent at times very American, at times very French.

"Look. I'm no con artist. I was born in Paris, but my parents are American. They are communist and chose to live in France where they felt there was real freedom of thought and speech. They're jazz musicians, too. My mom sings; my father plays the saxophone. They own a small club in Paris. See, here's their picture."

He removed a leather wallet from the inside pocket of his jacket, extracted what looked like a photograph, and thrust it toward Dru.

Dru hesitated, then sighed and rolled her eyes again. She couldn't believe she was even talking to this man. She took the picture anyway, practically snatching it from him.

She studied it. It showed the man, a young woman who resembled him enough to be his twin, and an elderly couple who obviously were their parents. It could not have been taken more than two or three years ago.

"That's my twin sister," the man said, reaching out and touching the face of the young woman in the photograph.

His fingers seemed to linger on her face. Dru thought she heard a slight catch in his throat as he said the words "my twin sister" and she looked up quickly, just in time to see the cloud in his eyes.

He looked down, took two cards from the wallet and handed them to her. Again he spoke before she could say anything.

"Those are my parents' business cards. You can call them right now if you like. There's a phone on the corner. I'll pay for the call myself." He waved to the phone booth at a few steps away. "I have a master's degree in finance, but I wanted to see the world before I settled down," he continued, looking intently at Dru. "So I joined the French navy, to the dismay of my parents, of course. I'm in port for just today. My name is Theron. Theron St. Cyr. And here is my ID."

He removed another card from his jacket pocket. This one was a bit bigger than the business cards. It was laminated and bore what Dru assumed was the seal of the French navy. His picture was on it.

Dru studied the family photo, and the alleged business cards, and his navy ID.

She sighed. *And a goddamn sailor too!*

She looked up into Theron St. Cyr's face, held his gaze for a moment, and then shrugged.

Oh, what the hell! "Okay. I'm going to walk along La Canebière to the Vieux Port and find a place to eat some *bouillabaisse*. You can come if you like," she said.

She made it sound friendly enough, but not overly inviting.

Theron St. Cyr nodded and smiled broadly. "So you know about *bouillabaisse*," he said eagerly as they crossed the street. "I know just the place where you can get a good one. And I'll give you a tour of Le Quartier Noir. I'm sure you would want to see what it can be like for black people in France," he said.

"Le Quartier Noir? You mean there's actually a neighborhood here where all the black people live? I don't recall seeing anything about that in the stuff I read about Marseille."

"Yes, there is a Quartier Noir. And, of course, it wouldn't be listed in the kind of books you would read. It isn't exactly a tourist attraction, you see."

"Will I have time to see it, though? I have an early afternoon train."

"You will have time. I promise."

Theron St. Cyr turned out to be the kind of personal guide that the well heeled would happily dig deep into their pockets to hire. Aromas of palm oil and lamb stew and grilled fish announced their arrival in Le Quartier Noir. Dru stopped several times to stare, not so much at the buildings, but at the people. She guessed that they were immigrants from

North and West Africa. They did not look like Arabs, like the North Africans she had met. These were black-skinned Africans.

She saw no women.

The men were very tall—over six feet, many of them—and lanky, with small, cloudy, deep-set eyes. Many of the older ones wore their native clothing—long, brightly colored robes and pointed, soft white shoes that looked like slippers. Some of them had that familiar empty look on their faces.

A shadow fell across Dru's face. She had seen these streets before, with their conflation of colors all along the sides. And black, blue-black, faces bearing every mark of people who had made friends with time from sitting on the steps and learning how each hour walks, and where it goes and why.

Oh, yes. These streets. These prophets. She had seen them before.

"Makes you think of Harlem, doesn't it?" St. Cyr said, looking at her intently.

"No," Dru replied, shaking her head. "It makes me think of Flatbush. Flatbush, Brooklyn."

They walked in silence for a while, Dru absorbing everything, her heart racing a little with the emotion of being so physically close to an Africanness she had never before experienced.

A man approaching them from the opposite direction caught her attention, a tall, lean man with erect shoulders, dressed all in black. His hair, jet black and shiny, fell in waves to his shoulders. He walked with long, purposeful strides, his hands cutting long swathes forward and back, forward and back, with soldier-like precision.

He seemed to be staring right at Dru. It was not a friendly stare.

Hypnotized, Dru kept her gaze on him as the distance between them shrank. The man looked like a very dark-skinned European. Not a white person with a deep tan. A naturally dark-skinned Caucasian.

He could be North African. Algerian, maybe? There were lots of them around Marseille.

Or maybe he's a gypsy, Dru thought. Back home he would have passed easily for Hispanic.

Now they were close enough to each other for Dru to see that the man's eyes were as black as his hair. Obsidian eyes, Dru thought. She had read that description somewhere. And boils on his face. Ugh! Lots of them.

And yet he was so striking.

Dru's eyes remained as riveted on the stranger's face as his were on hers. Sunlight bounced off the gold chain around his neck.

They were almost abreast of each other when the man suddenly shifted his gaze to St. Cyr. Hatred shot from his eyes then. Hatred so raw that Dru caught her breath and instinctively moved closer to St. Cyr, who slipped his arm around her waist and drew her closer still. Firmly, wordlessly.

Their hips touched. Dru glanced up at him. He was looking directly into the man's eyes. His face was calm, but there was a small smile on his lips that seemed mocking. Not once did his eyes leave the man's face, though Dru was certain that he was aware of her own eyes on him.

No one had broken stride.

These guys know each other, Dru thought. Goosebumps tickled along her arms and spine. She returned her gaze to the stranger. His scowl had deepened. His eyes hurled thunderbolts at St. Cyr and he brushed roughly against him as he passed, muttering something in a language that Dru did not recognize. St. Cyr kept on walking, not saying a word. He kept his arm casually around Dru's waist for several steps, then eased it away.

Dru could not help stopping and turning to watch the man with the obsidian eyes as he strode rapidly away without looking back. "Wow! That was weird!" she exclaimed, still staring at the man's back. "That is one nasty son of a bitch. Do you know him?"

She turned back expectantly to St. Cyr, but he had walked ahead a few paces. Hearing her question, he stopped and waited for her to catch up with him.

"Well? Do you know who he is?" Dru said impatiently as she caught up to him. "He said something to you in a funny language. And he looked at you as if he could kill you. Who is he?"

St. Cyr shoved his hands into his pockets and hoisted his shoulders negligently. "He's just one of those crazies you find in this neighborhood. Forget it."

Dru looked at him quizzically. St. Cyr returned her gaze, but remained mute.

Dru shook her head and sighed. It was obvious that he would not relinquish whatever it was that he was holding back.

She shrugged, annoyed. *Oh, well. It's your problem. I'll be out of here soon.*

Aloud she said, "Well, if you say so. You know these folks better than I do."

"Yes, I do. So come on, let's move on. There's a lot to see yet."

It didn't take long for Dru to become engrossed again in the sights of Le Quartier Noir. She asked many questions and St. Cyr answered them all. More than once his answers showed a sensitivity that gave her pause, and she would glance at him quizzically.

St. Cyr pretended not to notice. His thoughts were still on the man with the black eyes and gold chain. They had crossed paths before.

He hid a smile.

Yeah, you lose again, Ramy, my friend. You can curse me all you want. I still got to her first. This one is mine.

2

Lower Manhattan, New York
August 20, 1986

"Okay, gentlemen, here's what's before us. There's nothing official on The Street yet, but analysts are worried that a crisis is looming for European and American carmakers. Not enough people are buying cars. The Japanese are in the game with blood in their eyes. The Arabs have us by the balls again with their manipulation of oil prices. That's sending gasoline prices through the roof and forcing people to limit their driving, compounding the car sales situation. Detroit is shitting bricks. Anyway, a few government types on both sides of the pond have tuned into what the analysts are thinking and they're not happy at all, to put it mildly. They have every reason not to be. As we all know, auto manufacturing is the heartbeat of the European and American economies, but most especially ours. If plants begin to close, the chain reaction can hurl us into a crevice so deep it will make the Depression look like we merely stumbled into a ditch."

Lawton Pilgrim, CEO of the world-renowned consulting firm Pilgrim, Boone and Associates, paused and let his gaze move slowly around the mirror-bright mahogany conference table. He settled it for a few moments on each of the five faces turned toward him.

The men around the table met his gaze with equanimity. The legendary Pilgrim stare was not meant to intimidate but to embrace, to excite, to challenge.

These men knew this. They were the firm's keenest analytical minds, the innermost circle of an institution whose reach extended into the most hallowed chambers of the world's financial and political power brokers.

Pilgrim Boone was the juggernaut these power brokers unleashed in times like these, when trouble was nothing more than the faintest flicker on their mental radar screens. The firm made sure such flickers faded and died before they became persistent blips. Drawing on its massive network of "associates" in key cities on every continent—even, it was said but never proven, behind the Iron Curtain—the firm delivered reports, studies, forecasts, and recommendations to clients for fees that made the national budgets of most Third World countries look like an inner-city child's allowance.

The men and women who gathered intelligence for Pilgrim Boone were an invisible army operating silently in their respective areas of expertise. Their identities were unknown even to each other. Ostensibly employed elsewhere, they did their work for Pilgrim Boone on the side. They were former and current government officials, university professors, graduate students, union officials, scientists, experts in every industry. Some were even journalists.

Pilgrim Boone's clients never asked how or from where the information delivered to them was gleaned. They simply took each word as gospel and acted accordingly. They benefited from the results of those actions. They were grateful. They were loyal. They slept well.

"A client has asked us to come up with a plan to get auto production lines rolling faster, a way to put more American and European cars, buses, and trucks on the roads. Not just in our own country, but in every corner of the world—North, South, East and West," Pilgrim continued.

"East? Did you say *East*? Are we going to overrun Moscow with Mustangs now? Chevys in Kazakhstan? Surely you jest, Lawton!" Grant Featherhorn's eyes twinkled as he looked around, laughing, to see if anyone else was enjoying his observation as much as he was.

No one was, although they all smiled, including Pilgrim.

Pilgrim ran a very relaxed ship. He understood and encouraged contrarian thinking. He himself, ten miserable years after graduating from Notre Dame, had finally chucked aside the family's proclivity for public service and launched the consulting business with Carter Boone, his best friend in high school and college. He used his family name and clout to snare their first clients and, instead of scrambling for a Washington, D.C., headquarters address, as everyone else in the business seemed to be doing, he looked for space in the Wall Street area.

"I'm going there because money is the root of all power and I want to be near it," he told his father, who had long ceased to be surprised by anything his eldest son did or said.

"Near to which one? Money or power?"

"Both."

"Oh, give it a rest, Lawton. You were born into money and power. You don't have to move an inch to be near either," his father, a U.S. senator from Massachusetts, had said with a yawn. Born working class, his father had married into a wealthy family and had used his wife's fortune and connections to fulfill his political ambitions. "If you want to go wallow in that old pig run then just shut up and do so. Don't try to justify it with grandiose pronouncements about money and power."

It was the most he could expect by way of a blessing from his father. But it was a blessing, nonetheless, he had sighed with relief. He couldn't stand family conflicts.

The mind was not meant to be straitjacketed, was another of Lawton Pilgrim's favorite sayings. Keep it loose and free and you get the best it has to give.

Grant Featherhorn, more fondly known as The Flower Child, took that philosophy to heart. He lit up a joint in his office three times a day—at eight in the morning, which was an hour after he arrived at work; at noon on the dot; and at six in the evening, half an hour before he went down to the town car that chauffeured him between his townhouse in Brooklyn's Park Slope and the firm's headquarters on Water Street. He himself never drove. A phobia since childhood, he would say to his colleagues, waving the subject away without further explanation. And riding the noisy, smelly, sardine-can-like subway was out of the question.

Pilgrim's smile widened at Featherhorn's feigned mockery, deepening the creases in his tanned face.

"You laugh, Grant. But before this century is over, American and Western European cars will be rolling in those very streets. Mark my words," he said amiably.

"Oh, I don't disagree with you at all, Lawton," Featherhorn said. "It just sounds funny, coming from a man your age. So many of your peers are so busy hating Communism that they can't see that whole bloc of the world as a market for Western goods and services. The doddering old farts."

Pilgrim chuckled and ran his fingers through his thick, salt-and-pepper hair.

"Don't forget hearses. Nobody mentions hearses."

The nasal whine of Wilfred Cunningham cut the air. "It's always cars and buses and trucks. But I submit to you that with the structure and discipline of colonial rule removed, the death rate in these newly sovereign nations will skyrocket. Why? Greed and power struggles, followed by the decline of social services. They've already started to kill each other. Hearses, my friends. There's growth in hearses *and* the limousines that trail them."

Cunningham's labyrinthine analyses invariably took him much farther out on the proverbial limb than his colleagues.

"Brilliant timing, Willy," Pilgrim said.

Everyone laughed. Pilgrim was in his fifties and had the aura of a man in his prime. A third-degree black belt in Tae Kwon Do and a vegetarian, he was in better shape and better health than any of his juniors around the table and they knew it.

"Seriously, Willy. We know that every human being is the potential owner of a car, but how many individuals can own a hearse, or would even be interested in owning one, for chrissakes?" Damian Bettencourt, a third-generation Syrian American and the only non-Anglo-Saxon in Pilgrim Boone's Inner Circle, sounded irritated.

"Who's talking about getting people to own hearses? I'm simply saying we should be selling fleets of them to these emerging nations!"

"Oh, stuff it with the hearses, Willy! I still say we made a big mistake when we didn't bring that Japanese kid into the firm. Those old fogies in the boardroom are so anti-Japanese they can't see any advantage in having Japanese on staff. With a project like this we could use some Nipponese minds on our side. Japan is our firm's weakest link, if you ask me," grumbled Tom Briggs.

Briggs was the real brain behind the thesis that had won his college professor a Nobel Prize in economics. He could not prove that the original work was his, so he had seethed in silence when the prize was announced. He suspected, but never tried to confirm it, that it was his girlfriend at the time, now his wife, who had forced the professor to relinquish his coveted chair at the university by setting him up in a masterfully devised sexual harassment trap.

The professor, a married father of three, was given the option of going quietly into retirement or facing a scandal in the press. Briggs's girlfriend-turned-wife never mentioned the matter, except to exclaim, "Well, whaddya know," when Briggs told her about the professor's departure.

During his recruitment interview with Pilgrim, Briggs found himself speaking for the first time of his work on the prize-winning thesis. He spoke without bitterness or self-pity. He was simply recounting the facts of his life. Pilgrim believed him.

"Oh, I don't know if we need to focus that heavily on Japan right now, Tom. If Europe and America go down, Japan will tumble right along with them," said Jocelyn Raeburn.

Raeburn had a way of glaring at everyone as if he expected them to start giggling at his name.

"Everything the Japanese know about manufacturing cars they've stolen from the Europeans, starting with Mitsubishi ripping off the Fiat in 1917. Datsun, which we know as Nissan today, ripped off the Austin in 1930 and did the same to BMW in the 1960s. And it was America—the Pentagon, no less—that gave Japanese car manufacturers a new lease on life in the 1950s when they were in the toilet. Toyota was so broke it wasn't even making cars any more, just trucks. Then the Pentagon decided to order trucks from Toyota. Fifteen hundred, I believe it was. Why? Ah, the way the mind of Washington works! Thank God we're beginning to learn that business and politics *should* mix. It was right after the war. Japan was still weak and the geniuses in D.C. were worried about Communism spreading from North Korea. So they pumped money into the auto industry as part of the plan to shore up the Japanese economy. It began with that order of trucks. The boom came a decade later."

"But that's precisely the point. However they may have started out, there's no stopping them now. The way the Japanese government works hand in hand with industry, I bet you they've already worked out all kinds of strategies to slice into the market," countered Briggs.

"He's right. The Japanese are making small cars and people seem to love them. They make a lot more sense than our gas guzzlers," said Featherhorn.

"It's not Japanese carmakers and the Arabs that we should be worrying about. The Arabs can't keep up this oil thing forever and the word is that there's a lot more oil in Africa than there is in all of the Arabian Peninsula. We've simply got to start selling more cars and trucks and buses to the Third World. Make them our customers no matter what their economic situation is. That's where the population numbers are. We've got to make it so that they not only *have* to buy, but it's also *easy* for them to buy," said Raeburn.

Raeburn's colleagues knew better than to say anything about his first name in his presence. But they took him to task about his refusal to speak to his father because of it. The way Raeburn told it, his father had given in to his lunatic mother who had so craved a daughter that she refused to believe that the baby the nurse brought to her in the hospital was a boy. She named him Jocelyn, a name she said she just had "a thing" for.

"Let it go, J. You've proven your point by becoming the man you are today. It's the man behind the name that counts. Have a heart and talk to the old man, for God's sake," his colleagues would plead.

And, "Goddamn it, J., you won't be a man until you get that monkey off your back."

It was like talking to a brick wall. He had not spoken to his father since his last and most glorious defense-of-manhood fight, when he was in the sixth grade and broke the nose of one of his classmates. He was expelled immediately, but he had swaggered out of the principal's office with his chest sticking out and his head held high. For, as the Little League coach who had intervened in the fight hauled him by the scruff of his neck to the principal's office, he had seen respect in the eyes of his classmates for the first time. Later that night, his father had whipped him with an old leather belt, yelling about the shame and disgrace his firstborn had brought on his household for behaving like a common Irish street brawler and predicting that he would turn out just like his drunken grandfather.

After his parents went to bed, Jocelyn walked out of the house with two stuffed duffel bags and went to live with the same grandfather on the poor side of town. He left a note for his parents saying where he was. They neither called nor went to get him. He knew exactly what they were thinking: he was bad news for his younger siblings, so good riddance. Jocelyn did not care. He loved his grandfather.

"Which brings us back to the task at hand," Pilgrim said somewhat reluctantly but firmly. He enjoyed listening to his young team at play. They were all more than a quarter of a century his junior. He had personally recruited each of them straight out of graduate school. Age had been a key factor in his recruitment policy.

Studiously avoiding the Ivy League, he had sought out young men who were neither softened by privilege nor embittered by want or slight. He wanted graduates who had studied the gamut of social, economic, and political structures, all the isms, past and present, and knew the fallout from each one. He wanted minds as sharp and defiant as those he saw in the emerging nations, minds that did not toe the line of popular thinking, minds that drew no satisfaction from being white and right all the time. The recruits for Pilgrim Boone's team of analysts must be able to see only the brilliance or idiocy of an argument, without being encumbered by distractions like race and color and creed.

"Okay, synthesizer. What do you have?"

Damian Bettencourt leaned forward and spoke in a measured voice.

"Simple. We get the developing countries to rip up their rail lines, we make credit easily available to them to build regular roads, and then we get the auto companies to come up with enticing purchase plans for vehicles—cars, trucks, and buses."

"And hearses," mumbled Cunningham. It was a principled but half-hearted stance for a cause that even he himself had already given up as lost.

The minds around the mahogany table locked silently into Bettencourt's proposed solution. Jackets had long come off and ties loosened. Two bottles of imported water—one still, one sparkling mineral—had been placed with a Hoya crystal glass at each person's place. They had not been touched. Coffee and tea stood at the ready on an antique sideboard. That, too, had not been touched. There was no cigarette smoke, no cigar smoke, no kind of smoke, just five young men slouched in their chairs, staring into space.

Pilgrim rose quietly from his seat at the head of the table and stood at the gleaming plate-glass window overlooking the East River, his hands shoved deep into his pockets, his fingers curled in loose fists.

He smiled to himself as he counted backward from sixty.

He always gave the men exactly one minute. He could almost hear their brains clicking, almost see their inner eyes darting back and forth as scenario after scenario whizzed by as if on the screen of an old microfiche machine. He knew that on the door outside, superimposed by a small magnet on the square of polished brass that announced CONFERENCE ROOM, was another square of steel that read:

BRAINS IN ORBIT
ENTER AT YOUR OWN PERIL

It had been placed there, as usual, by whoever was the last of the five to enter the room. Featherhorn, this time. No one dared enter the room when that sign was up. Not even Lawton's own secretary, Miss Hatherby, a trim, fear-inspiring spinster who had been with him from the time he had started the firm.

Lawton no longer remembered when the sign first appeared and he did not care. It had become a respected practice. He himself dutifully retrieved it from the tiny wall cabinet in the corridor and placed it outside the door when he was the last to arrive.

God, how he loved these men. He felt a thrill of excitement, like a warm current of electricity, tingling through his body. He couldn't wait for what was about to happen.

Zero!

He turned from the window and at that precise moment their thoughts exploded into the open.

"Third World governments will never buy it. Railroads are good for their countries. They're a cheap way to move people and farm produce and they're low maintenance. Those guys will never buy it."

"I second that. The people in power in those countries are well educated and smart, and they're all socialists. They'll see such an idea as a capitalist plot to further enrich the rich nations, not to mention the multinational corporations, 'the bastions of capitalism.' Not that they're wrong about that."

"Oh, I doubt that. Most of these Third World leaders are essentially ordinary city boys enjoying the chance to show off their mastery of the flair and oratory of the European colonials who taught them in school. They know, or care, nothing about business, really. They are true products of the information they were fed by their colonial masters and later by their socialist heroes, both of whom taught them to be contemptuous of business. And that is precisely how they behave. Like civil servants. What did one of their own say about them? That they're 'armchair socialists who have learned to balance a teacup on their knees,' or something like that. Some of them act like they still can't believe they're prime ministers and presidents."

"That was Dr. Eric Williams who said that great line about 'armchair socialists' learning to balance a teacup on their knees, wasn't it? He was the first prime minister of Trinidad and Tobago, the petroleum islands. Now *there* was a man who had no blinders on when it came to capitalism and the games capitalists play. If he were still around we would have a hell of a time trying to sell the Caribbean on the idea of ripping up their railroads."

"But the ones who are there will be suspicious anyway. They know history and won't trust anything coming out of the West. How do we get them to buy into the idea?"

"By appealing to their desire to stay in power until they die, and at the same time convincing them that they're securing the people's welfare. We remind them, subtly, of course, of how nasty an unhappy bourgeoisie can become. Keep driving home the importance of making life comfortable for the bourgeoisie, with cars and good roads to drive on in the city. At the same time, we sell them on the idea of building roads that will link their villages and even their neighboring countries, roads that will make it easy for farmers in their brand-new trucks to drive their produce to the markets in the cities and towns, roads that brand-new, modern buses will drive on to take the people where they want to go, whether they live in the city or in the rural areas. And, best of all, roads to get their children to school on time."

"I can see it now. Nation after nation rallying behind road-building schemes. A road going from, say, Guyana to Brazil and on to Argentina. A Pan-American highway even, linking North, Central, and South America. Any nationalist's dream."

"What about Asia and Africa? You can't rip out the railroads in Africa. Those railroads support all those mining industries. In fact, the same is true in the Caribbean and South America. Even tiny Guyana has its bauxite and manganese, and all that gold and diamonds."

"I don't think Damian is talking about touching the private lines that the mining companies built and maintain on their own. Even if we wanted to, those companies wouldn't let us."

"How do the governments make money in all this? So far, all we're telling them to do is borrow, borrow, borrow and spend, spend, spend. Somebody's bound to raise that issue. Aside from keeping the lumpen proletariat and the bourgeoisie happy, how do they make money for all the social schemes they're talking about? You know, hospitals, schools, housing—all that basic stuff every self-respecting human society needs?"

"Taxes. They can slap all kinds of import taxes on the cars and trucks and buses. Hell, they can even put tolls on the roads."

"Perhaps get the multilateral lenders to throw them some free money, a few grants here and there for going along."

"So who exactly is going to sell them on all this?"

"Why don't we let the clients figure that out? I don't think that's part of our assignment."

"He's right. Christ, they've got to use their own brains at some time."

"True, but you know they'll ask for our ideas on that."

"We've spoiled them. They've become intellectual sluggards."

"That means, gentlemen, that *we* are running the free world."

"Big deal. That knowledge is hardly fungible."

"Running the free world, my ass. The clients tell us when to jump and how high. They can reject what we tell them at any time, and there isn't a damn thing we can do about it."

"Show me precedent."

"So when they ask for our recommendations along those lines…"

"We tell them to make the very same socialists the messengers. It's easy. In each of those regions—Latin America, Asia, the Caribbean, Africa, the Middle East—there's bound to be at least one head of state who thinks he and his country are better than all the others. Single them out and butter them up. Inflate their egos with praise about how well they're running their countries. Get them to feel like they're on equal footing with the big boys. Invite them for tête-à-têtes with the heads of state of the main auto manufacturing countries and throw them the line. They'll bite."

"And all the rest will follow."

"Can we really get away with telling them how well their countries are doing? Surely they know the truth since *they're* the ones running the show."

"You jiggle the numbers a little. It's been done before."

"What if no one bites?"

"You put someone in power who will."

"They'll still need independent parties to help grease the wheels."

"Use local consultants. There's a whole bunch of bright guys out there who can do the job."

Just as suddenly as it had exploded, the room fell silent. Lawton Pilgrim sat up straight. During the debate he had slipped down into his chair, his head on the headrest, eyes closed, his fingers interlocked on his flat stomach. He had followed every word.

He sat up now and spoke. "Any moral issues for American voters? Anything liberals or conservatives can rip apart?"

"Nothing whatsoever. Nobody's killing anybody."

"Or selling arms or pushing dope."

"We're just selling cars and trucks and buses."

"And…"

"Keep a lid on it, Willy. You did your Custer's Last Stand already."

"Keeping American autoworkers employed."

"Power to the people!"

Lawton sighed. "Great! I want each of you to take one aspect of this discussion and give me a written report on it based on what was said today. When I get them back, I want to see the problem defined as perceived by our client and analyzed according to what's real and what's hypothetical. And I want to see the recommendations, defined and analyzed the same way, with names named on all fronts. We'll meet here again at the end of the week to put it all together and go over it again. I know you're all working on other projects, but this one takes priority. Good day, gentlemen."

3

Georgetown, Guyana
August 20, 1986

Nelson Roopnaraine stood on the sidewalk on Lamaha Street and surveyed the rusting carcass of the Morris Mini Minor, wondering how he was going to haul it out of the trench. He needed it to boost the skimpy load of scrap metal he had collected over the last several days.

It was about two in the afternoon and the sun was angry. Those who weren't at work or at school were taking refuge indoors or under their houses. Thick wooden or cement pillars held their homes several feet above the floodwaters when the rainy season came.

Nelson had paid one hundred dollars at Mayor and Town Council for the right to remove the old car, plus an extra twenty to a clerk to make sure the document stamped APPROVED would not disappear on its way from the office in the back. It was that extra twenty that had put him over the top. Stingy old Janairaine Singh had stormed out of the bureau sucking his teeth and cursing to high heaven about whose *rass*—Guyanese for 'ass'—he was going to fix.

That they both had gone after the wreck in the first place was a sign of how bad business was becoming. Scrap was in short supply these days.

Nelson's father complained bitterly every time he checked off the loads that came in. "Every blastid t'ing is plastic, plastic, plastic! Soon ahwe gwan see kyars mek outta plastic! Mark my words!"

And the scrap runs kept netting smaller and smaller loads.

The constant worry that plastic was replacing good, strong metals to the point where even cars made of plastic were imaginable drove old Roopnaraine's blood pressure to heights that would leave him in bed. He advised Nelson to remove the car from the Lamaha before Janairaine Singh got his hands on it for the steel.

"See dat rusty kyar in de Lamaha? Bettah move it out before Jainaraine get 'e han' pun um. Dat ol' kyar full wid scrap," he told Nelson when he could no longer stand the dwindling reserves in the backyard.

The elder Roopnaraine spoke only Guyanese Creole, the earthy patois born of the languages spoken in cultures that had left their imprint on the tiny South American country. That Creole is peppered with influences from the indigenous Indians, European tongues, and the tongues of those whom the Europeans brought in from Africa and Asia to work on their plantations and in their rice paddies and sugar factories.

Nelson's father, a first-generation Guyanese who grew up in a small village on the East Coast, spoke Creole with the distinct accent of an East Indian, rolling his r's and pronouncing his t's and d's as if the tip of his tongue kicked the sounds out from the roof of his mouth. His parents had been brought to Guyana at the turn of the twentieth century to work as indentured servants in the rice paddies and cane fields.

Guyana was British Guiana then.

Roopnaraine Scrap Metal Co., Ltd. was Nelson's father's own creation, built up from a pushcart operation he started when he grew tired of fetching and carrying for Toolsie Persaud Enterprises on Water Street. He had refused to farm rice like his parents and brothers. Instead, he moved to Georgetown to try his hand at "somet'ing else." He would push his cart around the city in the sweltering, five-degrees-north-of-the-Equator heat, calling out in his rich singsong: "Scrrraap aiyan! Scrrraap aiyan!"

At his cry, housewives—or the children sent by their mothers who were too ashamed to be seen hustling for a few pennies—would come running with old pots and pans and broken pieces of this and that. The "scrap aiyurn man," as they called Roopnaraine in their city accent, would select the items with great ceremony, weighing them in his hands and rejecting those that were not pure iron. He would pay for his selections with the big round pennies that went a very long way in those days.

Around three in the afternoon, he and the other scrap iron vendors would make their way to the big Sprostons dock on Lombard Street, near to the sawmills, to sell their load.

The rear of the Sprostons yard and sawmills faced the Demerara River, forming a continuous line of wooden docks. Once his business was done, Roopnaraine would stand on the Sprostons dock and watch the men unload the ships berthed along the riverfront or load them up with lumber and scrap. Sometimes he was lucky enough to see one of the huge vessels sailing down the river, sounding its horn in short, sharp blasts to announce its safe arrival from across the Atlantic.

And as he watched the men and the ships and their comings and goings, he would feel a warm thrill throughout his dark, bony frame, and he would thank God once again that he was part of this commerce without end, which meant his children would always be well housed and clothed and fed and schooled. And his wife would have gold in her teeth and jewelry bought at Portuguese Pawnbrokers Ltd. High-carat gold. With fine filigree work.

The scrap that he and the other vendors sold to Sprostons traveled on these very same ships to steel mills in Europe and America to feed the construction and auto industries in those countries. Sprostons would also sell to local ironmongers, who blasted it and beat it into shoes and other accessories for the horses and donkeys that pulled the wooden carts used to transport everything from people to farm produce. And into simple tools and cooking utensils—coal pots, and the wok-like *karahis* to burn sugar for black cake or to deep-fry pancakes on Shrove Tuesday, *floats* for Wednesday's salt fish, and *pholourie* to sell to school children. And the flat, heavy *tawas* to bake roti and *dhal puri*.

There was no love lost between the ironmongers and the scrap vendors. The vendors refused to sell directly to them because Sprostons paid them more.

"Dem na pay good money like 'Praston," old Roopnaraine explained to Nelson, who sometimes worked the city with his father during school holidays.

By the time Nelson came full-time into the business, after graduating from a technical college in Trinidad and Tobago, his father had already bought four lorries and employed enough drivers to go around the city and out into the outlying districts to collect scrap.

Increasingly, the lorries traveled east along the Atlantic coast, as far as Berbice County, or in the opposite direction to the towns along the west bank of the Demerara River and sometimes across the river to Parika and into Essequibo County. They would be gone for a week or two on these longer trips, but the loads they brought back were growing smaller and smaller.

But the yard on Lombard Street was still buying.

Nelson scratched his head as he contemplated the wreck of the Mini Minor. The car had been sitting in the Lamaha trench for years and was half-covered by muddy water. It had ended up there following a collision with another car and had remained stuck, held fast by the mud. The driver, fortunately, had been thrown from the car before it plunged into the water and had escaped serious injury.

All efforts to pull the wreck from the Lamaha had failed and the Mini Minor soon became Lamaha Street's most commonly used landmark.

"Meet mi pun Lamaha Street by de Mini Mainuh," or, "De house 'bout t'ree doors before yuh reach de Mini Mainuh," or "If yuh pass de Mini Mainuh, yuh pass de place," people would say when giving directions.

As Nelson studied the wreck, a man rode by on a bicycle and called out with a mocking laugh, "Lookin' fo' de murmaid, Roopnaraine?"

The man's laughter trailed behind him as he pedaled away, speeding up in case Nelson decided to chase him, or throw a stone at him. Nelson ignored the taunt.

Five minutes later, a donkey cart came along. The donkey clip-clopped smartly. The iron chains around its belly jangled loudly. The loose boards of the cart clattered. The combined effect was part of the hum and rhythm unique to Georgetown.

The driver of the cart was no more than fourteen. "HOH! HOH! HOH!" he commanded the donkey, pulling hard on the reins to bring the cart to a halt near Nelson. "Mornin', Uncle Nelson," he said with a grin. His white teeth gleamed against his dark skin.

Nelson returned the greeting. "Mornin', Solomon. How come de kyart empty?"

He had known Solomon since he was born. Solomon's family were his neighbors. Patrick Ogle, Solomon's father, operated a transportation service comprising one donkey cart and one dray cart. Solomon, a first-class dunce in school, had been put in charge of the donkey cart. Nelson always thought it was the best thing Patrick could have done. Solomon was a born salesman. He talked his way into such lucrative seasonal and long-term contracts, hauling this and that for the businesses on Water Street, that his father was now contemplating buying a lorry to expand the business.

"Ah jus' going fo' pick up a load o' plantain now. Yuh drap somet'ing in de Lamaha?"

"Nah! Ah jus' tryin' fo' see how ah kyan pull out de ol' kyar."

"Oh-oh!" The second "oh" was almost an octave higher. " 'Cause when I see dis person standin' up so, starin' in de trench, I seh to meself, 'Eh-eh! Dis person like 'e lookin' fo' de murmaid.' Den I see it was you an' I seh, 'Ah hope Uncle Nelson ain' lookin' fo' no murmaid.' Den I seh yuh must be drap somet'ing in de trench. But is only de kyar yuh studyin'." He sounded relieved.

Nelson sighed. "No, Solomon. I ain' lookin' fo' no murmaid. Yuh bettuz guh lang before yuh fahdda seh I got yuh idlin' in de street." Solomon's father was notorious for the close eye he kept on his business. Word of the slightest aberration seemed to reach him by magic.

"Awright, Uncle Nelson." He made a hissing sound out of the side of his mouth and tugged on the reins. The donkey responded instantly, setting off at a trot.

Nelson sighed again and turned his attention back to the rotting vehicle. "Guyanese people! Is only we does believe in stupidness like murmaid," he grumbled.

40

The Lamaha trench, named after the street, is one of the main arteries in Georgetown's grid-iron canal system built by the Dutch in the eighteenth century to drain floodwater from the city. Guyana's coastal plain is seven feet below sea level and Georgetown, sitting smack on the Atlantic Coast, floods easily during the torrential rainy season. The canal system, a network of trenches and gutters, collects most of this water and empties it into the Demerara River, which in turn flows into the Atlantic Ocean.

A shiny blue Ford Cortina slowed and rolled to a stop in front of Nelson's pickup. A man in a white shirt jacket and black, knife-seamed trousers emerged from the driver's side. He approached Nelson with a loud, jocular greeting.

"Wha' happenin', Nello boy? Lookin' fo' de murmaid?"

Nelson recognized the voice. He sucked his teeth without bothering to turn around. "Yuh know, I sick o' hearin''bout dis blastid murmaid! Do I look like a damn fool to you, Compton?" he snarled.

Compton Dalrymple was permanent secretary in the Ministry of Transportation. He and Nelson had been friends since elementary school.

He laughed at Nelson's irritation. "Well, wuh de hell you expect people fo' t'ink wid you stan'in' up like duh, starin' in de trench?"

The mythical mermaid had style. According to the lore, she made a surprise appearance once every few years. All of a sudden, rumors would spread through Georgetown about mermaid sightings. Sometimes she appeared in the Botanical Gardens on Vlissingen Road, sitting on a huge, round, water-lily frond in one of the ponds. Other times she was sighted on the bank of the Lamaha, her tail dipping in the water.

The trench itself had claimed the lives of nine adults and five children over the years and, as a result, the population had endowed it with a spirit of its own, a spirit that was as alluring as it was treacherous. The beautiful mermaid who tended her long black tresses with a tortoiseshell comb as she lured her victims into the water with her soft eyes was the embodiment of that spirit. After an absence of five years, she had been spotted recently on the bank of the Lamaha, near Irving Street.

"Well? What are you doing?" Compton asked, switching to crisply articulated English in that easy manner common to the well educated and the socially privileged.

Nelson responded by indicating the wreck with his chin. Compton looked at the rusty skeleton and burst out laughing again. "Nelson, don't tell me you want to pull out de ol' kyar!"

"That is exactly what I want to do," Nelson said wearily. "Stop laughing, man, and give me some ideas!" He emphasized "ideas" so that it came out "iDAZE."

Compton shook his head slowly. "Boy, I can't help you there at all. You know the Lamaha. Once she brackle somet'ing she ain' loosin' it at all. Why do you think the Mini Minor is still sitting there? Because the Lamaha holding it tight tight!"

"It is still there because nobody has tried to pull it out since it went in," Nelson replied heatedly. "When is the last time you saw somebody trying to get it out? Eh? Tell me! I bet if I get a powerful enough winch I can take it out."

"Awright, awright, man. Tek it easy. Don't go on so, man. Look, lemme see. The only people I know with that kind of winch—one that is working—is that Venezuelan outfit that's building the road to Linden. And I doubt they will lend it to you, not even if you ask to rent it."

"Well that's a start. I didn't even think of them. Bet if I pay one of their workers a small piece I can borrow it for a night."

"You mean the scrap business is so bad, man?"

"If? It squeezin' we balls. And it supposed to get worse. Plastic is king. They're making everything out of it these days."

"Hah! I think you're right about that, boy. Last time I was in Japan with the *Kabaka*, I saw with my own eyes. Cars in factories made out of plastic. Real (he pronounced it "rayle") kyars that drive on the road! Out of plastic!"

Kabaka was one of those African words that flavored the patois spoken in Guyana. It is of Luganda origin, the language spoken by the Baganda people of Uganda, and is the title used for a chief or king. In Guyana, it was ascribed to Linden Forbes Sampson Burnham, the country's first prime minister, now deceased, who took on the persona of a traditional African chief and began to appear in public dressed accordingly, in flowing white robes.

A long moment passed as Nelson and Compton looked at each other, contemplating the insidiousness of the plastic invasion. As usual, each knew what the other was thinking. Invariably, their thoughts were the same on most issues and this time was no exception. If cars could be made of plastic, then nothing was sacred anymore. Plastic was the genius of cheapness gone mad, for what other logic could explain it but the desire to cut costs? You don't have to mine plastic. It's a chemical produced in a lab.

Compton tapped the side of his Cortina as if to reassure himself that the car he was driving was made of metal. "Boy, I tell you. At this rate, the only iron we will see in Guyana will be de train line," he said, pointing with his bottom lip to the rails that ran along the far side of the Lamaha canal. He sounded dejected, commiserating with his friend and contemplating the dubious future of Roopnaraine Scrap Metal.

Nelson turned his head listlessly in the direction indicated by Compton's bottom lip. His eyes settled with disinterest on the railway. He started to turn his attention back to the Mini Minor when his head snapped back to the railway. He stared more intently at the rails. They seemed to wink back at him as the broiling sun glinted off their back.

Nelson's eyes narrowed and his brow furrowed, as if a puzzle was beginning to make sense.

Compton watched him closely. His eyebrows angled down in suspicion as Nelson became more preoccupied with the train line.

"Nelson!" he said sharply. He could read his friend like a book.

"What?" Nelson said, turning to him a face that was a mask of innocence.

"If I were you, I would get that thought out of my head!"

"What thought?"

"Dat one about tearin' up de train line."

Nelson looked at him and said nothing. Then he turned again to look at the iron rails.

Compton followed his gaze.

43

Both were silent as they stared at the shiny iron rails. The train line ran the entire width of Georgetown and continued sixty-five miles along the coast to Rosignol in Berbice County. On the other side of the Demerara River, it picked up at Vreed-en-Hoop *stelling* and ran eighteen or so miles to Parika, in Essequibo County.

Someone had planted beds of callaloo, the local spinach, in the rich black soil between the Lamaha and the railway. The callaloo ran free and luscious. Its dark-green leaves, thick and round, were almost ready for picking.

Compton said, "De train really ol' an' rickety, Nello."

"I know," Nelson replied.

"An' nobody talkin' 'bout gettin' new ones."

"Is true."

"So is only a matta o' time before—" Compton's voice faded away.

Nelson finished the sentence in his mind and made a sound that seemed to blow out of his nostrils. "Hhmm!"

"Hhmm!" Compton echoed.

Silence filled the space between them.

Compton spoke first. "The *Kabaka* will never agree to it." His voice was soft and whispery.

"He could be convinced." Nelson's voice came back soft and whispery.

Compton said nothing.

Nelson's lips eased into a shadow of a smile. He didn't have to look at Compton. He could read him like a book.

4

On the platform at Gare Saint-Charles, Dru shook hands with Theron St. Cyr. She thanked him for the tour of Marseille and for keeping her safe from the city's lowlifes.

"Let me take you to your seat," St. Cyr offered, picking up her bags before she could protest.

He boarded the train and walked along the corridor ahead of her, peering through the glass door of every compartment until he found one that was almost empty. The only occupants were a young Asian couple who looked like student tourists. They sat very close to each other near the window, their heads buried in a French-language newspaper that the man was holding. Two backpacks were stored in the rack above their seats. There was no luggage in the rack above the seats facing them.

"This one looks comfortable enough for you, Dru," St. Cyr said.

The couple looked up as he opened the door and entered. He greeted them with a friendly *bonjour* and proceeded to place Dru's bags on the empty rack.

The couple returned the greeting and went back to reading the newspaper.

Dru squeezed past St. Cyr and flopped down on the seat with a loud sigh. After all the walking she had done with St. Cyr, she was ready to put her feet up.

She looked at the couple sharing the compartment. *Now what in the world is a fine-looking man like him doing with a mouse like that?*

She masked the thought with a warm smile and greeted them, deliberately speaking English. They looked up and returned the greeting with vigorous head nods and smiles that outdid hers.

"Going all the way to Paris?" Dru asked, continuing in English.

The man answered, bowing his head and smiling. "Yes. Paris."

"Me, too. Paris," Dru said.

The man spoke again. "American?"

"Yes. And you?"

"We're Japanese."

She sighed contentedly. *Looks like I've got decent company again. This could be interesting.*

She said good-bye to St. Cyr again, sticking out her hand in a preemptive strike against any move he might make to subject her to that idiotic European two-cheek kiss.

St. Cyr made no such move. He grasped her hand in a tight thumb-wrap, the way men do when they really like each other. He gave her that intent look again.

Dru was just beginning to feel uncomfortable when he broke into a smile. It was a smile that she could not read.

"Good-bye, Dru. Perhaps we will meet again."

He turned abruptly and left the train.

He stood on the platform outside her compartment and she stood at the window, listening incredulously to his advice about being careful and not trusting strangers on the train no matter how genuine they seemed.

"You've got to be joking," she laughed when he paused for a reaction from her.

"Am I laughing, Drucilla?"

He wasn't. Then suddenly he was.

"But you've got good instincts. And, of course, you've got that…

that…how shall I say it? That fighter look you gave me." He made a pitiful attempt to slide his head and cross his eyes.

Dru burst out laughing.

"Oh, please! Don't even try. You just don't have it in you. You've got to be East Flatbush–born and bred. Besides, only women do it," she said.

"Show me."

"Why should I put myself on display for you?"

The train's departure whistle raked the air. Dru jumped. "Jeez!" she exclaimed.

"Show me," St. Cyr insisted.

"Come on, Theron, be serious."

"Like this?" He tried again.

"Stop it," Dru laughed. "You look ridiculous. It's like this."

She showed him a black face and rolled her neck. "Satisfied?"

Before he could respond, the whistle blasted again and the train began to pull away, slowly gathering speed. Dru leaned farther out of the window and waved.

"I had a great time. Thanks again," she called.

"So did I. It was my pleasure," he called back.

"Good luck!"

"And the same to you!" He stood there, grinning and waving.

No running beside the train like in the movies, thank God, Dru thought with relief. But it would have been nice, she added wistfully, then laughed at herself.

She sat back in her seat and sighed. Well, that didn't turn out too bad after all. Interesting man, Theron St. Cyr. Clearly well educated. He hadn't lied about that. Blasé, as in sophisticated. Worldly. Warm. Witty. And she had felt safe with him, especially when they had run into that weirdo on La Canebière. Now that she thought of it, she liked the way he had put his arm around her waist and drawn her close without even getting fresh. His body had felt so lean and hard. She could still smell his cologne.

Dru closed her eyes and moistened her lips. No doubt about it, Theron St. Cyr was an exciting man. The kind of man she wouldn't mind spending time with. Getting to know. Perhaps learning to love. He certainly had the right ingredients.

But not now. He was too deep and she wasn't ready for that kind of depth.

She had picked up on the sadness in him almost immediately, though he had said or done nothing in particular to show it. In the hours they had been together, not once had Theron St. Cyr tried to bare his soul to her. Even if he wanted to, she knew he would have sensed her disinterest. He was the perceptive type.

The sadness was in the words he used sometimes, the pictures he drew with his words when he was describing places, and the way life is in those places. She had not pried into it. Her being with him was not about that. She was in Marseille for a few hours and she intended to make the most of her tour, not knowing if or when she would ever come this way again. There was no need to complicate things by getting personal with a total stranger whom she would never see again anyway, nice as he was.

So they had talked about Marseille and its history and Le Quartier Noir. About the rest of France. Paris, especially, and how it was for black people there. They even compared notes about Italy and Spain and Portugal.

Dru sighed again and yawned. The Japanese couple were hidden behind their newspaper. It made her recall her first encounter with St. Cyr.

She smiled and closed her eyes again. She couldn't help thinking about him. Theron St. Cyr was an unexpected surprise on the wind she was riding.

She sighed. *Bye, Theron. This is my time.*

After Europe there was graduate school, and after that a career, whatever it was going to be. Her heart wasn't set on any one thing. She'd just see where the wind took her. Maybe she'd work at the United Nations, or teach at a university in Latin America or Africa until she found her true calling. She didn't see herself as a college professor. Too ivory towerish. She'd be writing scholarly books and papers that the real world couldn't read. There'd be no in-the-trenches action.

At least not enough for me. And certainly not the kind that would thrill me.

Maybe I could work for one of those big consulting firms that are beginning to represent the interests of developing countries. Like Pilgrim Boone. They must have been shocked when I turned down their internship. It was flattering. It would have led to a real job with them, I'm sure.

For a fleeting moment she wondered if turning them down was the smartest thing to do. She had told only her brother about the offer and he had told her to follow her heart. If they really wanted her, they'd be there with another offer down the road, he'd told her. So she had followed her heart.

One thing she was sure of: Whatever career she ended up in, it would be something international. The name Drucilla Durane was going to be known, and not necessarily for a notoriety that brought out the TV cameras. No, she didn't really care about that kind of fame or glitz or glamour. She just cared about making a big difference in whatever field she chose, to be known in an industry as someone who shook things up.

For the better, of course.

So she had not given St. Cyr her phone number or address in the States, even though he said he visited New York pretty often and probably would end up living there one day. It was the right decision. She had things to do. And in the final analysis, you just never knew what lurked behind the charm veneer of strangers. Marseille was still a port city that all sorts of con artists drifted in and out of.

※

St. Cyr watched Dru's train disappear over the horizon. He forced himself not to think of the emptiness that had suddenly planted itself in the pit of his stomach.

As soon as the train was out of sight, he sighed heavily and began to make his way slowly toward the yawning station. He stared at the ground as he walked, his lips pursed tight with the effort he was making to keep his mind off Drucilla Durane.

He did not want to think of the hours he had spent with her and how much he liked her. Really liked her. He did not want to think about how warm and intimate it felt when she'd moved close to him in the Quartier Noir as Ramy approached.

Ramy!

The thought of his nemesis made him straighten up and quicken his pace. Inside the station he hurried toward a bank of pay telephones, barely beating a nervous-looking man to the last empty booth. The man flung up his arms in frustration and spun away wildly in search of another phone bank.

St. Cyr inserted a few coins into the box and dialed a number in Paris. Someone picked up on the third ring. St. Cyr heard the person fumble with the receiver before dropping the phone on what sounded like a bare wooden floor.

St. Cyr cursed and jerked the receiver away briefly as the clatter assaulted his ear.

A sleepy, irritated voice said, "Oui?"

"*Merde*, Michel! You nearly took my ear off!"

The voice became contrite. "Sorry, *mon vieux*. Just trying to catch up on some sleep. I've been working overtime all week with these damn reports. What's up?"

"Didn't mean to disturb your sleep, man, but I've got another pick up for you. For tonight."

The man he called Michel groaned. "If it has to be tonight, can you get someone else? I'm down to the wire on these reports. They're all due tomorrow."

"It's your turn, Michel. We can't afford to mess up this deal. You know what the alternative is if we do. She's a gem, Michel. We've got to keep her."

Michel groaned again. St. Cyr continued, his voice softening a little.

"It won't take long, Michel. You know that. Just a matter of picking her up and dropping her off. You'll be back home in no time. You've got to do this one. Ramy was already onto her and he's pissed as hell that I snatched her away. Knowing him, he kept a tail on her and knows she's heading to Paris."

Michel sighed. "Okay, okay. Gimme a second to get a pen and some paper."

St. Cyr held the phone away from his ear again as Michel fumbled around noisily on the other end.

"Okay, I'm ready now. What do you have?"

"Are you sure you're wide awake?"

"I'm wide awake, Theron. Just give me the damn details."

"About twenty-one. Black American. Arriving around eight. Cute. Big Afro. Wearing a short black dress with little pink and green flowers on it. White sandals. Italian made. American Tourister luggage. Gray. Name is Dru. Drucilla Durane. You got all that?"

"Yeah, I got it all. I'll pick her up."

"Great. Be sure to take her to the new place, not the old rat hole. Oh, and Michel, this girl's no fool. She's got street smarts. Be extra courteous. We don't want to lose her. She's textbook perfect."

"Don't worry. I'll handle it."

"And one more thing. Don't pan this off on Faustin like you did that other time. And you know what happened there. I don't have to remind you."

"No, you don't have to remind me, Theron. I said I'll be there tonight and I will." Michel didn't bother to hide his annoyance.

"I'm warning you, Michel. Keep Faustin away from this one! He's a loose cannon."

"All right, all right! Jesus! Can I go back to sleep now?"

St. Cyr hung up and walked out of Gare Saint-Charles, turning in the direction of the docks. He smiled to himself. It was a good day. A very good day. Drucilla Durane was his best find yet.

Michel Daubuisson pressed down the receiver hook, then released it, listening for the dial tone. He dialed quickly when he heard the sound. He'd just have to take his chances with Faustin. It was a straightforward assignment. The details were clear. Theron wouldn't have to know a thing.

"Qui est à l'appareil?" The voice that answered was that of a man expecting a call from a lover.

"Ce n'est que moi, Faustin. Ça va?" Michel's voice was that of a man who knew he was asking a favor that would not be granted without a string of insults.

51

"Oh, it's you. What the hell do you want this time, brain boy? You're tying up my line."

"Calm down, Faustin. Have some sympathy for a poor brother who hasn't seen a bed in forty-eight hours."

"Like hell you haven't. What do you want, Michel?"

"Theron just called."

"I'm hanging up."

"No, wait! Please. Help me out just this last time. I promise I won't bother you again. After this week I'll be free to jump back into things. I'll even take over your turn for a month. I promise."

"I've heard that song before, Michel. You're not the only one with obligations, you know. And as for that ungrateful Theron, that worthless good-for-nothing who wanders the earth, handing down orders like he's some kind of messiah! I bet he warned you not to call me. He did, didn't he? Why doesn't he—"

"I know, Faustin, I know. And I agree with you. But let's not bring all that up again. Not tonight. My head can't take it. He's given me an assignment for tonight that I just can't do. I just can't! I have to finish these reports for tomorrow and there's a lot more to do than I thought. You don't want me to fail, do you? Not after all the money you've loaned me to pay for this course."

"So why don't we just let this one go? What difference does it really make anyway?"

Michel let the question hang for a moment before he replied. His voice was measured and quiet when he spoke.

"You should be the last one to ask that question, Faustin," he said.

A long silence ensued.

"What does she look like?" Faustin said gruffly.

5

L awton Pilgrim's eyes filled with pride as he watched his protégés file out of the conference room, talking animatedly and smacking each other on the back in genuine camaraderie.

He did not have to warn them about duplicating each other's reports. Each would know instinctively what the other would write about. After so many years, they just vibed that way.

He caught himself and chuckled at his use of their word, *vibed*. Even after the door had closed behind them, he could hear their laughter and easy banter with the secretaries.

He stood up and moved again to the window overlooking the East River. It was just after noon on a sweltering late-August day. Hundred-degree temperatures had been sucking the life out of the city for the past few days and more of the same was predicted for the week ahead.

Everywhere he looked he saw stillness or sloth. Even the cars on the Franklin D. Roosevelt East River Drive seemed too overcome with heat to speed.

A barge stacked three levels high with red, yellow, and gray containers idled in the river. A Circle Line ferry crowded with tourists inched north toward Bear Mountain. Pilgrim could see some of the tourists fanning themselves. He smiled. He had not taken the three-hour ferry ride since he was a kid in elementary school.

Over to his right, a lone seagull swooped and sailed, its white wings spread wide. It was magnificently graceful. Pilgrim loved to watch seagulls, though he always mused that God must have been a bit jaded by the time he got around to creating them. Such beautiful creatures in flight, but what a letdown when they opened their mouths and emitted their coarse, grating caw. Like a beautiful woman with bad breath.

He turned away from the window and walked slowly to his chair at the head of the conference table. He stood behind the chair, trailing his fingers absently along a seam in the tightly stretched brown leather. His eyes followed the trail, seeing nothing. His thoughts were on the future of the firm. He had to come up with a strategy for its survival.

He scowled. The CPA firms were beginning to sink their claws into the consulting market.

His terrain, goddammit!

Touche Ross. Deloitte, Haskins and Sells. Andersen. Price Water-house. Ernst & Young. Peat Marwick. They were the nobility of accounting. They audited the books of the country's top corporations. Their reports provided a close-up view of these corporations' financial health. Analysts at investment banks pored over these reports when assessing stock values.

But now the corporations were moving into more complex waters, with mergers and acquisitions and management styles with fancy-schman-zy labels. And the CPA firms had a bug up their behinds thinking that, since the corporations were their clients already, what could be so wrong about advising them on reorganizing their operations so that everything ran smoothly after a merger or an acquisition. Pretty soon, Pilgrim fumed, they'll all start acting like full-fledged consultants, recommending this and recommending that about everything under the sun—doing the very things that Pilgrim Boone built its reputation on. One or two of them had already set up small consulting units.

It stinks, Pilgrim growled, driving his fist into his palm. We're heading for trouble. It's a rotten conflict of interest when you advise companies on operations then turn around and audit their books. You'll have to make your audits look good no matter what the real deal is. Hell, it's your advice they're taking!

He had said as much to a couple of his golfing buddies just this past weekend. One of them served on the Financial Accounting Standards Board, the private-sector organization that sets the standards for financial reporting.

"I don't know what you guys are doing at FASB, but you had better open your eyes," he had said darkly.

His buddies had laughed at him. It will never get that far, they said. Somebody in the government will stop them. They were willing to bet on it.

"You just keep on doing what you're doing and let someone else worry about the CPAs, Lawton," the FASB buddy had said.

Pilgrim decided there and then that he wasn't going to take any chances. He would position Pilgrim Boone to keep it solidly ahead of the pack.

As he ruminated on the situation now, his thoughts came to rest on the discussions earlier in the day about emerging markets. An idea struck him. An idea so simple in logic and execution that it was almost obscene that he had not thought of it before.

What if Pilgrim Boone began to offer its services to Third World governments that want to win favor with Washington? To companies that wanted to make inroads into the American market for their goods? No start-ups or microenterprises. Just established companies that could afford to pay for Pilgrim Boone's services, companies that had long-term visions of being listed on the New York Stock Exchange, say.

Asia would be the most likely place to go trawling first. And Latin America—Brazil, Argentina, Venezuela. Africa? South Africa for sure. Maybe oil-rich Nigeria, if you could get past the corruption. Other countries have oil but nothing's being done about it yet. There's Congo Kinshasa, of course, with all those diamonds and minerals. Other than that, there's nothing in that god-forsaken land that's worth the trouble. At least not now.

It would mean hiring people with ethnic or cultural ties to those places and putting some of them on the Inner-Circle track. The same skills and education would be required, of course. A master's degree, top third of their class, competence in a second language, formal studies in the politics and economics of the region, thinkers outside the box.

Pilgrim rubbed his hands in excitement as the strategy took shape. In his mind he went over the list of graduates he had been keeping his eye on since their junior year in college. Unknown to them, of course.

Funny the way things happen. For the first time his list of potential recruits had included minorities. Two of them. A Korean-American man and an African-American woman. He had not gone out of his way to choose minorities. These two just happened to be so damned good. The woman in particular. Bold as brass, this young woman was. Had the balls— the tits—to turn down a summer internship with Pilgrim Boone to go cavorting all over Europe. No graduate had ever turned down Pilgrim Boone.

Pilgrim felt warm inside. He liked that kind of spunk. Here was a person who knew where she wanted to go and everyone else be damned. Including Pilgrim Boone.

Damn, I like her!

As far as he was concerned, Drucilla Durane had a job at Pilgrim Boone whenever she was ready to show up. He was sure she would.

6

D ru watched the big black Citroën out of the corner of her eye.
Her heart was beating a little faster than normal, but she still
felt pretty safe. There was enough of a crowd around to deter a kidnapping, if that's what the people in the car were planning.

What an ugly car, she thought. Looks like an alien bug. Even worse
than the Volkswagen. Europeans must have some kind of fetish about
bugs.

The Citroën had followed her from the station. This is what you
get when your train screws up—a stalker, Dru thought. She should have
been on her way to Geneva by now, but the train had stalled on the way
to Paris and she had missed her connection, she and a whole lot of other
people. She had not planned to stop over in Paris until she returned for
her flight back to New York. She had given herself a few days to do the
tourist bit then.

The next train to Geneva was early in the morning. She would have
to find somewhere to spend the night. Nothing fancy. A *pension*—hos-
tel—was all she needed. Or, she could sleep in the station with all the
others, which is what the Japanese couple had decided to do. With her

budget, it would make sense to do likewise. Not to mention the fact that there's safety in numbers, bedding down in the station with the other passengers.

She decided she would sleep in the station, but she would walk around outside first, stretch her legs a bit before settling down to a night on a wooden bench. She put the bigger suitcase into a locker and walked out onto the street.

It was dark, but there was still a lot of hustle and bustle in the area. She should be fine as long as she didn't wander into any of the side streets. Maybe she'd even find a decent hotel with a good bathroom in the lobby where she could wash up. She didn't trust the ones in the station.

She crossed the street and turned toward the bright lights. The Citroën that was parked in front of the station pulled out and eased along the street behind her. Dru picked up the sound of the car matching her pace and she turned suddenly, her eyes briefly making four with the driver's. She faced front again and quickened her pace. The Citroën accelerated.

Dru stopped in front of a small bakery and pretended she was checking out the cakes and pastries in the window, but kept her eye on the reflection of the Citroën in the window. She saw the car pull into a parking space right in front of the bakery. A scruffily dressed man with a sour expression on his face emerged from the driver's side and started walking toward her.

Terror filled her. Her heart pounding, she hurried into the bakery, thanking God it was still open. The man came in after her. Dru moved to the far end of the counter where a few people were waiting to be served. The man kept coming toward her, his unpleasant face drawn into a scowl.

"Stay away from me!" Dru cried out in English as he came within a few feet of her. She hoisted her overnight bag, ready to strike. The man stopped abruptly and stared at her in genuine astonishment. Everyone else stopped what they were doing and stared at both of them.

"I beg your pardon?" The man spoke British English with a mild French accent.

"I said stay away from me or I'll smash your head in," Dru threatened.

She looked around wildly at the people in the store. "He's—this man is following me! I don't know him!" she cried. She caught herself and switched to French. She spoke the language fluently. She had studied it since the sixth grade and excelled in it in high school and college. She was even a life member of the French Institute Alliance Française.

Faustin stared stonily at the American woman before him. This I don't need, he thought angrily. If that son of a bitch Theron knows what's good for him, he'll keep away from me for the rest of his life. "Aren't you Drucilla Durane?" He spoke politely, trying hard to keep his anger under control.

Dru lowered the overnight bag a fraction. "Who the hell are you? How do you know my name?" she demanded.

"Look, Mademoiselle Durane. I'm sorry if I alarmed you. Theron St. Cyr asked a friend to watch out for you at the station, but that friend could not come so he asked me to come instead. Very much against my will, I might add. My name is Faustin Daubuisson. Didn't Theron tell you that someone would meet you in Paris?"

Dru shifted nervously from one foot to the other, but kept a defiant eye on Daubuisson. The shop patrons rolled their eyes and resumed minding their own business. One or two of them muttered something about uncouth, loud-mouthed Americans.

"Theron said nothing of the sort to me. Why the hell didn't he?" Dru said.

"How should I know? Perhaps he was so intrigued by your beauty that he forgot. Look, I was asked to do a favor and I'm doing that favor. Now, if you have no business to do in this place with these cockroaches, I'd be grateful if you came along with me," Faustin said, switching to French for the last sentence and glaring at the people who had made the disparaging remarks about Americans.

Dru looked around with distaste and stuck out her chin. "I most certainly do not have business in this place," she said haughtily.

"Good. Then let's go." He turned and walked out of the bakery without looking back to see if she were following him. His determined gait made it clear the he did not care whether she did or not.

"Where are we going?" Dru asked when she got into the car.

"I'm taking you somewhere to spend the night," Faustin said.

"Hey, wait a minute. I appreciate Theron's—your kindness, but I'm perfectly all right at the station. My train leaves early in the morning and I don't want to miss it. I've already missed one."

"I'm afraid you have no choice. These are my orders."

She didn't like the way that sounded, but she kept quiet. Best not to risk antagonizing this Faustin Daubuisson any further. He clearly was in a foul mood. She had made a fool of him at the bakery. He was built like a wrestler, too.

The car seemed to float up on its wheels when Faustin turned on the ignition. Dru had driven in a Citroën in Spain, but that had been a smaller one, not this big ugly thing.

Once it got rolling, the big ugly thing purred so softly she had to listen really hard to be sure that the engine was running. She had to admit it was the smoothest ride she had ever had in a car. It was like riding on air.

⁜

Michel slammed his fist into the wall. It was a brick wall—one of the reasons he had rented this apartment—and it hurt like hell. But he was so angry with himself that he didn't mind the pain. He had forgotten to tell Faustin to take Theron's new girl to the new place, and now he could not reach him on the phone. Faustin must have left early.

Michel kicked the wall, and kicked it again with such force that his head snapped sideways and knocked his thick, wire-rimmed glasses askew.

"*Merde!*" he shouted as he adjusted the glasses. "*Merde! Merde! Merde!*"

He paced the floor. He was beginning to get a headache. There was absolutely nothing he could do about his screw-up. He would never make it to the train station in time, even if he drove at breakneck speed. Faustin and the girl would have left long before he got there.

He walked into the bathroom and leaned over the sink, shaking his head. How could he have been so careless? How could he have forgotten? Faustin was still not used to taking the pickups to the new safe house. They had only gotten it a month ago. Theron had put up most of the money for the deposit on the lease. After that fiasco with Faustin and the Canadian girl at the old safe house, he had insisted that they find better accommodations. *Merde! Shit!*

He looked at his reflection in the small mirror above the sink. Maybe Faustin will see that this girl is quality like Theron said and he'd take her to the new place. But in his heart of hearts he knew no such thing would happen. When it came to these assignments, Faustin operated like a robot. To him the women who came off the trains all bright-eyed and innocent, like this Durane one, were all the same. They were open invitations to those who ran one of the world's oldest and most lucrative businesses. You picked them up and deposited them as quickly as possible.

Faustin loathed having anything to do with them, he and Theron knew, but the three of them had committed themselves and none of them could back out now. Not after Tabatha.

Michel felt the nausea swimming up into his throat and it was all he could do to keep from retching. He splashed cold water on his face and didn't bother to dry it. He stared again at his reflection in the mirror, as if he were contemplating the face of a stranger. He watched his lips move in a silent prayer. After a while, he dragged his hand over his face and turned away from the mirror. *God help her*, he said aloud.

⁜

Faustin stopped the car in front of a walled-off property in a narrow cobblestone street.

The wall was rough cement. Its sickly gray color meant it had never seen a coat of paint. Two sheets of rusty corrugated zinc leaning into one another at a rakish angle served as the gate. Someone had cut a hole into each of the sheets and run a thick iron chain through from one side to the other. The ends of the chain were tied together and secured with an odd-looking steel contraption.

Dru had no idea where she was, but she knew she wasn't far from the train station. It had taken less than ten minutes to get there. And just to be on the safe side, she had kept her eyes peeled for landmarks.

What she saw when they entered the courtyard made her stomach drop. Right away she thought of making up a story about having to get back to the station to meet someone. She had forgotten about it, she would say. But even to her that sounded weak.

She contemplated making a sudden dash for it, but Faustin was walking too closely behind her. He could grab her easily.

Her fear mounted. She hoped she didn't show it. She took a deep breath and studied the structure before her. It was the most ramshackle dwelling she had ever seen. Light shone from some of the windows, dulled by thin, shabby curtains that drooped in the middle.

"Is…is this where I am to stay?" she asked, feigning insouciance.

"Yeah," Faustin replied gruffly. He seemed to have grown morose during the short drive from the station. He was a short man. Shorter than she was and she was only five-foot-five, which was really short in her family.

The man had wide shoulders on a muscular build. African blood was the most prominent of the ethnic scramble that gave him chiseled features, jet-black hair that seemed to be making up its mind about whether to lay flat on his head or rise up in curls, and skin the color of cocoa mixed with milk. He looked like many of the West Indians in Brooklyn. Like her father's parents, in fact. They had migrated to the United States from Guyana when they were in their thirties. They had settled in Harlem, where earlier West Indian immigrants had established a community. Her own father had been born a year after their arrival.

Her grandparents hadn't been all that happy when he married her American mother and bought the house in Brooklyn. They got over it when she, Dru, was born. She had grown up with her younger brother in the comfort of her parents' two-story, three-bedroom brownstone, spoiled rotten from the rivalry between her two grandmothers as they vied for her affection.

As Dru's thoughts fell on her family and all the other honest, hardworking families she knew, she became enraged. *Maybe these Euroblacks think every black person in America lives in this kind of run-down place. Well, they'll have to think again,* she thought.

She whipped around. Eyebrows dragged together in a ferocious glare, she opened her mouth to set Faustin straight. Before she could say a word, she felt his thumb and forefinger press deeply into the upper part of her arm and she gasped in pain.

"Don't. I'm not in the mood," Faustin said in a low voice.

Dru clamped her mouth shut. For the second time that night she felt utter terror.

Faustin led her around to the side of the building. They went up a flight of rickety wooden stairs and walked along an even more rickety corridor with such huge holes in the floor that she had to step over them to move forward. There were apartments on either side of the corridor. The doors were closed, but Dru could see eyes peering through the slats where the planks in the walls had started to come loose. Here and there, where the holes were large enough, she could make out the figures of children and women moving about inside the apartments. They looked like Arabs. She saw no men. There was the smell of cooking, the same fragrance of saffron that had emanated from the Middle Eastern restaurants along La Canebière and in the Quartier Noir in Marseille.

I've got to stay cool. Dear God, please let me stay cool. Her heart thudded so hard against her chest that she was sure Faustin could hear it. She should talk. Talking would drown the noise.

"Do you live here?" she asked timidly. She tried hard to keep the terror out of her voice.

"Not hardly. The studio where you will stay belongs to someone else who is, er, away for a while. I myself live quite far from here. You will stay here until I come back to get you in the morning." Faustin actually sounded pleasant.

She was surprised by his even-tempered tone. She relaxed a little.

Like hell I'll stay here. I'll be leaving right behind you, shepherd boy.

At the end of the corridor, Faustin stopped at a heavily chained and padlocked door. Dru's stomach somersaulted. She wanted to scream when he opened the door and motioned her to go inside, but she thought twice about it. Who would come to her rescue? The fear in the eyes she saw peering at her along the corridor was no less than the fear she felt.

Dear God. Please save me. Her mother's face flashed before her and she fought to keep back the tears.

It was a studio, just as he'd said. One big room that served as living room, dining room and kitchen, and a tiny alcove with an oversized brass bed for the bedroom. The alcove was separated from the rest of the room by a thin, dingy curtain that made a mockery of the notion of privacy. At least the sheets on the bed seemed clean.

The mismatched pieces of furniture looked like they had been snapped up whenever the owner of the studio passed a pile of discarded junk on the sidewalk. Knickknacks of every shape and material adorned every available surface, collecting dust. Clothes, towels, and sundry articles of cloth hung on nails that stuck out from the walls. A ceramic sink near the stove—it might have once been white—was half filled with dirty dishes. Grease had congealed into a brown crud on the dishes.

And yet, there was a pleasant smell throughout the studio, as if someone had burned some kind of incense not very long ago.

"It's not much, but it's just for a few hours. And I can tell you it's far safer here than sleeping at the train station," Faustin said. He had softened his voice, sensing Dru's trepidation.

Dru could not believe her ears. This was safe? It was a goddamn prison. She felt like choking Faustin.

"The bathroom is outside, three doors down the corridor, on the left. You'd better go while I am here," Faustin said.

"I don't need to go," Dru said coldly.

"Are you sure?"

"Positive." It was almost a snarl.

"Suit yourself then," Faustin shrugged. "I'll leave you now. I will see you in the morning at six. Good night."

He didn't wait for a reply. He went out and closed the door firmly behind him. Dru moved quickly toward the door and pressed her ear against it, listening for his footsteps. She heard nothing at first. He must have paused just outside the door. She stood back, taking shallow breaths. Maybe he forgot something and would open the door again.

Then she heard the sound, the metallic sawing of the chain being pulled tight, the click of the padlock. Footsteps hurried down the corridor.

Dru went rigid. No! He didn't do what she thought he did! He couldn't have done that!

She flung herself at the door, turned the knob, and pushed. The chain rattled but it did not give. She locked both hands around the door-knob and shook it as hard as she could. It still did not open.

She heard the Citroën rev up and she went berserk. She pounded the door with her hands and screamed.

"Let me out! Please! Somebody help me! Let me out! Help! Help!"

No one responded. No one came.

She screamed until she was hoarse. Finally, she sank down on the floor and cried. She wailed loud and long, as if she had no hope of coming out of this hellhole alive.

Gradually, her sobbing eased to a whimper. She did not know when she fell asleep.

The sound of voices snatched her out of her sleep. She raised her head and remained still, listening, trembling. She heard a door open and close. The voices disappeared.

She squinted at her watch in the half-light. Four o'clock. She had to find a way to get out before Faustin came back.

She scrambled to her feet. Her bones ached. She needed to pee. She looked around for a container she could use. Nothing. She eyed the sink. Steeling herself, she walked over to it and picked the dishes out one by one with her fingertips, placing them in a pile on the floor.

When the sink was cleared, she hoisted herself up, wrinkling her nose, muttering in disgust. The sink wobbled under her weight, but it held fast. She relieved herself, climbed down and turned on the water.

She kept it running and went to tackle the door once again. She tried shaking it again and again.

It's not going to happen, idiot. You're wasting time.

She ran to one of the two small windows overlooking the courtyard and opened it. Too high up, she decided. She'd break a leg if she jumped.

She felt the panic rising in her. Sweat beaded on her forehead and in her palms. She ran back to the door. She'd have to break it down somehow. She looked at the hinges. They were old and rusty. There were three sets of them—top, middle, and bottom. Each one was held fast by two screws. Some of the screws were already straining out of the wood. They had flat heads with deep grooves. She should be able to turn them with a screwdriver, if she could find one, or with a sturdy knife.

Dru's heart pounded as she searched the cupboards and the counter next to the sink for something she could use. She soon found a knife that looked sturdy enough. She ran back to the door and began to work at the screws, starting with the hinge at the bottom. It was harder than she expected. The screws were made of iron and had rusted. The knife kept slipping out of the groove and her hands grew too clammy to maintain their grip for long. She needed a sturdier tool, something that would give her a better grip. She dropped the knife, dashed back to the kitchen area, and rummaged around the counter again. She did the same under the sink, tossing pots, pans, dishes, and strange-looking implements aside until she found a screwdriver-like instrument. The handle was made of roughly hewn wood.

She raced back to the door with it and set to work again on the bottommost hinge. The handle of the tool was crude, with sharp edges and knobs in the wood. Within minutes her hands began to blister. They burned so much that tears came to her eyes. But she had to keep going. She could not stop.

She switched the tool from hand to hand to relieve the soreness, but the blistering and stinging pain worsened. Some of her tears fell on the raw blisters when she looked at her palms and the salt made them burn so much that she cried out.

I will not give up, she told herself. I will die trying rather than die at Faustin's hands.

Slowly, after what seemed like an eternity, the screws began to come loose. Before she knew it she was at the middle hinge. This one was easier than the first, but it still took more time than she expected. The blisters were worse and the pain slowed her down considerably. But she was making progress. She could taste freedom now.

She had to climb on a chair to reach the top hinge. The legs broke as soon as she stood with her full weight on it and she fell hard to the ground. With a loud wail she picked herself up and dragged another chair to the door. This one held, but it was lower than the first one and she had to strain to reach the last hinge. Now she had to contend with both the pain from the blisters and the ache from stretching.

Tears poured down her cheeks. This was the toughest of the three hinges. She looked at her watch. It was five-forty. Faustin was coming at six. Her train was leaving at six forty-five. Once she escaped from the studio she still had to collect her suitcase from the locker in the station and at least try to wash up a bit in the public bathroom. She didn't need a mirror to tell her she was a mess.

And she had to get something in her stomach, even if it was just coffee. The last time she had eaten was on the train. Theron had made her buy a whole dinner to take with her.

The thought of Theron made her think of Faustin. Two criminals. Dear God! Keep him away, please. I beg you. Just let me get away in time.

Suddenly the top hinge came loose. She scrambled down from the chair and eased the door away from the wall. Restricted by the chain, it fell at an awkward angle. Dru set it as straight as she could so that there was enough space between it and the doorframe for her to squeeze through.

She grabbed her overnight bag, wincing as the handle touched the raw blisters in her hand, and pushed it through the space. Then she slung her shoulder bag across her chest, picked up her sandals and squeezed herself through.

I'm free! Sweet Jesus, I'm free!

On the other side of the door, she picked up the case, tiptoed down the corridor and flung herself down the rickety steps two stairs at a time. There was no sign of life anywhere. At the bottom of the stairs she slipped on her sandals and took off again.

She drew up sharply at the gate. *What if it's padlocked?* she thought, horrified.

She reached for the strange-looking contraption that Faustin had seemed to open with ease. It came apart almost as soon as she touched it. The zinc sheets fell to the ground, banging loudly against each other.

She didn't wait to see if anyone had heard the noise. She leaped over the zinc and bolted down the street. She looked back only once—when she reached the corner. No one was following her. And there was no sign of Faustin's car.

Her heart pumping, she raced around the corner and sprinted away. Thank God for those landmarks! she thought. She ran until she reached the station. It took her less than five minutes to retrieve her suitcase from the locker. She glanced at a clock on the wall. Six forty-three. Her train was leaving in two minutes. No time to get coffee and no time to wash up. I'll just have to wash up on the train. Maybe I can buy coffee and a sandwich on the train, too.

Frantically, she scanned the big black board for the number of the platform her train was leaving from. There it was. Ignoring angry glares and looks of disdain, she pushed through the people who were milling around and ran as fast as she could.

She heard the first whistle. *Oh, please let me make it.*

She almost collided with the conductor. "Take it easy, Mademoiselle. You've made it," the conductor said, chuckling.

Dru climbed aboard, found an empty compartment and sank down on the soft leather seat. As the train pulled out of the station, she burst into tears. Her body shook uncontrollably as the reality of what she had gone through began to sink in.

Suddenly, she laughed out loud. *Here comes the sun, and I'm alive and well.* She laughed hysterically. She looked at her palms and the sight of them made her laugh more.

These are the scars of freedom. This I did to myself to escape from a fate I don't even want to think about.

The laughter evaporated as suddenly as it had begun. Dru grew sober. Soon, her sobriety gave way to rage. And rage to hatred.

Theron St. Cyr was vermin. If anyone had told her that she, Drucilla Durane, Flatbush-and-street-smart, could be conned by a pimp on the prowl she would have been so insulted she would have cursed that person out. She had no doubt that pimping was St. Cyr's game. The classmate who had recommended *Europe on 5 Dollars a Day* had also given her the rundown on Europe's underbelly. She had spent a long time describing the abduction and sexual enslavement of women and girls.

It was big business, she had said. Grossing billions of dollars a year.

Theron St. Cyr was a slave trafficker with a first-class abduction act. *God help the poor innocents who did not get away, and the ones to come who will not.*

She was lucky. She would be a lot more careful now.

She shivered as the train pulled away from the station. She had the strange feeling that Theron St. Cyr would cross her path again. And not in Europe. In America.

When he does, I will take him down, so help me God, Dru swore.

⁓⁓⁓

Faustin stared at the collapsed door in disbelief.

With trembling hands, he undid the padlock, uprighted the detached panel, and leaned it against the wall outside the studio. He stepped inside quickly. His eyes swept the studio as he made a beeline for the makeshift bedroom. The bed had not been slept in.

He knelt beside it on one knee, lifted the ragged bedspread that hung down to the floor and peered underneath. He had to blink several times before his eyes grew accustomed to the darkness. The dust made him sneeze twice. There was no body under the bed. Dru Durane had not been assaulted and left for dead in the studio.

Breathing a sigh of relief, he rose to his feet, walked into the living room, and stood there. He looked around, perplexed. He saw no sign of a struggle. The place had been looted, naturally. What else could one expect of the "neighbors"? But that was the least of his worries. There was nothing of value in the place.

Dru Durane was the focus of his attention. It was clear that she had broken out on her own. He wondered what time she had left the studio. He looked at his watch. If she was lucky, she had made it safely to the train and was about to leave France. It would be pointless to try to pursue her.

He kept looking around, at a loss for what to do. How fleeting these encounters are, he thought.

There was no evidence whatsoever that someone named Drucilla Durane had ever been there, nothing that singled her out from what was left of the stale clutter in this ravaged room, or from the ones that had come before her. She had vanished, as so many before her had done.

He wondered if Ramy's men had picked her up. He would never know. No one ever knows. These girls were windblown creatures.

Sometimes, when he had finished his part and they were out of his life forever, he would spend hours wondering if they were real. They were so beautiful. All of them.

Like Tabatha.

Tabatha!

Angrily, he kicked away the broken chair. Scattered about the floor, almost hidden in the detritus of the looting, was the story of Dru Durane's escape. He saw the dinner knife. The long, rusty screws. The three heavy hinges that had held the door in place swung from the door. The clumsy screwdriver he had made in metal shop when he was in high school.

He picked up the screwdriver, turning it this way and that. He saw the blood on the handle. It wasn't quite dry.

Yes, she was here. Here is her proof. She was no dream.

Absently, he put the screwdriver in the inside breast pocket of his jacket. He stared at the gaping hole in the doorway. He would have to repair the door right away, of course.

He set to work.

He would not tell Michel that Dru Durane had run away from the studio. He would make sure the next one didn't, for indeed, there would be another Dru Durane.

Tomorrow, and the day after that, and all the days after that.

Life guaranteed it.

7

June 15, 1998

"**B**ad news, Dru."

Lawton Pilgrim's sober voice on the telephone confirmed the suspicions Dru had been harboring in the two weeks since their return to the United States.

There had been no word from Jamaica. No phone call, no letter, no e-mail, nothing.

This time, no news definitely is not good news, she had told herself at the end of the first week. She had finally put the nagging feeling into words, said it out loud, just this morning, while she was showering.

They screwed us, the bastards.

"Let me guess. We didn't get the contract," she said to Lawton now. The lightness in her voice surprised her.

"Right!"

Dru heard the *thump* as Pilgrim's fist smashed into his desk.

"They went with BMG. Branford Mellon, for God's sake!" The words grated between his teeth.

"I'm not surprised we didn't get it," Dru said coolly.

"Well, I damned sure am!"

Dru jerked the receiver away from her ear a second before Pilgrim's fist crashed down on his desk again.

Pilgrim's voice was strident. "This was a done deal as far as everyone was concerned. Everyone. On both sides. The prime minister himself said as much when we met before we left Jamaica! Good God, Dru, what—"

He stopped abruptly. Dru waited, but he did not continue. She heard his quick, angry breathing gradually slow and return to normal. Lawton Pilgrim was not given to lengthy indulgences in what he called "leech emotions." He was far too disciplined.

"Anger, hate, frustration—they suck the sense out of you like leeches. And when you've got no sense, you're just taking up space on this good earth, fella. Nothing more than a breathing carcass, that's what you become." Dru had heard him say this to his chief financial officer, who was cursing and railing against the unmoving traffic on the George Washington Bridge that had made him late for an important meeting with his counterpart at Goldman Sachs.

Dru remained silent, giving Pilgrim the time he needed to calm down.

"I just don't understand it," he continued after several minutes, sounding bemused. "What the hell could have happened?"

Dru had never heard him sound like this. Lawton Pilgrim perplexed? Didn't happen. Anytime he walked into a negotiating session, you could put your head on a block that he had already figured out every possible argument, every possible scenario that could come up, and how to turn it all to his advantage. He was a master negotiator. He knew when to cajole, when to suck up, when to show contempt, when to walk away. And he knew the precise moment when he had hooked his fish and it was time to start reeling in.

She found it odd that this unusual display of anger and exasperation didn't really surprise her. She was taking it in the proverbial stride. Maybe I *am* a cold bitch like the rumors say, she thought. She shrugged away the thought. As far as she was concerned, Lawton was entitled to blow some steam. Losing this deal was a hard blow for Pilgrim Boone. She knew it. Everyone else in The Circle knew it.

Hell, it was a hard blow for her, too. She was going to be the firm's point person on the account, if they had gotten it.

Pilgrim Boone had pursued this particular contract for more than a year. Contracts from developing countries that wanted to attract investment from rich countries—they were called Foreign Investment Strategies contracts, or FIS contracts—were coveted in the consulting world. It was multifaceted work that gave you an in with the movers and shakers in the client country, an in that led to all kinds of other contracts from both the government and private businesses.

FIS work entailed reviewing and, in most cases, revamping entirely the country's policies and the regulations that governed the way foreign investors behaved. Whoever got the contract would have to assess the country's traditional and nontraditional industries to determine which ones were strong enough to compete globally, and which ones could be shored up to capitalize on domestic, regional, and global demand. Once all these reviews, assessments, and determinations were completed, the consultant was in a position to draw up a priority list of investment needs. Often, the client country would ask the consultant to go even further and assist in designing specific investment projects, vetting all proposals submitted, and selecting the right investor.

Consultants milked these contracts for all they were worth. The money good, they could be leveraged to win similar contracts in other countries.

Dru ruminated on all that could have been theirs. *Hers.* It would have been the first FIS for which she took the lead. She would have reported to Grant Featherhorn, of course, since he headed the firm's Latin America/Caribbean division. But *she* would have been the one in the trenches. Organizing, supervising, making contacts, making decisions. Suffering the blisters, relishing the bliss.

The thought of it, the nearness of it, excited her even now. She had done all her homework and she had been ready. She liked the country. She had roots in the Caribbean. She cared.

She had watched her peers make their mark in Eastern Europe while she waited hungrily for the opportunity to work her ass off to help put this one little Caribbean country on the right track, to see that it, too, got the proper—no, *enabling*—environment that would bring in tons of investors who could do what they had to do with the least amount of regulatory or bureaucratic hassle or breakdown in the infrastructure, like blackouts and water shortages.

It would have been a win-win situation for everyone involved. And now someone else was going to have it all. It would be Branford friggin' Mellon, one of the Johnny-come-lately bulldogs, taking on the Jamaican banking system to make it easier to do hard-currency transactions. *They* would get the credit for getting rid of usurious interest rates, for making sure checks cleared in five days max instead of thirty-plus, as was the practice at certain banks when the checks of small businesses needed to clear. *They* would be the ones seeing to it that the ministries and state agencies were lean and efficient; that the legal infrastructure dealt with cases competently, fairly, and expeditiously; that rules and regulations were transparent, with no divergence between what was on the books and what was practiced; that the whole damn civil service was free of corruption; that the labor force was decently paid; and that utilities worked all the time.

It wouldn't be Dru Durane looking out for the local entrepreneurs who kept the economy going when the national budget was on the ropes. All of a sudden, everyone was braying about the importance of entrepreneurship, a point she had been making for years. The more entrepreneurs were able to expand their businesses, hire workers, and build fancy homes, the more money they put into local banks instead of their mattresses or accounts in the States, the better off the economy and the more the government could brag about the correctness of its policies.

Yes, they would have to make sure the local business people were happy. That happiness, a measure of local investor confidence, was an important gauge for foreign investors.

So maybe nobody could achieve all of the above. But *she* certainly would have given it her best shot because she cared. It would have been tedious work, but it was work that she had already carved out for herself and the team she would have put together from both Pilgrim Boone and local Jamaican consultants. The contract would have positioned Pilgrim Boone to go after a good chunk of the development money being freed up in Washington and in multilateral institutions for the Caribbean private sector. Money channeled away, at long last, from investment in government projects that either never saw the light of day or never were completed.

All this had eluded Pilgrim Boone because of *her*. The black girl from East Flatbush, Brooklyn, whom many people referred to as "the ice queen" or "the frosted bitch."

Lawton had practically salivated over the contract. In his eyes, awarding such a contract to Pilgrim Boone was a no-brainer.

"No firm in America is our equal when it comes to this kind of work and we've got the track record to prove it. I'd like to see one of these consulting wannabees take this one from us," he had declared to The Circle, rubbing his hands gleefully.

Wilfred Cunningham, bald, fat, and still given to silly ideas, had been skeptical.

"We would be the logical choice if it was just American firms in the running. But there's Brits, Canadians, even Frenchies in the mix, and the Caribbeans love to play us against each other," he had said.

"I very much doubt they would go for a non-U.S. firm, Willy. America is the big kahuna for the developing world, and Jamaica especially. We've got the pot of gold. This is where they're all casting their nets. It's America that they want to impress most," Pilgrim had argued confidently.

Sure enough, when the FIS contract was simultaneously put out for bid in Europe and North America, the inside scoop was that a U.S. firm was sure to win it because the Jamaican government, backed by its business and professional elite, wanted their country to be Washington's most favored nation in the region, financially and policywise.

So shameless was Jamaica's pursuit of this status—one well-known local radio announcer even went so far as referring to a news report from Washington as "the news from our nation's capital"—that other Caribbean nations joked that all that was left for Jamaica to do was to switch from driving on the left side of the road to driving on the right side of the road.

Jamaica was one of the biggest and most influential members of the Caribbean Community. Pilgrim Boone had wined and dined the ambassador and every minister and permanent secretary who showed up in New York and Washington, whether they came on official business or for private reasons. When the bid came out, Lawton himself had headed the team that traveled to the island to make the necessary presentations on behalf of the firm. Three trips the team had made. Dru had accompanied them on all three. On the third trip, Lawton had met with the prime minister for the first time. The local associates who had arranged the meeting had been compensated handsomely by Pilgrim Boone, even though the prime minister had agreed to spend only a few minutes with Lawton.

Those few minutes had stretched to an hour and Lawton was grinning from ear to ear when he emerged from the meeting. He took the entire team and their local "associates" to lunch. He ordered champagne and proposed a toast. When he raised his glass, he uttered just three words: In the bag.

The response was a boisterous eruption of hear-hears, pounding on the table, guffaws, and the clinking of glasses.

Now this.

Two weeks after the team's triumphant return to New York, the surprising call had come to Lawton from the head of the investment promotion agency herself. It wasn't about losing the money. The retainer the country was prepared to pay was laughable compared to what the average corporate client paid in America.

No. It wasn't the money.

What made this loss so painful and potentially damaging was the signal it would send to the other developing countries Pilgrim Boone wanted as clients.

So far, the firm had not been able to land any clients among the Group of Fifteen advanced and rapidly emerging economies. Landing the accounts of a tiny West African country that few people had heard of, another in Central America, and one more in the Pacific was as far as they had gotten in the developing world. Still, Lawton had used those contracts to begin cultivating Pilgrim Boone's image in the press as the friend of developing countries. He would seize every opportunity to show off his Emerging Markets Team, letting the world see that its ethnic make-up reflected the people of the developing world. He made sure the team members had high-profile speaking engagements on development issues, that they were seen with visiting delegations, and that they got on the most important talking head shows on TV.

The message from Pilgrim Boone's media relations department was that this was the firm that would do right by poorer countries, the one that would keep them in Washington's good graces. Favorable policies, substantial aid packages, and a river of private investment would come from their association with Pilgrim Boone.

For all Lawton's cunning, winning those first clients had been a hell of a hard sell. Officials from developing countries hadn't yet caught on to the idea of spending hundreds of thousands of dollars to polish up their image. This was especially true of officials from Africa and the Caribbean. Moreover, many of them were suspicious of American consultants, believing that they really worked in the interest of America alone and that, in the end, they sold everyone but America and themselves short. A few saw the logic of the idea, but they could not get past their development priorities when it came to allocating funds that already were in too short supply. Image was a cosmetic thing. Education and health care were not.

"You make a great deal of sense, Mr. Pilgrim. But this cannot be a priority for my government now. The opposition would nail us to the cross if we were to put money into public relations instead of infrastructure and things like education," one ambassador had said in response to Lawton's pitch.

Lawton had persisted with the same patience, precision, and shrewdness that he had used decades ago to build Pilgrim Boone into the behemoth it had become, the same stick-to-itiveness when he had to go it alone after the untimely death of Carter Boone in a plane crash.

He countered the ambassador's argument. "We're not talking about public relations, Excellency. We're talking about development, about taking those very priorities you talk about to a higher level. We're development strategists, not a PR consultancy."

The ambassador did not see a difference and said so. "Anyway, the World Bank has given us all the consultants we need for the moment."

This was said with such finality that Lawton dropped the matter and switched smoothly to a discussion of the country's chances in this year's soccer World Cup competition. It was his signature strategy: deflect, parry, and punch. Even if the punch came much, much later.

It was only now that developing countries were coming around. They were beginning to understand that American lawmakers and investors really liked it when a highly reputable American firm was involved in cleaning up a poor country's act.

But something had gone terribly awry with the Jamaica contract. Dru knew exactly what it was. She had known it the moment she was introduced on that last trip as the one who would be the lead on the account.

Poor Lawton just didn't get it. How could he? A different dynamic was at play here, one that the Lawtons of this world never encountered. Its vocabulary and the accompanying gestures were so subtle that they flew right past people like Lawton.

But Dru knew all the telltale signs: eyes opening wide in surprise, but only for the smallest fraction of a second; eyelids fluttering in swift recovery; then the all-teeth smile that failed to hide the hardening in the eyes from those who knew the language.

There was the ever-so-slight stiffening in the hand extended in greeting. The almost imperceptible turn of the shoulder so that it wouldn't *really* look like the back was being turned. The stubborn formality in the exchange of words whenever an exchange was unavoidable. And always, always that determinedly polite smile.

Oh, yes. Dru knew it all.

What the hell happened, Lawton, is that thing between some of us black folks, she thought grimly, black people refusing to give their business to other black people. It didn't matter how qualified the blacks were.

Dru recalled when she was planning her first trip to the island—years ago, for spring break with a group of college friends—someone had remarked that it was a place where privilege was accorded to left-over colonials, Syrians, Chinese, coffee-cream blacks and dark-skinned blacks who had *good hair*, good money, Britishy accents and white or near-white wives.

"Those people? They don't like anything blacker than themselves, you hear me?" Dru remembered the girl saying. She was from another island.

Dru couldn't remember which one, but it was somewhere in the eastern Caribbean.

But that's true for black people everywhere, even here in America, Dru had argued.

"Not like there. You'll see," the girl had said with a knowing smile.

Over the years, Dru had run into the same thing in other parts of the Caribbean and even in Africa—this passing over of black professionals, no matter how good their credentials, in favor of whites. She found it most prevalent in cities and big towns, among the pockets of people who had clawed their way to money and membership in circles absorbed with their own pretensions to nobility and class and entitlement. Most of the time it made her angry, but sometimes she found herself laughing outright at the pretensions.

Of late, she simply ignored them. Outside of those sorry-ass little circles were the real people, thank God, the masses who had no delusions about who they were, where they came from, or where they needed to be, who let it be known that no one was greater than they were because their greatness came from old, old traditions and from the Almighty.

What a world, Dru sighed.

She spoke patiently to Lawton now. "So we lost this one, Lawton. It's not the end of the world. There are many others to win."

"Don't give me that trite bullshit, Dru! I know there are other fish in the sea. What I want to know is why we didn't hook this one! And what do you mean, you're not surprised?"

Dru sighed. Maybe she *should* give Lawton her take on what happened.

"I'm waiting for an answer, Drucilla."

Dru sighed again. She knew that tone.

"Okay, Lawton. You asked for it so I'll give it to you. Just don't give me any righteous outrage when you hear what I have to say, okay?"

"Get to the point, Dru."

"We lost the contract because they're uncomfortable with someone like me handling the account."

There was a long silence before Lawton responded.

"What are you saying, Dru?" He spoke very quietly.

"I'm saying that I believe they would be more comfortable with someone who fits the physical image of the kind of person they have in mind for the job. I do not fit that image, Lawton."

Another long silence.

"I see," Lawton said finally, still in that very quiet voice.

Dru released the breath she suddenly realized she had been holding. She did not have to go any further. Lawton understood.

That did not mean the matter was over, but at least no words of indignation would be hurled into the air. Lawton would settle the score in his own way. She could tell by the quiet of his voice, a quiet that spelled danger. It was the proverbial calm before the storm, more like the calm before the hurricane, when it came to Lawton Pilgrim.

As she waited for him to speak, she thought of the two occasions on which she had seen Lawton in action, wreaking vengeance on those who had made themselves his adversaries. The first time was right after she joined the firm. It was over an article in the press about an affair alleged to be taking place between Lawton and one of his administrative assistants. The girl in question had had a little too much to drink at a gala event, and had bragged about an alleged affair to a reporter for one of the monthly gossip tabloids.

The reporter and his paper ran with the story without checking the facts. They had pieced together all sorts of circumstantial evidence to paint a picture of the taciturn Pilgrim as a womanizer. They even juxtaposed photos of Pilgrim with those of various young women on the fast-track to the boardroom, never saying that he really was not in the company of these women, but simply happened to be attending the same functions they were at the time.

The day after the story appeared, Lawton summoned the assistant to his office, where he had already assembled Phil Beckenstein, a lawyer from the firm that represented Pilgrim Boone; Marlene Driscoll, head of the human resources department; Elaine Panelli, who sat on the newly created Ethics Committee of the Wall Street Chamber of Commerce; and, much to her own surprise, Dru herself.

In front of all of these people, Lawton asked the girl to explain the origin of the newspaper story. The poor girl broke down, sobbing that she had been drunk and was just kidding around; that she did not know she was talking to a reporter. It wasn't meant to go that far.

She begged, pleaded, groveled for a chance to redeem herself. She would be a slave for Pilgrim Boone if that was what Mr. Pilgrim wanted.

She was fired on the spot, with no severance pay. She got not a dime more than the money she had worked for up to the very hour of the meeting. Months later, when she realized that she was blacklisted and would never again find a job in any consulting firm of good repute, even if she had sued Pilgrim Boone for harassment, the girl committed suicide. She left a note saying how sorry she was for the shame and disgrace she had brought on a wonderful man and on her family, and that it was she who had a crush on Pilgrim and had made up the whole thing about an affair after she had been drinking.

Well, I guess the liquor lobby will come out with guns blazing, Dru had thought dryly when she read the news of the suicide.

It didn't end there.

Throughout the ordeal, Lawton had refused to speak to the press, not even to the biggest bylines on the society and business pages of the cream of the publications crop. Once the girl confessed, he filed separate suits against the offending reporter and his newspaper. The charges were reckless disregard for the truth, defamation of character, and malicious intent. His lawyers proved them all.

Even after his victory in court, Lawton made no statements to the press. The day the court decided in Lawton's favor, the head of Pilgrim Boone's public relations department announced in a brittle voice to the microphones shoved in his face outside the courthouse that Pilgrim Boone had no comment to make on a matter that American jurisprudence had laid to rest.

On the second occasion, the head of a small, upcoming accounting firm had caused Pilgrim Boone to lose a hard-won account by suggesting at an elite, private gathering of financial analysts that Pilgrim Boone's growth strategy was "risky and unwise."

Lawton and the accounting firm's CEO had been college roommates for a year and they still saw each other socially. This "friend" was not being malicious. At least that's what he told everyone afterward. Besides, he complained, wasn't the gathering off-the-record? Street talk in a private home? Nobody had said anything about the press being there. He was merely giving his candid, objective view of the booming consulting industry and how accounting firms were taking advantage of that boom. All he had done was note that Pilgrim Boone was in a very vulnerable position because its growth strategy put so much store in countries whose economies were not on solid footing. Wasn't that the plain truth?

"Lawton is my good friend and we talk business all the time, but I worry about him. Anyone who's as heavily exposed as he is in the emerging markets could be in for a rough tumble," the CEO had declared earnestly during the gathering. "I see a lot of signs in Asia that tell me the bubble is going to burst soon. There's just too much money flowing too freely into places it shouldn't be flowing to. It just can't continue. And when it goes bust in Asia, Latin America and all the rest of the developing world will feel it. I wouldn't be surprised if we soon begin to see a whole lot of red ink on the financial statements of firms that are heavily exposed in emerging markets."

A small mention of these sentiments appeared in *The Wall Street Journal*'s "Heard On The Street" column the next day, with Pilgrim Boone prominently mentioned. Neither Lawton's friend's name, the location of the gathering, nor even the names of others who had been there had been mentioned.

Even though the columnist expressed confidence in Pilgrim Boone's decision to "go where few still dared to go," and that the fundamentals of the firm were sound enough to enable it to weather any storms in the emerging markets, the mere speculation on the possibility of trouble, and a suggestion of unwise business decisions were enough to raise a few eyebrows.

The subsequent buzz, albeit short-lived, was too much for the telecommunications giant that had engaged Pilgrim Boone to study the landscape in developing countries and come up with a few investment options.

The company's board of directors was dominated by some of the most conservative names in American business. It had been hard enough to get them to consider investments in Canada and Europe, let alone "the poverty-stricken, debt-ridden, communist-prone Third World." But, swayed by Lawton Pilgrim's passionate reasoning, they had finally agreed to go forward with the Pilgrim Boone study, the results of which they would take "under advisement," they said.

The "Heard On The Street" column sent them scurrying back into the corner from which they had so reluctantly ventured. They pulled the plug on the Pilgrim Boone study that very week.

Lawton got the bad news from the company's chief executive himself over lunch at Bouley Restaurant.

"Sorry, Lawton, but you know my board. A bunch of tight-asses. They just don't like the buzz about Pilgrim Boone. Everybody knows it's all hogwash, but I've got to abide by what they say. They dragged me in and went on and on about protecting the interest of our shareholders. Sorry, old man. I have no choice."

Lawton had accepted the decision graciously. Inwardly, however, he was seething. He had expected the buzz from the *Journal* piece to blow over without any damage.

He didn't seethe for long. Beginning with the columnist, who refused to reveal his source, he harangued everyone who had attended the analysts' meeting until he was able to figure out and confirm who the loudmouth was. He was devastated to learn it was his good friend, but he decided to bide his time before he took action. He would let the buzz fizz.

A year later, at a fund-raiser to launch the governor's re-election campaign, he let it slip within earshot of a reporter for *The Financial Times* that the Securities and Exchange Commission was about to launch an investigation into the accounting practices of a certain aerospace company.

Dru was standing next to Lawton at the time. Lawton's position within earshot of the reporter was no coincidence. He knew every important reporter by face and by name. The reporter immediately approached Lawton for more details, but Lawton feigned annoyance, telling the reporter to go digging elsewhere and threatening to sue him and his paper if he was quoted in connection with any story about an SEC investigation into the aerospace company.

The following week, *The Financial Times* broke the story about the SEC investigation, backing it up with statements from anonymous sources and even a "neither will confirm nor deny" from the SEC itself, which was as much an admission as any.

Neither Lawton Pilgrim's name, nor that of Pilgrim Boone, was mentioned in the article.

That was the beginning of the end for Lawton's ex-friend's accounting firm. The aerospace company was its biggest client, and its management suspected that someone in the accounting firm had spoken out of turn.

That's the way it was with Lawton. He was fair but he was no saint. Hurt him and he would hurt you back. He fought an ugly, down-in-the-gutter fight.

Dru felt sorry for Jamaica. It had no idea what it had gotten itself into by snubbing Pilgrim Boone.

But like Lawton, she was no saint. She didn't feel sorry for the island for long. Hell, she groused silently, it wasn't her fault that, in this day and age, some black folk still behaved as though they came from a better breed of slaves than everyone else. *They deserve what they get, the arrogant Uncle Tom bastards.*

Dru was on high ground, comfortable in the knowledge that she was on the good side of Lawton Pilgrim. She intended to keep it that way.

In the privacy of her office, the phone pressed to her ear as she waited for Lawton to speak, she rolled her neck and pushed away a thought about "consorting with the enemy" that tweaked at her conscience. *The enemy isn't always white folks. Sometimes it's black folk who hate themselves.* She heard Lawton say, "Let's talk in a couple of days, Dru," and hang up.

⁓⫞⫞⁓

Dru put down the phone, closed the file she had been studying when Lawton called, and stood up abruptly, causing her swivel chair to roll back into the wall with a thud.

Glancing at the clock, she stepped from behind her desk, stepped out of her shoes, and kicked them aside. She closed the door, stood in the middle of the floor, and let her body go limp. She uttered a contented sigh as she arched her back, balled her hands into tight fists, lifted her arms, and pushed them up toward the ceiling with all the tension of a weightlifter struggling against his personal best. Her stockinged feet were planted a hip's width apart and she pressed them down as hard as she could, flattening them against the floor. Her mind told her body that she was in the grasp of two powerful, opposing forces, one holding her down by the ankles, the other pulling her up by the wrists, stretching her torso, and stretching it more.

She held the stretch for as long as she could hold her breath, then she let go, exhaling slowly and collapsing her body so that her head and limbs hung limp again. She rolled her head from side to side, counting to ten, then rotated her shoulders, ten times backward, ten times forward. Finishing the rotations, she pulled herself erect, neck long, eyes on the horizon, to lift the spine. She closed her eyes, bent her knees just slightly, then turned her waist to the left, held it for an instant, then turned to the right, held it, back again to the left and again to the right. Her arms swung loosely with each turn.

She opened her eyes, inhaling and exhaling deeply, and remained motionless.

Stand like a tree, her instructor's voice said.

After a minute she shook herself, retrieved her shoes from beside her desk and slipped them on. God, that felt good, she said aloud as she plopped down at her desk and pulled the folder to her.

The telephone rang. She reached for it.

"This is Dru," she said, her voice relaxed and mellow.

There was a brief silence before the voice on the other end of the line said, "Hello, Dru. This is Theron St. Cyr."

8

June 15, 1998

A heated argument between Andrew "Livuh" Goodings and Reginald "Macky" MacPherson, minister of transportation, was taking place over drinks in the family room of MacPherson's home.

Goodings had dropped by unexpectedly for a nightcap with his boyhood friend, now his neighbor in the posh Prashad Nagar community where the elite of Guyana were bedding down for the night in homes costing millions of Guyanese dollars, guarded by armed ex-policemen and ferocious pedigree canines.

The minister was delighted by the surprise visit. His wife and children were spending the August holidays with his mother-in-law in Essequibo County and he was feeling particularly lonely and restless this night. He had a lot on his mind.

After a third round of rum and Pepsi—fealty to Pepsi ran deep and fierce among Guyanese—the conversation between the minister and Goodings landed on the subject that pained them both, but to which they were always drawn when they drank.

"I don't care what anybody says, Macky. There is no way anybody born and bred in this country can justify such an asinine decision,"

Goodings declared passionately. "Whoever heard of ripping out a country's entire railroad system? *Especially* in a small, poor country like Guyana, where country people depend on that train to get to town and back. Good Christ, man! What the hell were those guys smoking?"

Goodings was so angry that his generous bottom lip flapped furiously, giving the impression of someone shaking a piece of liver, hence his nickname. "Livuh" was the kinder nickname, the one he accepted from his closest friends. More malicious individuals called him "Lipticus" or "Lebba Lip," *lebba* being the local lexicon's pronunciation of *liver*.

Teasing about his lip had been the most ruthless in elementary school. His classmates drove him crazy simply by tapping on their bottom lips with their index fingers. And they did it with an almost absent expression, as if they were lost in thought and the last thing on their minds was Andrew Goodings' lip.

Although he was bright enough to be admitted to Queens College, the elite high school in Georgetown, Goodings was so devastated by the death of his mother just a week before classes started that he never recovered enough to make good grades. He barely scraped through to the sixth form, often finishing at the bottom of his class. Many who knew his potential called it a blessing in disguise when his father sent him, at eighteen, to Florida to live with an uncle. A year later, while still employed as a driver for a surveying company, he enrolled in the civil engineering department at the University of Florida.

At twenty-five he had a master's degree from the University of Texas at Austin and headed north to work for the Port Authority of New York and New Jersey. He took early retirement from his position as a senior engineer in the bridges and tunnels division, sold his house on Long Island, bought a two-bedroom fixer-upper condo in Harlem—"because it's wise to own a piece of real estate in America"—fixed it up, and rented it out for a handsome amount that was deposited directly into his Carver Federal Savings Bank account. He moved back to Guyana with his American wife and took up residence in the house they had built in the exclusive Prashad Nagar community six years ago, and which had been rented to the Japanese Embassy for those six years.

In the States, Goodings had seen his three children through college and helped each one buy a house. After they were all married and had started families of their own, he began to think of going back to Guyana. The children and grandchildren could visit. It would be good for them to get closer to his half of their roots, he thought. The winter cold was beginning to eat into his bones. He wanted to be buried in Guyana, he told his friends in New York. His wife said she loved him enough to follow him wherever he went.

At a private farewell party his closest friends threw for him at Henry House in Brooklyn, he stood straight-backed at the microphone and recited the words of M.A. Coussou's "My Native Land," one of Guyana's most moving patriotic songs. When he came to the final verse his voice rumbled with passion. His bottom lip trembled. With his right hand splayed over his heart, his left arm flung toward the heavens, he squeezed his eyes shut and sang out the words in a rich bass:

> *And though I rove o'er hill and dale*
> *And brave old Neptune's foam*
> *O'er crags and rocks and mossy dells*
> *I still will turn me home*
> *For when at length I come to die*
> *I want no gilded tomb*
> *Just let me rest within thy breast*
> *Where thy sweet flowers bloom.*
> *Where thyyy sweeeet floowwuurs blooooooom!*

The Guyanese among the gathering stood and joined him when he got to "Just let me rest."

As soon as Goodings arrived in Guyana, Macky MacPherson put him on the payroll as a senior adviser to the transportation ministry. No one—not in the ruling party, not in the opposition, the civic watch groups, nor the press—uttered a word against that decision.

Macky looked at his friend now with mischievous eyes. He liked to play the devil's advocate with Livuh.

"But Livuh, we built roads when we did away with the train lines, man. Gave the people cars, modern buses. All kinds of high-powered lorries. I don't hear anybody grumbling about that," he said slyly.

MacPherson had been named transportation minister even though he was a member of the opposition party. It was a brilliant move by the ruling party, proof positive that the president had risen above the political bloodletting, had taken the high road in the interest of the country, as he had promised to do during his inaugural speech.

A graduate of the University of the West Indies, MacPherson had worked his way up in the transportation industry from his days as a clerk with the municipal bus company in Georgetown. Everybody agreed he was by far the most competent man for the job.

"Macky knows the topography of Guyana like the back of his hand," *The Chronicle* had said in its editorial. And, indeed, he knew where and how to build roads that would not be flooded out by the rains, where to bridge the rivers, the best location for an airstrip in the hinterland. Most of all, he knew the commuting patterns of the people in the villages, towns, and cities.

Macky sipped his drink and arranged his huge bulk more comfortably in the Berbice chair. He sighed contentedly. It was a relief to be talking to his friend.

"Are you listening to me, Macky?" Livuh demanded impatiently, his voice rising. "I'm not saying we shouldn't have built new roads and brought in vehicles that people could afford to buy. All I'm saying is that we should have kept the train lines. What was wrong with having both?"

"But you know as well as I do that was not the way the deal went down," said Macky, his eyes piercing Livuh's.

Macky was a fan of black-American sitcoms and movies that starred black Americans, which he pirated with a state-of-the-art satellite dish on his roof. Every so often he liked to test his knowledge of the lingo.

Livuh sucked his teeth. "Man, Macky man, don't talk to me 'bout no deals. All o' you betray we country. Bunch o' damn fools," he said, switching to Creole to emphasize his frustration.

Macky studied his glass. He shook it to let the water from the melted ice cubes mix with the rum and Pepsi. After a while he looked up and nodded at Goodings. "Is true. When you come to think of it, is really true. We sell out."

He sipped his drink slowly and continued in a sober voice. "But the Americans and Europeans put a hell of a lot of pressure on us, Livuh. All kinds of people—World Bank people, IMF people, Paris Club people, aid people, everybody who lend development money—all o' dem was coming in here telling us that road was the way to go. I tell you, money was flowing for roads, man. The money people said that they wouldn't give us anything for railroads. Not a red cent! You don't think we knew it was better for us to keep the railroad? But what were we supposed to do? The trains were old and decrepit anyway. We had no money of our own to replace them. And as for getting help from our socialist friends, hmph! They had other priorities—Africa, Latin America. Guyana was small peas to them."

Macky paused and took a big swallow of his rum and Pepsi. Livuh swirled the liquor in his glass and waited for Macky to continue.

"That was the time when we wanted to get closer to the Americans. The Americans knew it, too. I tell you, they had us by the balls, Livuh. They had that big-shot consulting firm tightening the screws behind the scenes all the time. You know which one: Pilgrim Boone. The same one that is now trying to get us to buy airplanes from Savoy Aerospace. Slick outfit. Roped in Nelson Roopnaraine and Compton Dalrymple to work over the people closest to the president. Those two made out like bandits. Pilgrim Boone paid them a hundred thousand dollars U.S. each. A hundred thousand dollars! You know what money like that can do in Guyana? Especially back then?"

MacPherson sucked his teeth and cut his eyes away from Livuh.

Goodings said, "Didn't anybody call Pilgrim Boone to task for violating its own country's Foreign Corrupt Practices Act? It's against U.S. law for American companies operating overseas to pay bribes."

"No case. Pilgrim Boone formally contracted Roopnaraine and Dalrymple as local consultants. Had them write up some stupid feasibility study that probably ended up in the rubbish, and paid them for it. The payments were legitimate consulting fees. Besides, who wanted to take on

Pilgrim Boone? They say old man Pilgrim is one vindictive son of a bitch when he gets ready."

"But Dalrymple was permanent secretary at the time. How did he get away with being a consultant?"

"The money was passed through his brother's consulting firm. For all intents and purposes, it was the brother's firm that Pilgrim Boone hired. Of course, Roopnaraine was in the clear. He was a private individual."

"Mmm! Mmm! Mmm! Greed is a hell of a thing," Goodings said, shaking his head. "So right after that, Dalrymple resigned from the ministry and went into business with Roopnaraine, right?"

"Right. That's when Roopnaraine Scrap Metal Co., Ltd. became Roopnaraine and Dalrymple, Traders & Consultants Ltd. And guess who got the contract from the government to dig up the railroad *and* dispose of the iron? Man, I can't even begin to imagine how much they made selling the scrap alone!"

"A triple killing. No wonder they're multimillionaires."

"Big fancy office on Brickdam. Yuh been deh yet? Hanh! Man, you should see inside!"

"Traders I can understand. But consultants in what? What's their specialty?"

"Nothing and everything. It's a clever way for them to attract all kinds of business, especially from foreigners. But you know, when you come to think of it, Livuh, is it really greed? Dem boys jus' got business smarts. Plastic was kicking the shit out of Roopnaraine's scrap metal business, and the party wasn't putting Dalrymple no higher than permanent secretary. Nah! It wasn't greed. Wuz nutten more dan dey tekkin advantage o' de opportunity. Dey ain' kill nobody. And in the end, the *Kabaka* coulda said no, right?"

Goodings closed his eyes and leaned back until his head rested on the chair back. He took a deep breath. "So I suppose Pilgrim Boone is going back to them again on this airplane business," he said.

Restless, he opened his eyes and leaned forward again, dragging his hands down his face.

Sometimes, like now, he wondered why he cared. Why he'd come back to spend his last days in a country that seemed not to care about its own well-being. He might as well have stayed in the United States with his memories of the Guyana he knew as a child, the old Guyana he bragged about to Americans. The warmth and beauty of its people and walking without fear at night. Its greater than 80 percent literacy and the brilliance of its scholars and cricketers. The majestic St. George's Cathedral—tallest wooden building in the world. The magnificent hardwoods coveted by nations far and wide, including America itself. Didn't Americans know it was Guyana's greenheart that buttressed the Brooklyn Bridge, he would say with his chest high. The longer greenheart stayed in the water the harder it became. Yes, he could have stayed in America and bragged about the Guyana of which he was proud.

But home was home and it had called him back.

He was sure he heard envy in Macky's voice when he responded to his question. "Of course, Pilgrim Boone is going back to them. Wouldn't you? They delivered for them before."

Goodings sighed again. Neither man spoke for a long while.

Goodings broke the silence. "So, if I understand it correctly, Pilgrim Boone is trying to sell Guyana on the idea of establishing an air transport system for travel into the interior, right? But the opposition, and quite a few people in the president's own party, want the railroad back. Am I right?"

"Right."

"Pilgrim Boone, of course, is operating on behalf of Savoy Aerospace, which says it would give Guyana excellent—their word—terms on a fleet of small planes if we opt for air transport over rebuilding the railroad."

"Yes. Same kind of deal as before, only a different mode of transportation and a different client. Last time Pilgrim Boone was working for the U.S. auto industry. This time it's the aerospace industry. Savoy has been kicking ass in the last five years, clawed its way to number two with all kinds of merger deals."

All of a sudden Goodings chuckled. "Would serve them right if the president started talking to Embraer in Brazil and Airbus in France. They

93

make good planes." He burst out laughing, throwing himself back in his chair. "Maybe they should even be talking to the Chinese."

MacPherson roared. "That's a good one, Livuh. I could see it now. Big splash in the papers and on TV. Mek Pilgrim Boone suck salt!"

They laughed until tears rolled out of their eyes. Still laughing, Macky got up, picked up the two empty glasses, and walked over to the liquor cabinet. He broke open a new bottle of El Dorado Gold, splashed some on the floor and muttered a toast to the souls of his ancestors, then refilled the glasses. He poured some Pepsi into both drinks, added fresh cubes of ice, handed Goodings his glass, and raised his own. "To Guyana!" he said, still chuckling.

"To Guyana!" Goodings echoed.

They were pensive as they savored the liquor. For a while, the only noises in the otherwise still night were the distant bark of a dog and the sound of ice tinkling against glass. Unaware they were doing so, the two men shook their glasses in unison, making circular motions. Each man's eyes were fixed on the play of light on the ice and the golden liquid in his glass.

Again it was Goodings who broke the silence. "Seriously, though, Macky. Where does the president really stand? What's his thinking?"

Macky's reply was matter-of-fact. "You know how it is with Quartapint. The consummate politician. Wants it both ways. Likes the attention from America. The air transport proposal is sweet. It makes sense. Would be a boon to our fledgling tourism industry. But he knows the train line is more practical for now, and would be more popular with the people."

He paused, sipped his drink, and continued in a mellow voice. "Deep down, he knows we got the shorter end of the stick on the railroad deal. Sure we got something out of it, but we lost much more. Set us back on the bigger transportation picture, not to mention our plans for agro-industry. Farmers just couldn't move their goods fast enough. Quartapint doesn't want his government to make the same mistake. All these years he's still getting away with blaming the *Kabaka* for our stagnant economic growth."

"So what does he want you to do?"

"Just what I am doing. He told me to talk it over with you. See what you had to say. He trusts your judgment."

"I don't know, Macky. Something about it doesn't sit right with me. How come all of a sudden Savoy Aerospace is interested in little Guyana? Who is really pushing this deal? It's easy to assume that Savoy Aerospace just wants to sell planes. And nothing's wrong with their wanting to do that. That's how they make their money. But we need to find out what those guys really want from Guyana beyond selling us a few planes. And what will happen to us if we decide not to buy them? What if we decide to rebuild the train line instead? These corporate giants have long arms."

Goodings sounded grim. He and Macky had never gotten this far before. The railroad lament had always ended with each of them taking turns at berating the "treachery" of people like Roopnaraine and Dalrymple. Too many Roopnaraines and Dalrymples were cropping up in Guyana. There were too many people who cared more about getting rich than seeing the country progress. Corruption had spiraled way out of control. It was sucking the blood out of Guyana. Something had to be done. And soon!

But tonight they had moved into new territory. The two men silently acknowledged this as they held each other's eyes.

Thoughts of Pilgrim Boone filled MacPherson's head. The firm was back on the scene in full force, again at the behest of one of the world's most powerful corporations, not that it had been totally absent since its success with the railroad-auto business. Pilgrim Boone executives breezed into Georgetown every so often to conduct one feasibility study or another for various U.S., European, and Asian mining and lumber interests. As far as MacPherson knew, they had never approached the government itself with a mega-infrastructure proposal, as they had done in other parts of the developing world. He often wondered why, but he would dismiss the question almost as soon as it came into his head. Why should he waste his time trying to second-guess Pilgrim Boone?

"You sure you're not being paranoid, Livuh? I find a lot of people who lived in the States see a plot in everything," he said carefully, wanting to draw out his friend's thinking.

"And with good reason. Listen to me, Macky. I spent forty years over there, more than half of them working for one of the biggest contract-peddling organizations in the country. I was an insider, privy to a lot of deals. Believe me, 95 percent of the time things were not as black and white as they seemed. There was always a subdeal, always somebody deep in the background whose special interests were being catered to. If there's a plan for Guyana, if there's someone's special interest deep in the background, we need to know what it is."

"So what should we do?"

"I know someone who can scope out this whole thing for us. A guy named Theron St. Cyr. French-American. Black guy. He's got a small firm that does excellent work. Behind-the-big-picture work—"

MacPherson cut him off with a groan. "Not another consultant."

"St. Cyr is good. Damned good. The Port Authority of New York and New Jersey used him once to take a second look at a dredging contract awarded to a big-name contractor. The waste disposal component didn't ring right with one of the top Port Authority guys, who had political aspirations and was avoiding anything that smelled the least bit rank. It was a hush-hush deal when they brought in St. Cyr. Seems a few of the port's board members also were uneasy about the contractor's connections, but they didn't want word of their uneasiness to get out.

"Anyway, St. Cyr came in and did the job quietly. He told them that the waste was being recycled too close to a reservoir. The contractor was livid when he heard what went down, why the port held up their first payment. He even threatened to sue St. Cyr, whose name had been leaked by one of the board members. But the Port Authority stuck by St. Cyr. They didn't write off the contractor. That would have created all kinds of hell. You know, interested parties and all that. They only made the contractor redo the proposal with better provision for the waste. A few months later, state environment officials found a tiny runoff into the reservoir from an old paper mill in the area. Nothing toxic was going in, at least not yet. But if the dredging waste had been disposed of in the same area, God knows what would have happened.

"After that, St. Cyr was signed on as a regular. Good man. Solid balls. Integrity." Goodings pounded a fist on the side table to emphasize "balls" and "integrity."

96

MacPherson suddenly felt tired. He had reached his limit of rum and Pepsi. Livuh was making things too complicated with all this Port Authority business. Still, he had to admit, he'd been asking himself the same questions that Livuh had raised. Why this lust for Guyana all the time? Somebody always had a grand plan for his country. The British, the French, the Dutch, the Jews, crazy Jim Jones and his suicide cult. Avaricious Venezuela claiming a third of the country as part of its territory for no other reason than the oil that was yet to be exploited. Christ! When would it end?

MacPherson was a man who studied the history of nations, and the relationships between nations, and the part each of those individual histories and relationships played in shaping the current state of the world. He harbored dreams of one day writing a book on the subject. From all his readings, and from the news reports he captured via his satellite dish, he had tucked away in his memory all sorts of little dots that he knew he would connect when the day came to write the book.

Now, as he pondered the idea of his country in the grand design of those with limitless power and wealth and influence, he delved into his encyclopedic store of little dots. Was there something magical in this land of eighty-three thousand square miles and barely half a million people that others saw and the Guyanese didn't? It had to be more than the gold, the diamonds, the bauxite. Perhaps someone saw it as the Caribbean's Singapore or Malaysia. An eighty-three-thousand-square-mile factory churning out all sorts of goods for buyers around the world? That wouldn't be so bad, would it?

Perhaps a haven for people running from high taxes, now that Bermuda and other islands were under the microscope. A military beachhead maybe? But in preparation for war between who and who?

MacPherson sighed heavily.

"Don't let it weigh so much on you, Macky boy." Livuh spoke gently. "We could bring in St. Cyr without a word to anybody. What is there to lose? He'll either find a clean deal or a dirty deal."

"Yes, but what will it cost us? How will we pay for his services?"

"Don't worry about that. He owes me a favor for that first Port Authority contract. I was the one who introduced him to those folks."

Macky sighed again. "Okay. Let's bring him in, then. But make sure he knows that discretion is the name of the game. I know nothing about this. I'm not even sure I want to meet the fella."

"You'll never have to worry about St. Cyr and discretion, Macky. The man breathes it."

Macky stood up, drained his glass and stretched. "Livuh, you're either a godsend or, as you Americans say, a pain in the ass," he said.

Livuh laughed and stood up. "I'll take that as a compliment."

He looked at his watch. "Well, it's way past midnight. I stayed here longer than I intended to. I'm off. Need my beauty sleep."

They shook hands at the door.

"Good night, Macky. I'll talk to my guy tomorrow and give you the particulars."

"Ahright. 'Night, Livuh."

9

June 16, 1998

"**D**id you hear what Pilgrim Boone did to Jamaica, Compton?"

Nelson Roopnaraine stood in the doorway of Compton Dalrymple's office, a thick sheaf of papers in his hand. He was on his way down to the accountant's office on the first floor. The government was demanding more than the firm had already paid in taxes, a demand with which he had no intention of complying.

Roopnaraine looked like a man who was feeding from the fatted calf. The gold ring with a huge nugget that he wore on his left middle finger and the gold chain-link bracelet he wore on his left wrist gleamed as he absently shuffled and reshuffled the sheaf of papers. The pounds of prosperity that generously expanded his girth were set off by a custom-tailored gray suit, light-blue shirt, and blue-and-gold tie. His jet-black hair no longer was slicked down with coconut oil as in the old days. It was airbrushed light, with a few wisps strategically arranged on his forehead. His thick eyebrows had been plucked into gentle contours. His nails had been manicured for twenty dollars U.S. at Savitri's, the salon of choice for everyone who was anyone in Georgetown. The scent of Old Spice Classic smacked the air with his slightest move.

Dalrymple abruptly stopped the dictation he was giving to his secretary and looked at his partner.

"No. What did Pilgrim Boone do to Jamaica?" He, too, exhibited the physical weight of prosperity. And, like Roopnaraine, to whom he had introduced his own tailor, he was resplendent in a summer-weight gabardine tan suit, white shirt, and olive-green bow tie. Gold adorned a finger on each hand and both wrists. The smooth-shaved, baby-bottom skin of his face and manicured nails marked another job well done by Savitri's. Cartier glasses and Diesel cologne bought in from Atlanta completed the image.

Dalrymple and Roopnaraine were your corporate Dapper Dans *par excellence.*

"Took away the G-15 summit from them. Got it moved to Trinidad and Tobago," said Roopnaraine, his voice almost breathless with awe.

"Don't be an ass, Nello. You can't move the summit like that. All fifteen of those countries voted for Jamaica to be the host this year."

"Well, Lawton Pilgrim seems to have gotten that decision changed. That's what you get for pissing that old bastard off."

"What do you mean pissing him off? What did they do to him?"

"I thought you knew, man. They strung him along on their FIS contract then gave it to Peat Marwick."

"Why would they want to do a stupid thing like that?"

"Maybe somebody didn't like the idea of a l'il black gyal in charge of the account. You know how some o' we people t'ink," Roopnaraine said seriously. Roopnaraine held the view that the human race was divided into black people and white people. Anyone who was not European was black because that was the way the white-controlled world treated all non-whites. And in the eyes of whites, if you were black you were inferior. Not that he believed this inferiority crap one bit. It was just the way white people lived in a world where they were outnumbered, but had the power of money and weapons of mass destruction.

"All white people?" Dalrymple asked in surprise the first time Roopnaraine expressed this view. Dalrymple saw eye to eye with Roopnaraine on most issues, but this was not one of them. He could not accept that all whites believed in the master race theory.

Not even a breath passed between his question and Roopnaraine's vehement answer. "Every last one o' dem, plus dem who t'ink they white! But white man ain' bettah dan nobody. And in Guyana, nobody bettah dan nobody. All o' we is Guyanese, an' as Guyanese, we got bigguh t'ings fo' worry 'bout! Like how fo' grow rich in a rich country that's poor."

Today, Roopnaraine was in no mood for verbal sparring on the subject. "There is no way Lawton Pilgrim would let such a low blow go by. No way," he said, slapping the sheaf of papers against his palm for emphasis and unleashing another burst of Old Spice.

"What makes you so sure Lawton Pilgrim is behind the G-15 change, if indeed there is a change? I didn't hear anything on the news."

"What's the matter with you, man? Isn't that why we get paid big money? To know the news before it makes the news?" Roopnaraine tut-tutted, shaking his head. "You let me down, Commo. I got wind of a sudden venue change from some people at the Caricom Secretariat. Then I put two and two together, and Drucilla Durane all but confirmed my four. She said she had never seen Pilgrim so furious when he found out that he had lost the contract to Peat Marwick."

"You believe her? She may be telling you that just to put pressure on us about delivering this airplane deal. You know how cold and calculating she is."

Roopnaraine laughed. "She isn't cold at all. She's quite nice to me in person and when she calls. You're just saying that because she won't give you any."

The pretty secretary coughed. She crossed and re-crossed her legs daintily, trying hard to suppress a snicker.

Dalrymple gave her a hard look. "I'm a happily married man, in case you have forgotten, Mr. Roopnaraine," he said with a straight face.

"Since when did that ever stop you, sweet boy?" Roopnaraine countered with a slow smile.

The secretary could not contain herself. She exploded into a fit of coughing, hastily excused herself, and, sputtering that she had to get a drink of water, rushed from the office.

Roopnaraine stepped aside with a deep bow as she ran past him.

"You're such a fool, Nello," Dalrymple said. "Try to be serious. We've got to get more aggressive with the minister on the air transport proposal. He's dragging his feet."

"I think he's been talking to Lebba Lip. He doesn't make a move without checking with that man. And you know Lebba Lip. Man got a mind like de CIA. Don' trus''e own mudda."

"His mother died when he was twelve years old, Nello."

"Well, he don' trus' she spirit."

Dalrymple feigned shock. "Nelson Roopnaraine talking about *jumbee*. I thought you didn't believe in such things—*jumbee*, and mermaid, and moongazer, and *baccoo*—all of those spirits that populate our wonderful folkloah." He ended with a mock British accent.

"Very funny, Mr. Dalrymple. You should take your own advice about being serious. Let's invite Minister MacPherson to lunch this week."

"Good idea. You set it up."

"Okay. You know, Jamaica should make amends to Pilgrim Boone. They might get the summit back."

"You mean they should suck up to Pilgrim Boone?"

"Ouch! Those are unkind words, Mr. Dalrymple." Roopnaraine made a big deal of contracting his body and sucking in air through his teeth as if he had been stung by a bee.

"I wouldn't worry about it. Where the hell is that grinning hyena?" said Dalrymple, stabbing one of the buttons on his phone with his thumb to summon his secretary.

10

Drucilla froze.

It couldn't be. Not after all these years. After all those dreams.

"Hello? Dru? Are you there?"

Twelve years. *Twelve years* had passed and the ordeal still haunted her, tormented her in her sleep. It got so bad sometimes that she would cry out and bolt up in bed, sweating and trembling.

That was what had killed the one serious relationship she had had in all that time. She had refused to see a therapist and Anthony—God how she had loved that man!—just could not take the screaming and the sweats and the shivers anymore.

"Dru?" Theron St. Cyr sounded anxious.

Dru took a deep breath. *This bastard made me lose Anthony!*

"Yes…yes. I…I'm here."

Why was she stammering when her thoughts were so clear? She heard St. Cyr sigh with relief.

"I suppose I caught you by surprise. I hope it is not a bad time for me to call." His voice was apologetic, warm.

Dru heard the faint French accent, so much harder to detect now, almost nonexistent. But it was there, in the formality of the "it is not" instead of the more conversational "isn't," in the slight catch at the back of the throat over the "r."

Suddenly, all the horror, all the fear and despair of that night in her ramshackle prison in Paris came at her in a rush. Her stomach somersaulted. Her head buzzed.

The man saying her name so easily on the other end of the line, talking to her so comfortably, was the man who had put her in that prison.

Theron St. Cyr!

Rage boiled in the pit of her stomach. How dare he call her! How dare he say her name as if she were his friend! What did he think? That she would forget? That she would forgive?

The twirly cord that ran from the receiver to the base of the telephone shook violently. Dru sprang to her feet, her face tight and hard.

"As a matter of fact you did not catch me at a bad time, Mr. St. Cyr," she said with asperity. "How did you get this number?"

"'Mr. St. Cyr!' Whoa! *This* Dru I remember. But why does she surface again? Why are you so angry with me, Dru?"

Why are you so angry with me, Dru? The rage in the pit of Dru's stomach rushed upward and crested in her head. Theron St. Cyr was mocking her. The man was daring her to be nice to him!

Dru drew her breath and opened her mouth to respond, but before she could say anything there was a light knock on the door and Grant Featherhorn stepped into her office. He closed the door softly behind him and leaned against it laconically, his arms folded across his chest, his languid gray eyes fixed on Dru's.

All the fight fled from Dru.

Her jaw dropped in disbelief. She stared at Featherhorn.

The gall of the man! Bad enough that he had not even waited for her to say, "Come in." But to just stand there so rudely. Couldn't he see that she was in the middle of a serious phone conversation?

She covered the mouthpiece with her free hand and mouthed that very question to him between clenched teeth.

Grant Featherhorn did not even blink.

"Aren't you going to respond?" St. Cyr's voice was plaintive now.

It was too much for Dru. "Excuse me!" she barked into the phone. "There is an unpleasant situation in my office and I have to deal with it!"

She covered the mouthpiece again and addressed Featherhorn, fixing him with eyes that glinted like points of steel in the sun. "This is a very private conversation, Grant," she said caustically.

"This is company time, Dru," Featherhorn drawled back with a smile.

Dru turned her back to him. Grant Featherhorn was a partner in the firm. A member of the Inner Circle. And he was her nemesis.

When she joined the firm, she and four other recruits had been assigned to senior partners who would prepare them for membership in Pilgrim Boone's Inner Circle. She had been assigned to Featherhorn and, in their first moments alone, after all the gladsome introductions, in the privacy of his imperious office, he had made it clear that he thought she did not belong on Pilgrim Boone's fast track to the executive suite. That, to him, she was there solely because Lawton Pilgrim felt compelled to wave the flag for affirmative action.

He did not speak those words outright. Grant Featherhorn would never do such a thing. He was the firm's lovable resident liberal. A graying, longhaired charmer, maddeningly svelte and handsome, who frolicked with people in high civil rights places.

What tipped Dru off that he was a closet racist, flower child image be damned, were his condescending remarks when he and she were alone. That's when he would use expressions like "your people" and "your kind."

He would correct her pronunciation with long-suffering patience: "It's '*pen*cil' not '*pin*cil,' Drucilla. And it's '*Wed*nesday,' not '*Wid*nesday.' Sooner or later you'll have to lose your people's accent and learn how to speak like someone who really belongs in the upper echelons of Pilgrim Boone."

He would reel off names of blacks who had been "accepted into some of our most exclusive social circles" and who spoke "so well."

"Close your eyes and you'd never believe there was a darkie in the room," he would say with a gleam in his eyes, goading her.

Darkie!

Dru would bite her lip, swallow hard, and vow silently that this man would not win his war against her.

Making it into Pilgrim Boone's Inner Circle was important to her. She needed to prove to herself, and to a whole bunch of people who had their eyes on her, that she was *that* good. The color of her skin may have gotten her in the door, but that was not what was going to keep her in the building *and* get her into the Inner Circle.

She told no one about Featherhorn's haranguing. Not even her brother—her one and only sibling who knew just about all of her secrets, all her heartaches. Featherhorn was the kind of individual who would never slip up. He would never inadvertently reveal his true nature to anyone in the firm.

At least not to anyone who mattered.

So who would believe her if she complained?

Dru knew she was totally on her own in this and she was absolutely certain that Featherhorn knew this. Just as she was absolutely certain, much later in the mentoring period, that he knew that she knew he could not keep her out of the Inner Circle. For she was one of Lawton Pilgrim's chosen, and there was not a damned thing he or anyone else could do about it.

Unless she quit.

Away from the eyes and ears of everyone else, Featherhorn tried to make her quit. When she made it into the Inner Circle—it seemed a lifetime ago—he looked straight into her eyes, smiled, congratulated her, and wished her well.

Dru would never forget that smile. It had made her shiver.

Theron St. Cyr's voice penetrated her thoughts. "I tell you what, Drucilla. Evidently, I made a mistake calling you."

He paused. When Dru said nothing, he continued, his tone distant and formal. "Perhaps it is because, as you say, something unpleasant has developed at your office. Clearly, however, it's not a good idea for us to be on the phone together. At least not at this time. So I will give you my phone number and you can call me if you would like us to meet again. If I do not hear from you, I promise you I will not call you again."

He recited his number.

Maybe it was because Featherhorn was in the room and she did not want to have to explain why she was holding a phone to her ear and not saying anything. Maybe it was because she wanted to know exactly where to find Theron St. Cyr when she finally found a way to bring his ass down. Whatever the reason, Dru grabbed a pen, pulled a notepad toward her, and wrote down Theron St. Cyr's telephone number.

When St. Cyr finished reciting the number, he did not ask Dru whether she had written it down or not.

Dru spoke stiffly into the phone. "Yes, I think this is the proper way to deal with it. Good-bye."

She put down the phone. It was the best thing to do, she told herself. She could not rail at St. Cyr as she wanted to, not with Featherhorn installed in the room. This was personal business. She would never play into Featherhorn's hands. Would never give him the opportunity to even *suggest* that Drucilla Durane's private life was troubled and risked compromising her work.

She planted her hands firmly on her desk, raised her head, and spoke to Featherhorn. "It was very rude of you to come into my office and just stand there while I was on the phone, Grant," she said icily. She no longer held her tongue with him, not since she had come to realize that he was powerless to keep her out of the Inner Circle.

She sat down, tore off the sheet on which she had written St. Cyr's number, and placed it between the pages of her leather-bound day planner.

Featherhorn watched her movements without saying a word. He waited until she closed the day planner and lifted her eyes to his again before he spoke.

"What about Guyana, Dru?" he asked quietly, ignoring her remark about his being rude.

"What *about* Guyana, Grant?" Dru said, echoing his quiet tone, deliberately ignoring the fact that he had ignored her comment.

"Where are we with the air transport deal, Dru?" He spoke patiently, as if to a child.

"We're moving along well with it, Grant." She responded, as if to an old man who had become senile.

"It doesn't seem that way, Dru."

Dru shrugged. "Our people down there are meeting with the transportation minister again this week, Grant."

"And what can we expect the outcome of that meeting to be, Dru?"

"We can expect the outcome to be satisfactory, Grant."

"Just satisfactory?"

"The term seems appropriate. The Pilgrim Boone motto is temperance in all we do and say, is it not?"

Silence flooded the room. Grant spoke first.

"I understand someone named Andrew Goodings exercises an extraordinary amount of influence on the minister and the president."

"I would say that understanding is flawed."

It wasn't exactly a lie. "Extraordinary" was an exaggeration.

"I am told also that this Goodings is a rabid nationalist who would rather see a new railroad system in place than an air transport network."

"I, too, have been told the same about him."

All through this tit-for-tat conversation, Featherhorn had not moved an inch. He kept his eyes fixed on Dru's, his voice even. At six foot five, his wavy salt-and-pepper hair styled in a page boy, he was a casual but commanding figure. He was not a handsome man by any means. But his height and his air of ownership gave him that *présence* that made even his peers bow and scrape before him.

Dru was not in the least bit intimidated. More than being mentored by Featherhorn, she had been schooled in the art of verbal fencing by Lawton Pilgrim himself. Over the years, she had seen Lawton in some of the most grueling negotiations. She had studied every one of the moves he drew from what he described as his arsenal of diplomacy-cum-martial arts.

"If you are having trouble with this deal we can always get Sharon to help you. She's on a first-name basis with all the Caribbean ambassadors and just about all the heads of state in the region." Featherhorn said, his eyes narrowing just a tiny bit.

Dru smiled. "You're panicking, Grant. There's no need to reach into the trash bin."

To Dru—and, for that matter, most of the staff at Pilgrim Boone—Sharon Brinkley was a blonde, blue-eyed slut who never saw a male executive, official, or diplomat she did not like. Race, color, or creed did not matter to her. The combination of high rank, two legs, and a penis was enough to crank her negotiating skills into high gear, though she insisted coyly that she did not have to sleep with the men she negotiated with. She was always brought in as a last resort on deals that really mattered and she almost always delivered.

Featherhorn returned Dru's smile. His intention had been to push Dru's famous mouth button by mentioning Sharon Brinkley and he had failed. The indignant, defensive tirade he hoped for did not materialize. Quite the contrary, the relaxed composure of the woman before him bordered insultingly on boredom.

It dawned on Featherhorn, then, that this Drucilla Durane would give him more trouble than he had anticipated. Fury settled behind the mask in his eyes. Not a nerve in his face quivered in betrayal. He and Dru remained smiling at each other for a long moment, each fully aware of the hatred simmering between them.

Eventually, Featherhorn turned and opened the door. His movements were calm. He left without a word or backward glance. He did not close the door behind him either.

"Good riddance!" Dru said under her breath. She sank into her chair the moment he disappeared from her doorway.

All of a sudden she felt boxed in. She needed to get out of her office. Out of the building. She needed a vacation, period! She hadn't taken any real time off in God knew how many years. How could she, with Featherhorn breathing down her neck as she slogged her way up the Pilgrim Boone hierarchy. Featherhorn and all those jealous bitches on the fifty-first floor, the ones in middle management, waited eagerly to see her screw up. Some even tried to make her screw up. The little black girl from Brooklyn who was Lawton Pilgrim's pet!

'Pet,' my foot!

She had slogged. And it was worse now that she was in the Inner Circle. Oh, sure, Grant Featherhorn had eased up a little, if you can call switching from racist remarks to biting sarcasm "easing up." Maybe the "easing up" had more to do with the fact that she had learned how to handle him than with any change in his behavior. All she knew was that one day she did not go home and cry her eyes out, and her eyes had stayed dry since that day.

She worked harder than the others in the circle. She loved her work, loved the thrill of the negotiation, of taking potential clients through possibilities they had never dreamed of. She loved watching for that moment when they made that crucial mental leap and she could relax because she knew she had them. Then she would close.

She had no illusions about the weight that the name Pilgrim Boone carried. But she was still a black woman in a white, male-dominated world. Lawton had given her jurisdiction over the Caribbean and sub-Saharan Africa, and even there her blackness still mattered, sometimes in a good way, sometimes in a way that hurt. Her gender mattered, too, though it mattered more with Africans than with West Indians. She had to bring in those accounts. She could not let Lawton down. She couldn't let *herself* down.

She sighed—a long sigh—and rolled her head around. She really needed to get away. She rolled her shoulders and chuckled as an image of her Aunt Petal flashed across her mind.

"Aunt Petal would say I need a husband more than I need a vacation," she muttered.

Aunt Petal was her great aunt on her father's side. Eighty years old and as irascible as a hen with new chicks, sometimes she sounded as if she had just landed from Guyana: "Now you listen to me, you Drucilla! I don't care how much degree you have or how much countries you been to. I don't care if dem Pilgrim Progress people you work for make you Queen of de Roundtable. If you don't have a man to squeeze you up and chil'ren to make you remember yuh pooh-pooh does stink, den all dem odda t'ings don't matta, you hear me? Dey don' matta one bit! Take what I tell you, yes!"

Ever since Dru could remember, she had heard her Guyanese family describe her as "Aunt Petal to a T." She was the image of Aunt Petal in looks, character, and especially "that mouth!"

Dru swiveled her chair around to face the window. Aunt Petal's admonition aside, which had a lot of merit to it, she conceded grudgingly—it wasn't as if she didn't want to get married and have kids—she really needed a vacation. The odd day off here and there didn't count. Since she had made the Inner Circle, her business trips doubled as her vacation. It wasn't much, but at least she was away from the pressures of the office.

Staying in the best hotels, compliments of Pilgrim Boone, she would use her free evenings—yeah, right!—to have a good workout in the hotel gym, then relax in the pool or the Jacuzzi. Afterward, she might take a walk if it was safe enough, or indulge in a long dinner, a drink in the bar, or maybe enjoy casual dancing and conversation with a business associate she met on the trip.

But right now she would settle for a long walk to rid herself of feeling she was suffocating.

After the Jamaica fiasco she had to bring in Guyana. Fast. Lawton did not blame her at all for the way the Jamaicans had acted. Still, she felt responsible for the loss of the contract. Lawton had put the squeeze on the Jamaicans big time, meeting with top officials of the fifteen leading developing countries and persuading them to call for a change of venue because of the high crime in Jamaica.

His meetings with these officials were not cloak-and-dagger affairs. And Lawton himself never uttered a word against Jamaica. But it didn't take much to connect Lawton's meetings with subsequent calls from the same countries for a change of venue. Trinidad and Tobago was the venue most often mentioned as an alternative.

Jamaica had come crawling back to Pilgrim Boone and the calls subsided, hosting the G-15 summit countries was that important to

111

them. Not only would it send their national ego further into orbit, it also would be a boon to their tourism industry.

They didn't come back with the same contract. People have to be allowed to save face, Dru shrugged. They came back with a juicy one for an urban renewal study covering Kingston, the administrative capital, and all the main towns, including Montego Bay, the tourism capital, and May Pen, capital of the sugar and citrus region.

Although she did not let Featherhorn know it, Dru was every bit as concerned about Guyana as he was. Things were moving far too slowly. Roopnaraine had told her about that troublemaker Goodings and all his we-the-people blabber.

Maybe she should go down there herself. Talk to Goodings and MacPherson. Win them over. Assure them that she shared their ideas about rail travel and that she saw no reason why those ideas could not be implemented as well, but, most important, she would press home the point that Guyana needed to move forward at the same pace as other nations of its size and potential. This could happen if people and commerce moved faster from point A to point B, which air transport would do.

She would let Goodings and MacPherson know that while they could always build a railroad system, a deal like this for an air transport system, with all kinds of concessions and perks, came around only once. The offer could easily be taken elsewhere, and where would that leave Guyana?

She would remind them that her own interest in Guyana went beyond something as mundane as an agreement with Pilgrim Boone. With her, it was a matter of her birthright. She would be earnest and passionate because she truly believed all those things.

Yes. That was exactly what she needed to do: Get on a plane to Guyana. Roopnaraine and Dalrymple had come through for Pilgrim Boone before. But that was more than a decade ago, and she did not think they had it in them to do it again. For one thing, the new president was a much younger man—so young, in fact, that Guyanese had nicknamed him "Quartapint," Quarter Pint—who was still very much in salt-of-the-earth mode. That meant he was likely to decide with his heart. Either she or someone close to him that she could win over would have to influence that heart.

Yes, she would fly down to Guyana this very week and take the blasted bull by its blasted horns herself, she thought, using one of Aunt Petal's favorite expressions.

She swiveled around again to her desk and punched a button on the phone.

"Yes, Dru?"

"Leona, I need you to book me on a flight to Guyana. Departing Wednesday, returning the following Monday. And you can book me into the Pegasus, too."

"You got it, Dru. Want me to set up any appointments for you while you're there?"

"Yes, but not right now. I need to make a couple of calls first. As a matter of fact, as soon as you get the flight and hotel reservation arranged, call Roopnaraine and Dalrymple. I'll talk to either one of them."

"I'll get right to it."

"Thanks, Leona."

"Oh, Dru—"

"I know, Leona, I know. A bottle of fifteen-year-old El Dorado. You got it."

Leona giggled. "Thank you, Dru. You know how much my husband likes it since you introduced him to it."

"Yeah, right, Leona. You and I both know who the real rummy is in the family."

Leona giggled again and cut the connection.

Dru sat back in her chair with a smile. Leona was one hell of an assistant. She was the only black one on the executive floor and, true to her name, she watched Dru's back like a lioness guarding her cub.

Dru had insisted on hiring her own secretary when she joined the Inner Circle. She knew what she wanted—needed, rather: a mature, efficient black woman who knew the ropes, one who was familiar with the nasty little games men and women played in corporations in order to reach—and stay in—the upper ranks and, at the same time, one who knew how to earn the trust and respect of the foot soldiers, from executive assistants to mailroom clerks. Equally important was one who liked herself.

Leona had been with IBM for twenty-five years when she was pink-slipped in the company's last round of layoffs. At sixty, she was too young, too healthy, and too full of joie de vivre to stay home, but too old for a job market overrun by eager beaver college graduates willing to take any job in any blue-chip corporation for any salary, as long as the pay was enough for them to afford their one-fourth of the rent at an address in the newest lipsticked slum. She had been referred to Dru by the wife of Dru's pastor.

With Guyana being taken care of, Dru felt a little more relaxed. "Now for you, Mr. St. Cyr," she said aloud.

Her face hardened as her thoughts returned to Theron St. Cyr. She reached for her day planner, opened it to the sheet of paper with his phone number, and stared at it. How was she going to deal with him? She had vowed to make him pay for what he had done to her. In all the years since she had written that contract into her heart, she had dreamed only of seeing him suffer.

She hadn't bothered to contact the French police or the American Embassy. How could she? What would she say? That she had gotten into a car with a total stranger at a *train station* in Paris? That he had imprisoned her in an apartment with chains on the door but she had managed to take the door off its hinges and escape? And what proof did she have that St. Cyr was involved?

The whole thing sounded bizarre, even to her. Except that she had lived it.

And when she returned to New York, whom could she complain to? The French Embassy? The NYPD? That would have been a laugh! They probably would have grilled her about what *she* did to get herself invited to the man's place.

So she had bided her time, knowing in her gut that one day she would see St. Cyr again. She imagined him begging her for mercy after she did whatever it was she was going to do to him. That part she had never worked out. She always told herself she would figure it out later. In her dreams he would be down on his Euro-pimp knees and she would spit in his face and laugh as she walked away.

Or as they took him away to prison.

The dreams were daydreams and sleep dreams. They were so real she would come out of them trembling with the thrill of revenge. Like the thrill she was feeling right now.

What gave him the right to talk to her so casually? What gave him that comfort level?

A thought struck her and she turned to her desktop and logged on to the Internet. There might be something about him on the Web.

At the prompt she typed in his name. Four entries came up. She clicked on the first entry. It brought up the transcript of a presentation Theron St. Cyr had made a year before at the Schomburg Center for Research in Black Culture, an iconic institution in New York City's Harlem community. His presentation was about black Americans who had migrated to France in the second half of the twentieth century. Below the title of the presentation was the presenter's name: Theron St. Cyr, Chief Executive Officer, Trans-Global Solutions, Inc., New York/Atlanta/Paris.

Trans-Global Solutions.

Dru had never heard of the firm. She scanned the presentation, stopping every now and then at a passage that caught her attention. St. Cyr's account of black life in France for his Schomburg audience was as captivating as it had been for her twelve years ago in Marseille. There was the same sensitivity, the easy humor, the deep introspection.

He must have wowed them. The snake!

Dru closed the document and used the computer's Back button to return to the list of entries for "Theron St. Cyr." She clicked on the second entry. It was a repeat of the Schomburg lecture. A click on the third entry brought up a news item about the Port Authority of New York and New Jersey's annual spending with minority-and women-owned companies. Trans-Global Solutions was mentioned as the recipient of a contract to study urban traffic patterns, part of a massive transportation improvement project the Port Authority had just undertaken for the airports in New York and New Jersey. St. Cyr's name was cited as Trans-Global's CEO.

The fourth entry took Dru to *The Network Journal,* a monthly business magazine that she subscribed to but had little time to read from cover to cover. Theron St. Cyr's name appeared in the magazine's latest "40 Under Forty Dynamic Achievers" edition as one of the top black entrepreneurs under forty years old. A biographical note read: "Theron St. Cyr, 38, CEO, Trans-Global Solutions, Inc. New York, Atlanta, Paris. Born Paris, France. B.A., Economics; M.A., Finance, Strasbourg University, France. Special Officers' Corps, French Navy. M.Sc., Environmental Engineering, New Jersey Institute of Technology.

Dru's head swam. Theron St. Cyr was conning the world with his little Trans-Global setup and his college degrees and his special-officer-of-the-French-Navy crap.

What happened to due diligence? Didn't anybody dig deeper than the credentials people threw at them? What about character? What about morals? Don't people care about those things anymore? Is it only about what school you went to, who you know, how much money you make, and how young you are when you're making it? Is that it?

Dru shoved herself up from her chair and paced the floor, furious. As she passed her desk a second time, she stopped suddenly and stared straight ahead.

Why do people believe him? She asked the question out loud. That was the problem. People *believed* Theron St. Cyr. There was nothing about him that sent shivers up your spine. Nothing that told you to be wary. He was totally, utterly believable.

Dru circled her desk and dropped into her chair.

Well, you can't con me anymore, Theron St. Cyr. Either you're out of the slavery and prostitution business altogether, or you're still in it and Trans-Global is a front. Whatever. You're in my territory now, and I know exactly what you are even if nobody else does.

She clicked off the page on her computer screen and began a search on Trans-Global Solutions. There were five entries, the same four from before and one other that gave the Web address for the French-American Chamber of Commerce in New York City. Dru clicked on the address. The chamber's home page came up. Dru moved the cursor to the menu and clicked on "Member Directory." A log-in prompt came up. She sucked her teeth, went back, and clicked on "French-American News." She scanned the page quickly.

Nothing. Not about Theron St. Cyr; not about Trans-Global.

She clicked on "Events" and scrolled down impatiently. She was pulling the cursor so fast that she shot right past the highlight before it registered that she had actually seen it.

She scrolled back slowly until she came to it. There it was, highlighted in yellow. Trans-Global Solutions. Next to St. Cyr's name, which was on a list of featured speakers for an upcoming seminar on "Doing Business with New York State and City Agencies."

There was nothing more. No link to anything else. No Internet address for Trans-Global Solutions. Not even a listing with a postal address.

Keeping it low, you snake in the grass, Dru muttered.

Frustrated, she logged off the Internet and propped her face in her hands. St. Cyr had built a wall of decency around himself.

"Oh, but it's soon coming down, Theron," Dru whispered.

A plan was already forming in her head.

⁓⫷⫸⁓

Grant Featherhorn dialed a number in Caracas, Venezuela. Someone picked up on the first ring.

"What news?" The man who spoke had a heavy Spanish accent.

"There could be trouble in Guyana."

"What kind of trouble?"

"The president could be swayed in a direction we do not like."

"By anyone in particular?"

"Do the names Reginald MacPherson and Andrew Goodings mean anything to you?"

"I have dealt with MacPherson. He's the minister of transportation. But this Andrew Goodings I do not know. Who is he?"

"Does it matter now?"

There was a slight pause before the man replied.

"No. It does not matter now. And Lawton Pilgrim?"

"What about Lawton?"

There was brief silence before the man spoke. "I see. He does not matter either. You are sure of this?"

"I am sure of it."

Featherhorn hung up.

11

"Those friggin' cheapskates! That's the trouble with consulting for these small businesses. They want you to move heaven and earth for them, but they whine about paying you a retainer or how high it is! I tell you, Theron, we don't need this aggravation any more. Those days are over, man. *Over!* Know what I told them? I told them to go to the Service Corps of Retired Executives. Let *those* guys take on that kind of headache for no pay. See if *they* could turn them into the next friggin' Microsoft. And do you know what they said when I told them that? You want to hear what those jokers said, Theron?"

St. Cyr was paying little attention to Faustin's ranting. He wanted to focus on Drucilla Durane, come up with an explanation for her strange behavior. He already knew where Faustin's argument was going. He had ridden many times with him on this high horse of indignation. As far as St. Cyr was concerned, trying to hook the accounts of small businesses with big potential was what most consulting firms did while they waited for the big accounts to bite. It's what kept the cash flow flowing.

But Faustin, always the impatient one, did not see it that way. It was a waste of time, he would remonstrate. Too little money for way too much work and way too much frustration. Better to suck wind until the *real* clients came in than to deal with these jerks, he'd grumble.

"What did they say?" St. Cyr asked absently.

"Those jokers had the nerve to say—I swear to God they said this, Theron—they had the nerve to say, 'Oh, we've been to SCORE already. They're good business technocrats but they can't do anything for us at our level. They don't have the market savvy and the contacts you guys at Trans-Global have. Besides, everybody says you guys are the best.' That's what they said. How do you like that?"

St. Cyr laughed. "They said that?"

"As God is my witness. Barodi himself came on the line and gave me the spiel. The guy's a friggin' nutcase."

"So what do you want to do, Faustin? Drop them altogether? Seems to me you've got them right where you want them. They as much as admitted they can't do without us."

Faustin did not reply aloud. Instead, he dropped his eyes to the floor and muttered something about being "sick and tired of having to fight for a decent retainer from people who want to suck the life out of you."

At least, that's what St. Cyr thought he heard.

"Tell you what, then. Let's ditch them." St. Cyr said with finality.

Faustin's head jerked up. "Naaah! I think I can bring them in."

"With your soft touch, no doubt."

Faustin ignored him. "Did you ever call the Durane girl?"

"Yeah, I did."

"So?"

"So what?"

"Did you get her?"

"Yeah, I did."

"And?"

"And what?"

"*Merde,* Theron! What did she say?"

"She didn't say anything."

"What do you mean she didn't say anything? *C'est pas possible!* After all this time? She must have said *something.* Good, bad or indifferent."

"Why are you so—" St. Cyr broke off petulantly as the phone on his desk buzzed. He rammed a finger at the speaker button. "*Oui, Celine. Qu'est-ce qu'il y a?*"

There was a pause before the voice replied. St. Cyr knew that what that pause meant. It was his secretary's way of letting him know that she did not appreciate his tone.

"A Mr. Andrew Goodings in Guyana is on the line for you, Mr. St. Cyr," Celine said coolly in English.

Mr. St. Cyr. Not *Theron.* She was mad all right. St. Cyr softened his tone. "Thank you, Celine. Tell him I'll be with him in a second."

He looked at Faustin. "Sorry, *mon cher.* This might take a while."

Faustin held up his hands. "No problem. Catch you later."

St. Cyr waited until the door closed behind Faustin, then settled himself more comfortably in his chair and picked up the phone. This had to be a very serious call. His relationship with Goodings was not the thinking-of-you-so-I-called-to-say-hello kind.

"Andrew! How good to hear from you. How is Guyana treating you? Or should I say how are *you* treating Guyana?"

"Theron, my good brother. Glad I caught you. I half expected to hear you were off somewhere in Europe. Guyana's a pisser but what can I say? Love her like a fool. That's why I'm calling you."

"I always tell people that I'm the last person to come to for help with affairs of the heart, Andrew. But for you I'll give it my best shot. What's up?"

"Got a big favor to ask, Theron. I can't go into details on the phone. What you know of me is all that you'll have to go on when you make your decision."

"Okay, I'm listening."

"I have a project I'm working on and I need the kind of help I can get only from you. I'd like you to come to Guyana to take a look at a few things. Won't take more than a few days."

St. Cyr did not hesitate. Goodings had gotten him his first consulting contract with the Port Authority of New York and New Jersey's Construction Management Division under its minority vendor program. It was actually his first contract with such a large organization. After that, it was as if the floodgates had opened. There were many other contracts, not just with the Port Authority, but also with some of the Port Authority's biggest corporate contractors.

That's the way it worked with these minority contracts, St. Cyr soon learned. Once you got in and proved you could deliver, you stayed in. Getting in was the hard part, for there was a clique of "approved" minority firms that always got the contracts. Approval rarely had anything to do with whether you paid the annual $300 fee to certify that you were indeed minority-owned and operated. It was who you knew. Government, private sector, it made no difference. With government contracts, everyone knew your company was a shoo-in if certain elected officials and people of influence (POIs) gave you the nod.

Everyone knew who those elected officials were, just as they knew who the POIs were. Vendors sucked up to the elected officials shamelessly. Campaign contributions, birthday party donations, complimentary invitations to 250-, 300-, 350-dollar luncheons and dinners—with VIP seating, acknowledgement from the podium, and a photo-op for the press—jobs for a girlfriend, kid, and/or distant relative. Wives were off-limits.

Hey, all's fair in love and business, the vendors argued. "Besides, we're the ones creating the jobs."

St. Cyr didn't suck up. He had no idea why Goodings pushed so hard to get Trans-Global into the mix. He had never asked and Goodings had never volunteered an explanation. Neither of them had known the other before their first meeting.

Not that Trans-Global wasn't up to the job. But there were some well-established, well-connected firms in the running and Trans-Global was little more than a start-up at the time.

After he got to know him, after he heard him mumble umpteen times that "the last shall be first and the first shall be last," he suspected that Goodings simply took pleasure in shaking up the status quo.

Whatever the reason for it, that first break with the Port Authority literally swooped Trans-Global up from anonymity. For the small, uncompromisingly efficient firm that knew far too many days of famine than feast, the proverbial ship had finally come in.

Goodings had never asked them for a favor. Until now.

"How soon do you want me there?" St. Cyr said.

"This week, if you can get away. There's a round-trip ticket waiting for you at BWIA. And you'll be staying at my home."

St. Cyr chuckled. So did Goodings.

"What can I tell you, Theron. My father was a Rosicrucian and from the time I was a little boy he taught me the importance and art of studying the character of every man, woman, and child who crossed your path for more than a fleeting moment. But I think you, too, have learned those lessons, Theron."

St. Cyr responded soberly. "I learned much later in life than you, Andrew, and I would venture to say under much more painful circumstances. If there is a flight on Wednesday, I will be on it."

"There is one. I will be at the airport to meet you. Thank you, Theron."

"Not at all. Gives me a chance to see a country I've heard a lot about."

"Well, I hope you won't be disappointed. Guyana is not the place it used to be when I was growing up." Goodings's voice was suddenly heavy with hurt.

"Yes, I can imagine. But, hey, new times, new challenges, new opportunities, right?"

Goodings laughed. "Easy for a young man like you to say. I'm not sure how much more of these new times this old body can handle. Anyway, I won't keep you. Call me only if you're not traveling on Wednesday. There's only one flight that day so I know when to be at the airport."

"Okay, Andrew. Want me to bring you anything from New York?"

"Naaah! Ain't nothin' there I can't live without. See you in a couple of days. Have a safe flight." He hung up.

St. Cyr sat forward, elbows on his desk. His intertwined fingers formed a tight fist under his chin. He had read enough in Andrew's words to conclude that something big was about to go down in Guyana, something that had to do with the country itself. This wasn't a private thing.

Love her like a fool. That's why I'm calling you, Andrew had said. The fact that Andrew had called on him meant American interests, possibly European as well, were involved.

St. Cyr turned to his desktop and logged on to the Internet. A search on "Guyana" brought up the usual country site with links to "Latest News" and "Newspapers." He clicked on "Latest News" and found only one item, from Reuters, about the latest hit in a six-month crime spree allegedly perpetrated by escaped convicts who were heavily armed. This time the gunmen had slain three antidrug enforcement officials, one at a time, in their own homes.

St. Cyr closed that window and went back to the "Newspapers" link. He clicked on the first publication on the list, *The Guyana Chronicle*. It was that day's edition. He scrolled through the page of general news. Only one item caught his attention.

NO DECISION ON AIR TRANSPORT PROPOSAL

President Sankar today told the Georgetown Chamber of Commerce and Industry that, contrary to rumors, the government had reached no decision on a proposal brought to it by the American consultancy Pilgrim Boone on behalf of a major American aerospace company, to establish an air transportation network throughout the country. The President said, however, that he expected to make a decision before the end of the month, "after we have exhausted consultations with the various representatives of the Guyanese citizenry."

Chamber members have publicly squabbled over the proposal, with opponents calling for the restoration of the national railroad before any consideration is given to instituting an air transport system. The opposition People's Democratic Party also has come out against the proposal. PDP leader Raymond Cambridge has stated that an air transport system would benefit only American aircraft manufacturers and a few wealthy Guyanese at this time. He argues that rail would better serve the interests of the average Guyanese and the country as a whole.

Meanwhile, sources in the transportation ministry say Pilgrim Boone is pushing for a quick decision and has engaged local Guyanese consultants Nelson Roopnaraine and Compton Dalrymple to help make its case to the government.

In a related matter, *The Chronicle* has learned that two senior transportation officials from Venezuela arrived in Georgetown this week for meetings with Transportation Minister Reginald MacPherson. Venezuela has long advocated an interlinked air transport system serving all of South America.

St. Cyr sat back in his chair when he finished reading the article, locked his hands behind his head and stared up at the ceiling. He knew instinctively that this was the "project" that Goodings wanted to discuss with him. Goodings was fascinated by the air, rail, road, and water networks of America and the rest of the developed world, and lamented the fact that developing countries seemed to pay little attention to such things. This St. Cyr knew.

One of his biggest dreams, Goodings had told him once, was to visit Japan to see the magnetic levitation trains that "race the wind." In his spare time he was learning everything he could about the history of transportation in America and about the evolution of ITS—intelligent transportation systems that combined precollected data and communication technology to seamlessly move vehicles from border to border, he had said.

St. Cyr recalled the time when he and Goodings had run into each other at a Port Authority dinner. It had been their first encounter in months. After the dinner they had gone to a nearby bar to catch up and Andrew had spoken with quiet hurt about the number of times he had offered, when he was much younger, to contribute his knowledge and experience to Guyana, to help get the country started on an efficient, sustainable transportation system, he had said. One designed with vision.

He had submitted paper upon paper to the ministry about ways to open up the interior of the country with rail and road, piece by piece, connecting it eventually to Brazil, Venezuela, and the rest of the continent. But he had never heard "so much as a peep from a single soul."

"I guess those boys didn't want to deal with a small fry like me," he had said, knocking back a vodka straight.

The more St. Cyr thought of the article he had just read, the more he was convinced that something was bothering Goodings about the Pilgrim

Boone proposal, which, he was sure, came straight out of Savoy Aerospace, one of Pilgrim Boone's long-standing clients.

And that visit by the Venezuelans. Was it mere coincidence?

St. Cyr stood up abruptly and went to the door. Celine was at her desk. Her cubicle was just a few feet away from his office. He strolled over and stood beside her until she looked up.

"Sorry I was so abrupt before, Celine. Would you reschedule those appointments I have on Wednesday for next Tuesday or Wednesday. I have to go to Guyana. There should be a ticket for me at BWIA. Check on it with the airline and confirm me for the Wednesday flight, returning Friday."

"Sure thing, Theron. Do you need a hotel?" She was her old chirpy self again.

Women! It took so little to keep them happy, St. Cyr mused.

"No, I'll be staying with Andrew Goodings in Georgetown. I assume you took his phone number when he called so you have that in case you need to reach me."

"Of course."

"Thank you, Celine."

St. Cyr returned to his desk and buzzed Faustin's office. Faustin himself answered.

"Sorry about that, old man. Looks like I have to go to Guyana on Wednesday for a couple of days. Let's have a drink this evening."

"Sure thing, man. Theron, about Drucilla Durane—"

"Oh, for God's sake, Faustin, why are you so obsessed—"

"That day I met her in Paris, she ran away during the night." The words rushed out as if a dam had broken.

"*You* met her in Paris? She ran away? I told Michel to pick her up. And what do you mean by 'ran away'?"

"She broke down the door and ran off before I got back the next morning. She must have thought she was in danger. You know how creepy that old studio was," Faustin said defensively.

"The old studio? Faustin, what the hell are you talking about?"

"What do you mean what the hell am I talking about? Michel with his goddamn reports couldn't pick her up at the station like you asked, so

I went instead. I took her to the studio for the night the way we always did with the girls. I left her there, padlocked the door and everything. But when I got back in the morning, I found the door off its hinges and she was gone."

There was a long silence.

"Theron?" Faustin's voice was tentative.

"What?"

"She didn't want to talk to you, did she?"

"What do you think?"

"Sorry, man. At least she made it out intact."

St. Cyr did not respond.

"Well, you can't argue that she didn't, Theron," Faustin said plaintively. "Look what she's done for herself since. She's a hotshot at Pilgrim Boone. *Pilgrim Boone*, Theron!"

St. Cyr sighed.

"You can't be more wrong, Faustin. She did not make it out intact."

12

Gazing into the infinite expanse of baby-blue sky and cotton-ball clouds from his business class seat on BWIA Flight 425, Theron St. Cyr decided he had to make things right with Drucilla Durane.

It was the morally right thing to do. It was a matter of pride. Besides, her connections could prove invaluable.

"Hot towel, Mr. St. Cyr?"

The flight attendant's voice was rich with the flavors and cadences of the Caribbean. In one hand she held a small silver tray packed with tightly rolled, steaming face towels. In the other, a pair of silver tongs hovered in dainty repose above the tray.

St. Cyr stared blankly at the tray. His thoughts were locked on that morning in Marseille a lifetime ago.

"Towel, sir?" The flight attendant's voice rang as prettily as ever.

St. Cyr's thoughts zoomed back to the present, just in time to catch a quick curl of irritation at the corners of her mouth before she pasted on the smile again.

Normally, especially on flights that lasted more than five hours, he would have killed time by trying to smooth that edge and wrest a genuine smile from the flight attendant. It was an ancient and pleasurable game. A virile man; a pretty woman; a chasm between them. What else was he to do?

But this was not one of those times.

"Er, yes. Sorry, I was a bit distracted. Yes, thank you," St. Cyr said, cupping his hands to receive the towel.

The attendant clung to her smile, dropped the towel into his hands and moved on.

The damp, fragrant heat of the towel brought St. Cyr fully back to the present. He shook out the square of soft cloth, pressed it to his face and took a deep breath, savoring the invigorating effect of the heat and the subtle herbal fragrance he could not identify. He was far more tense than he realized. He had left home just after 5 a.m. to catch the 7:15 flight to Georgetown.

He held the towel hard against his face until it went cold, and then dropped it next to the half-empty glass of orange juice he had placed on the tray beside his seat. He picked up the glass, drained it, and leaned back against the soft leather, eyes closed. His thoughts rolled back to the day Faustin gave him the whole sickening account of his encounter with Dru in Paris, from their confrontation in the bakery near the train station to his return to the empty studio the next morning. He had omitted nothing as he described the condition of the studio when he found it, not even the part about the blood on the screwdriver. Then he had declared, dragging out that irritatingly clinical precision he resorted to when he was being defiant in his guilt, that no matter what Theron thought of him from then on, he just could not hold back any of the facts about the "episode" with Drucilla Durane. After all, he, Theron, needed to know the whole truth if he planned to "take action to remedy the current situation."

Even now Theron could feel the fury that had boiled in him that day as he listened to Faustin. The scene replayed itself in his head, reeling itself out frame by frame as if it were a movie. Theron saw himself heaping his foulest French on Faustin and topping it off in English, his voice rising above the happy-hour cacophony of Two Steps Down, a popular lounge for professional blacks in the brownstone neighborhood of Brooklyn's Fort

Greene. A hush swooshed down on the lounge then whooshed away. Faustin dropped his head and accepted his flagellation wordlessly.

"I warned Michel not to send you. I warned him," St. Cyr muttered. His anger was spent but the gravity of what had happened in Paris settled on him like lead.

Faustin was defensive. "I didn't want to go. I hated going. You both know I didn't like to do that. It was too painful. But Michel begged and begged and I gave in."

"He was supposed to take her to the new apartment."

"He never said so. I didn't even know it was ready. If I had known, I would've taken her there."

"She wasn't like the others. She was different. Jesus Christ, Faustin, any idiot could see that."

"Yes. I knew that as soon as I saw her. But I had nowhere else to take her. I couldn't take her to *my* place, or to Michel's."

Theron continued as if he hadn't heard Faustin. He spoke as if to himself, his voice thick with resignation. "You should have heard her on the phone. Voice like a dagger. It's as if she wants my blood."

"I can imagine. She'll get over it."

"Like hell she will! After all these years she sounds as if it happened yesterday! Don't give me that bullshit about time healing all wounds!"

The hush swooshed down and whooshed away again, leaving in its wake raised eyebrows, knitted brows, and fierce glares. Faustin warned in French, between gritted teeth, to keep it down before they were thrown out.

Theron flicked his wrist dismissively, but continued in a lower voice. "She'll never get over it. Not that type of girl. Drucilla Durane hates me."

"That's because she doesn't know the truth."

"What the hell difference does truth make? The truth is whatever you perceive it to be."

"So we change the perception."

"And this 'we' would be who exactly? You and me?"

"You, me, one of us at least."

Theron burst out laughing, knocking over his drink.

"You're drunk, Theron," Faustin said disapprovingly, mopping up the spill with a fistful of paper napkins.

Theron stopped laughing abruptly and looked straight at Faustin. "No, I'm not drunk, Faustin," he said quietly. "Just think of the irony of the whole thing. There I was, playing God with my grand plan to outwit the Ramys of this world and look what happened. I became the Ramys of this world in the eyes of the one woman from that whole lot that had real street smarts."

He paused, looked down into his near empty glass. "She was so... different," he said. His voice was barely more than a whisper.

Faustin said nothing. St. Cyr continued, his voice steady, pensive. "Maybe you were right all along, Faustin. Maybe we never should have gotten involved in that kind of thing."

The flight attendant's voice, still lilting and silky and over-rehearsed, wafted into his thoughts.

"Your menu, Miss Durane."

Then *her* voice. "Thank you."

Theron's spine snapped into a straight line. He waited. When he did not hear the voice again, he sprang forward to stand up, only to be firmly restrained by his seatbelt.

He fumbled impatiently with the buckle, freed himself, and stood up so abruptly that his head collided with the luggage bin above. Ducking, he turned toward Drucilla's voice. It had come from one of the rows behind his. There were no more than eight people in business class and they sat well away from each other.

The attendant was already moving down the aisle.

Theron scanned the rows. Only one woman sat between him and the dark-blue curtain that separated business class from Coach. She was alone, in the window seat three rows back. She was bent over, as if reading, so that Theron saw only the top of her head.

No Afro. Permed hair. Too many years. Hairstyles change. People change.

Theron fastened his eyes on the top of the woman's head, willing her to look up.

She didn't.

He stepped into the aisle and walked toward her, his heart hammering. He paused when he reached her row, taking in the figure bent over the menu.

Then, "Drucilla?"

She looked up, recognizing the voice, recognizing *him*, instantly, in spite of the years. If she was startled she did not show it. Her face was stone. She said nothing, just kept her eyes on his, unblinking.

For a moment Theron could not speak either. They remained locked in a stare until Theron blinked.

"What a coincidence meeting you thousands of feet above the earth. This must be heaven." He knew it sounded pitiful but it was the best he could do just then, in that moment, standing before her at last.

Dru cut her eyes away from him and bent over the menu again.

After their exchange on the telephone, Theron more or less expected the cold shoulder. It surprised him, nonetheless. Marseille was never far away from his mind.

He steeled himself and tried again. "I'd like to talk to you, Dru." Even he was surprised at how firm his voice sounded.

"No, you don't. You don't want to talk to me because you don't want me to make a scene." Acid dripped from Dru's softly spoken words. She had not bothered to look up when she spoke.

"You're right. I don't want you to make a scene. But I would like to speak to you." St. Cyr felt his nervousness ebbing. He leaned his elbows on the back of the aisle seat in the row before hers.

"And what would you like to say to me?" Dru asked, her eyes traveling with deliberate slowness from the menu to his feet and up along his body until they made four with his.

Theron could not help but smile. It was Marseille all over again. Only this time the wall between them was several inches thicker than the wall between ordinary strangers.

Dru's eyes were flat and cold, but they were on his. However little it was worth to her, he had her attention. So soon after they had spoken, it was more than he had expected.

A tremor darted through him. "May I sit?" He did not wait for her answer. He lowered himself into the aisle seat in Drucilla's row and turned to face her.

Dru watched him, her face blank.

"I need to explain what really happened in Paris, Drucilla."

Not even a blink.

"Sadly, you misunderstood the whole thing," Theron continued earnestly. "Faustin…we were not going to hurt you. Quite the contrary, we—"

Dru's eyes crossed.

"May I take your towel, Miss?"

The attendant with the fake silk in her voice was making her cleanup rounds. Deliberately ignoring Theron, she beamed a meaningful look at Drucilla. Dru read her message: If the gentleman is being a nuisance I'd be happy to rid you of him.

"Why certainly, thank you," Dru said brightly, reaching across the empty seat between herself and Theron to hand the attendant the towel. Locking eyes with the woman, she beamed back: I'm okay. Grateful for the offer of help. Will let you know if things get out of hand.

Theron felt the exchange between the two women even though his own eyes had not left Dru's face.

The attendant floated away and Dru turned her attention back to St. Cyr, her eyes moving once again with calculated patience. "You were saying?" she said, with a raised eyebrow.

St. Cyr pressed on. "Faustin told me what happened. That you took off the door and ran away. He saw your blood on the instrument you used."

"So?" The second eyebrow arched up.

"You have to believe me, Dru. We were only trying to save you from those people who prey on women and girls traveling alone, especially women who are as young and as lovely as you were then."

Dru's lips pursed. Her eyes narrowed the teeniest bit.

"I'm sorry. That came out wrong. You're still young and lovely, Dru." An awkward smile, a rush forward. "I'm sure you remember that man in the Quartier Noir. The one who brushed against me. You said he was weird. That man's name is Ramy. He is part of a gang that abducts women and sells them to the highest bidder—slave traders, body-part traders, pimps, sexual deviants, you name it. He had already spotted you and was after you. Believe me, you would not have escaped. But I intercepted him, you see. That's why he was so angry with me. He—"

He broke off lamely. It was clear from the expression on Dru's face that she did not believe a word he was saying.

He sighed and looked past her, beyond the window into the endless silver blue sky. He couldn't blame her. If he were in her place, he wouldn't believe him either.

Twelve years too late, his story was pitifully ludicrous.

The silence between them was long and raw.

Dru spoke first. "Right. And I suppose you are following me to Guyana to make sure Ramy and his gang of abductors do not get to me."

St. Cyr bristled. "Don't flatter yourself, Dru. You are not the only one who travels on business."

"Oooooh! Mr. St. Cyr is offended. Naughty me. I am sooo verree sorree, Mr. St. Cyr. It was not my intention to hurt your feelings." Her lips puckered coquettishly as she taunted him.

St. Cyr struggled with the anger that roared into his head and lost. "That attitude does not become you, Dru," he snapped.

"Now don't *you* flatter yourself, Theron St. Cyr. I don't give a rat's ass what a lowlife like you thinks about what becomes me or not!" Dru snarled back, thrusting her face toward his.

They glared at each other.

The attendant cruised by yet again, coughing to announce her presence. She lingered long enough to beam a concerned look at Dru.

This time, Dru ignored her.

St. Cyr relented first, summoning to his mind that moment an hour or so ago when he had decided Drucilla Durane's approval was worth fighting for.

"What can I do to make you believe me, Dru," he said softly, rising to return to his seat.

Dru looked up at him, her mouth twisted in an ugly smile. "Not a goddamned thing, Mr. St. Cyr. Not a goddamned thing!"

13

Andrew Goodings checked his watch for the umpteenth time and sucked his teeth in disgust. He shifted irritably from one foot to the other and glared at the two uniformed agents idling on either side of the door that led to Customs, Immigration, and the passenger lounge.

The door was wide open. The line that waited in front of it was long and untidy as family and friends clung to their last moments with those departing for a new life in the United States. The first-time travelers stood out, their innocent Third World faces changing from excitement to fear and back. The handful of seasoned travelers feigned boredom and kept looking at their watches. The agents, engrossed in their conversation, ignored the line. This line was like any other on any given day: It represented a planeload of Guyanese running away from home.

Goodings sucked his teeth again and cut his eyes at the agents as if *they* had delayed the flight from New York just to spite him. If looks could kill, they would have been dead an hour ago.

"You shouldn't be so angry, man. Don't you know by now what BWIA really stands for?"

There was laughter in the voice that came from the woman standing next to him. Goodings sized her up: attractive, mid-to-late forties, average height, average weight. She wore tight black jeans, an oversized blue linen shirt unbuttoned to within a hint of her bra, and dark glasses. White strappy sandals showed off dainty, professionally manicured toenails lacquered fire-engine red. A length of bright blue silk hung from the back of the wide-brimmed straw hat on her head.

Goodings scowled at her, sucked his teeth yet again, and moved away. Midweek, the waiting room was almost empty. With no tourism industry to speak of and an economy so politically befuddled that much of the investment destined for the Caribbean bypassed it altogether, Guyana was hardly a favored port of call for international airlines. The lone BWIA flight coming in from JFK was bringing back mostly Guyanese traders, family members for a wedding or funeral, and perhaps a few government officials.

The woman's mocking voice floated above the quiet.

"Well, aren't you a sourpuss, Andrew Goodings! How well I remember the days when you couldn't bring yourself to walk away from me!"

She could be Guyanese. It was hard to tell from her accent. She sounded like a Guyanese who had lived abroad for a long time—in the United States, perhaps with a stint in England.

Heads turned. Chuckles and giggles rippled through the waiting room.

Goodings stopped in his tracks as if someone had thrown a stone at his back. He turned to face the woman and stood still again, squinting at her. Slowly he started walking toward her.

All eyes in the waiting room kept pace with him.

A plump woman with a no-nonsense air seized the opportunity to champion the cause of wronged women everywhere.

"You tell 'e aff, gyurl! Dese blastid men t'ink dey could jus' suck we like cane den dash we 'way like de peelin'! Tell 'e aff good an' proppah!"

More chuckles and giggles. Everyone looked expectantly at the woman, hoping she would indeed give Andrew Goodings a good and proper telling off.

"And who invited you to push your mouth into the people's business? You're damn presumptuous, lady!" The man who challenged the plump lady was short and skinny.

The no-nonsense woman swung her bulk toward him and looked him up and down, her hands planted on her hips. "Did you speak to me, Mister?" she asked haughtily, switching to straight English as much to match his highbrow tone as to make clear her ability, and intention, to do him serious harm.

She rolled forward, one hand on her hip, the other aiming her index finger at the skinny man's forehead.

"Whom else am I talking to?" her accuser declared. He planted his feet apart and stood his ground.

The lined shuffled closer. A few picked sides and gleefully egged on their favorite. One of the uniformed agents stood up, stretched, and said loudly to his companion, "Just look at them. Dog buy rum, cow drink it, pig get drunk. Everybody minding somebody else's business."

He ambled over to the gathering crowd. "Okay! Okay! Break it up! Break it up!" he ordered, elbowing aside the onlookers. "Y'all Guyanese don't have no shame? Y'all don't know how to behave at a big international airport like dis?"

"Well, hear he! Look at what he callin' a big international airport! Like you never been away, brudduh. Yuh should see what a real airport look like!"

Laughter.

Goodings, meanwhile, was staring at his accuser. Hard as he tugged at his memory, he could not place her.

"Excuse me, do I know you?" His bushy eyebrows formed a sharp V as much from suspicion as from the effort to recall her face.

"Sure you do, Andrew," she said softly.

"I do?"

"Ah! You don't remember. I'm offended." She pouted.

"I don't mean to offend you, Miss. But I just can't place your face at all. Where did we meet?"

The woman smiled and looked around quickly. No one was paying them any attention. All eyes were on the plump lady, the skinny man, and the Customs and Immigration agent who were embroiled in a boisterous melee.

The woman touched Goodings lightly on the arm. "Come on. Let's move away from all this commotion. The flight's not due for another hour at least. That's if it comes at all. BWIA! But Will It Arrive?" she laughed. She hooked her arm through his and led him outside to a grassy patch under a frangipani tree in full red-and-yellow bloom.

Not a soul cast an eye in their direction. Word of the goings-on inside had spread and everyone who was lingering outside—self-appointed baggage handlers, taxi drivers, handicraft vendors, currency changers, those meeting an arriving passenger, and the usual compliment of street entrepreneurs sniffing around for a quick deal—was trying to get into the terminal for a firsthand look.

"You still don't recognize me, do you? Sit down and I'll refresh your memory," the woman said mildly. Her smile teased as she arranged herself on the grass with exaggerated modesty.

Goodings remained standing. Georgetown was a very small place. Word got around like fire in a cane field. The last thing he wanted was to find himself in trouble for cavorting at Timehri Airport with a pretty woman who, for all he knew, was some big shot's property.

He himself was somebody's property. He thought of his wife.

"I...I don't..."

"Oh, sit down, Livuh," the woman commanded, pulling him down beside her.

That did it. Only people who knew him well dared use that name to his face. He relaxed.

"There. Is that so bad?" the woman pouted coyly.

She took a slim, sterling silver cigarette case from her purse, clicked it open, and proffered its contents to him. "Here. Have one."

Goodings looked at the cigarettes and held up his hands.

"Don't tell me you gave them up."

"I'm trying to, actually."

"So you haven't had one in quite a while, eh? No wonder you're so wired."

She lit one for herself, tossed her head back, sent a perfect ring up to the sky, and sighed with genuine pleasure before turning back to Goodings. "A strong-willed man like you, I don't think one cigarette will turn you back into an addict. You need something to calm your nerves. Go ahead. Take one. They're your favorite brand—or used to be."

Goodings looked at the cigarettes again. Marlboros. This woman knew him, all right. He sighed with resignation and took one.

She was right. He could use a smoke. He didn't know why he felt so uptight, as if someone were following him, watching him. He was only meeting a friend at the airport. How could anyone know who Theron St. Cyr was? And why would anybody be watching him anyway? He was putting too much drama into this whole thing about Savoy Aerospace.

The woman wiggled closer. "I'll light it for you. I always lit your cigarettes for you, remember?"

He didn't. But he did not say so.

"I know you don't," she said softly.

Her lighter matched the cigarette case.

Slim. Shiny. Expensive.

She cupped the flame expertly. Goodings inhaled deeply and exhaled. His shoulders dropped and he leaned back against the tree.

"That's better," the woman said happily.

They smoked in silence for a while.

The woman spoke first. "You're sure you don't remember me, Andrew?"

Goodings looked at her. "I'm sorry. I just don't. I've been trying, but for the life of me I can't remember who you are," he said apologetically.

The woman sent another perfect ring up to the sky before she answered. "Poor Andrew. And I used to mean so much to you." There was genuine hurt in her voice. "Perhaps if I took off my sunglasses—"

She reached up to remove the sunglasses. As she did so, the long, intricately painted nail of her little finger caught Andrew on his bare thigh.

Shorts and sandals will be my standard attire when I go home, he had announced jovially at his farewell party in New York.

He flinched at the sting of the scratch. A thin line of blood appeared.

"Oh, no! Oh, I'm so sorry. What have I done!" the woman cried, pressing her palm to her face.

"Please, please. It's just a little scratch," Goodings said, holding up both hands to keep her from throwing herself on him. He scooped up the blood with his finger and thrust the finger in his mouth.

"I don't know why I like to wear them so long," the woman wailed. "My mother always told me my vanity will get me in trouble. Oh, Andrew, does it hurt?" Her eyes were wide and appealing as she reached tentatively for his thigh. Andrew moved his leg deftly out of her reach.

"No, it doesn't hurt. You were about to remind me who you were." An edge had crept into his voice. He wasn't superstitious, but the sight of his blood seemed to underscore the strangeness of this encounter.

Just then, a loudspeaker crackled. "Announcing the arrival of BWIA Flight 425 from New York!"

The woman squealed and scrambled excitedly to her feet. "Well, what do you know! It's here already! Here it comes, Andrew! Here it comes!"

Before Andrew could move, she dashed off toward the building. She did not look back. Not even once.

That was the last time Goodings saw her.

Much later, as his heart collapsed from the poison he had unknowingly inhaled when he smoked the Marlboro laced with the powder of tiny dried leaves from a plant that grew deep in the jungle of his beloved country, he remembered thinking, that day at the airport, that no girlfriend of his had ever called him Andrew.

And just before he died in Theron St. Cyr's arms, he thought how curious it was that the woman had never shown him her face, nor told him her name.

Strange, too, how he knew that she had killed him.

⁓⁕⁓

"*Dígame!*"

The man answered the phone the Castilian way, although he had lived in Venezuela all his life and had visited Spain no more than three times.

"It is done." The woman's voice was hushed.

"Good. Was there any difficulty?"

"None. I gave him a special cigarette. It's made from the leaves of a deadly plant that the Makushi tribe of the Rupununi savanna has used for centuries during special ceremonies. There's a way to prepare the leaves so that you get a safe 'smoke,' one that gives a mild but long-lasting high. The formula is known only to certain initiated elders. Unfortunately for Goodings, some very enterprising tribesmen have created a different kind of market for the leaves. His blood has already begun to thicken and in a couple of hours it will be moving like sludge in his veins. His heart will pump faster and harder to compensate and eventually it will give out. It will be all over before the night is through. No trace of the poison will show up in the autopsy. The thickening of the blood lasts only for a few hours, just long enough to trigger a heart attack. By the time they cut him open, his blood will have returned to normal, so it will be as if his heart simply gave out. Everyone will attribute it to the rigorous exercise routine he put himself through. He was a vain man."

The man chuckled. She was good. He had left the method of execution entirely up to her. "You did well. And the people you used?"

"They created the perfect diversion. A fat woman about to give a skinny man a good ass-whipping? Mmmm! You can't get more entertaining than that in my country."

"You will take care of them appropriately, I am sure."

"I have already compensated them. Unfortunately, the woman was killed in a car crash on her way back to the city from the airport. She was in a taxi. Guyanese taxi drivers are notoriously reckless. As for the man, I believe he will accidentally drown in a day or so."

The man on the phone tut-tutted. "May all their souls rest in peace," he said dryly.

"Indeed."

The secure line between Caracas and Georgetown abruptly went dead.

The woman eased open the bathroom door, tiptoed into the bedroom, and replaced the cell phone in the purse on her dresser. In the silvery slivers of moon and starlight she caught sight of her reflection in the mirror and paused. She touched her face. It was an arresting face. Amerindian. "A Makushi face," those who could tell the difference between the indigenous Indian tribes would say. The high cheekbones, wide-set, piercing Oriental eyes under thin, perfectly arched eyebrows, a gently sloping, almost bridgeless nose, and surprisingly full lips gave her face a sensuousness most men found hard to ignore.

She smiled at her reflection, reached up, pulled a hairpin from the fat twist of blue-black hair at the nape of her neck and shook the tresses free. They fell like silk almost to the middle of her back.

She turned from the mirror, tiptoed to the bed, and dropped her satin robe on the floor. For a moment she stood there, naked, contemplating the sleeping, heavyset figure sprawled on her bed under the mosquito netting. The man lay on his stomach. He, too, was naked, the sheets barely covering his buttocks. The woman's nipples hardened as she stared at him. She liked it when he stayed the whole night at her house, which he rarely did. She understood, of course. Wife, children, reputation. None of that counted tonight.

She lifted the net and slipped noiselessly into the bed.

Compton Dalrymple, a light sleeper, felt her weight and her movements as she settled beside him. He stirred, raised his head from the pillow and turned toward her, his eyes half-closed.

"What's the matter?" he mumbled drowsily.

"Sshhh. I just went to the bathroom. Go back to sleep," she whispered as she snuggled closer.

"Not a chance," he said. He rolled over and pulled her on top of him.

14

The black Cadillac limousine rolled quietly onto the pier that led out to the Pilgrim family's private marina on the Hudson River in Nyack. It came to a stop just a few feet from the end.

The chauffeur, a craggy-faced, elderly Irishman in formal black livery alighted and walked away from the vehicle, his gait slow and burdened, his shoulders drooping. At a discreet distance, he stopped and leaned against the wooden railing, his face turned upward in an appeal to the sky. What, he asked in his mind, was the reason for this terrible thing that was making his eyes wet.

Off to the right, the Tappan Zee Bridge stretched mightily between Westchester and Rockland Counties, another testimony to civil engineering's dominion over time and space and the elements.

The quiet of the late morning matched the mood of the limousine's lone passenger, who stared out at the river from behind tinted windows. Minutes ago, Lawton Pilgrim had dried what he thought were his last tears for a life that, he still found it hard to believe, was rapidly coming to an end.

He sighed.

Images of the people, places, and conquests that had filled that life tumbled one after the other into his consciousness, intimacies fleetingly renewed, each one rolling away as another took shape. He knew he would summon these images back again and again. They would help him to bear the pain as the cancer slowly devoured him.

Three months, perhaps sooner, his doctor had said earlier that morning.

"Yes. If I had a chance to live all over again, I would live exactly as I did before," he said aloud. He shook his head emphatically. "Exactly as I did before," he repeated.

Reluctantly, he pushed aside his memories and turned his attention to the firm he had built. He would have to implement his succession plan much sooner than he had expected.

He smiled. As usual, he had not been caught unprepared. He had drawn up the plan months ago, never dreaming he would have to put it into effect so soon. He had given himself another three years as CEO before he would retire and turn the company over to Grant Featherhorn.

He shrugged. He would meet with the Inner Circle one evening after everyone else had left, maybe in the next two or three days, after he had straightened everything out in his mind. He would give it to them straight. He was dying and he was naming Grant Featherhorn his successor, effective immediately.

Well, maybe not immediately. He still felt fine. No need to rush things.

His choice would not sit well with one member of the circle. As for the others, they all were brilliant thinkers who had no interest whatsoever in running Pilgrim Boone. Too much suck-up and wave-the-flag crap went with that territory. And too much blood and too much guts. They weren't cut out for it. Oh, no! That bunch would accept his choice with a relief they wouldn't know how to hide.

Lawton Pilgrim pictured that look on their faces as he announced Grant as his successor. He laughed out loud. The thought of Drucilla Durane's reaction sobered him. Grant and Dru may have succeeded in hiding their feelings from the rest of the firm, but he, Lawton, had seen the tension between them blossom over the years into full-fledged hatred. He had seen it only because he kept a very close watch on the relationships among his senior-most staff, for he truly believed that Pilgrim Boone's success in attracting the clientele it did was largely due to the perception that the foundation on which the firm's management was built was solid as a rock. The company gave off good vibes at every level. That was a boast few of its peers could make.

People who negotiated contracts, he felt, had inner radar that picked up the slightest sign of discord in the upper ranks. No one would be foolish enough to entrust work of a sensitive nature to a firm whose management team had "issues" with each other. The risk of sabotage out of spite was too great.

Dru's explanation of the loss of the contract with Jamaica notwithstanding, Lawton suspected that someone's radar had picked up the tension in the Featherhorn-Durane relationship. It possibly was contributing to the foot-dragging in Guyana. He was aware, of course, of Grant's true sentiments about people of color and what their place should be in society. He had deliberately made him Dru's mentor to test Dru's mettle. If she was going to function in the top ranks of Pilgrim Boone, she would have to learn to handle bigots like Grant; she'd have to suppress her natural response to such people and focus only on getting their business.

Lawton had found out about Grant years before, when a lawyer contacted him discreetly, saying that his client would go public with his story if he were not compensated for Featherhorn's behavior. His client, the lawyer said, was a young black man employed by a personal entertainment service that catered exclusively to the rich, famous, powerful, and all combinations of the three. Featherhorn was a patron of this service. His preferences were young and black, male and female. The young man in question was not the first to be physically abused and subjected to racist remarks by Featherhorn, the lawyer said. But he was the only one with the evidence to do something about it. He had video and he had audio.

Lawton met the lawyer and his client at the lawyer's pretentious uptown offices at Fiftieth and Fifth, reviewed the video and audio, and wrote a check on the spot for a million dollars, payable to the client. Before he took leave of them, he made it clear to both the lawyer and his client that it would be most unwise to allow even a hint of what had transpired in that office to surface anywhere, ever. When he left with the tapes—he didn't bother to ask if there were copies floating around somewhere in the cesspools of New York—he knew that the matter had been laid to rest permanently.

He had never said a word to Grant. Every human being wrestled with at least one demon, he reasoned. Who was he, Lawton Pilgrim, to chastise another for his or hers? Grant Featherhorn was far too important to Pilgrim Boone. As for Drucilla, she needed no one's help to stand up to Grant. She was that strong, that proud, that driven. He was sure of it.

For the umpteenth time since he had hired her, Lawton congratulated himself on his choice. In an age of gender and ethnic correctness, the brains and creativity wrapped up in Drucilla Durane had been a tremendous advantage for the firm. That she would leave after he was gone, he was certain. He regretted that, but so be it. He needed Grant's perfect mix of arrogance, power lust, charm, and gutter savvy to keep Pilgrim Boone at the top of a world that seemed to be changing as fast as they made new-fangled telephones. That world was increasingly an enigma to the Lawton Pilgrims that dwelt in it.

The CPAs had grown bolder and bolder in their greed: Arthur Andersen, Deloitte, Touche, Ernst & Young, Price Waterhouse, Coopers and Lybrand, Peat Marwick—all of them. Double-dipping bastards. *Too bad I won't be around to see the SEC clip their goddamn wings.*

He savored a feeling of vindication as he thought of Arthur Levitt, Jr., chairman of the Securities and Exchange Commission. After he got to the SEC in 1993, Levitt unleashed a crusade against the accounting firms. He argued that the inherent conflict of interest between their auditing functions as accountants and the massive sums they earned as consultants to the same clients had corrupted the reporting on which the country's entire financial system depended. Investors had lost billions—eighty-eight billion was the going figure—as a result of that corruption.

It's obscene! Lawton's smug smile morphed into a scowl. *And I bet the bastards will be running after Dru with all kinds of offers the moment word gets around that she's left Pilgrim Boone.*

146

The thought made him angrier still. It would make sense for Dru to join one of the big accounting firms. What else could she do? Start her own firm? That's a laugh! A Drucilla Durane wouldn't last a year on her own without a Pilgrim Boone behind her and she knows it. She's got two strikes against her: she's a woman *and* she's black. Wall Street won't stand for that. It's a fact as ugly as sin, but that's the way our world works. *Her* world. The one she's used to.

No. Dru's no fool, Lawton thought with a mixture of sadness and pride. I taught her everything she knows, he said under his breath. Everything. And to think it will all go to one of *them*! Christ! Isn't life a son of a bitch sometimes!

The feistiness went out of him. A heavy feeling overtook him, creeping along his bones and into his heart, weighing him down. He thought of the word "melancholy," that draining combination of utter futility and fatigue. *That's how I'm feeling: melancholic.*

He reflected that this was the way he felt the day he crafted his succession plan months ago, at the height of the Jamaica fiasco. It had hit him, then, that the years of manipulation to stay ahead of the pack, the years of stepping into the ring with men and women of lesser souls but unfathomable power, had finally begun to wear him down and it was time to begin to let go.

Perhaps it was then that the cancer started, he thought bitterly. He shrugged away the thought. What difference does it make when it started? It's here now. Killing me.

He punched the air, a quick one-two, his face contorted in anguish. His mind screamed: Why me? How could a man like me get lung cancer? I don't smoke. I exercise! Every day! I eat a careful diet! There must have been symptoms. How could I have missed them and let this damn thing get so far?

The doctor had responded kindly when he had shouted those very questions at him. Cancer does not discriminate, he'd said. "And it is not uncommon for men who drive their mind and their body as hard as you do to dismiss any telltale signs," he'd added. Mercifully, he did not mention what they both were thinking: Lawton should have been having annual physicals. He hadn't had one in three years. He just didn't have the time. No, that was not true. The truth was that he hated going to doctors.

Oh, well, Lawton shrugged now. He would not dwell on the consequences of his foolishness. Not with so little time left.

So little time.

A wave of fear rolled over him. He reached for the drink he did not remember pouring. Vodka, straight. His hands shook as he lifted the glass to his mouth.

He did not want to die. He was afraid of dying. He wasn't prepared for death. How *does* one prepare for a thing of such *finality*?

Lawton sat his empty glass on the small bar that had been built into the side of the limousine and wept again.

***

Dru watched with interest as Theron St. Cyr embraced a much older man dressed in shorts, a loose shirt-jacket, and sandals. The man had that person-of-means look. A Mr. *Some*body. Connected.

Dru studied the man's face. No sleaze there, she thought. Hope the poor guy knows just what he's dealing with. St. Cyr is probably setting him up for a swindle big time.

She could not help noticing that the man seemed genuinely fond of St. Cyr. He had embraced St. Cyr a second time and kept his arm around his shoulders as they walked out of the terminal.

"The man in the shorts is someone you should know. That's Andrew Goodings, the spoke in the wheel in our project. The other one, the young, good-looking one who just came in on your flight, him we've never seen before."

The voice was close behind her. It sounded amused.

Dalrymple!

Dru swung around and nearly bumped into a grinning Compton Dalrymple. Nelson Roopnaraine stood beside him. He, too, was grinning.

"Whoa, don't jump. It's only us," said Roopnaraine. He held out his hand. "Welcome back to Guyana, Dru. It's good to see you."

"Yes, nice to have you back in G.T.," echoed Dalrymple, using the popular name for Georgetown. "How was your flight?"

Dru smiled and shook hands with the two men. "Hey, Nelson, Compton. Good to see you, too. My flight was okay, thanks."

"And your family is well, I trust?"

"Oh, yes, indeed, thank you."

"You must be glad for this little break from the stress of New York," Roopnaraine volunteered warmly.

"In a way, yes," Dru answered politely.

"Of course, we don't mean to imply that Guyana does not have its ups and downs," Dalrymple said with a laugh.

"Of course not. I wouldn't dream of interpreting it that way," Dru said. The touch of impatience in her voice was not lost on the two men. They glanced at each other knowingly. Time to cut the fellowship among humans. Americans were so predictable. With them it was always hurry. Hurry! Hurry! Let's get down to business! And for all Dru's touting of her Guyanese roots, she was very much the American business executive.

Roopnaraine took her by the elbow with one hand and grabbed the handle of her rolling leather suitcase with the other. "Let's go," he said, steering her toward the exit.

Dalrymple followed a half step behind. Dru watched him out of the corner of her eye. It seemed that he waved and returned a greeting every two or three steps he made. People still called him "P.S.," a throwback to his tenure as permanent secretary in the Ministry of Transportation.

Hard to believe he was that good, Dru thought testily. She did not think very highly of Roopnaraine and Dalrymple, especially Dalrymple who always seemed to be undressing her with his eyes when he thought she was not looking. In fact, beyond their contractual obligations to Pilgrim Boone, she did not think of them at all.

She'd been turned off at their first meeting by their tomorrow-will-do, no-problem attitude. She had suffered through their small talk about how they hoped she and her family were well, and about the latest political goings-on in New York and Washington—which, to Dru's surprise, they were very familiar with—before getting down to the business at hand. She was well aware that this was their culture, that it was typical of the Third World markets that Pilgrim Boone was going after, and that she had to put up with it for the firm's sake. But that didn't mean she had to like it.

That's what's wrong with these countries, she ranted to herself time and time again. The world is rolling by and they're still laughing and making small talk.

Still, she was flattered that both Dalrymple and Roopnaraine had come to meet her. They may be caricatures to her but they were big-shots in Guyana, as far as big shots went. And after her run-in with St. Cyr on the flight, it was a relief to be in friendly company.

So be nice to them, Dru. It's only for a few days.

She smiled amiably at the two as they led her outside and responded amiably to their inquiries about Lawton Pilgrim and Grant Featherhorn.

When she stepped outside it was as if she had slammed into a wall of heat. It hit her full in the face. She felt her hair go limp and within seconds she was soaked under the arms. Sweat ran down her back, along her spine.

She had worn a silk blouse that she thought would keep her cool, but it was already clinging to her body.

"Whew!" she exclaimed, fanning the heat away from her face. "So much for all the hype about silk being cool. I will never get used to this heat no matter how many times I travel to the tropics."

"Not to worry. We'll be out of it in a minute. The car is just over there. It's air-conditioned," Dalrymple said, quickening his pace.

"God bless air-conditioning!" Dru sighed. She looked around quickly, wondering if she would catch sight of Theron St. Cyr and the man who had met him. It vexed her to think that she was more interested in seeing St. Cyr again than she was in seeing the man who supposedly was holding up closure on one of the most important deals of her career.

You need to rearrange your priorities, Durane, her inner voice chided. "Tell me about it," she muttered irritably.

"Sorry? You said something, Dru?"

Roopnaraine. Mr. Solicitous. "Oh, nothing. Just talking to myself. The heat, I guess," Dru said quickly with a shrug.

Just then, she spotted St. Cyr. He was about to get into the front passenger seat of a late-model Jeep with tinted windows. Andrew Goodings was already behind the wheel. St. Cyr was laughing.

Probably at his own stupid joke, Dru thought resentfully. Her gaze lingered on him. Theron St. Cyr clearly was a man at ease with himself. He had paused to take off his jacket and was now rolling up his shirtsleeves. He was still laughing, his face creased with mirth.

Dru's gaze took him in from head to toe. *So he still works out.*

He was lean and fit. His slacks were a perfect fit, as perfect as the ones he'd been wearing in Marseille.

It was as if she were seeing him for the first time. And once again, as she had so many years ago, she thought that he was not a bad-looking man at all.

A flicker of doubt played into her mind, causing the crease in her brow to deepen. How could a man like this be such a demon? Could the story he told on the plane be true?

They were unwelcome questions, darting waywardly into her eyes and causing her face to reflect a curious mix of perplexity and annoyance.

As if drawn by her gaze, St. Cyr turned his head and looked straight at her. Dru frowned and looked away hastily, only to encounter Dalrymple's cool gaze. Dalrymple did not say a word, but the corners of his mouth crinkled in a smile.

Dru bristled. *Is that a mocking smile on his goddamn face?* She could practically read his dirty mind. She feigned nonchalance. "You know, that man looks a lot like someone I met in Europe years ago. Oh, well, they say we all look alike."

Before Dalrymple could comment, she turned to Roopnaraine who was holding open the door of his shiny black Toyota RAV4. "Why thank you, Nelson," she said sweetly. "So good of you to remember I don't like sitting up front. You Guyanese drivers make me way too nervous."

She stepped into the car and settled herself behind Dalrymple, who had already climbed into the front passenger seat. "And off we go!" she said brightly as soon as Roopnaraine started the car.

Dru wanted them to take the old route into the city, not the highway that bypassed the villages and small towns that told her the real story about the country. Roopnaraine obliged. On the way she asked pointed questions about the state of Guyana's economy, and the political mood of the country. Was the flash headline on CNN the other day about an attempted coup true? Should the president's subsequent upbeat address to the nation in which he outlined his vision for the country be taken seriously? Has the transportation minister made any statements on air or rail transport?

She hoped she was giving the impression that she was trying to gauge whether it was worth it to Pilgrim Boone to pursue as costly an investment as an air transport system in Guyana, given the government's foot-dragging on the proposal. She wanted them to think that the investors were wavering on the deal. *That* should light a fire under them, she thought. Force them to push harder with the government for fear of losing thousands of dollars in consulting fees.

Dalrymple and Roopnaraine reeled off reason after reason why Pilgrim Boone should not even consider pulling out. The more Dru kept up her questioning, deliberately injecting doubt into her voice, the more the men grew agitated. Their voices rose as they tried to persuade her that there was no need to worry.

Dru smiled to herself. Good. Now they'll go on the attack.

As they rounded the bend near the old Diamond Sugar Estate, the foul smell of the factory wash that Guyanese fondly referred to as "G.T. perfume" seeped into the car.

Dru made a face. "Ooof! I guess nothing can be done about that horrible smell," she said in distaste, then switched the subject abruptly. "You know, I was kind of surprised that both of you showed up to meet me. I expected to see just one of you, or your driver, knowing how busy you are. This tells me how much value you place on this deal. Oh, yes, I've been keeping track of you guys. You're well known out there. And I see you've opened offices in Trinidad and Barbados. Everyone's coming to you now."

Roopnaraine smiled appreciatively at her in the rearview mirror but said nothing.

Dalrymple preened. "Yes. I must say we've worked very hard at building a reputation for efficiency and 100 percent delivery. I hope what everyone is seeing now is the result of all that hard work."

"And that's exactly why I want you to pull this one off. I know you can do it." Dru was sincere.

Dalrymple was touched. "I know it seems like slow going to you, Dru. But we won't let you down."

"Thanks, Compton. Now tell me about Andrew Goodings. What's the deal with him?"

The more Dalrymple and Roopnaraine recounted what they knew, the more exasperated Dru became. "I just don't understand why, if he is such a patriot and wants to see real progress in Guyana, he is holding up a project like this? My God! For a country that has more jungle and rivers than people, what else but progress would air transport bring!"

Roopnaraine swallowed before answering her, determined to stay calm. "People say he's still furious about the railroad being torn up. He claims our leaders don't really understand the role transportation plays in economic development. So it's not that he's against putting in a high-tech air transport system—of course, you know we already have privately operated planes going back and forth between the city and the interior, but nothing in the league of what Savoy is proposing—it's just that he thinks we should put our energies and resources into rail first. He doesn't think air is in Guyana's best interest right now and, after that business about the railroad, he's suspicious of the big push for it."

"Nobody is saying rail is not important. I don't see why both can't be done at the same time. If someone is coming to the table with something that clearly is needed, it doesn't make any sense to me to hold out on them, especially when no one is coming to the table with the other stuff. Is there a proposal for rail on the table?"

Dru's voice had risen with indignation. She was beginning to dislike this Goodings intensely. Who was he? What gave him the right, the power, to spit in the eye of Pilgrim Boone! Because that's exactly what he was doing. She knew the type: a low-level functionary, an insignificant retiree with an American pension and an American Social Security check that allowed him to live like a lord in his own rice republic. Here he was, feeling he could now hoist his balls at big, bad corporate America for all the wrongs big, bad corporate America had done to him in the big, bad concrete jungle. He was just the type that would click with Theron St. Cyr.

"Well! Is there a proposal for rail on the table?" she repeated heatedly.

"The government talks about restoring the old line, but as far as we know there's no concrete plan or proposal, right, Compton?"

"Right. Just talk."

"Just talk," Dru mimicked scornfully. They're not even upset, she thought resentfully. "I want a meeting with him," she said coldly.

"On what pretext? Officially, Goodings has no role in the discussions. Even if we succeed in arranging a meeting, he can easily tell you he doesn't know what you're talking about." Roopnaraine was all brisk and business now.

"I'll take that chance."

"Fine. But that still does not answer the question of pretext. How do we bring the two of you together?"

"Nelson's right, Dru. Goodings doesn't hang around, not even with the American expatriates. That makes a chance meeting him highly unlikely."

"This is Guyana. A small country whose people are known for their hospitality. Why don't I simply call on him at his home? Unannounced. That's not unusual, is it? Besides, we're both New Yorkers. We'd have a lot in common on that score. Then I can come straight out and say something about wanting his input on how to move our proposal forward. Massage his ego by saying that Pilgrim Boone has heard of his reputation as a transportation expert and his closeness to the minister. He'd buy that. Hell, he'll even appreciate my candor. He's a New Yorker, shoo."

"Sounds like a plan to me. What do you think, Nello boy?"

Roopnaraine ignored his friend. "So, your intention is to...?" He let the question hang.

"Persuade him to give up his opposition to the deal."

"In that one meeting?"

"Yes. In that one meeting. We're running out of time to get this done. We're *all* running out of time."

Dru locked the door of her hotel suite as soon as the bellhop left and peeled off her damp clothes. She hurried over to the air-conditioning unit below the wide glass windows and stood naked in the full blast of its cold air.

"I know it's crazy to do this, but I'll die if I don't," she murmured. "How in God's name can human beings live in this kind of heat three hundred and sixty-five days a year? Phew!"

Half a minute later, she went into the bathroom, pulled a fluffy towel from the stack on a shiny brass stand and wrapped it around herself. She walked back into the bedroom and threw herself across the bed. She reached for the telephone, pressed the button for overseas calls, and dialed her brother's cell phone number.

Halfway through dialing, she stopped and put the phone back on the nightstand. She rolled off the bed and retrieved her own cell phone from her pocketbook. *I'm not paranoid. You just never know*, she thought grimly.

Her brother was a principal investigator at a small law firm in Washington, D.C., that the U.S. Department of Justice had recently contracted to build a financial crimes database.

"Need a favor, brother mine," she said without ceremony when her brother answered.

"Only if it is within reason. You like to climb way out on those limbs and, as you know, I am deathly afraid of falling out of trees."

"Awwww, come on, Lance. You make me sound like one of those James Bond floozies."

"Oh, don't give me that pouty voice. It won't work this time." He sighed. It worked all the time. "Okay, Dru. What's up?"

"All I need is information on a man named Andrew Goodings. Born Guyanese, U.S. citizen. Worked at the Port Authority of New York and New Jersey until his retirement three years ago."

"That's it?"

"Well, while you're at it, check on a guy named Theron St. Cyr. He's pals with Goodings. Just landed in Guyana."

"And I suppose you just landed there, too. How's that deal going?"

"Working on it."

"Ooookay! Check your e-mail in an hour."

"Thanks, Lance."

15

The executive jet touched down gently on the stretch of tarmac high up in the Pakaraima Mountains of Guyana, about fifty miles from the Venezuelan border.

It was a beautiful aircraft. The spitting image of a Citation Mustang, Cessna's breakthrough model that was awaiting certification in the United States before it could hit the market.

But it wasn't a Mustang. While the Federal Aviation Administration snailed through the certification procedures, a maverick baby boomer from Boston had swooped in and started to manufacture look-alikes in Brazil. He used a stolen copy of the authentic Mustang design, but modified it just enough to keep Cessna's legal bloodhounds at bay. People with very deep pockets and very secret missions were buying up the look-alikes even before they rolled off the production line.

The one that had just touched down in the Pakaraimas had been the very first off the line. In honor of that distinction, the maverick baby boomer had the factory inlay a horse's saddle in gold on the tail of the aircraft. Nothing garish. A tasteful size, just big enough to be seen from up close.

The maverick baby boomer was Jackson Stone, a billionaire who loudly and shamelessly declared himself a modern-day Robin Hood. In private, he chuckled that every good deed he did was more for himself than for the masses that benefited from it. Good deeds, he said, were his wall of protection. An impenetrable barricade between himself and those who would thwart his success.

And true enough, the half-hearted attempts to shut down his factories in Asia, Africa, and Latin America invariably ran into a wall of workers, spouses, children, even the elderly and the infirm. Jackson Stone's factories had brought them jobs, and schools, and medical clinics, and decent houses, the people shouted angrily at the authorities. *And what have you given us but empty words?* they yelled.

They wanted nothing fancy, the workers proclaimed. Nothing state-of-the-art. Just basic, ordinary things that took the shadows out of their eyes.

The authorities knew when not to mess with the salt of the earth. The doors of Jackson Stone's factories remained open.

"Doin' good deeds ain't nothin' but good business sense. Heck, I count my return on those measly investments in the billions!" Stone would laugh.

His factories pirated every top-of-the-line, name-brand item, from jogging suits to the aforementioned jets, and sold them all over the world, even in the United States. Few wasted their time wondering how he got away with it. Even his most avid detractors conceded, grudgingly, that all was fair in trade and war. He committed a third of each factory's annual earnings to feeding, housing, and doctoring as many of the earth's wretched as he could. He paid Uncle Sam his due, gave generously to the Democratic, Republican, *and* Independent parties, got himself branded by the press as America's lovable bad boy philanthropist, and dodged every bullet of jealousy fired in his direction.

It helped a great deal that he was "a living, breathing, American Adonis, born into a poor Irish family in Bensonhurst, Brooklyn, a college dropout," as one bedazzled news reporter once described him.

"I am the American dream: poor but ballsy blue-eyed boy makes his way to the top with no college degree," he told his friends. Not a soul argued with him. When he branded his Mustang knock off "Sali," borrowing from the popular Wilson Pickett song "Mustang Sally," opinion page and talk show pundits shook their heads and roared with laughter. So did most of America's business brass, though they did so in private so as not to offend Cessna.

Now, as the golden-saddled *Sali* bounced along the runway, three young Indian men dressed in combat fatigues emerged at different points from the surrounding bushes. Each one carried an AK-47, cocked and ready. Not one of them was older than eighteen. They stood guard silently as the *Sali* rolled to a stop behind the aircraft that had touched down just minutes earlier, another *Sali*.

The door of the arriving jet swung open. A man in dark glasses and an impeccably cut summer-weight wool suit stepped into the doorway. From a distance he cut an impressive figure. Trim. About six-foot-four, two hundred pounds, give or take a few. Dark-skinned, though more of a Mediterranean hue than Latin American.

Up close, his square-jawed, handsome face was cruelly marred on the right side by a scar that formed a jagged crescent from his temple to the corner of his mouth. It was a trophy from his first fight in a bar in the slums of Caracas.

His bearing exuded arrogance and inspired fear. This was a man who was used to commanding and to being obeyed.

He descended the metal staircase with measured steps, a half-smile on his face, head held high, turning slowly in a studied, piercing sweep of the clearing. The moment his foot made contact with the earth the three combatants simultaneously lowered their rifles and saluted smartly. The man did not return the salute. He stood still at the foot of the staircase, his back as erect as if he had had military training.

Behind his dark glasses, his jet-black eyes continued to sweep the thick foliage that encircled the airstrip. He cocked his head slightly and listened intently, as if filtering the raucous brawl of the hundreds of species of birds, howler monkeys, and other fauna that inhabited the Pakaraima region. He scanned the skies beyond the mountaintops, where the sun was making its laborious ascent to noon.

And he waited.

The combatants cocked their rifles again and they, too, waited.

No one spoke.

Suddenly, there was a break in the foliage and another figure emerged into full view. Startlingly pale in the tropical sun, the graying, middle-aged man who strode onto the runway wore the casual business attire of an American executive attending a meeting in the tropics: khaki Dockers; pale-blue oxford shirt open at the neck; navy-blue jacket of some new high-tech blend; laced leather brogues; and designer dark glasses.

He walked quickly and confidently toward the one the Indians called Sickle Face, his hand outstretched in greeting, his face grim.

"We meet again, Alejandro. How are things in Caracas?" It was a boyish voice. High-pitched. Full of charm. Devoid of warmth.

Alejandro grasped the outstretched hand. "They are well, my friend. And for you? How are things in New York?"

The resonant timbre of Alejandro's voice contrasted sharply with the high pitch of the American's. His heavy accent was more Spanish than Venezuelan. It was the accent of his father, a Basque revolutionary who was educated in Madrid and who fled to Venezuela after bombing the headquarters of the Guardia Civil.

The American frowned and shot a quick glance at the three guards. Voices carried in the mountains.

Alejandro nodded toward the staircase. "Shall we go aboard?"

"New York is not pleased," the American said when they were settled in the soft leather seats of the custom-appointed aircraft. "Things are moving much too slowly in Georgetown. But this sudden death of Andrew Goodings. A little too obvious, don't you think? Too convenient, the timing. The old man has already made comments to that effect. He is very shrewd."

Alejandro fixed his obsidian gaze on the American and smiled a slow smile. "It had to be done. You know it was the only way to handle him." His tone was patronizing.

"*Something* had to be done. Perhaps this was not the most prudent thing to do."

"You sanctioned it, my American friend. We understood each other that day. On the phone."

Grant Featherhorn ran his fingers through his thick salt-and-pepper hair, sighed, and looked away. He leaned back in the seat and stared up at the ceiling, chewing his bottom lip.

He sighed again. "Yes, you are right. It was the only way."

They were silent.

"And now?" said Featherhorn after a while.

"I meet with Minister MacPherson later today to discuss my proposal to develop an eco-resort and conference center here in these mountains. It is a project the Guyanese government desperately wants. Needs, in fact. Foreign investors are staying away. Too much crime. Too much trouble with the opposition. Blacks and Indians killing each other over who did what during the elections and who should rightfully be running the country. The place seems to be disintegrating and the government appears to be at a total loss as to what to do. A project like mine would give the president something to brag about to the international community. He could say it is a sign of renewed foreign confidence in Guyana; that no one would invest in the country if they were not satisfied that the government has a tight grip on things."

Featherhorn's eyes narrowed as he watched Alejandro light a cigarette. He thought irritably that the Venezuelan's movements were affected to the point of being effeminate.

"Fools!" he snapped. "If they want a sign of renewed foreign investor confidence, then why won't they go forward with Savoy's proposal?"

Alejandro inhaled deeply, blew out the smoke through his nostrils, and then continued as if Featherhorn had not spoken. "But I have made the issue of transportation a determining factor. Clever, don't you think, my friend? I am insisting that the government provide adequate air transportation to my resort. I have impressed upon them, *all* of them—the president, Minister MacPherson, the tourism minister, the commerce and interior ministers, all of them—that this would demonstrate their commitment to the project. But they have been stalling. Understandably, of course. But, in the long run, foolishly. They plead they have no money, therefore they want *me* to be responsible for the transportation. I have said I cannot leave myself that exposed when the situation in the country is so uncertain. So we have been at a stalemate for the last month or so."

He paused again and inclined his head with an air of modesty, misreading Featherhorn's silence as approval of, even admiration for, his negotiating acumen. "It is now time to play hardball. I plan to say to Minister MacPherson that I am well aware of Savoy Aerospace's interest in setting up an air transport network in Guyana to better access its interior and its neighboring countries, of its offer to sell the government a fleet of small planes on very attractive terms. I will state to him in no uncertain terms that I would consider it very bad faith, very bad faith indeed on the part of the Guyanese government vis à vis my project if Savoy Aerospace's interest were dismissed. You see my point?" He stared at Featherhorn expectantly.

Featherhorn nodded, concealing his annoyance. Alejandro's voice and the roll on his r's had deepened as he became caught up in the drama of the scenario he described. Of course, he saw the point. Alejandro Bernat's money was behind some of the most exotic and successful eco-resorts in Latin America. If Guyana continued to balk, he would threaten to walk away from the project. And if he walked, he would not go quietly. No way! The Alejandro Bernat he knew would create a stink in the press. And he would not do it in Guyana's local media either. This was the kind of story that would be lapped up by news organizations in Europe and North America.

Featherhorn pictured the whole thing in his mind. Bernat would set up the reporters he had access to, feeding them information about his discontent with Guyana's investment environment. He would cite the hallowed names of Savoy Aerospace and Pilgrim Boone as fellow victims of the Guyanese government's ineptitude. Before long, the press would be seething at the gall of some dirt-poor rice republic to turn down investments that so many other countries coveted. By the time Bernat was through, the poor little country would be hard-pressed to get even its own émigrés to consider investing there.

Hell, it was brilliant! Using the press was a textbook Pilgrim Boone tactic.

Suddenly, Featherhorn could not help grinning. There was no need to say more on that subject. He was relieved, actually, that Bernat had things so well figured out.

He nodded to Bernat. "You know of the Pilgrim Boone woman in Georgetown?" It was more a statement than a question.

"Yes, I do. I have not seen her, but I have heard much of her. A Black American woman, is it not so? Of Guyanese extraction, I believe?"

"Yes. She's very smart. And very much like Pilgrim himself. Approaches negotiations the same way. *He* was her real mentor. As much as she wants this deal to go through, she, too, will ask questions about Goodings' death."

"Ah, my friend. You worry too much. We, too, have our woman in Georgetown. Her name is Leila. She is an Amerindian woman who is very loyal to us. I will assume that you know who the Amerindians are. She despises the government of Guyana for what it has done to her people: robbing them of their tribal lands, leaving them defenseless against the Canadian mining companies and the Malaysian timber concerns. Venezuela was smart enough to give them sanctuary when they rebelled during the Burnham regime. Our woman, she was just a little girl at the time of this rebellion, but she knows intimately the story of the men of her family and of her tribe who died. She is strong in her vow of vengeance. She will see to it that your woman does not ask too many questions. She is discreet and most efficacious. Goodings is a fine example of her work."

Featherhorn felt his skin crawl. Alejandro was going too far. "Alejandro—"

Bernat cut him off. "Perhaps you are tired after your long flight from New York. And the thought of making that very journey back in…" His voice trailed off as he raised his arm and looked at his gold Rolex, "just over an hour, I am sure it must make you doubly tired. Let us relax and have a drink. We still have a lot to discuss, assuming Guyana will act wisely."

He chuckled and leaned closer to Featherhorn, his voice amused and intimate. "This meeting between us, Grant. You said it was necessary to put things in perspective. Surely that does not mean it has to be unpleasant."

Featherhorn shrugged. He knew Alejandro Bernat well enough not to be fooled by his chummy demeanor. Challenging Bernat's unspoken but obvious plan for getting Drucilla Durane out of their way would put him on Bernat's wrong side, a place he had no desire to put himself in. Oh, well, too bad for Dru, he thought. She should have gotten out of Pilgrim Boone long ago. He had tried hard to make her do just that. The stubborn fool. She had to prove how tough she was, didn't she? Well, this is what you get when you play tough in the wrong game. She's on her own, now. It's no secret that Guyana isn't the safest place to be.

Bernat patted Featherhorn on the arm. He spoke kindly. "Relax, Grant. There is too much at stake for us in Guyana to be distracted by unknowns. Now, let's toast our good friend Jackson Stone and these amazing Mustang Salis."

16

That face.

    That bearing. Tall, svelte.

The walk. Long, heavy strides.

And his hair. So thick. So black. Curling down to his shoulders.

The color of his skin was like the flesh of old tamarind, a fruit she grew up seeing in her home. A deep, burnished brown.

What a striking man, Dru thought. He reminds me of someone.

Fascinated, she stared at the man through the tinted windows of Dalrymple's SUV.

Dalrymple had picked her up at her hotel and brought her to the Ministry of Transportation. On the way he told her that he and Roopnaraine had called in a ton of favors to get her a meeting with MacPherson that very afternoon. She had been adamant about the meeting, refusing to be swayed by their protests about protocol and short notice.

"You're supposed to have the clout to pull off something like that. That's why Pilgrim Boone paid you the outrageous retainer you asked for," she had said tersely.

She and Dalrymple had just driven through the gates of the ministry on Battery Road when she saw the man. She had singled him out from the crowd of people coming and going in the ministry compound not only because he was so tall, but also because he seemed familiar.

She scanned the man's long, thin face more intently, her brow drawn tight with the effort to jog her memory. His eyes, set deep under bushy, perfectly angled eyebrows, seemed unusually small. His lips were thin and unsmiling. The lift of his head caused his chin to jut out slightly, adding to his air of absolute power. The longer she stared at him, the stronger she sensed she had seen him before.

Dru squeezed her eyes shut and tried to place the man in her past. Where would she have seen such a man?

Suddenly she knew. *Marseille!* He reminded her of the man in Marseille all those years ago. The man Theron St. Cyr had called "Ramy."

Ramy! He whose nearness had made her skin crawl. He who had made her huddle close to Theron St. Cyr. The one who, if what St. Cyr said on the plane was true, would have kidnapped her all those years ago had he, St. Cyr, not reached her first. Could this be the same man? Would Ramy be this old? This guy seemed to be in his late forties.

You simply would have disappeared and you never would have escaped alive, Dru. Believe me.

Dru shuddered as she recalled St. Cyr's words. He had sounded so earnest, so sincere. Was he telling the truth?

She pushed the question aside and brought her focus back to the stranger approaching the SUV. Dalrymple had stopped, waiting for the parking slot that was being vacated by a mint-new, silver-gray Honda Accord.

Did this man really look like Ramy? Dru was beginning to doubt herself. Maybe Ramy was on her mind because Theron had brought him up on the plane in that laughable attempt to clear his name, she thought with disgust. Did he think she was stupid?

Still, she struggled to recall details of the face of the man in Le Quartier Noir. No clear picture emerged. It was too long ago. She had seen him only that one time, that one weird moment when he strode by and shot pure hatred at Theron St. Cyr.

It's this man's look and the way he carries himself that reminded her of Ramy, Dru concluded. The darkness that seems to emanate from him. The same aura of evil clings to this man as it had to Ramy.

The man had almost caught up with the SUV now. His eyes were fixed on the darkened windows of the SUV as if he could see right through them. Dru tensed, sinking her fingernails into the arms of the seat. She stared back at the man, unable to look away.

A memory stole into her head. *There are evil people on this earth*, the old woman on the train in France had said to her. *Good people always sense their presence. If ever you sense such a presence, be on your guard. It is a sign of bad things to come.*

Dru blinked, surprised at the awakening of yet another memory from those heady days in Europe. Theron St. Cyr's reappearance in her life had flung open a door in her mind. First Ramy, now the old woman.

Dru blinked again. The stranger was so close she could see beads of perspiration on his forehead, compliments of Georgetown's blazing heat. She saw the pockmarks.

Didn't Ramy have pockmarks on his face, or was it boils? And she saw his eyes. Obsidian eyes. Liquid black orbs that were unreadable.

Dru shivered. She had always told herself that she was not superstitious. But, Ramy or not, she could not help thinking that the sight of this man was a bad sign indeed.

"Here we are, Dru. We got here ahead of time, but you might be lucky. The minister may have finished his work early, or he may not have had anything to do today." Dalrymple hoped Dru would pick up on his sarcasm. He was still smarting from her gall. The idea that she could get an audience with a minister of government whenever she wished was a common attitude among big foreign investors. They seemed to think that their investments entitled them to 24-7 access to the top officials of whatever poor countries they were investing in. He'd heard the same complaint from colleagues in the islands and in Africa. These investors would never expect the same in America or Europe, Dalrymple fumed silently as he waited for Dru to step out of the car. He had pulled into the slot vacated by the Honda and had already opened the door on his side.

Dru heard Dalrymple's voice but his words were meaningless sounds. She wasn't paying attention. She had turned her head to follow the stranger as he strode away.

"Are you okay, Dru?" Dalrymple didn't mask his impatience. *What's gotten into her now?* he wondered.

Dru turned to face the front of the car again, but did not respond to Dalrymple. Questions were pounding in her head. Could this man be Ramy? No, it couldn't be. This one looked too old. Ramy would not have aged that much. Back then he seemed to be not much older than Theron. Sure, twelve years had gone by, but twelve isn't twenty. Maybe he had plastic surgery. It would make sense for him to do that if, as Theron claimed, he was a criminal and wanted to disappear into a new life.

So if it is Ramy, why is he here? And why now, when St. Cyr was here too? Were they friends after all? Partners in some heinous plot? They *had* to be. It was too much of a coincidence, their being here at the same time, in this out-of-the-way city, of all places! Not New York. Not Paris. Not Marseille. Not some place teeming with hustle and bustle and bright lights and starry-eyed girls looking for adventure and magic, girls who could easily be lured into their vicious net.

Dru's hands suddenly felt clammy. She rubbed them up and down her thighs. Ramy and St. Cyr were either working together or against each other, and whatever they were involved in had to do with the business that had brought her to Guyana. That was the only explanation that made sense. This guy was at the same ministry she was visiting. And St. Cyr was with the same man who was holding up Savoy's proposal.

Her head throbbed. If Ramy and St. Cyr were pursuing their own transportation deal in Guyana, then Savoy and its representatives—i.e., Pilgrim Boone, i.e. Drucilla Durane—may be standing in their way.

She thought again of St. Cyr's words to her on the plane. *You simply would have disappeared and you never would have escaped alive, Dru. Believe me.*

Given what she had just figured out, those words sounded very much like a threat couched in the same charm and earnest concern St. Cyr had exhibited in Marseille. He was telling her what he *and* Ramy were capable of doing to her.

For the first time since that terrifying night in Paris, Dru felt desperately afraid. This was not one of her nightmares that she would awaken from. There would be no big relief the morning after. Evil was here, in flesh and blood. She had sensed it.

She covered her face and moaned. This couldn't be real. Of course, that man wasn't Ramy. It was the nightmare again. But this was daytime. How could she have a nightmare in the daytime? Was she going crazy?

"Oh dear God! Dear God! What's happening to me? Whatever it is, make it go away! Please make it go away!"

"Dru! Dru! What's the matter? What the hell is wrong?" Dalrymple had grabbed her by the shoulders and was shaking her roughly. "For God's sake, Dru. Tell me what is going on!"

Dru dragged her hands down her face and clasped them tight in her lap. She stared at Dalrymple as if she did not recognize him. Her breathing was heavy and jagged.

She looked around wildly, her eyes searching in the direction she had last seen the man. He was gone. Of course, he was gone. It was an illusion. It wasn't Ramy. Just someone who reminded me of him.

Following her cue, Dalrymple looked around, at the same time tightening his grip on her shoulders. "What is it? What or who did you see?"

"I saw…I saw…a man. An evil-looking man. He reminded me of someone I met—saw—many years ago." Her voice was hoarse and cracking. Her eyes were still wild and darting.

"Who is it? Where is he? Where?" Dalrymple's head snapped from side to side as he scanned the compound.

"He…he's gone. He's gone. I don't see him anymore. He's gone. But he was here. Just a minute ago I saw him. Coming toward me." Her voice rose hysterically.

Dalrymple shook her again, more gently this time. "It's all right. It's all right, Dru. No one is going to hurt you here," he said reassuringly.

It was all he could say. Dru's behavior and her outburst were shocking. The frosty Drucilla Durane he knew could never lose it like this. And even if she did, she would not do so in front of him, not the way she looked down on him and Nello, perched on her high Yankee horse.

So what was this all about, then?

He wondered if she was on drugs and hadn't had her fix. You never knew with Americans, even the best of them, these high-octane executives and high-society types—if you would excuse the pun, he chuckled inwardly. He'd seen some of them in action himself and read enough about others. Maybe Dru was part of that crowd. Hadn't she acted a bit weird at the airport too? Hale and hearty one moment and lost in space the next. He couldn't wait to tell Nello.

All of a sudden he felt ashamed. You're lying to yourself, Dalrymple. Dru Durane is no druggie and you know it. So what if she went off every now and then. A woman like her must be overloaded with stress. And with the government taking so damned long to decide on Savoy, the white boys are bound to be putting all kinds of pressure on the poor girl. So give her a break, Dalrymple! She's entitled.

Dalrymple's eyes softened as he stared at Dru. He eased his grip on her shoulders and dropped his arms. He smiled awkwardly. Like we say, "Only knife know what in pumpkin belly," he thought.

The image of a knife plunged into the soft belly of a pumpkin flashed through his mind and brought him up sharply. Once again, his brow crinkled with concern. Something or someone seemed genuinely to have set her off. But whatever or whoever it was, it would have to be dealt with later. That is, *if* she wanted to. Right now, he had to get the situation in hand, get her to pull herself together. This meeting with the minister was important. Neither he nor Nello had been able to get a one-on-one with MacPherson since the last Pilgrim Boone visit. The minister had dodged them with repeated excuses about being tied up with Quartapint. But the minute he had heard Dru was in town, he had agreed to meet her.

"Either he's got a crush on her or he frighten ol' Lawton Pilgrim," had been Nello's explanation. Whatever. The meeting was on and he, Dalrymple, would be there. He wasn't going to say much. While Dru and the minister talked, he would be watching and listening closely to the minister for clues, anything that would tell him which way the decision would go. He was good at sifting through the hyperbole.

He spoke to Dru in a voice that belied his concern. "Try to calm down, Dru. The person is gone. And look! You're almost right on time for your meeting now. We have to start walking up."

Dru dragged her eyes to his face. His features slowly registered in her brain, his words slowly took on meaning. She thought of how she must have looked, how she must have sounded, how he seemed to be pitying her. Her face grew hot with embarrassment, which swiftly gave way to annoyance. She didn't need Dalrymple's pity. Her eyes hardened as she looked at him. She rolled her neck slightly, waiting for his smirk to appear.

It didn't. Instead, Dalrymple was looking at her quizzically. She held his gaze, neck-rolled again and said nothing.

Still no smirk.

The fight ebbed from her face, her eyes. Dalrymple was genuinely flummoxed.

Dru took a deep breath and swallowed. "I'm sorry, Compton. You must think I'm nuts. It's a long story, but I assure you I'm not crazy," she said with a weak smile. "And I'm not on drugs, either. I know that's the first thing you probably thought."

Dalrymple noted that she had called him by his first name. It pleased him. Still, he put on a face of one dutifully aggrieved. "How could you say, even think, such an ugly thing, Dru," he said, his voice heavy with hurt.

Dru laughed. Under the circumstances, his predictability was comforting.

She felt almost back to normal. The pounding in her head eased. She had imagined the whole thing. She must have. Ramy walking toward her in Georgetown, Guyana, indeed! How could she have allowed herself to get so carried away? She had simply seen someone who reminded her a lot of Ramy.

It's because he had that same evilness about him, she told herself. The feeling that he was a bad sign. Bad for the meeting and therefore bad for the whole Savoy deal. That's what had set her off.

She sighed, relieved that she had a reasonable explanation for her behavior. She had to get a grip on herself. These past few weeks have been crazy, what with trying to close on Savoy, Grant on her back, Lawton supportive but clearly anxious, St. Cyr surfacing and behaving as if he had done nothing wrong, the hastily arranged trip to Guyana. Not to mention Georgetown's unforgiving heat! Her brain was frying, literally and figuratively. No wonder she was starting to imagine things.

I never should have given up yoga, Dru thought. I wrapped up my life when I stepped onto the corporate ladder and handed it over to Pilgrim Boone. That's what I did.

She sighed again. What else could she have done? What else was she supposed to do with her loan-shackled college education and her European experience? Wasn't she supposed to reach for the top? Blast her way through all the ceilings?

The sudden blast of a car horn startled her out of her thoughts. Dalrymple was still looking at her like a man unfairly wronged. A few parking slots down from their SUV a shiny black Mercedes Benz with the ubiquitous dark-tinted windows was backing out. The driver blasted the horn again. Two young women were slow-walking directly in front of the car. Simultaneously, they turned their heads, cut their eyes at the driver, and slowed their pace, exaggerating the roll of their hips.

Dru looked at the Mercedes curiously, wondering if the stranger was in it. No point dwelling on him, she told herself, and turned back to Dalrymple. She owed him an apology. She would put the stranger out of her mind.

"Yeah, you're right," she said to Dalrymple. "Suggesting that you would think I'm on drugs was an ugly thing to say. You would never think a thing like that. Come on, let's go see Minister MacPherson."

⁂

Reginald MacPherson stood somberly as his secretary ushered Dru and Dalrymple into his office. He leaned across his cluttered desk and shook hands with them, Dru first.

Dru was thunderstruck by his appearance. This was not the affable, energetic man she had met before. Never mind the exquisite manners. The man whose eyes seemed barely able to meet hers was a shadow of the man she had expected to see. Standing before her was a man in torment. Or was it defeat? His face was ashy and drawn, his shoulders sagged. Dark circles stained the skin under his vacant, reddened eyes.

The confident smile Dru had plastered on her face as she walked up the wide mahogany staircase to his office fell away instantly. She stammered as she shook hands with him.

"It's...it's good to see you again, Mr. Minister."

Dalrymple, equally appalled by MacPherson's appearance, muttered something unintelligible. The two were on very cordial terms. They met frequently at various political and social functions, and once in a while MacPherson would seek Dalrymple's advice on a sensitive matter having to do with ministry operations.

When the minister spoke his voice was hollow, a sound emanating from a body that seemed to be hemorrhaging its own life. "Thank you for coming, Ms. Durane, Compton. Please have a seat." He waved vaguely to the chairs facing his desk and dropped into his own.

They waited for him to continue, but he seemed to have drifted away, no doubt to whatever was responsible for his obvious torment.

Dru's mind reeled. Her heart pounded. Though she couldn't explain it to herself, somehow she knew that the man she had seen downstairs—the man she knew now was not Ramy, but someone just as sinister—had something to do with the way the minister looked.

Dru shivered. The presence of evil in the room was palpable.

Once again, though less than ten minutes had elapsed, she found herself struggling to overpower fear. She glanced at Dalrymple, who seemed to be fiercely contemplating the Marjorie Broodhagen original on the wall behind the minister's desk. She knew he was trying to save the minister face by not staring at him. She had no way of knowing that he was frantically trying to recall his grandmother's teachings about protecting yourself from *obeah*, Guyanese witchcraft.

"Forgive me, Ms. Durane." MacPherson's voice was thin and far away. "I'm not sure I can be of any help to you at this time. You see, I lost a dear friend quite suddenly last night." He paused, momentarily overcome. He pulled himself together quickly and turned to Dalrymple. "You may not have heard yet, Compton. We've been keeping it quiet because it's all so strange, so very strange. So I must ask you not to say anything to anyone. I don't mean Nelson, of course, because that would be like asking you not to breathe."

The minister smiled feebly at his own joke, but his eyes drifted away as he continued to speak, more to himself than to his guests. "What I cannot understand is that he was in such perfect health. A little blood pressure, that's all. And which of us doesn't have that. His certainly wasn't serious enough to cause anything like what his doctor is talking about."

He paused again, shaking his head. Then he looked straight at Dru. "My friend's name is Andrew Goodings. He supposedly died of massive heart failure. But there's still the autopsy to come." He slumped back in his chair, one arm folded across his chest, the other hand holding his forehead.

The horror in Dru's gasp seemed to envelop the room. No one spoke. Dru's hands trembled and she gripped the chair tightly. She closed her eyes, squeezing them tight as if to keep away the thoughts that came pelting toward her. She did not want to think of the man downstairs anymore. Nor did she want to think of Theron St. Cyr, whom she had seen getting into Andrew Goodings's car. She did not want to think of Andrew Goodings himself, a man who seemed to have been in good health, enjoying life. And most of all she did not want to think of the question that was trying to claw its way through all the others.

Would she be next?

She sat like a rock. She would not move. She would not speak. Moving, speaking, they made room for thought. She was determined not to think. Not now.

It was Dalrymple who broke the silence. "I'm sorry to hear this, Macky. You have my deepest sympathy. And please convey the same to his wife and family for me. Goodings and I had our differences as you know, but this…" He shook his head in disbelief. "This is a terrible, a most shocking loss. We all know how close you two were. Is there anything I can do?"

He meant every word. Goodings' death was bad news in more ways than one. Very bad news indeed. If someone had bumped off Lebba Lip, and Macky seemed to be hinting that someone had, it meant an even longer delay in the Savoy decision. It could be weeks. Everyone knew where Goodings had stood on Savoy. People who had already positioned themselves to benefit from the spin-off contracts and the side deals that went with such a project had cursed him to high heaven. Some of them did so publicly, some privately. Every last one of them would come under suspicion, not to mention himself, Nelson, the Savoy Aerospace reps who dropped in from time to time, and Pilgrim Boone. Even *Dru*.

He turned to her. She seemed to be in a daze. He thought she was overreacting. After all, she hadn't known Goodings. The first time she ever saw him was at the airport. He wondered if the episode downstairs had anything to do with the way she was acting now. Hadn't she said she knew the man Goodings met at the airport? What the hell was going on?

He turned back to MacPherson, waiting for his answer. MacPherson had slumped deeper into his chair, his chin on his chest. He stirred, wiped a hand across his face, and sighed. "No, Compton. I don't even know what to do myself. Perhaps later I may need your help."

The sound of the minister's and Dalrymple's voices shook Dru out of her daze. She had to say something. "My condolences, Mr. Minister. What a shock it must be indeed." It wasn't enough. She had to say more. She had to know. "It must be awful for Theron St. Cyr," she said.

The minister's head jerked up. "Who?" he demanded.

Dru was taken aback by his vehement reaction to St. Cyr's name. "Theron St. Cyr. Mr. Goodings met him at the airport yesterday. They seemed to know each other well. Mr. St. Cyr was on the same flight I took from New York."

"And how do you know this Mr. St. Cyr?" MacPherson was suddenly transformed. Gone was the tortured shadow of a man. His voice commanded. His eyes pierced.

The shroud in the room lifted. MacPherson stared at Dru, fixing her like a bug.

She was thrown off guard, but she didn't flinch. "I met him several years ago in France," she said evenly.

"And do you know why he is here?" The question was almost an accusation.

"I beg your pardon?"

"What is the reason for Mr. St. Cyr's visit to Guyana?"

"I have no idea, Mr. Minister." The conversation had devolved into an inquisition and she resented it. What the hell was he trying to prove?

The minister tried again. "You did not speak to each other on the plane?"

"We did, but we did not discuss each other's reasons for traveling to Guyana. We are not exactly on friendly terms, Mr. Minister." Try as she could, she couldn't keep the edge out of her voice. She could feel Dalrymple's eyes on her grow cold.

The minister suddenly sighed. He seemed relieved. Anguish overcame him again and he slumped in his chair once more. "So you have no idea what Mr. St. Cyr is doing in Guyana? Why he was met by Mr. Goodings?" His voice was tired.

Dru's voice remained crisp. "No, Mr. Minister. I do not."

The minister closed his eyes and leaned back in his chair. Dru kept her eyes on him. Her mind zigzagged. If she played her cards right, she could turn this scene to her own advantage. She spoke again, the edge gone from her voice.

"But I suppose it would be reasonable to surmise that his visit has something to do with the very reason for my own visit to Guyana, the very matter I came to discuss with you today. I do know that Mr. St. Cyr heads a consulting firm that specializes in the rather unpopular field of proposal investigations, doing the due diligence, if you will, on proposed project participants and processes. Your government has delayed its decision on our client's proposal. Perhaps you have doubts about the motives behind that offer. Perhaps Mr. St. Cyr was called in to assist in clearing up those doubts."

She had spoken off the top her head, the words coming together with a will of their own and making it seem as if she had given prior thought to Theron St. Cyr's visit to Guyana. But now that she had spoken them, she realized that they conveyed a perfectly plausible answer to her own questions. Maybe they were what she wanted to believe. Maybe she needed to believe them because that other explanation was too terrifying to contemplate.

Or...

No. She wouldn't go there.

She went anyway.

Could it be that she had it all wrong about what had happened in Paris, that St. Cyr was telling the truth on the plane? Could it be that she really wanted him to be a good guy, to still be the sensitive, at times taciturn, man who had walked her around Marseille?

A part of her refused to give up the belief she had clung to for the last twelve years. *Stop it! Stop it right now! You can't afford to drop your guard. Not now.*

Before MacPherson could speak she blurted out, "And what if Mr. St. Cyr had a conflict of interest?" There! She'd done it. She'd planted a nugget of doubt that would undermine whatever trust MacPherson and Goodings had put in Theron St. Cyr. She hoped she sounded as if she knew more than she was going to say.

Dalrymple's eyebrows arched. He pursed his lips and stared at Dru with admiration. She was one smooth operator. How the hell could he have thought she was on drugs! Which druggie could put two and two together so fast? Whatever this St. Cyr did to her—and he must have done something to her, the way she had looked at him at the airport—she was paying him back for it now. Not only that, she's cornered Macky. But grief or no grief, Macky could deliver a bite like red ants. If St. Cyr is his boy, like Dru said, he'd protect him all the way.

MacPherson studied Dru's face for a long moment. In the end he decided that she was telling the truth. She did not know why St. Cyr was in Georgetown. Her conjecture was just that. Conjecture. And this business about a conflict of interest? He shrugged it away. Besmirching the integrity of your opponent was an old tactic in business. He had no reason to doubt Andrew's account of the man.

"Do you know a man named Alejandro Bernat, Ms. Durane?"

Dalrymple could barely suppress his smile. There it was. The Mack attack. Throw her off balance. He saw the surprise in Dru's eyes, saw it disappear almost instantly, saw her eyes go flat as she steeled herself. This time he couldn't suppress the smile. Yes. Dru Durane was one smooth operator. He had to give her that.

Dru repeated the name, pronouncing it carefully. "Alejandro Bernat?" It was not familiar to her. "I'm afraid I do not, sir. Should I?"

"No. Never mind."

Dru's turn. She leaned forward and spoke earnestly.

"Do you have doubts about the motives behind Savoy Aerospace's offer, Mr. Minister? Because if you do, I will do anything in my power to erase those doubts. Pilgrim Boone is known for its integrity. Its clients are of high moral repute. We do business with no other kind. Without such integrity, our company could not have survived all these decades, especially in the position it occupies."

The minister hesitated for a fraction of a second before replying. "I am touched by your enthusiasm and your sincerity, Ms. Durane," he said gravely. Troubled was more like it, he thought. Surely such a smart woman could not be so naïve? He had already concluded that either Pilgrim Boone or Savoy itself was involved in some way with Andrew's death, directly or indirectly. It might not be Pilgrim himself, but someone in one of those two companies was a killer. Instinctively, he ruled out Dru Durane. Not her. Something of this magnitude would be dealt with at a much higher level. The Dru Duranes of this world were the decent face others put on their machinations. And, unfortunately, they often ended up being the fall guy.

But surely she should at least question the timing of Andrew's death, given the pressure on her company to deliver for its client. He continued, "However, I must ask you to be patient a little longer. Try not to worry. The deal may well turn out in your favor."

He stood up and extended his hand. The meeting was over.

Dru rose from the chair. In spite of MacPherson's encouraging words, she felt hollow inside. She needed more than encouraging words. She needed a decision in her client's favor. But at this point, Pilgrim Boone and Savoy Aerospace were no closer to any decision than when she had entered the minister's office. Lawton Pilgrim wouldn't blame her, but Grant

Featherhorn would. And it would not be pretty when he did.

She held her head high and shook the minister's hand firmly, her face grim. She told him again, in a crisp voice that belied the sinking in the pit of her stomach, how sorry she was about Mr. Goodings's sudden passing and expressed hope that he would be able to meet with her again soon so that she could allay any fears he may have about Savoy's intentions.

MacPherson saw through her stoic façade and felt guilty. Even in small talk during their previous meetings, he had never mentioned that they were related by marriage. He was sure she didn't know the relative that had married into his family, but *he* knew. And in countries as small as his, those relationships carried obligations that everyone expected you to honor. He should be taking care of Dru. He should be seeing to it that she got what she wanted. The fact that she was "from away," that she had not grown up in Guyana at all, was all the more reason he should be looking out for her.

But his hands were tied. At least for the moment. She'll get what she wants in the end, he mused. The president will decide in favor of Savoy. Bernat, that crapaud-face, had pretty much sealed that outcome.

Everyone would just have to wait. He could not let Andrew's death pass like one of those you read about so often in the newspapers: *Retired Guyanese-American dies of—stroke/heart attack/cancer/pick-any-one—after returning to Guyana fewer than five years ago.* No, Andrew deserved a more honorable mention. There had to be an inquiry.

17

Andrew Goodings had been murdered.

The fact that Andrew's own doctor was baffled by the sudden-ness of his death only reinforced Theron's belief that his friend had been killed. It wouldn't surprise him either if the autopsy showed nothing out of the ordinary, he told himself, nothing but massive heart failure, which is what all the signs were pointing to. There were ways to engineer a killing so that the autopsy gave no clue as to the real cause of death.

Someone wanted Andrew out of the way and that meant only one thing: There was more to Savoy Aerospace's proposed project in Guyana than met the eye, just as he had suspected.

Once again, Theron reviewed everything he had learned from An-drew as they drove into the city from the airport. Andrew owed no one any money, cheated no one, coveted no one's possessions, no one's power. He lived the private life of a retiree: He was involved in his church, fundrais-ing and curriculum guidance for his old high school, the Lion's Club, the Georgetown Cricket Club, and his small circle of friends.

The one subject he spoke out publicly on was the country's trans-portation infrastructure. His insistence that rail, not air, was what Guyana needed most at this time had earned him a few detractors, particularly among tour operators and the owners of the small eco-resorts, inns, and bed-and-breakfast lodges that were cropping up in the interior. They countered Andrew's arguments just as passionately and publicly as he made his. But nothing Andrew had said suggested that this was anything more than a difference of opinion, or that he had reason to fear for his life. In fact, he seemed to enjoy meeting and debating his detractors, which he said he often did at the cricket club.

He recalled Andrew's words: "I would give it to them good and proper, Theron. Mind you, they all admitted, and without shame, that they had their own business interests to consider, but then they would argue that even if they weren't involved in it, tourism was a big help to the economy. And I would agree with them on that point. But it's the timing, man. The timing. Tourism can wait. The masses of people can't."

Theron paced back and forth in his room. Despite Minister MacPherson's best efforts, word about Andrew's death had leaked out and family and friends were beginning to gather at the Goodings home where he was staying. The commotion drifted upstairs to his room: an anguished wail every now and then; an exclamation—Jesus of Nazareth passeth by!—as some skeptic finally accepted the truth; Andrew's wife, distraught, calling to her husband; a voice raised in prayer; and strains of a hymn.

Theron stopped pacing. He sat on the bed and buried his face in his hands, recalling those final moments with Andrew. Andrew had fought death like an enraged animal, gripping at and twisting in Theron's arms until his strength finally waned, the shock in his face turning to fear when he knew he had lost his fight, the rasping sounds in his throat ebbing until there was no sound at all.

It had been an agonizing death that came in the wee hours of the morning. The pain first struck just before they reached Andrew's home. Andrew had talked all the way from the airport, about Savoy Aerospace and what it was proposing to do in Guyana, about the pressure from Pilgrim Boone, the minister's misgivings and his own, about how Guyana had been tricked into doing away with its rail system and how the promised highways and bridges across the Demerara River to accommodate the thousands of vehicles that choked the city and outlying towns had never been built.

Theron had listened intently, saying little. He had been intrigued, as usual, by Andrew's passion. He had made up his mind long before Andrew had finished his story that he would put Savoy Aerospace under a microscope the moment he got back to New York. He would pick apart every contract the company had ever signed; scrutinize its leadership and every bank account it had established; and peel away its decision making, its contacts and relationships in and out of America. And he would do the same with Pilgrim Boone. If that's what it took to put Andrew Goodings's mind at ease he would do it gladly. He owed the man that much.

Then, in the middle of a sentence, Andrew had doubled over the steering wheel, groaning in pain, one hand gripping his stomach. The car had almost run off the road, but Theron had grabbed the steering wheel and righted it just in time. Andrew had managed to slow the car to a stop and they had remained there for several minutes, Andrew writhing in pain, and he not knowing what to do.

He was about to get out of the car to get help from a nearby house when Andrew suddenly straightened up. The pain had passed. He was fine, he said, though he felt weak. They weren't far from home, he told Theron, just a couple of more streets.

By the time they reached the house, it was as if nothing had happened. Andrew insisted he was fine, that the pain had gone completely. He attributed it to something he must have eaten, joking that his stomach was still very much American and that it sometimes rebelled against all the spicy Guyanese food he loved. He didn't want to talk about it once they entered the house, he'd said. It would upset his wife and he didn't want to do that.

When they resumed their conversation after dinner that night, after Mrs. Goodings had gone to bed, Andrew raised the notion of Guyana being used as a drug transshipment point. "Think of it, Theron. Jamaica is under the U.S. Drug Enforcement Administration's blanket now. So are all the Andean countries. We're the only one that's free and clear. We have no history of drug trafficking so the DEA isn't watching us. The small-scale stuff carried out by those deportee criminals the United States keeps dumping on us—you'd think they were already criminals when they left Guyana as babies or little kids—DEA doesn't have time to bother with that. On the other hand, we can be reached from Colombia by land or by water, both of which are treacherous and slow, but certainly doable if the cartels have no choice. But they do have a choice: Air. Not a damned soul is keeping tabs on their airspace."

"So you think drug interests could be manipulating the Savoy deal? With or without Savoy's complicity?"

Andrew's shoulders sagged. "I don't know what to think, Theron. But I'm not ruling out anything. It's just too much damn pressure, man!"

Then the pain hit him again. His last clear words were something about a woman who said she knew him, but who would not show him her face, and a cigarette she had given him to smoke even though he'd told her that he had quit. The words made no sense to Theron, who by then was cradling Andrew in his arms and shouting for Mrs. Goodings.

A hesitant knock on his door brought him back to the present. He rose from the bed, crossed the room, and opened the door. A young man in his late twenties introduced himself as Andrew's last son, Paul. He had just arrived from New York, he said, and had been told that Theron was the last person to see his father alive. He wanted to know what had happened, true, but it was a good excuse to get away from the wailing and confusion downstairs.

Theron decided not tell him about Savoy Aerospace or Pilgrim Boone. Instead, he told him that his father, knowing Theron's interest in investing in the Caribbean, had urged him to come to Guyana to check out a potential opportunity and had invited him to stay with him. He described the ride from the airport, Andrew's garrulousness—"he talked almost non-stop about Guyana and its potential for industrial development"—his brief bout of pain and, later, the final struggle.

"I know your mother is inconsolable. He was gone before she got to the room. They never got a chance to say good-bye to each other, it was that sudden."

Paul wept softly as he listened to Theron.

"I plan to leave within the hour," Theron said after a brief silence.

Paul tried to control his tears. Sniffling, he gave Theron a baffled look. "Leave?"

"Yes. I've already reserved a room at the Pegasus. You will need all the space here for your relatives."

Paul drew a deep, ragged breath and steadied himself. "That's not necessary, Mr. St. Cyr. You're our guest. This is a big house. We have plenty of room. Besides, there are other homes where family members will be just as happy to stay."

"That's very generous of you, but I insist. And, please, say nothing to your mother about my leaving. She has enough on her mind. By the time she misses me it will be too late for her to do anything about it."

Paul didn't argue. He thanked Theron for being with his father in his final moments, said he would drive him to the Pegasus when he was ready and left the room.

Theron hurriedly repacked the few items he had taken out of his garment bag. He was anxious to get going. He had to get to Drucilla Durane before anyone else did.

⁂

She was striding across the lobby of the Pegasus, toward the elevators, when she saw Theron St. Cyr checking in.

Heads turned appreciatively as she walked by but she ignored them. She knew she was an attractive woman, dressed in an exquisitely tailored, knee-length linen dress, straight and sleeveless, the color of lilacs, but she was lost in her thoughts and so intent on reaching the elevator that she did not see St. Cyr approaching her. He caught up with her, reached out, and touched her lightly.

"Dru."

She jumped, startled, and turned sharply toward his voice, refusing to believe he would dare to accost her in a place as public as the lobby of her hotel, but there he was.

She gasped. Her hands flew to her mouth and she began to back away from him. Her face filled with horror. She thought for a mad moment that St. Cyr was either the killer or had had something to do with Goodings' death. She had seen him with Andrew at the airport.

"I had nothing to do with it, Dru. I was his friend," St. Cyr said harshly, as anger welled in him.

She didn't answer. She kept backing away from him as he came closer. Heads began to turn in their direction.

"Is this gentleman bothering you, Miss?" The security officer in plainclothes seemed to materialize like magic beside Theron. His voice was low and menacing.

Theron stood his ground, his eyes locked on Dru's.

Dru looked at the officer, unsure what to do or to say.

"Is he bothering you, Miss?" The officer's voice had dropped to a growl. The weightlifter biceps under his rolled-up sleeves rippled. He had spoken to Dru, but he hadn't looked at her once. He was sizing up St. Cyr, taking him in slowly from head to toe. He knew the type, apparently. Pretty boy. Sharp dresser. Show off. The type who spen' two mawnin' in America, get kick out, den come buzzin' roun' de Pegasus with a put-on Yankee accent an' t'inkin' he could pick up every Yankee woman who walk t'rough de door.

"Tell him, Dru. Tell him I'm bothering you. Tell him I want to do you harm. That I want to kidnap you, rape you, kill you, or whatever unholy acts you believe I want to commit against you. Go on." Theron's voice was as low and threatening as the security officer's.

Dru looked at Theron, then at the officer again. Her jaw worked from side to side as she struggled to make up her mind. She could see that the officer was itching for a physical confrontation with Theron. As for Theron, he had not taken his eyes off her. There was no mistaking his fury.

"Tell him, Dru."

Dru blinked, swallowed, took a deep breath. "No, officer. He's not bothering me. It's a private matter." Her voice was almost a whisper.

"Are you sure, Miss? You don't want me to escort you to your room? Place a guard at your room for de night? Is not a problem, you know."

"No, it's all right. I'll be fine, thank you."

Without so much as a glance at the officer, Theron seized Dru firmly by the elbow, marched her to the elevator and pressed the UP button. The few curious onlookers who had drifted toward them began to disperse. Dru held her head high and looked straight ahead.

The elevator chimed its arrival and the doors slid open. Theron tightened his grip on her elbow and ushered her into the car. No one else entered. The elevator *pinged* again and closed its door.

Theron released Dru's elbow the moment the door closed. Dru moved swiftly to the far corner, braced her back against the wall, and folded her arms. She stared at Theron with smoldering eyes. She wasn't afraid. St. Cyr would be a fool to try to harm her. If anything happened to her, there were enough people, including the hotel's very own security officer, who had witnessed the scene in the lobby. Any one of them could finger him. She was sure the security officer would watch to see when St. Cyr left the hotel and would come to her room to make sure she was all right. He hadn't look convinced when she told him everything was fine.

So what was St. Cyr doing at her hotel? And why was he carrying the same bag that he had arrived with at the airport?

By now she was almost certain he did not kill Andrew Goodings. No killer would want to draw attention to himself the way he had with that display in the lobby.

The scene in the lobby replayed itself in her mind and she became more infuriated. No one had ever bullied her like that. No one. Not in public. Not in private. Who the hell did he think he was? Well, she had fixed *his* business with MacPherson. The thought gave her a perverse feeling of glee and she rolled her neck.

St. Cyr looked at her through narrowed eyes and shook his head. "You know, Dru, you are so obstinate and suspicious that one day you will cause yourself great harm."

"The kind of harm that Andrew Goodings caused himself, I suppose!"

St. Cyr glared at her. Dru glared back.

"What floor?"

"Why do you want to know? You're not coming to my room."

"Yes, I am. What floor?"

She could tell from his tone and the granite clench of his jaw that it was futile to argue. "Seven!" She hurled the word at him, wishing it was a mallet that could smash his head into tiny pieces.

St. Cyr swung away from her to face the door and pressed the button for the seventh floor. He remained facing forward, silent, angled against the wall, arms folded, ankles crossed.

They rode in silence. The elevator ascended slowly. Dru stared straight ahead, but stole glances at St. Cyr surreptitiously. With each glance she seemed to read more into him. What was it that made him seem more than just angry? Was it the droop in his shoulders instead of the straight back of defiance? The bowed head instead of a stubborn tilt to his chin? That almost imperceptible sigh that had escaped on a breath without his realizing it? It was as though he carried a heavy ache in him, a big, deep hurt that rose up and caught him off guard and there was nothing he could do to stop it.

But wasn't that to be expected with the death of Goodings? They seemed to have been good friends. True. But this was something older than the death of Goodings. She had felt it, seen it, that day in Marseille, too. She had dismissed it at the time. Back then she was riding one hell of a whirlwind and he was a stranger she probably would never see again, so she had pushed it away.

In spite of herself, Dru smiled, softening her face as memories of those heady days whizzed by. That amazing old lady on the train, on her way back to France after visiting her daughter in Italy. I wonder if she's still alive. Why shouldn't she be? She seemed old then, but she couldn't have been more than fifty. When you're twenty-two, anyone over forty is old. Besides, with the kind of life she lived and her peace of mind, the old bird was probably healthier than a lot of people far younger. Twelve years isn't such a long time. She—

St. Cyr suddenly shifted his weight from one foot to the other and sighed again. The sigh was louder this time, though he seemed unaware of it.

The sound jerked Dru out of her reverie. Her face turned to stone again as she glanced at him. He was staring down at the floor.

St. Cyr must have felt her eyes on him for he straightened up all of a sudden and turned slightly toward her. Their eyes connected briefly before Dru cut hers away, tightening her jaw. But in that instant, in that tiny breath of connection, she had seen in his eyes the full measure of his mysterious pain.

Her heart quickened as she skimmed through every exchange, every encounter she had ever had with him. That day in Marseille—his arm around her waist, protective; his phone call just a few days ago—how excited and delighted he seemed to be talking to her again; his plea for understanding during the flight to Georgetown; the warmth with which Goodings embraced him at the airport; and now.

He's no killer, she decided. A man with a lot of baggage, yes, but not a killer.

How about kidnapping! What about Paris? Did you carry around twelve years of vengeful thinking for nothing? What kind of fool does that make you?

The voice in her head was harsh and resentful. She closed her eyes tight against its barrage of questions. She did not want to answer those questions. Not just yet. There were more pressing ones to deal with. Like, if St. Cyr did not kill Goodings, who did? And why did St. Cyr come to her, anyway? Did he think that she, or her people, killed Goodings? Would MacPherson and others in the government—or anyone close to Goodings, for that matter—think that? If they did, did they send St. Cyr to find out for sure? To make sure she didn't flee the country? Would they come after her in revenge?

Was her life in danger in Guyana?

※

The phone rang once.

"Dígame!"

"The American woman from Pilgrim Boone was with Andrew Goodings' friend today. The man he met at the airport."

There was a long pause.

"What were they talking about?"

"I couldn't hear. I was in the lobby of the Pegasus for a last-minute meeting with a friend at the same time they were there. They didn't arrive at the hotel together. Dalrymple took her there. He told me this morning that the two of them had a meeting with MacPherson. She was walking toward the elevators when Goodings's friend approached her. She backed away from him as if she was afraid he would hurt her or something. Then it looked as if they were having some sort of quarrel. A security man went over to them but he left them alone after a few minutes. They went into the elevator together. She didn't seem afraid of him anymore. Just angry. Really angry. I'd say those two have known each other for a long time."

"Is the man staying at the hotel, too?"

"So I was told. A friend of mine works at Reception. She told me he had just checked in today."

"Do you know his name? What does he look like?"

Leila described St. Cyr. "My friend at Reception told me his name is Theron St. Cyr."

The pause stretched into a full minute.

Leila smiled. She knew what was coming. A new assignment. Another twenty thousand dollars minimum. It would put her almost at her target. If Alejandro kept giving her assignments at this pace she would reach it in less than a year. She would retire, tell Compton she was tired of him, and move to America. Out West. Somewhere in the mountains. She would build a fabulous house on acres of land and maybe find a man to live with, a sexy young stud. No marriage. No kids. Ever. She liked being detached. That's why it was perfect with Compton. He had no intention of leaving his wife and he knew that she knew this. So there was never any stupid talk about commitment or marriage. Yes, she liked things uncomplicated. Life came and went too easily. She should know.

"So! You know this Theron St. Cyr," she said softly into the phone. "What do you want me to do about him?"

"No. I do not know this man," Bernat said, his voice slow and far away. "And there is nothing I want you to do right now. Nothing just yet. I will let you know when I am ready." He disconnected the call.

Leila closed her eyes and watched her dream wisp away. Maybe he was lying, maybe he was not, about his not knowing Theron St. Cyr. There could be any number of reasons why it took him so long to speak after she gave him the name. He could have been trying to place the name, or he could have been thinking through his next step. Maybe he was coming down from a high and just drifted off. She knew he snorted coke. She was sixteen the first time she saw him do it. It was on his ranch in Venezuela. She had been working in the kitchen and, thinking no one else was in the house, had wandered about only to come across him in his study. She had managed to sneak out before he saw her.

She had grown up on Bernat's ranch. There was a group that took care of Amerindians who fled to Venezuela after the rebellion and that group had sent her entire family to Bernat to work. In exchange for their labor they got a small amount of money, a tiny cabin in the village where all the other workers lived, and a small plot of land that they could use as they pleased once they had finished their chores for *el Señor Bernat*. Her family farmed the little plot and sold their excess produce to the lazy ones and the ones who drank away their money.

She saw Alejandro snort several times after that. When he finally realized that she had been watching him, he'd given it to her. Forced her to take it. And forced her to become his lover. Once she had resigned herself to being his lover, she began to enjoy it. She began to enjoy the cocaine, too.

Alejandro kept telling her how smart she was. He trained her to do special assignments, and those assignments took her to the United States and sometimes to Europe. Sometimes it was delivering drugs or cash. Other times it was spying on someone. The first time she killed for Alejandro was five years ago, in France.

She didn't mind any of it, though it had broken her parents' hearts. She liked the money, the clothing, the jewelry, the jungle-green Jeep Cherokee, the trips abroad. And the way Alejandro made her feel beautiful and important even though he never introduced her to any of his friends or took her with him when he traveled. She told herself she would enjoy whatever she got so that when it disappeared—she was sure that it would one day—she could say without regret that she knew what it was like to be rich and pampered.

Just as she had predicted, Alejandro grew tired of her. The expensive gifts, the free cocaine, the high life, all of it stopped the day Alejandro told her that the beautiful white woman he had brought home from Caracas was the mistress of his house. She really didn't mind, she told herself. She never wanted to end up hooked on cocaine for the rest of her life. She ignored Alejandro's edict that she would have to buy the stuff if she wanted it, and stayed clean.

And the rest of it? Well, it would have been easy to find other men to give her whatever she wanted. She was Amerindian, but she was beautiful and desirable in her own way. Alejandro had proved that to her and she would always be grateful to him for that.

Alejandro didn't release her or her family from their bondage to him. He still needed her for work. She was his best agent, he said. He paid her well. Extremely well. She could take care of herself. Soon, she would be free, but perhaps not as soon as she would like.

She shrugged, gave a little laugh, opened her eyes, flicked the phone shut. The memories, along with the last wisp of her dream, faded.

She shrugged again.

Whatever. Life played games like that.

18

"What's going on in Guyana, Grant?"

Lawton Pilgrim kept his back to Grant Featherhorn. He hadn't bothered to turn around when Grant walked into his office, and closed the door even though Grant had found it open. Instead, he had smiled to himself. It was so typical of Grant. He liked to give the impression to the people outside that his discussions with the big man were confidential.

Lawton was standing at his favorite spot at the huge plate glass window overlooking the East River, his hands clasped behind him, watching a seagull sail on the wind. If he was weighed down by the knowledge that he was dying, he didn't show it. He held himself as erect as he always did.

"What do you mean, Lawton?" Featherhorn's voice was languid.

Lawton swung around abruptly. He stared at Featherhorn for a moment, then shook his head and smiled. He walked slowly to his desk, sat down, and leaned back in the chair, his fingers forming a steeple on his stomach. He drummed his thumbs against his stomach, momentarily delighting in the flat, rock-hard return on his investment in an exacting exercise routine. Then his eyes clouded and for a while he concentrated on the Tiffany light fixture in the ceiling.

Finally, he lowered his eyes to meet Featherhorn's.

"What's going on in Guyana, Grant?" He posed the question in the same voice as before, not a decibel higher, not a decibel lower, not a trace of anything other than curiosity, pure and simple, in his question.

Featherhorn's guard shot up instantly. After thirty years with the man, he knew his ways. "That's a question we should be asking Dru, don't you think? Believe me, I myself would dearly love to know what's going on. But she hasn't contacted me since she arrived in Guyana. As far as I know, she hasn't contacted anyone since she left."

Pilgrim raised an eyebrow. "That's unlike her, isn't it? What about Roopnaraine and Dalrymple? Have you talked to either of them?"

"No, I haven't. They haven't called."

Pilgrim looked at him coldly. "And I suppose you did not see fit to call either one of them. What are you trying to do to her, Grant? Set her up for failure? Put her in harm's way in that godforsaken little republic? You never could get over the fact that she turned us down for that internship, could you? College kids, especially *black* college kids, aren't supposed to say no to a chance to intern at one of the world's most reputable consulting firms, are they? And especially when it's Grant Featherhorn himself who writes the letter, makes the phone call. You never got over it, did you?"

Featherhorn returned his icy gaze with a smile. "You must be very tired, Lawton. You're not making any sense. Come to think of it, you don't look yourself at all."

Lawton sprang forward in his chair and slammed both palms on his desk. "Don't give me any of your patronizing bullshit, Grant!" he said between clenched teeth. "Something stinks in Guyana and you know it. They're stringing us along and I want to know why. You should be talking to Dru every minute of every goddamned day she's there!"

He grabbed the phone and punched furiously at the intercom button. Miss Hatherby's voice, loyal, prim, and unflappable, sailed through immediately.

"Yes, Mr. Pilgrim?"

"Get me Dru Durane in Guyana!" Pilgrim barked.

"Certainly, Mr. Pilgrim."

Pilgrim stabbed the button off and picked up his conversation with Featherhorn. "And there's another reason why you should be talking to her. The place is a goddamned crime pit! It's *our* responsibility to make sure she's safe."

He threw himself back in his chair and steepled his fingers on his stomach again, breathing heavily.

Featherhorn knew better than to speak. He knew he had gone too far this time.

"What do we know about Andrew Goodings' death?" Pilgrim's voice was once again calm. Typically, his anger had dissipated as abruptly as it had arisen.

Here it comes, Featherhorn thought nervously. As much as he had anticipated the question, his heart still skipped a beat. He feigned disinterest to hide his nervousness. "Heart failure, I heard."

"Bull. It's too damned convenient, that's what it is."

Featherhorn shrugged. "He wasn't a young man."

"That's neither here nor there. I don't like it, Grant. It puts us in a compromising position. Someone down there's bound to start pointing fingers in our direction soon."

Miss Hatherby's voice, a wee bit pinched, clipped the air. "Miss Durane is on the line, Mr. Pilgrim."

Pilgrim sprang forward and hit the speaker button. "Dru?"

"Hello, Lawton. So you've heard." She sounded guarded, uptight.

"Are you all right? What the hell is going on down there? Why haven't we heard from you?"

Featherhorn leaned forward, all ears, though his face remained inscrutable.

"I had nothing to report, Lawton. I met with Minister MacPherson today and it didn't go well at all. I'm convinced he thinks there's more to Savoy's proposal than a mere desire to bring air transport to Guyana. Why? I have no idea. And the sudden death of his man Goodings makes matters worse."

"Why? What are people saying?"

"That Goodings was killed."

"I knew it! I knew it!" Pilgrim exploded, jumping to his feet and pacing the floor.

Featherhorn sat back in his chair and crossed his legs.

"There won't be any decisions until the reason for his death has been determined," Dru continued.

"Do you think they're linking it to us?" It was Featherhorn who asked the question.

A long moment passed. The sudden silence made Pilgrim stop pacing. He stared at the phone. The silence stretched out until Lawton Pilgrim could stand it no longer.

"I need an answer, Dru. Now!"

"It's possible," Dru said quietly.

Pilgrim strode over to his desk and leaned on it, his bony, manicured fingers splayed in two perfect semicircles. He leaned into the phone, his face red with outrage.

"What do you mean, "It's possible"? How the hell could anyone even think a firm of our reputation could be involved in such a dastardly act! It makes absolutely no sense! Is this a set up of some sort?"

"I honestly don't know, Lawton. I honestly don't know."

The fatigue and fear in her voice were unmistakable.

Lawton cursed silently. "Get on the next plane and come home, Dru," he ordered. "There's nothing we can do but wait it out."

Dru remained silent.

"Do you hear me, Dru? I want you to pack up and get back to New York ASAP!"

"And how would that make us look, Lawton? Don't you think I should stay around? Try to show them that we're blameless?"

"I don't give a rat's ass how it looks. I don't want you there a minute longer than the next flight to New York. Do you hear me, Dru?"

She sighed. Certain fights you just did not pick with Lawton Pilgrim. "Yes. Yes, I'll leave."

"Okay. You be careful now." He waited until he heard the phone click on her end, then turned to Featherhorn. "She doesn't like you, does she? Can't say I blame her, Grant. In your eyes Dru had two strikes against her when she came into the firm. She was black and she'd essentially told you to go fuck yourself. So you've made her life hell at Pilgrim Boone, you heartless bastard."

Featherhorn sat up, stunned.

"Oh, wipe that asinine look off your face. I know you, Grant. I know all of you. I studied you for years before I brought you into this company and into the Circle, just like I did Dru Durane. I know how each one of you thinks, what each one of you is capable of. Did you really think you could fool me? I knew what that girl was going through with you, but I kept her there because I knew she would fight you. And in fighting you she would become exactly what she became—one of the best in the firm. And that's all I cared about—what she could do for Pilgrim Boone, being as good as she was. She's never let me down."

"Lawton, I...I..."

"Shut up, Grant. Shut up and listen to me!"

Featherhorn shrank back in his seat, his stomach lurching. Lawton had never yelled at him like this. Why now? Did he know about Bernat? Did he know about his clandestine trip to Guyana?

"I'm dying, Grant. Cancer. Doctor says I have no more than three months."

Featherhorn's face collapsed in disbelief. He opened his mouth to say something but Lawton held up his hand and stopped him.

He said, "I've decided that I want you to take over after me. I don't have to spell out the reasons why, but I'll do so all the same. It's nasty out there. The Big Five are pulling accounts away from us. Those gluttonous bastards are now earning more than half their income from consulting. Christ! Last time I looked, consulting was growing three times as fast as the auditing business they're supposed to be doing. They've swindled the whole goddamned world with their fancy PR and merger gimmicks, hiring armies of Ivy Leaguers who don't know diddly about consulting!"

He paused. The look on his face warned Featherhorn to keep his silence.

196

"The fact is, Grant," he continued in a calmer voice, "if it keeps up like this, Pilgrim Boone will be out of the big leagues in less than five years, a distant memory in ten. We both know it. Oh, sure! We could have played the game, merged with Ernst & Young or Price Waterhouse or Andersen when they propositioned us. They all did, as you know. Even Peat Marwick and Deloitte and Touche. A merger with any one of them would have put us at the head of the pack. But we would have become just another rat in that pack and that's not us, Grant. That's not our race. Those guys will have a good run. They should enjoy it while they can because my gut tells me they'll be done in by their own greed. And when that time comes, I want Pilgrim Boone to be there, ready to claim our rightful place. Holding our nose and towering above the shit pile."

He stopped abruptly at the sound a low chuckle and glared at Featherhorn. The chuckle suddenly turned into a fit of grunts and ahems as Featherhorn struggled to wipe the grin off his face.

"Sorry, Lawton. I know you're serious, but that's one hell of an image." Featherhorn had recovered from his tongue-lashing and was feeling comfortable again, much more than comfortable. He was on top of the friggin' world. Lawton had just named him heir to the Pilgrim Boone throne! Well, good goddamn! And here he was, worrying for no reason at all. He could afford to banter.

Lawton's lips began to twitch, then he, too, started to chuckle. "Yeah! I guess it's one hell of an image," he said, laughing openly.

He soon became serious again. "All joking aside, you're the only one who can take them on, the only one who can keep Pilgrim Boone from slipping into oblivion, Grant."

He paused to study the effect of his words on the younger man. His eyes hardened as he caught the smirk before Featherhorn fixed his face into its usual mask of propriety. He leaned forward and addressed Featherhorn in a low, cold voice.

"Oh, don't let it get to your head, Grant. I'm not really paying you a compliment, you know. All I'm saying is that it will take guile to do the job that I want done and that's what you've got. Guile. All the ugliness that word conjures up, that's the real you. But this is not about you, fella. It's all about me. With you in charge, I get to go out smelling like a rose, knowing that my life's work won't fall apart after I'm gone."

He leaned back in the chair, holding Featherhorn in a steely gaze until Featherhorn's eyes veered away. He smiled. "You needn't worry, Grant. Everyone will go along with my decision. They'll all want to know that their interests will be protected by any means necessary, and having you at the helm will give them that assurance."

Pilgrim held up his hand and shook his head as Featherhorn opened his mouth to speak.

"There's one more thing, Grant. I want to win the Guyana contract for Savoy before I bow out, but I want to win it clean and fair. As I said, I go out smelling like a rose. So you tell me now and tell me straight. What business do you have with Alejandro Bernat?"

Featherhorn's jaw dropped.

Pilgrim steepled his fingers under his chin and waited, his eyes never wavering from Featherhorn's face.

Featherhorn's mind worked frantically. What should he say? How much did the old man know?

He decided to stall. Lawton might inadvertently give him a clue about how much he knew about his relationship with Bernat.

"Alejandro Bernat?" he repeated, tilting his head back and gazing up at the ceiling, as if in deep concentration.

Pilgrim's eyes glinted. "You're stalling, Grant. You want to know how much I already know about you and Bernat. You of all people should know better than to try that with me. I want to hear it from your mouth. What's your business with Bernat?"

Featherhorn knew he was trapped. He'd just have to brass-ball his way out. "Yes, I do know Alejandro Bernat. But why do you ask in that way, as if he's someone I shouldn't have anything to do with? Do you know something I don't know, Lawton?" he said calmly.

Pilgrim smiled. "Oh you're good, Grant. I'd forgotten just how good you are. Now, for the last time, I want to know what the deal is with you and Bernat."

The thought came to Featherhorn like the proverbial lightbulb going off. He could tell the truth and there was nothing Lawton would do about it because he could drop dead at any time and he intended to go out—how did he put it?—smelling like a rose. The last thing Lawton would want to do was drag the firm's name through a scandal, and a scandal is exactly what would break out if, upon hearing the truth, he went to the authorities or did something foolish like alerting Savoy. Pilgrim would be dead before he got a chance to crucify Grant Featherhorn in the press and restore the reputation of Pilgrim Boone.

It took a split second for Featherhorn to figure out all this, to realize that he, not Lawton, had the upper hand. Watching him closely, Pilgrim knew the precise moment Featherhorn gained that hand.

The eyes of the two men met and held. Featherhorn smiled benignly, acknowledging Pilgrim's acknowledgement of his own defeat. When he spoke, his tone was superior.

"No, Lawton. There is nothing I can tell you that I'm sure you don't already know. I have known Alejandro Bernat since you put me in charge of the Latin America division with a mandate to get to know personally all the movers and shakers in the region. That is exactly what I did. Bernat is a wealthy and powerful businessman in Venezuela. It is because of the intelligence we receive from him that we have been able to make the few strides we have in Latin America. That is, before Drucilla Durane came along. But we may yet win Guyana, in spite of her bungling."

Pilgrim felt himself shrink in his chair and hoped it was more a feeling on his part than an actual change in his physical demeanor. He had no one to blame but himself. He had created a monster in Grant Featherhorn and now that monster was out of control. He had checked out Alejandro Bernat through his Washington contacts. Bernat, he had been told by one of his sources in the DEA, was rumored to be the biggest drug lord in the hemisphere, but no one had any proof. Not even Washington's high-tech artillery could pin anything on him. Bernat was brutal. People were too scared to talk. Not even a million greenbacks could buy a snitch.

Pilgrim knew that Featherhorn had flown to Guyana for a secret meeting with Bernat, but Featherhorn did not know this. Pilgrim paid Featherhorn's pilot a handsome retainer to inform him of every move

Featherhorn made in the jet. The pilot could not say what the two discussed, but, instinctively, Pilgrim knew they were up to no good. Proof or no proof, Bernat was bad news.

So now Featherhorn had him in a corner and he had no fangs with which to fight back. He would not live long enough to bring the battle to a close. The one comforting thought was that Featherhorn would do everything in his power to keep his illicit dealings secret, for he was a man who craved public approval. Now that he knew he was about to take the helm at Pilgrim Boone, there was no way he would jeopardize that approval. Pilgrim Boone's reputation would remain intact after all, and he, Lawton, would go out smelling like a rose. His name would be given glorious mention in the annals of American business.

And yet—

How different it would have been if Maggie had borne him a son, he thought ruefully. But his poor wife had died childless, her spirit shattered. He had received a call once from a woman with whom he had had an affair shortly after he found out that Maggie could not conceive. What was her name? She was one of his assistants in the Paris office. A beautiful mulatto. She had said she was pregnant. Pilgrim refused to believe it at first. They had gotten together only once. He remembered the occasion well. He had been drinking. Everyone had been drinking. They had just closed one of their biggest deals in France.

But the woman insisted. She said she hadn't dated anyone for a year before her encounter with him. Everyone he queried about her, under the guise of considering her for a promotion, confirmed her propriety. She had been widowed a year earlier, they all repeated. Heart attack. Such a young man. Promising future in law. She was devastated, never dated since.

But he had known all this. He knew everything about everyone who worked for him.

Ashamed, panicking at the thought of what it would do to Maggie if she found out, he had sent the woman a money order for five thousand dollars, with a letter stating that she should do what she knew was necessary. He'd sent it to her home. He had never heard from her again. She left the company less than a month later and disappeared. He had thought of her often, wondering if she had had the child. There were times when, lonely and miserable, he would daydream of a son appearing out of the blue, an educated, accomplished man, with a lovely wife and beautiful children, his grandchildren. His skin would tingle with excitement, so real did the dream seem.

Once, only once, he had tried to track down the French woman. But for once his clout and immense wealth got him nowhere. The lips of the French were sealed. It had taken him years to accept that his father's bloodline would end with the death of Lawton Pilgrim, his parents' only child.

He returned Featherhorn's smile.

⁎⁎⁎

Le Meridien Pegasus is Guyana's premier hotel, a five-star delight rising nine floors above Seawall Road just off High Street, about half a mile from downtown Georgetown.

Seawall Road takes its name from the wide stone wall running parallel to the road along the Atlantic Coast. The wall keeps the ocean's waves at high tide from overwhelming the city and towns farther east. Started in 1870 and completed in 1882, the seawall is to Georgetowners what Central Park is to Manhanttanites. It's the place to walk, jog, fly a kite, eat parched *channa* or pop peanuts from a paper cone, steal a kiss, lose your virginity, feel the breeze, watch the tide, pass the time.

It's the city's signature Saturday or Sunday *lime*, the term Guyanese use for "hanging out."

The Pegasus was built almost a hundred years after the first brick was laid for the seawall. The hotel offers a breathtaking panorama of the city. From its roof you can follow the mud-brown sloth of the Demerara River until it disappears over the horizon, or watch "the great Atlantic, blown into a fury or asleep," as described in Valerie Rodway's song *O Beautiful Guyana*.

The trade winds roll off the Atlantic and linger around the hotel. They are not too strong, nor too cool. They are just the perfect breezes to temper the blistering heat of the day.

When Pilgrim Boone began negotiations with the Guyana government on behalf of Savoy Aerospace, it chose the Pegasus to lodge staff members traveling to Georgetown, shunning the venerable Tower Hotel and its claim to being the businessman's hotel. Away from the throb of the city, the Pegasus seemed the safer of the two. Tower, in the heart of the city, on Main Street, was too close to the thick of things, too readily accessible to any and everyone.

Dru shoved open the door to her suite and marched in, not bothering to hold the door open for St. Cyr. The door almost hit him in the face.

Dru kicked off her shoes in the airy, elegantly appointed living room, threw her briefcase into the nearest chair, and strode into the bathroom, slamming the door behind her. She was more furious with herself than with St. Cyr. She hated not being in control of a situation and twice in one day—no, three times—she had lost it.

And as if that weren't annoying enough, she was beginning to believe she might be wrong about St. Cyr, and she hated being wrong about her assessment of someone. She felt compromised when she failed to size up a person accurately. Wasn't she being paid the big bucks to be in control, to correctly assess the players in a negotiation? How else could she close a deal?

She scowled at her reflection in the mirror above the sink.

Outside, St. Cyr stood stiffly with his back to the French doors that led to the balcony, his jaw set, eyes glued to the door as he waited for Dru to emerge. The effort to keep up this stony façade kept his mind away from the deep hurt he felt. Dru still believed he had tried to kidnap her in France all those years ago. Why else would she grow ice cold in his presence on the plane, or even before that, when he contacted her on the phone?

And now, compounding that—rather, *because* of that—she believed that he had had something to do with Andrew's death. In her eyes, he was evil, she hated him, and she was afraid of him, her bravado aside.

Well, if that's the way she felt, so be it. *Tant pis pour moi.* Too bad for me. There was nothing he could do about a hatred that was so old, so deep, so determinedly misplaced. He would warn her about the danger she might be in and leave.

Dru emerged from the bathroom just as the phone rang. She grabbed it impatiently.

It was a call from Pilgrim Boone. Lawton Pilgrim himself. Even though she kept her back turned to St. Cyr and kept her voice low, she knew he could hear every word she exchanged with Lawton, especially with Lawton shouting.

She remained standing for the entire conversation. When it ended, she slumped down heavily on the sofa and stared at the floor for a long moment.

All of a sudden she seemed to remember that St. Cyr was in the room. She jerked her head up and looked at him resentfully.

St. Cyr stared back, the expression on his face indecipherable.

After a few moments, Dru blinked and sighed. "Well? What do you want to say to me?"

Her voice was so hollow, so devoid of fight, that St. Cyr was taken aback. He forced himself to keep his tone brisk. "Things have gotten ugly over this contract you're negotiating for Savoy, Dru. Andrew Goodings was killed because he stood in the way—"

Dru sat up sharply and cut him off. "How do you know about Savoy?"

"Andrew told me. He told me everything about their proposal to the government through Pilgrim Boone. He wanted me to check it out. He invited me to Guyana to talk about it. Not that he had proof of anything untoward. He just wanted to be sure Guyana wouldn't be compromised in any way, be stuck with a something nasty if the government decided to accept the proposal. Small, vulnerable countries like Guyana bear too many scars from their relationships with giant corporations, he said."

Dru flicked her wrist impatiently. "The man was paranoid. This is a Pilgrim Boone client we're talking about. If they had ulterior motives, they wouldn't be our client."

"Then why was Andrew killed?"

"What makes you so sure he was killed?"

"Oh, come off it, Dru. I know you believe he was killed."

"You're flattering yourself again, Mr. St. Cyr. You don't know what I think. You don't know me."

"Yes, I do, Dru. I do." He ignored the "Mr. St. Cyr."

Dru looked away, uncomfortable.

He continued. "But that's neither here nor there. The point is, you may be in danger. Lawton Pilgrim is right. Sorry, I couldn't help overhearing. You should leave the country."

Dru's head whipped around. "Why should I be in danger? I'm on the right side as far as this alleged killer is concerned, aren't I? I *want* this deal. And fast!"

"You're not on the right side if the killer thinks you're going to start asking questions about Andrew Goodings' death, even if only to make sure no suspicions fall on Pilgrim Boone and sully its reputation. And you definitely won't be on the right side of the killer once word get around that you're talking to me, hostile or not. You're a smart woman, Dru. Whoever killed Andrew knows that by now you're wondering about the convenience of his death. Wondering leads to snooping."

Dru shuddered and wrapped her arms around herself. His words made sense. But they were hard to accept. First Ramy, or someone like him, now a killer who might come looking for her.

"And I suppose you don't have any idea who the killer might be," she said coolly, locking eyes with him.

"I suspect someone in Pilgrim Boone knows something." His voice matched the coolness in hers.

Dru jumped up. Her long arms, tensed like steel rods, pressed hard into her sides. Her fists were clenched tight. She pushed out the words through gritted teeth and lips that barely moved. "Are you implying that—"

He didn't let her finish. "I'm not implying anything, Dru. I am stating loud and clear that someone in Pilgrim Boone knows something about the death of Andrew Goodings. That person may not have ordered the hit, but he, or she, sure as hell let it happen."

Dru froze, too stunned to speak. She recovered fast. "How dare you! *How dare you!* What makes you so goddamned righteous? What gives you the right to even suggest something like that? Do you think I would be involved with—"

"Whom do you report to at Pilgrim Boone?"

"Stop cutting me off. I'm the point person on Savoy!" She was shouting now.

St. Cyr sighed wearily. "Yes, Dru, but who ultimately oversees all operations in this region? Who makes first contact with the big wigs in every country? Sets up all the deals, then hands them over for management to the operational people at your level?"

He paused and took a step toward her. "And who's been acting strange about this particular deal? Putting unusual pressure on you to close quickly. Threatening to put someone else on the case, for instance?"

"There isn't—" Dru stopped abruptly. Her mouth fell open and she sank down on the sofa.

One name.

Only one name answered all of those questions.

"Grant," she whispered. "Grant Featherhorn."

St. Cyr sat down on the edge of one of the chairs facing the sofa. He leaned forward and looked at Dru intently. "Who is he and what kind of man is he?" He spoke softly this time. Dru was in that delicate place between cognition and incredulity.

She blurted it out. All of it. Her world shattering with each word, each sentence. She couldn't hold back.

Would she hold back if she could? The question crept up like a shadow behind the words now pouring out of her and she chased it away with a resolute nod of her head.

She began at the beginning, telling St. Cyr how Featherhorn had tried to goad her into leaving the company with his snide remarks. How, when that failed, he had made life hell for her, setting traps to make her screw up so that she would be fired, or at least kept out of senior management.

She told him about Featherhorn's threat to put Sharon Brinkley on the Savoy project when he knew that her own competence was not at issue.

And how the hatred between Featherhorn and she had come to a head that memorable day.

"It was the same day you called out of the blue." Her voice was steady, but barely audible. Her mind was racing even as she spoke. Featherhorn *had* to know something. St. Cyr was right.

She covered her face and moaned. "My God! My God! This is awful. This is so awful!"

"Is he capable of murder, Dru?"

Dru's hands fell away from her face and she shrank back into the sofa, staring at St. Cyr with uncomprehending eyes. Deep lines etched her brow. She seemed to be struggling to make sense of his question. Then, as the horror of the answer that crept into her mind sank in, she began to wring her hands.

St. Cyr snapped his fingers impatiently. "Answer me, Dru. Is this Grant Featherhorn capable of murder?" His voice was harsh. He needed the answer he knew she had. She wanted to scurry away from what she knew to be true. That's what she knew people did in their desperation to keep their world falling from apart.

"I don't know. I don't know. How would I know that?"

St. Cyr's expression grew even harder.

"He…he could be ruthless. I don't know. The whole thing seems so unreal."

"What about Lawton Pilgrim?" St. Cyr's eyes remained riveted to hers.

Dru knew he was mad as hell. She had made herself believe that he was the scum of the earth. That had to have hurt. She had made him out to be a man who preyed on women traveling alone; a man who abducted innocent women and did God-knows-what with them. She had carried in her heart for years the hatred that stemmed from this belief.

And less than an hour ago, in front of a lobbyful of people, she had backed away from him the way you backed away from something loathsome. She still thought that he was involved with Andrew's death. Her loyalty to Pilgrim Boone was that unassailable.

Dru sat up and shook her head vigorously. "No. Not Lawton. I just can't see it. The law is sacred to him. The firm is his whole life. It defines him. He would never do anything to compromise its reputation. Especially something as heinous as…as…" She couldn't bring herself to utter the word "murder" in the context of Lawton Pilgrim.

"Dalrymple? Roopnaraine?"

Dru laughed and shook her head again. It was a spontaneous laugh. "Are you kidding me? Puleeze! Not those two," she said scornfully. "Definitely not those two. They're in this for the money, and for the leverage of a relationship with Pilgrim Boone. Nothing else. But they can live without Pilgrim Boone and its money if things don't work out. For them, in a small country like this, there's tons of money they can make without having to deal in nasty stuff. Especially something like murder." She laughed again. "Uh-uh. Those two love themselves too much to get their hands dirty like that."

St. Cyr watched her closely as she talked and laughed.

"Yes, I think you're right. From what Andrew told me, and it wasn't much, Dalrymple and Roopnaraine are your typical middlemen, leveraging their contacts and connections like capital. Andrew didn't think they had any real influence in this particular deal. On the contrary, he thought Pilgrim Boone probably knew it was wasting its time and money with them but figured it wouldn't hurt to let the government see them in a relationship with a local enterprise." He was waiting to gauge her reaction.

Dru heard the edge in his voice, but she could not help smiling at the perceptiveness of the late Andrew Goodings. "Hmmm. Interesting," she said.

"Yes. Well, I'm sorry to say it, but your firm really is in a very suspect position, Dru. I'd be very circumspect about what I said in New York if I were you. Watch this Grant Featherhorn carefully, but don't let him know what you may be thinking about him. Say nothing to anyone about him, in fact. Not even to Pilgrim himself."

Dru's expression grew serious again. "This is so unreal."

St. Cyr stood up abruptly. "Yes, so it seems. But it is very real and you're way out of your league."

Dru was tired of defending herself. She looked up at him, frowning. Was he leaving? It surprised her that she didn't want him to leave. Not yet.

Not now, when she was so confused and afraid. She wanted him to go on talking to her. He was strong and sure and her world was collapsing. She wanted his words to assure her again and again that none of what she had believed about him was true.

St. Cyr saw her confusion, she thought. That was why he remained standing, half turned toward the door. He had warned her and, in the process, had managed to at least to shake her ugly perception of him. Good! But you don't wipe away years of anger and hate in a few minutes.

"So that's it, then," he said brusquely. "I've moved into the hotel here, so you can reach me easily if you need to. Let me know when you will be leaving for New York." He started toward the door before she could respond. "You don't have to get up. I'll let myself out."

He crossed the room in long, determined strides, his face gripped in an obstinate scowl.

He had almost reached the door when Dru said, "Do you think I had anything to do with it?" Her voice was pleading and defiant at the same time.

He stopped and stood still for a moment, his back to her. He turned slowly and studied her. She was standing, her arms wrapped tightly around her.

"No, Dru. I do not believe you are involved in the death of Andrew Goodings," he said evenly. His face showed no expression.

"What makes you so sure? I'm…was…am suspicious of you."

St. Cyr lost it then. "Good God, Dru! This isn't a game. I'm not going to accuse you of murder just because you suspect me of that and more. Just because you obviously see me as the most evil creature on the face of this earth. Use your common sense, for God's sake! Think!"

Dru's head dipped. Her eyes burned. She said nothing.

St. Cyr rolled his eyes. "I've had enough of this, Dru. As I said, I'm around if you need me." His hand was already on the doorknob when her words stopped him cold.

"I saw Ramy."

He whipped around. Dru watched him warily, her breathing shallow. The words had fallen from her mouth before she could stop them.

He came toward her slowly. His eyes had narrowed and he was looking at her in a way that alarmed her. She backed away from him as he came closer. She collided with the sofa and fell into it, leaning far back as he closed the space between them.

He stood directly over her, an inscrutable human tower.

"What did you say, Dru?" He spoke quietly.

"I saw Ramy. Today. At MacPherson's office."

St. Cyr let her words hang in the air for several moments before he spoke. "Ramy is dead, Dru," he said in the same quiet voice. "His body was found in an alley in Marseille, not far from where you and I were when we saw him. He had been stabbed several times. This happened five years ago. I myself went to the morgue, just to make sure."

Dru's hands flew to her mouth. "But…but he…this man had the same face. Same eyes. Obsidian. And even that terrible skin," she said weakly.

"There are evil men everywhere, Dru. And this part of the world is full of people who look like Ramy. You may well have seen a man who looked like Ramy and who had a dark aura. But I assure you, Ramy is dead. His devilish life finally caught up with him. You could not have seen him today."

St. Cyr's expression remained inscrutable. He held Dru's eyes for a long moment, then turned abruptly and strode quickly to the door.

It didn't make a sound when he closed it behind him.

⊰※⊱

Dru slowly picked herself up from the sofa and forced her feet to drag the rest of her body to the door. She secured the lock, leaned her back against the door, and closed her eyes.

She felt numb. What should she do now? She should eat something. She hadn't had a meal since breakfast. She rang room service and ordered a fish dinner. A thirty-minute wait. They were still serving tea.

She hung up and sighed. "Too early for dinner, Madam. So sorry, Madam. We will do our best to have it to you in thirty minutes or less," she said out loud, making a face and mimicking the accent of the voice on the other end of the line.

She looked around listlessly. She should start making arrangements to leave Guyana. Find out when the next flight left for New York.

Her eyes fell on the laptop she had left on the coffee table. She hadn't touched it since she arrived. She decided to check her e-mail and send off a couple herself. One to Leona, who must be frantic by now, not having heard from her. She was sure Lawton had checked with her before he called.

She opened the laptop, logged into her account, and pulled up her e-mail. There were two from Leona and one from Featherhorn. Judging by the time it had arrived, he must have sent it as soon as he had returned to his office after Lawton's phone call. She didn't bother to open it. He was the last person who should have anything to say to her.

There were a few others from business associates and clients, and one from Lance, her brother. Her heart skipped a beat. She had completely forgotten that he was going to send her whatever information he could dig up about Theron St. Cyr.

She clicked on his note.

Hi, Sis: Attached is what I found on the subject. Must say it's an impressive subject, with the looks to match. The kind of package I'd love to unwrap. Just kidding. You know how it is with me and Phil. Love you. Me.

Dru couldn't help smiling as she downloaded the attached zip file. She adored her brother. He was lot happier about coming out now that he and their parents had reconciled. Their mother and father had finally accepted that their son was not "going through a phase"; that he liked to be intimate with men, not women; that, in spite of his smiling "you never knows," he may never bear them grandchildren to carry on the Durane name.

And no, he had assured them with a laugh because he had seen the worry in their eyes and knew they would never ask, he would not be dressing as a woman, swishing his behind, hanging his wrist, or lisping the letter s.

They had embraced each other then, their parents relieved that their son would not bring "shame and disgrace on the family," Lance overjoyed that the family was whole again and at peace.

What a relief! It had been so ugly for so long. For a while her father had refused to even allow Lance's name to be mentioned in the house. His only son! He had chased Lance out of the house and ordered him never to return. He suffered a stroke two months later and everyone knew that it was "all this aunty-man business with Lance" that had caused it.

As for her mother, she had just cried and cried and wrung her hands a lot. Lance called her a month after he left home to let her know that he was in Washington and had found a good job and an apartment. He had been living with a friend and his family until then, he told her. She was relieved to hear from him, but she rushed him off the phone because his father was growing suspicious and she did not want to upset him. Lance did not call her again, but he kept in touch with Dru, and Dru would let her mother know how he was doing.

Dru could not say exactly when or why her parents came around to accepting Lance for what he was. She suspected it had something to do with her father's brush with death and his subsequent belief that he would be "called to meet his maker" sooner than he thought. He had never recovered fully from the stroke.

Anyway, things were back to normal with Lance, and soon Phil, his boyfriend, became a fixture at family gatherings. It turned out that everybody had figured out the truth about Lance a long time ago, but it didn't really bother them because he was still their Lance—handsome, intelligent, fun-loving, and kind. Too bad those good looks were wasted on men, the aunts and female cousins would tease him to his face. But, hey, they would say, variety is the spice of life, isn't it? And Lance would agree with a jovial "amen to that."

At first, Dru, fiercely protective of her brother, had been suspicious of this free-flowing liberalism in her otherwise very conservative extended West Indian family. For a long time, she kept her ears tuned for double entendres and snide remarks about Lance. When none were forthcoming she grudgingly conceded that her kin's feelings were genuine.

There were four items in Lance's zip file. One contained photographs of St. Cyr—an eight-by-eleven, black-and-white bust shot, the kind that would accompany a press release. Another showed him receiving an award. Dru squinted to read the French inscription on the plaque. She could barely make out the words because of all the curlicues in the lettering. She finally figured out that the award was being bestowed on Theron St. Cyr for his dedication to the protection of women and girls.

The third and last photo, from a newspaper clipping, tore at Dru's heart. It was taken at a funeral and it showed a distraught St. Cyr bent over a closed casket. Two men, one on either side of him, had their arms around his shoulders. She recognized one of them instantly. It was Faustin, the same man who had picked her up at the train station in Paris and locked her in that frightening studio. The third man resembled Faustin, though he seemed younger. His brother, probably.

All three were clearly torn up over whoever had died, St. Cyr and Faustin most of all. Their faces were twisted in pain. The picture must have been taken not very long before she met them. Both St. Cyr and Faustin looked the same as when she met them. The caption read, "The funeral of Tabatha St. Cyr, a budding jazz pianist, who was found brutally stabbed to death in Paris. Pictured left to right: Faustin Daubuisson, her fiancé; Theron St. Cyr, her twin brother; Michel Daubuisson, brother of Faustin."

Dru was stunned. She could not take her eyes off Theron's face.

Finally, she sat back and closed her eyes. Her breathing was heavy. She opened her eyes and stared at Theron's face again.

So this is it. Her mouth silently formed the words. He wasn't lying. *He wasn't lying.*

Memories of Marseille and Paris rushed at her. Her heart went on a rampage in her chest as the image of St. Cyr pushed itself forward. She saw him as she had seen him the very first time, heard his voice as they walked up and down the narrow, stepped streets and along La Canebière. His protective arm as they passed the man he called Ramy. His good-bye at the train station. Then Paris. And Faustin.

And wasted years waiting to avenge a wrong that had never been done to her.

Dru put her head down on the coffee table and wept. She cried for herself, and for Theron and Tabatha St. Cyr.

A brisk knock on the door, followed by an equally brisk "Room service!" stirred her to action. As soon as the waiter left, she resumed reading the files from Lance. There was the standard information about St. Cyr's parents and place of birth, all of it matching what he had told her in Marseille. His schooling and service in the French navy, and his firm, which she had already read about on the Internet.

She left the file about Tabatha St. Cyr for last. It was the longest. Lance had scanned an entire article in the magazine *Paris Match* that detailed the circumstances of Tabatha's death. Her kidnapping, St. Cyr's search for her, the discovery of her body, her funeral and Theron's personal pursuit of justice. The writer had interviewed several people for the piece, including Theron himself, and she had woven a story so vivid that, reading it, Dru felt as if she were watching the scenes in real time.

Tabatha had been kidnapped on her way home from Spain, where she had gone with her head full of dreams about playing with the great American jazz vibraphonist Lionel Hampton. Her parents had been close friends of Hampton's when they lived in the United States and they had arranged for her to meet him. Hampton was in Spain for a brief engagement, and did not want to go to France just yet. He would do so during his European tour scheduled for later that year.

Tabatha had rushed off excitedly to Madrid where she had indeed met Hampton and even joined him on the piano in an impromptu jamming session at a small nightclub. She had called her parents the moment she had arrived back in France, gushing about the experience and promising to visit them the very next day to tell them all about it. They never saw or heard from her again.

Theron and Faustin never stopped looking for her. In the process they learned about organized crime groups that had built the smuggling and exploitation of human beings into a multibillion-dollar industry with tentacles on every continent. They learned about the trafficking routes—young girls and women taken from China, Thailand, Korea, Laos, Cambodia, Burma, Vietnam, the Philippines, Malaysia and Indonesia; and from Mexico, El Salvador, Guatemala, and Peru. And still more from Romania, and Russia.

The principal destinations for these women and girls were Western Europe and North America, where they were sexually exploited or thrown into forced labor. They rarely made it out alive.

Theron and Faustin followed every lead, sometimes spending an entire night in the human cesspools that littered the Paris underground. Their efforts eventually paid off in a tip from a heroin addict who was coming down from his high and needed money for another fix. A girl had run away that very night, he said, and the King had sent the one called Eyes to find her. The addict told them that they were saying she had probably run toward the police precinct. They all did that when they ran away and that's why the King planted men all along that route.

When Theron and Faustin asked him to describe the girl, he kept pointing at Theron, his mouth slack, his knees sagging. Theron thrust him up against a wall and threatened to kill him if he did not speak. The junkie, protesting loudly, finally blurted out the words that Theron had been praying to hear: "Like you. She looked like you."

Tabatha was close to death when they found her. "We called her name. Many times. It was no use. She was already leaving us. But she opened her eyes, saw us, smiled, and then…then she died. She…she simply died," the writer quoted Theron as saying, even describing the tremor in his voice.

Dru shuddered as she read the description of Tabatha's mutilated body. It was the work of an animal. Tabatha had been stabbed and slashed repeatedly and left to die.

Shortly after the funeral, Theron, embittered by the powerlessness or unwillingness of the authorities to pursue Tabatha's murderers, launched a vigilante movement against the people who preyed on women. He and his recruits kept watch at the train and bus stations through which thousands of innocent women and girls passed daily, coming from the rural areas of France and from all over Europe, traveling alone on a thrill or a dream. Only a few came like that from Asia, Africa, and the Middle East, for those were places where the culture still did not permit women and young girls to travel alone to foreign lands. Those girls were taken in their own countries, sometimes given up by their own families in exchange for money to settle debts or to feed the rest of a starving family.

The vigilantes quickly learned to recognize the predators, just as the predators quickly learned to recognize the vigilantes. Neither side confronted nor attacked the other. The vigilantes simply formed a protective presence around anyone who fit the profile of a prey and that kept the evil ones away.

Women's rights organizations estimated that hundreds of lives were spared as a result of Theron's vigilantes. Although these successes on their own were too few to make a dent in the human trade, it was enough for the right people to take notice and shame the French authorities into action. Funds were hastily allocated for a specially trained squad of undercover police to be assigned exclusively to terminals and ports. Shortly after that, a coalition of women's groups from countries in the European Union presented Theron with the first "Tabatha Award." It was an honor that, from then on, would be bestowed annually on a deserving individual.

Dru took a deep breath and closed the file. She could not sleep that night, thinking about all that she had said and done to hurt Theron St. Cyr, when all he had ever done was try to keep her safe.

19

Roopnaraine stuffed the last piece of roti into his mouth, licked his fingers and leaned back in his chair with a contented sigh.

He had been craving a good *hassa* curry for weeks and Jean, his wife, had finally prepared it for him. More precisely, the maid had prepared it. The maid was much better with curry than Jean could ever hope to be, though Roopnaraine didn't dare tell Jean so.

Not that Jean was bad herself. Every Guyanese woman knew how to make a decent curry. After all, curry was a national dish. But Jean's curry just didn't have the *kick* that comes from the right combination of garlic and *achar*, the spicy pickled green mango. Still, he had pestered her about cooking curry *hassa* until she snapped back that it was easier to find *hassa* on Liberty Avenue in Queens or at Bacchus shop in Brooklyn than in Georgetown. The closest place to G.T. where you could find it was *till-away* up the East Coast, in the Corentyne region, she had argued heatedly.

"So if you know somebody in Berbice who could send you some hassa, Nelson, or if you got somebody in Brooklyn or Queens up dere in New York, you go 'long and ask dem to send it. And once dey send it, Nelson, I will cook it."

Jean had made this statement in a very reasonable voice, but with that emphatic inflection on the words "Nelson" and "New York" that spelled danger. Nelson had retaliated with the surest and safest tactic he knew— silence. And Jean hated not being spoken to. Nelson had kept it up for two whole days before she herself relented and telephoned a friend in Berbice. As if he, Nelson, didn't know that the *friend* was an old boyfriend he had run off, but who seized every opportunity to let Jean know that the flame she had lit in his heart all those years ago would glow within him "like de star o' Bethlehem" until he went to his grave.

Hoping for a little play-play when Nelson was not at home, the ex-boyfriend told Jean that on his next trip to G.T., which just happened to be the very next morning, he would stock her up with several pounds of the best *hassa* in Guyana.

Hassa was a strange-looking crustacean, no bigger than a croaker, with a dark, vertebrae-like carapace. Guyanese lobster, Jamaicans jokingly called it. And indeed, once it was cooked, the shell was easily pulled away, leaving a length of succulent, yellowish meat that was lobsterlike in consistency.

Ex-boyfriend and fish had arrived as promised. Jean hurried him away as soon as he handed over the bundle and made Sundrawattie, the maid, swear that she would not breathe a word to Mr. Roopnaraine about who delivered it. "Just tell him you didn't see when it came, you hear, Sund-row'tie?"

The aroma of curry hit Roopnaraine and Dalrymple at the gate as they arrived for lunch. Roopnaraine made a beeline for the kitchen as soon as he entered the house and uncovered the pot on the stove. Were it not for Dalrymple's scornful remarks about how stupid some people carried on when they saw food, not to mention Sundrawattie covering her face and giggling, he would have seriously humped Jean right there in the kitchen in gratitude. He settled for an exuberant embrace and a handful of Jean's bottom.

Just as Nelson had done, Dalrymple leaned back in his chair and patted his stomach. "Boy, I got to hand it to Jean. This is really good food. I don't know the last day I had *hassa*. They exporting every damn thing to America now, talking about how much money they making. Everything is for America! America! America! Like if Guyana don't have people living here. Like if we mustn't eat. Like if we can't pay for food. Even *labba* heading for America. *Labba!* That nasty rat-meat! I see it with my own two eyes at Bacchus shop. I tell you, Nello, for me one-one, I would leave all dem Yankee Guyanese to punish up there with spaghetti and meatball. If they want to live in America they should learn to eat American food. You don't agree with me, Nello? Why should they have it bake and cake?"

Roopnaraine had heard this all before. He kept his eyes closed and remained silent. Dalrymple sighed and called out to Jean. "Aye, Jean! Put some of that *hassa* in a bowl for me to carry home, gyurl. And wrap up two *roti* with it."

Jean sucked her teeth. "Does my house look like a restaurant to you, Compton Dalrymple? Why don't you ask that buck woman you're cheating on your wife with to cook curry *hassa* and roti for you!" The pot cover clattered and Jean addressed her husband. "Nelson, when you miss me I gone."

They heard the kitchen door slam, followed by Jean's three-inch heels clip-clopping on the driveway as she headed to her car. She was taking an afternoon class in computer programming at one of the private technical schools that were springing up all over the city.

Roopnaraine sat up, laughing. "Eh heh! See what I told you? The whole of Georgetown know your business. Jean vex like mad about it and not she alone. Anyway, don't worry 'bout de roti an' curry. Sundrawattie gon tek care o' yuh. But you better straighten out your business fast, man."

"All right! All right! Leave that alone. Let's get back to the matter at hand," Dalrymple said, flicking his wrist and switching to straight English. "As I was saying on our way here, this business with Livuh is nasty business. I vote we cut loose from the contract with Pilgrim Boone. Find a way to ease ourselves out of it without anybody losing face. I just don't want anybody looking at us funny, pointing fingers and making remarks. I don't want my name called in no murder business."

"But is there any real proof that it was murder?"

"What more proof do you want? You already put two and two together but you just don't want to admit that you got four. Come on, Nello.

A big, healthy, strapping man like Livuh drops dead out of the blue. The man used to jog and he wasn't no young yam. Everybody knows there was no love lost between him and the Savoy people. I tell you, somebody put out that man's light. What's wrong with you, man? Besides, if the minister says it's so, it's so."

Roopnaraine leaned back in the chair and closed his eyes. He let a moment pass before he spoke. "Nobody in his right mind would think we had anything to do with it, Compton. People know us."

"I *know* people know us. But a lot of those same people are jealous of us. Remember what some of them said when we got our first contract with Pilgrim Boone? How the only reason we got it was because you let Grant Featherhorn go down on Jean. Remember?"

Roopnaraine scowled at the recollection. It had not taken them long to figure out where the rumor had originated. But word of it, and the name of its author, had gotten back to Jean before either of them could say or do anything about it, and she decided to take matters into her own hands. She never asked her husband or Dalrymple if they had heard the rumor, although, she admitted later, she assumed both had.

The opportunity for revenge presented itself sooner than she expected, at a frou-frou reception at the American ambassador's residence to celebrate America's Independence Day.

Knowing how much Fenton Latchman was in awe of the United States, Jean deliberately wrangled an invitation for him. Without making it seem obvious, she sought him out at the reception, and, hooking her arm amiably through his, she laughed and joked with him until he felt comfortable enough to confess to her that he would give anything to be personally introduced to the ambassador. Yes, he had shaken the ambassador's hand on the greeting line, but that didn't count, he argued. The greeting line was just a polite formality, and the ambassador most likely had already forgotten his name. He simply *had* to make an impression on the man who represented the most powerful nation on earth. He couldn't come so close, eating and drinking in the ambassador's *pryvit* residence, and leave without stamping the name and face of Fenton Latchman indelibly on his mind.

Besides, it was getting harder and harder to get a visa to America without the right connections. What better connection than the ambassador himself?

Latchman told Jean that he had seen her exchange warm greetings with the ambassador as if they were good friends. He did not know, and she did not tell him, that she had met the ambassador just the previous week, at a small ceremony marking his donation of several boxes of books to the National Library, where she worked as a librarian.

Feigning reluctance, Jean led Latchman over to the ambassador, who, it so happened, was speaking to a group that included Nelson, Dalrymple, and the American deputy consul general. She refused to look at Nelson, knowing that he had already guessed she was up to no good when he saw her arm in arm with Latchman.

With the most innocent smile, Jean introduced Latchman to the ambassador as "one of Guyana's leading businessmen." She paused only briefly before she went in for the kill, her expression cold and hard. "And, Excellency, Mr. Latchman also happens to be the man who has the distinction of single-handedly compromising the integrity of one of America's most venerable consulting firms, Pilgrim Boone."

"Oh?" the ambassador said, looking intently at Latchman, ignoring his extended hand. "And how did Mr. Latchman accomplish such a feat?"

"Oh, I'm not so sure you want to know the sordid details, Mr. Ambassador. Suffice it to say that Mr. Latchman has come to regret his, shall we say, his error in judgment?" Jean's voice was pure honey. She was enjoying herself.

Latchman stood like idiocy personified. His unshaken hand was still extended toward the ambassador, his face frozen in a foolish grin.

Dalrymple and Roopnaraine, who had given up trying to catch his wife's eye in hopes of staving her off, shifted nervously from one foot to another and tinkled the ice in their glasses. The deputy consul general cocked his head and looked amused. He was a man in his thirties who had won notoriety throughout Guyana for his adulation of the Guyanese personality with the words "that truly delightful spirit, that inimitable verve, so singularly Guyanese." Those words, spoken in a televised interview, had earned him the moniker "Inimitable."

The ambassador smiled icily at Latchman and addressed Jean. "Well, now, Mrs. Roopnaraine, you've aroused my curiosity tremendously. Please don't spare me the sordid details."

Jean inclined her head graciously. "If you insist, Mr. Ambassador."

Latchman's face crumpled. His unshaken hand finally fell to his side and he whispered frantically to Jean, "Ow, Mistress. Don't do me so. Mi wicket down a'ready."

"Come to think of it, I do remember hearing an ugly rumor about that contract," the ambassador said suddenly, before Jean had a chance to continue. "Yes, indeed I do. I had not yet arrived in Guyana, of course, but it was such a vile piece of gossip that the American community here still mentions it from time to time. Naturally, word of it got to me soon after I came. Now, Mrs. Roopnaraine, are you saying that Mr. Latchman here is the one who started that rumor? Then I am sure there is some mistake. Didn't you say Mr. Latchman was one of Guyana's most important businessmen? Surely someone of such standing could not stoop so low. Someone must have twisted his words into that unspeakable accusation, isn't that so, Mr. Latchman?"

Latchman lost no time darting through the opening the ambassador provided. "So it is, Mr. Ambassador. And in front of all of you, I apologize to Mrs. Roopnaraine for any pain caused by those wicked allegations."

"Your apology is accepted, Mr. Latchman," Jean said triumphantly.

"Good. Now what were you saying, Mr. Dalrymple?" the ambassador asked, turning his back to Latchman.

By the next day, the entire business community had heard of the scene at the ambassador's residence and from then on, Latchman had been nicknamed "Wicket Down."

Roopnaraine dragged his thoughts back to the present. "So who do you think killed him, Compton? You think Dru knows anything?"

"Nah. But I think this Theron St. Cyr that she and Macky were talking about knows something. Remember him? The fella at the airport? The one she was staring at with greedy eyes?"

"Oh, yes! She and Macky were talking about him? Why?"

"She so much as told Macky he was the one who killed Goodings. But Macky looked like he didn't believe her one bit. In fact, he looked like he was more sorry for her than anything else. By the way, you know a man named Alejandro Bernat?"

"Alejandro Bernat? Alejan—you sure Bernat is the last name?"

"Yes. Why? You know the name?"

"I heard something just the other day about a Alejandro. Alejandro something or other. It sounded like Bernat. But this Alejandro I heard about is supposed to be some big-time drug lord in Venezuela. Killing Guyanese youth over there left and right, I hear. He couldn't be the same person you're talking about."

"I don't know what this Alejandro Bernat does. But Bernat is the name I heard plain and straight. Nobody said anything about Venezuela, though. But then again, Alejandro is a Spanish name. Guyanese people don't name their children Alejandro. Where did you hear about this Alejandro and this business about drugs?"

Roopnaraine's belly was full and he was ready to tell a good tale. They had an hour yet before they would return to the office. He settled himself more comfortably in his chair, stretched out his legs and crossed his ankles, and locked his fingers behind his head.

"I was having drinks at The Lib'ry the other day with those boys from the Rupununi. You know who I'm talking about? The two who came to see us about finding a foreign investor for their farm project. Remember them? They said they didn't trust Guyanese. They called Guyanese people thieves. Said Guyanese would rob them blind before they could blink. By the way, don't forget you're supposed to call Willo in New York about their project. He said he had one or two leads, remember? Anyway, after two drinks—you know those people can't hold their liquor—these boys started talking about their escapades in Venezuela. You know how they cross the border like they're going from G.T. to Vreed-en-Hoop. Anyway, they started talking about how hard life was for some of them over in Venezuela. How all these young Guyanese suddenly got mixed up with drugs after they went to work for this man named Alejandro something. Big helluva ranch this man has, they said. The name sounded like

Bernat, but I could be wrong. They said he even had a Guyanese mistress at one time. One beautiful buck girl. Young. She was only a teenager when he took her. But he turned that little girl into something so nasty it killed her poor mother and father. Kill dem dead. This Alejandro apparently is a real big shot in Venezuela. He's supposed to be friends with all kinds of army and government people. But all the poor people know he's a big-time drug lord. Coke, what else? Runs the whole operation from his ranch. Dem Rupununi boys said planes fly in there all the time, even in broad daylight. But this Alejandro keeps a fancy office in Caracas with a cover-up business. Something to do with building hotels. But as for the ranch, those boys said every single worker who ever left ended up dead. And every last one of them was Guyanese. They know all this from crossing the border to sell gold."

Roopnaraine paused and shook his head. One look at his friend's face and Dalrymple knew what was coming next. Nelson denounced to anyone who would listen the wanton bleeding of Guyana's gold deposits. At the very least, he contended, the traders and the country should have something to show for all that good El Dorado gold. But there was nothing. Not even one good road.

Dalrymple listened patiently as Roopnaraine groused. "Boy, I tell you. This gold business gets me so blasted vex every time I think about it. Everybody is a gold trader these days, and it's every man jack for himself. Instead of all of them organizing and getting a good price? Nah! Each body selling for himself. So all of them end up selling out our country's gold cheap to *rass* in Venezuela and Brazil, then got the temerity to brag about how much money they're making, when it's the Venezuelans and Brazilians who mekkin' big money when they purify the gold and sell it to Europe and America. You don't see how ignorant we are? Venezuelans and Brazilians mekkin' more money sellin' Guyanese gold than Guyanese themselves! It's a damn shame!"

"So what happen with the two Rupununi boys, Nello?" Dalrymple interjected firmly.

Roopnaraine studied Dalrymple pityingly for a moment, as if his friend embodied the ignorance that afflicted the gold traders. Dalrymple grinned. This was nothing new. Nelson always got on one high horse or another when his belly was full.

Roopnaraine took a deep breath and picked up his tale. "Once, when they crossed into Venezuela, they came across a man who was on the run from this Alejandro. The poor fella was trying to get back to Guyana. It was a man they knew from long, from their village. He is the one who told them the story of Alejandro and the Guyanese who worked on his land. They said the same man's body was found the very next day, in the jungle, just near the border. He'd been shot dead. They suspect it was other Guyanese who work for Alejandro that did it."

Roopnaraine paused to drink some water. By then, Dalrymple had leaned back in his chair, one leg crossed over the other. He had closed his eyes, and his hands were clasped behind his head.

"You sleepin', man." It was an accusation.

"No, Nelson. I'm listening to you." Dalrymple said patiently. Then he added: "You really believe that story? You said you were all drinking. You sure it wasn't the liquor talking for those boys?"

"You don't know those people. I have had more dealings with them than you. Other people make up stories like that to impress others. But one thing Guyanese Indians don't do is try to impress. They have a whole different philosophy about life. With them, it's all about keeping it straight and simple. They don't complicate things the way we do. They don't try, like we do, to remake ourselves according to other people's perceptions of us."

Dalrymple laughed. His eyes were still closed. "What happen, Nello? You're getting deep in your old age, or is it all that curry *hassa* talking?"

"You can laugh. But I tell you I'm getting tired of the Tonto syndrome. I'm tired of bending over backwards to keep other people's egos intact. Tired of letting people get away with the idea that they are doing our country a favor when all the time they're either lining their own pockets or securing their own country's future. And don't tell me you don't feel the same way. I know you."

Dalrymple sighed. Nello was right, of course, but he didn't want to go down that road just now. The whole mess surrounding Livuh's death had gotten to both of them, more than either wanted to admit. He sighed again and changed the subject.

"Anyway, this Alejandro you're talking about doesn't sound like the same person. But then, who knows? Macky mentioned his name when he was going back and forth with Dru, but he didn't dwell on it. Just threw it out in one of his Mack attacks then dropped it."

"Did Dru know him?"

"No. She said she didn't recognize the name at all."

"But you think he may be someone to check out?"

"Aww come on, Nello. You know Macky. He doesn't drop names for dropping name's sake. There's bound to be a connection somewhere between this guy, the whole Savoy deal, and Livuh."

"So what do you think we should do, Sherlock Holmes?"

"Don't get sarcastic with me. Didn't I say right from the beginning that we should pull out?"

"That would be a bad move. You know what would happen if we did that? Not a single American firm would ever give us another contract. Word would get around that we can't be counted on when the going gets rough and no American would want to do business with us. Would you blame them? And if it's proven that Pilgrim Boone had absolutely nothing to do with Livuh's death, then we might as well close up shop and go plant rice."

"I think you're exaggerating. Anyway, don't we have clients from other countries? Even if the Americans drop us we would still get contracts from the Canadians and the Europeans. And especially the Asians."

"I wouldn't put my money on that. These foreign companies may be rivals with each other, but they stand on common ground when it comes to countries like ours. They take their cues from each other."

"Not the Asians. Not these days. Don't forget they were colonized just like us, which makes them very suspicious and very wary when they're dealing with Europe and Uncle Sam."

"Well, maybe you have a point there. But they're cheap and selfish. It's all about money with them."

"Like it isn't with everybody. So are you saying we should just fold our arms and wait for the *cungxi* to hit the fan?"

"What else can we do?"

"Shouldn't we at least talk to Macky? Impress upon him that we're innocent?"

"What makes you think we can get near him now? On our own, without Dru?"

"Well, I refuse to be dragged into somebody else's mess. There must be something we can do."

"What if…" Dalrymple hesitated, weighing what he was about to say.

"What if what?" Roopnaraine said impatiently when too many seconds had gone by and Dalrymple still had not completed the question.

"What if we went to see this Theron St. Cyr?"

"Theron St. Cyr?"

"Yes, Theron St. Cyr."

"You mean the same fella Livuh went to meet at the airport?"

"The very same. As I said, his name came up in the meeting with Dru and Macky. Dru dropped a strong hint that he might have been involved in Livuh's death."

"So why should we go to see him if he was involved? So he could kill us, too?"

"I didn't say he was involved, Mr. Roopnaraine. I said Dru *tried* to accuse him of being involved. Now here's a man who obviously was a good friend of Livuh's, this Theron St. Cyr, right? And Livuh was a good friend of Macky, true? So maybe, just maybe, Mr. Roopnaraine, the man Theron St. Cyr is also a friend of Macky. Macky clearly didn't buy Dru's attempt to discredit him. That, to me, is a very strong indication that Macky not only knows the fella quite well, but he also is convinced that he had nothing to do with Livuh's death."

"And you think we should persuade this Theron of our own innocence so that he'll put in a good word for us with Macky, who, then, would remove us from the list of suspects."

"You have a better idea?" Dalrymple said defensively.

"And during this meeting with Mr. St. Cyr, will we bring up the name Alejandro Bernat and the things that I heard about a Venezuelan whose name is also Alejandro and whose last name could possibly be Bernat?"

Dalrymple glared at his friend. He did not appreciate Nello's mocking tone. "The answer is yes," he said coldly. He sat up, his face set. "Now you listen to me, Nelson. I will go to see St. Cyr even if I have to go alone. And when I go, I will run my mouth about everything I've heard in order to keep the good name of Rebecca Dalrymple's son clean, you hear me? I don't care how farfetched it sounds, I will say it nonetheless."

"And what about Dru?"

"What about Dru? What *about* Dru? Miss Drucilla Durane will be on a plane to New York before you can snap your fingers. Mark my words. And once she gets back to New York, the impenetrable walls of Pilgrim Boone will come down around her. Small fry like you and me, on the other hand, have to live right here, in the middle of this mess, alone. That is, unless you can convince me that Pilgrim Boone will fly in their legal samurai to keep suspicion away from our door."

Roopnaraine sighed. For the first time in years he reflected on the choices they had made since the day he and Dalrymple stood beside the Lamaha and silently condemned the country's railroad to death. They hadn't bothered with the Mini Minor's rusting carcass after that. To this day it remained half submerged in the middle of the Lamaha, a monument of long suffering that had finally won the respect it was due when a contributor to *The Sunday Chronicle*'s op-ed page used it to position one of a string of a carjackings that plagued the city.

"The latest incident of this reprehensible crime form took place less than a chain away from the rusty Mini Minor in the Lamaha trench. If only that princess of endurance could speak! For, as usual, fear has buttoned the lips of those who could identify the perpetrators," the writer had penned.

Whenever Roopnaraine drove past the Mini Minor he would nod in its direction and say, "Okay, Princess." It was an acknowledgement of ownership. For, technically, the wreck belonged to him. He still had the letter from Mayor and Town Council granting him the exclusive right of removal. He and Dalrymple had parted company that day with an unspoken understanding. It had been easy for Dalrymple, who was still permanent secretary at Transport, to arrange a meeting with the Pilgrim Boone team. The contract was signed within a week.

Roopnaraine sighed again. If he had a chance to do it all over again, would he make the same decision?

"Absolutely," said Dalrymple. For the umpteenth time in as many years he had correctly read the mind of his oldest friend and business partner.

Roopnaraine laughed. It was a good-feeling laugh. The laugh you laugh when a burden is rolling away. So many times over the years he and Dalrymple had taken turns making each other laugh like that.

"Okay, then. Where do we find this Theron St. Cyr?"

20

Dru dropped her bag on the floor, leaned her back against the door, and exhaled a long, loud sigh.

"Oh, thank you, Jesus. Thank you. These four walls in Brooklyn never felt so good," she said aloud.

She closed her eyes and for a moment enjoyed the peace of listening to herself breathe. When she opened her eyes, she looked around the living room, lovingly taking in every piece of furniture, every painting, every knickknack: the colorful woolen rug from Aunt Petal; the sheer voile curtains her mother had made, the color of sunshine; and the grainy parquet floor that she still had not found time to sand and refinish.

She inhaled the calming scent of lavender that floated out of the old-fashioned potpourri dish on the antique half-moon table just beside the door. Her eyes settled on the plants in the far window and her eyebrows suddenly arched, as if she were noticing for the first time how tall and upright they stood. How you've grown, she thought fondly, remembering when she had brought them home as tiny seedlings that first weekend, in all that rain, after she had moved into the apartment. She had deliberately chosen plants that did not require much watering, knowing that she would have to travel often. And if she had to be away for more than a week, she would give Mr. Jackson, the super for the apartment building in the Crown Heights section of Brooklyn where she lived, twenty dollars to look in on them.

Mr. Jackson! Now *there* was a man who knew plants. His own apartment was like a tropical garden.

"I swear they're the reason I'm alive today," he told Dru the first time she stopped by his apartment to collect a package the mailman had left there for her. She had gasped in delight when he opened the door and she caught sight of the melange of flowers and foliage.

Mr. Jackson had continued talking in that clipped Barbadian accent as he limped over to the dining table where he had put her package. "Lord knows I wanted to hit my wife Clarissa, God rest her soul, so bad sometimes. What a mouth that woman had on her! Good God! But I knew I'da been dead before I even touched her. So I just walked away and tended to my babies here when she got me all riled up."

But Dru was never away for more than two weeks and Mr. Jackson didn't have to check on the plants more than twice. This time, of course, she'd been away just three days.

Three days. Was that all?

She walked over to the window and felt the soil in each pot. It was still damp. She had watered the plants the very morning she had left for Guyana.

Guyana.

She folded her lips into a tight line and turned away from the window. She went back to the door, picked up her bag, and walked down the hallway into her bedroom. A tiny red light flashed impatiently at her as she entered the room, drawing her eyes to the telephone on the nightstand beside the bed.

"Your mailbox is full," she said aloud, making a face as she mimicked the superior tone of the electronic voice that would greet her when she dialed her password to retrieve her messages.

She glared at the phone for a few seconds, and then addressed it harshly. "Give me a break, will you? Christ! I just got back from another continent. Do you mind if I take some downtime?" She rolled her neck and cut her eyes.

The red button blinked back insolently.

Dru sucked her teeth, dropped her bag on the floor, and looked around. Everything was as neat and tidy as she had left it. She hated coming home to a messy apartment. She liked the instant, comforting embrace of order when she entered her own space after a trip. And, of course, her mother's repeated exhortations from her teenage years would ring in her ears every time she prepared to leave home, "Make sure you wear clean, decent panties." She would pause for emphasis on "decent" and open her eyes wide, meaning, in those days, no bikini panties.

"And keep a clean home at all times like every self-respecting woman. Make up your bed before you leave your house so that if anything happens to you on the road and people have to carry you home they'll know you didn't come from trash. Don't you ever give anyone a reason to wash their mouth on you or this family. Do you hear what I say, Drucilla?"

Dru sank down on the side of the bed. The spread was taut. Not a single ripple.

She threw herself flat on her back and stared at the ceiling. The late evening sun pushed slivers of soft golden light through the Venetian blinds and sprinkled them across the bed and on the walls. It was that very quiet, strangely melancholy moment between daytime and nighttime. The time of day they called "the gloaming" in Guyana.

Gloaming. Even the word sounded sad.

Thoughts of Guyana brought up the image of Theron St. Cyr standing over her, looking at her with such cold eyes. Her heart raced as she recalled the moment. Her face flushed hot and she turned her head sharply to one side as though Theron himself were staring down at her from the ceiling and she did not want him to see the heat of shame in her face and in her eyes. Even now, nearly twenty-four hours later, the shame of their last meeting was still raw.

She had called him later that night, just before she went to bed, to say she would be leaving for New York the next day. She was calling because he had asked her to let him know when she was leaving, she had said quickly when he answered the phone. She had made her voice brittle and aloof to mask the humiliation she felt.

He had been just as distant, speaking to her in that very formal English he used when he was being impersonal. He thanked her for letting him know. She was surprised when he offered to accompany her to the airport, but she had declined, saying quickly that it would be too much trouble for him, a stranger in Guyana. Besides, her colleagues Roopnaraine and Dalrymple were taking her to the airport, she told him. She gave him her home number, explaining that it would be best to call her there if he found out anything that she should know. She didn't see any reason to give him the number of her cell phone.

It had pained her to decline his offer to accompany her to the airport because it meant giving up an opportunity to redeem herself in his eyes. She could have used their time together on the way to the airport to explain the whole business about seeing Ramy again. She could have told him that she now believed he had nothing to do with Andrew Goodings' death, that she knew about Tabatha, that she knew now that he did not try to have her kidnapped in Paris and sold into prostitution or slavery.

She couldn't say all these things to him on the phone. Not when he was so obviously disgusted with her, and rightfully so. She needed to speak her mind when she was in front of him so that she could see his reaction, read his eyes, his every gesture.

Trying to keep him on the phone nonetheless, she had asked him when he was returning to New York. He was noncommittal. "Perhaps in a few days. I need to check on a few things here first. Get some answers," he had said. He remained quiet after that and she had rushed off the phone, not knowing what else to say.

Lying in her own bed now, she angrily commanded herself to get a grip. Why was she making such a big deal of Theron St. Cyr and what he thought of her? Who the hell was he, anyway, with his pathetic little company trying to go up against the likes of Pilgrim Boone! A European that she probably would never understand, anyway! So what if he's black? So what if his parents are American? He's still European, he and his friend Faustin. He was different from all the other black people she was used to: West Indians, Africans, Hispanics. Not in a bad way. Just different in a strange way. She had interacted with a few European blacks before, but only at business meetings. Never socially. She couldn't put a finger on what it was that made them different.

She rolled over onto her stomach and laid her head on her hands. Europeans. She didn't know these people. Why should she waste her time thinking about them?

She closed her eyes with a sigh. Almost immediately, Theron St. Cyr's face loomed into vision. Irritated, she snapped open her eyes and flipped over onto her back.

The voice in her head was plaintive. *You're* the one who's strange, Drucilla Durane. The Savoy deal is in big trouble and that's what your mind should be focused on, not Theron St. Cyr, who's being paid by the Guyanese government to go meddling into the thing. Look at the way he questioned you. Get real, Dru.

Dru blinked guiltily. She didn't want to think about Theron. But she didn't want to think about Pilgrim Boone either. Not just yet. What about the stuff he had said on the plane about wanting to make her believe him? And how about his arm around her waist in Le Quartier Noir, pulling her close to him, gently, but so firmly? He liked her then.

The voice would not let up. So he liked you. Your doorman likes you, too. St. Cyr's a charmer. You know that. His arm around your waist was for protection. End of story. As for now? Take a wild guess, bright girl. You're no longer a college kid running around Europe trying to find herself. You're Pilgrim Boone. Think what you and your connections could do for his company if he's on good terms with you.

Dru covered her ears to shut out the voice. She rolled from side to side, hugging herself tight, as if doing so would quell the trembling that had suddenly seized her. But the tremors did not stop. She knew what was happening. Her mind was being overwhelmed. The organized, comfortable world she had grown used to over the years was in total upheaval. She was on the verge of losing a deal that could cost Pilgrim Boone the huge Savoy account; a man had been murdered and her boss, a man she thoroughly disliked, might be involved; and she had lost her cool in the presence of a man who, she conceded grudgingly, was the epitome of cool himself, humiliated herself in front of him, a man she barely knew.

A blast of rock music from the clock radio on the nightstand shattered her thoughts. She rolled over on her side, slammed her free hand on the off button and flopped back down on the bed. She hated rock. She'd been promising herself to get rid of the clock radio for a month now, ever since it had developed a mind of its own and rolled from station to station, blasting out its latest musical fixation whenever it felt like it. I'll get rid of it tomorrow morning, first thing, she thought. And this time she meant it.

Still, she had to admit, the noise seemed to have steadied her. She wasn't trembling any longer.

Suddenly, she burst out laughing. Ice princess indeed! A man bullies her in public and she agonizes about what he thinks of her! So you're not frozen inside after all, Drucilla Durane. What now? What do you do about Theron St. Cyr?

The answer came back instantly. Nothing. Absolutely nothing. He was kind to you all those years ago in Marseille. Probably saved your life. Today, you're on opposite sides of a battle for a contract that your firm is counting on you to deliver. And right now, Dru, you're not delivering. Meanwhile, he, as far as you know, still has the confidence of the Guyanese government.

Dru took a long, deep breath, infusing herself with renewed resolve. Reason was in control once more. She had no doubt she would hear from St. Cyr as he got deeper into his investigation of Andrew Goodings' death and its possible connection to the Savoy proposal. But that was business. And as long as it was business, she could handle it, she told herself firmly.

Or could she? Could she really still handle business?

All of a sudden she wasn't so sure. Pilgrim Boone had trained her to be as impersonal as a hangman when the need arose. She was the "ebony star" of the company. The highest of the highbrows in consulting knew her name. She had dined with heads of state and ministers of government and policymakers and powerbrokers. Everything seemed to be falling apart now. Two contracts in a row. First Jamaica, now Guyana. And now this complicated stranger into whose orbit she was being pulled against her will.

What the hell happened? How did she get to this point? Could she have brought in Jamaica if she had dealt with the prejudices—or was it fear—of the Jamaicans with more understanding? Could she—should she—have shown more sensitivity?

Perhaps. But what had she done instead? She had rolled her eyes and her neck and stalked away, making it clear to everyone who was watching her—and she knew that all the Jamaicans in the room were—that, as far as she was concerned, Jamaica could shove its turn-of-the-century prejudices up its ass because a backward little speck of land like that wasn't worthy of Pilgrim Boone's attention anyway. And she, Drucilla Durane, was Pilgrim Boone personified, whether they liked it or not.

Shame consumed her again. Had she really become so caught up in the Pilgrim Boone persona that there was no Drucilla Durane anymore? All in the pursuit of what? Contracts that increasingly benefited the partners of Pilgrim Boone more than the countries they were signing up?

There! She'd said it! She'd finally given voice to what she had avoided acknowledging for so long.

What happened to the Dru who, at twenty-one, told the same Pilgrim Boone "later for your internship," then rode the wind on a Eurail Pass? The Dru who could take a deep breath and identify no less than five different scents in the air. Who could close her eyes in a noisy train station and discern the different nations in the timber of the voices around her. Who delighted in doing all of those things.

Where was the Dru who instinctively knew a culture's attitude to time because that attitude was loud and clear in the cadence of footsteps? And where was the Dru who matched the colors of Le Quartier Noir with the souls of a people two worlds away? When did that Dru disappear? Was she gone for good?

I want you back, Dru said aloud. I want *me* back.

The telephone rang. She let it ring until it stopped and her greeting kicked in. She heard the faint click before her voice finished saying, "Have a great day," and she shrugged. Whoever it was obviously did not want to leave a message.

Good. She was not yet ready to deal with the world beyond her apartment. Besides, there was no more room in the message bank.

She pushed herself up on her elbows and remained in that position for a few minutes. Then she turned on her side, rolled off the bed and stood up, dragging the back of her hands roughly across her eyes as if to wipe away the vision of what she had become.

It was dark, she observed with surprise. She stared absently at the window and wondered when the sun had finally sunk and why she had not noticed the darkness before, even though she had been wide awake.

Had she really been awake?

She was moving toward the light switch beside the door when the telephone rang again. She ignored it and kept on walking. This time, the caller hung up as soon as the ringing paused to switch over to voice mail.

She turned on the light and stood before the mirror over the dresser, scrutinizing her face as if she were seeing it for the first time in a long time. She turned away and began to undress.

The telephone rang again. She stopped undressing and stared at it. She was sure it was the same caller. Who could be so insistent? It couldn't be her mother. She usually called late at night, around eleven.

She decided to answer it. She picked up on the last ring before it switched to voice mail.

"This is Dru," she said tonelessly.

"I called to make sure you had arrived safely."

Just like that. No greeting. No waiting for her to respond either. Theron St. Cyr's voice was without emotion but courteous.

He continued. "I called twice before, but there was no answer. You must have arrived home only a few minutes ago. You had no trouble, I hope."

Dru sat down hard on the bed, the receiver still clamped to her ear. Her mouth opened but nothing came out.

"Are you there, Dru? Are you all right?"

Somehow, despite the numbness she felt, Dru managed a smile. Two familiar questions. She had put him through this before. Was it really such a short time ago? "Theron," she began. She stopped, and then tried again. "Theron…" She didn't know how to continue.

He misread her hesitation. Perhaps she had company. "I'm sorry. How

236

very inconsiderate of me. You are only just arriving home and you must be very tired. I simply wanted to make sure you were safe. Good—"

"Theron, no!" She didn't mean to raise her voice, didn't mean to sound so urgent. But she could not let him leave like that. Not again.

She dropped her voice to its normal pitch, trying to hide her embarrassment, hoping she could convey to him that it was different with her now, that she knew the truth. She had to win his respect again because he was her link to the person she once was. He could help her find her way back to that person again.

"Don't go, Theron. Don't hang up." The phone was still pressed hard against her ear. Her free hand twisted and untwisted the twirly black cord that wriggled from the receiver to the cradle on the nightstand.

Theron caught the urgency in her voice and thought the worst. "Dru! Are you in danger? Is someone there with you?" His voice whipped across the distance like a blade hurled through the air.

"No, no," Dru said hastily. "No, I'm fine. There's no one here. I'm all right. I'm sorry I shouted like that. I just—" She broke off, flustered.

There was a long silence. Dru worked her bottom lip, biting it from one side to the other. Her fingers abandoned the twirly cord and attacked a clump of bedspread.

"You just what, Dru?" Theron said evenly.

She had to say something. She owed him an explanation for screaming out his name and begging him not to go. Otherwise, he would think she was insane. As if he didn't think so already.

"I'm sorry, Theron. I keep giving you reasons to think I'm crazy, don't I?" she said, wondering if she really sounded as rational as she thought she did. "I guess everything is just hitting me all at once and there's really no one here to talk to about it."

St. Cyr remained silent for a while, and then said quietly, "I see." He waited again, giving her time to continue. When Dru said nothing, he spoke again.

"Dru, listen to me." His voice was firm, but gentle.

The back-of-the-throat roll of his French accent seemed more pronounced. He was being kind, Dru thought, her heart pounding at the stark maleness of his voice. It was obvious. He thought that she had lost it and he was being kind. That's all.

She listened to his words while her eyes fixed on an invisible object on the wall across the room.

"I will be back in New York in a few days. I will see you then, if you wish. It's up to you. But you should get some sleep now. This was not an easy trip for you. You should go right to bed. I will call you when I get back. That would be okay with you?"

Dru let the question hang for a moment. Then she said, "Yes. It would be okay. Please do that." Her voice was devoid of emotion. She felt numb. Instead of his respect, she had gotten his pity.

"I will. One more thing, and this is very important, do not mention to anyone the matters we discussed when we last met. Goodnight, Dru." He hung up before she could respond.

Dru sat motionless, her eyes still riveted on the invisible object on the wall. The receiver hung limply from her hand. Then she sighed and replaced the receiver. She stood up, finished undressing, turned out the light, and lay down naked on her bed, on her stomach.

She fumbled around with her toes until she got a good grip on the folded coverlet at the foot of the bed, wagged the folds out, and lifted it up far enough for her to reach down and grab it with her hand. She pulled it across her buttocks and settled her head on the double-stacked feather pillows.

She moved mechanically. Not a thought was in her head. She had shoved them all away. She was tired of thinking. She just wanted to sleep.

21

The knock on the door startled Theron.

He had been staring at the password prompt on his laptop screen for the past—he glanced at his watch—fifteen minutes, trying to figure out what was going on in Drucilla Durane's head. Where he stood with her. Where she stood with him.

He glanced at his watch again. Yes. Fifteen minutes had indeed gone by since he had put down the phone after his strange conversation—no, not conversation—exchange. After his strange *exchange* with her.

He knew he had hung up abruptly. He had to, or he would have said something he would have regretted, with Dru sounding the way she did, diffident and needy.

Did he want to be involved with *that* Dru? He had sought her out in New York because he genuinely liked her. That is, he liked the Dru he had met in Marseille. He also wanted to renew their friendship because he thought that she could lead him to new business for his firm. But now—

As soon as he had put down the phone, he had opened his laptop, still bemused, mechanically going through the motions of logging on.

He would check his messages. Do some more searches on Guyana. On Savoy. On Andrew Goodings.

A name, a link, something might turn up.

Then the need in Dru's voice hit him again and his fingers rebelled. He tried again to read behind her voice, analyzing every nuance, every inflection, every breath. She had practically screamed his name. Begged him not to hang up. She, Dru, who had recoiled from him barely twenty-four hours earlier.

He felt a rush of warmth. Dare he think it? Had she in those twenty-four hours changed her mind about him? Had she learned something about him that made her realize that he was not the evil creature she made him out to be?

If only it were so!

Maybe she was having a nervous breakdown. The woman on the phone was not the confident, defiant, risk-taking Dru he knew. And there *was* that crazy talk about seeing Ramy. Had she cracked under the pressure of closing the Savoy deal, under the suspicions surrounding Andrew's sudden, inexplicable death, the thought that someone inside Pilgrim Boone might be implicated in that death?

The knock on the door was sharper this time, startling him again. He stood up, frowning. He approached the door cautiously, his body tense. He was expecting no one. The evening maid had already come and gone. If the front desk needed him for anything they would call first. No one would—no one *should*, the hotel had warned when he checked in—show up unannounced.

He stopped a few inches from the door. "Yes? Who is it?" He made his voice gruff, a warning to whoever was on the other side of the door.

"Mr. St. Cyr?"

Theron did not recognize the voice, but he noted the educated pronunciation of his name, the unmistakable authority of the tone. The voice belonged to someone "with position," as the Guyanese would say.

"Yes?" He kept his own voice harsh, but moved closer to the door and waited.

"Good evening, Mr. St. Cyr. We're sorry to disturb you, but we'd like a word with you, if you please. I am Compton Dalrymple and my partner, Nelson Roopnaraine, is with me. We are the principals of the firm Roopnaraine and Dalrymple, Traders & Consultants Ltd. You've probably heard of us?"

Theron ignored the question.

"Why didn't you call up first, which, I'm sure you know, would have been the proper thing to do since we do not know each other?"

"Point well taken, Mr. St. Cyr. But it is an unusual circumstance that brings us here. It concerns—"

Dalrymple paused, and then continued in a lower voice. Theron imagined him looking around furtively and leaning into the door.

"It concerns your friends Drucilla Durane and Andrew Goodings."

Theron's entire body went rigid at the mention of the two names that were most on his mind. He let the man's statement hang in silence for a few seconds.

A slight shuffling and whispering on the other side of the door told him that his silence was having its desired effect. He smiled grimly. Good. Silence is as effective a defense weapon as any other.

"Mr. St. Cyr?" The same voice, this time with a hint of irritation, just enough for Theron not to miss.

"Give me a minute, please," Theron said. He tiptoed back to the desk, picked up the phone and dialed the front desk. It was picked up before the second ring.

"Good evening. This is the Front Desk. Sharon speaking. How may I help you?"

St. Cyr recognized the voice of the young woman who had registered him earlier. The one with the watery gray-flecked eyes and the playful, bucktooth smile.

"Hello, Sharon. This is Mr. St. Cyr. Has anyone asked for me this evening?"

"Oh, Mr. St. Cyr. Didn't Mr. Dalrymple and Mr. Roopnaraine get there yet? They came just a short while ago. They asked me for your room number, I gave it to them and they went straight up. They said you were expecting them. They should have reached your room already."

"No. They have not yet arrived. Are you sure you saw them? I mean, you do know what they look like?"

If the girl was offended, she did not show it in her voice. "Yes, I'm quite sure I saw them, Mr. St. Cyr. Mr. Dalrymple and Mr. Roopnaraine are very well known to us at the Pegasus. They are well known in all of Georgetown, for that matter. Not to worry, Sir. They should be there any minute now. They may have run into someone they know and stopped to chat. Those gentlemen know just about everyone who stays here regularly."

"As a matter of fact, I think I hear them now. Thank you, Sharon." Theron put down the phone and went to open the door. He immediately recognized Dalrymple and Roopnaraine as the men who had met Dru at the airport.

The black one smiled at him apologetically. Theron did not return his smile. The East Indian looked like he thought that being there was a waste of his time. Theron ignored him.

"Please come in," he said. He kept his voice formal and addressed only the black one.

Dalrymple and Roopnaraine stepped in. Both men looked around quickly, as if to make sure St. Cyr was alone. Their movements were identical, Theron noticed with amusement.

He waved them to the two armchairs in the room. He had not taken a suite, figuring he would be at the hotel for no more than a couple of days. A suite would have been an extravagance he never would have been able to justify to Claude, his firm's eagle-eyed accountant and chief financial officer.

He swung around the chair at the desk, sat down, and faced his visitors, his eyes riveted on Dalrymple. He waited for one or the other of them to speak. The Indian one, obviously Roopnaraine, judging by the name, still had his mouth set.

Dalrymple spoke. "Again, we apologize for the intrusion, Mr. St. Cyr—"

"You mentioned Andrew Goodings and Drucilla Durane. What about them, Mr. Dalrymple?"

Dalrymple bristled at the slight. Roopnaraine tried to hide a smile but Theron caught it. It was an I-told-you-so smile. His eyes met Roopnaraine's and held. They assessed each other, not sure whether they should continue pretending to ignore each other or not.

"Okay, Mr. St. Cyr. We'll dispense with the civilities," Dalrymple said crisply. He sat forward in the chair and fixed Theron with a cool but candid gaze. This scenario was nothing new for someone who used to be a Senior Government Official.

Now it was Theron's turn to try to hide a smile. He was well-schooled in the body language of senior government officials. Theirs was a universal language.

A flicker of his eyes in Roopnaraine's direction told him his attempt to hide his smile had failed. Roopnaraine was staring at him intently.

Theron sat back in his chair, folded his arms across his chest, and waited for Dalrymple to continue. He had already decided that these two had something revealing to say.

"No doubt you've confirmed our identities with Sharon at the front desk. That's good. It means we won't be distracted by any dark suspicions," Dalrymple continued dispassionately. "And by now, Mr. St. Cyr, you should also have learned that we are intermediaries for Pilgrim Boone in the negotiations on Savoy's proposal. Understandably, the government's consideration of that proposal has virtually stalled. But it had stalled long before the death of Andrew Goodings. We know that the reason for the stand-down has to do with the questions raised by Goodings prior to his death. What those questions were, however, we have absolutely no idea. We do know—everyone knows—that Goodings was a zealous nationalist. There's no telling what he saw behind Savoy's proposal. For our part, it was a straightforward deal that we were in a position to facilitate: Savoy wants to set up an air transport system in the interior of Guyana, and once that system is in place, Savoy will make a ton of money selling and servicing the planes to keep it going. Everyone else wins, too. Guyana and the Guyanese people will benefit from the new investment in the interior that would certainly follow the establishment of a proper transportation infrastructure. Tourists will have easier access to our amazing hinterland. Foreign investors will consider exploiting the wealth of that hinterland. And my company wins as facilitators of the whole thing. Yes, everyone wins. That is how we saw this deal. That is why we went into it."

He paused. His eyes narrowed and he leaned closer to Theron.

"Then, all of a sudden, Andrew Goodings dies. You can imagine, then, that nothing will move forward pending the outcome of a full investigation of what is already being spoken of as the convenient removal of a spoke in the wheel. This puts my firm in a very poor light to say the least, given our connection to Pilgrim Boone, which had every interest in bringing the Savoy discussions to a speedy close in their favor. People are beginning to draw conclusions that are not flattering to my firm, Mr. St. Cyr."

"And what does all this have to do with me?" Theron knew the question was naïve, but he felt he needed to ask it, if only to interrupt Dalrymple's pompous soliloquy.

Dalrymple looked at him with contempt. "Don't insult our intelligence, Mr. St. Cyr. We know you saw Drucilla Durane with us at the airport just as we saw you there with Liv—Andrew Goodings. What exactly your connection is to all this, we do not know for sure. We did an Internet search before we came here and found out about your firm and the kind of work you do, so we assume that Goodings brought you in to quietly check things out behind the scenes."

Dalrymple paused, but his gaze never wavered from Theron's face.

Dalrymple was no novice at wielding the weapon of words. One made it, and survived, in government by doing so. Well before his appointment to the Transportation Ministry, he had learned to accurately read the effect of words spoken in certain tones in certain situations. He had become a master at eliciting whatever response he desired from someone after spending just a few minutes in that person's presence. These were skills that have contributed tremendously to his success in consulting. How many times had he told Nelson that politics and consulting were on the same psycho plane? Whatever psycho-tactics got you what you wanted in one of those fields, you could be damned sure the same tactics would get you what you wanted in the other.

Theron St. Cyr's stubbornly impassive expression told Dalrymple that he had guessed right: St. Cyr was a snoop for the government. Fair enough. Governments, too, were entitled to their share of due diligence.

"Have you ever heard of a man called Alejandro Bernat, Mr. St. Cyr?" Dalrymple asked abruptly.

St. Cyr frowned. Instinct told him that Dalrymple had spoken truthfully so far. Their reason for coming to see him was clear. They believed Andrew had been murdered and they wanted their names to be free and clear of any association with that murder. They would use every piece of information they had, raise every connection, however absurd it might seem, to preserve the image that brought them contracts with the likes of Pilgrim Boone.

Which was why the name that Dalrymple had thrown out—this Alejandro Bernat—was a name that he knew was the link he had been searching for.

"No, I don't know that name," he said. "Why?"

Roopnaraine, who also had not taken his eyes off Theron, knew there and then that the standoff was over. They had crossed the line to the side of trust.

He turned away from Theron and looked knowingly at Dalrymple. Dalrymple returned the look with a smile. Then both men turned back to St. Cyr at the same time, as if on cue.

Theron studied them anew. The tension had disappeared from their faces. It occurred to him that, up till now, from the time both men had entered his room, they had engaged in a ritual with which he was very familiar.

He relaxed. He was beginning to feel a certain *sympathie* toward these two. Like him, they were consultants. It was all about the contract.

They told him everything. Almost. About their relationship with Pilgrim Boone. How it started, how it had gotten to where it was. They told him about the meeting with Dru and MacPherson at which Dalrymple was present. About the mention of the name Alejandro Bernat and the possible tie-in with the Alejandro in Venezuela. About their horror at the news of Goodings's death. About their conviction that it was murder.

They did not tell him about Dru's attempt to implicate him in the murder, although they had come prepared to tell him even that. In that uncanny way they shared, in that knowing between them that required neither words nor eye contact for confirmation, each had decided that the information about Dru had no place in their conversation with St. Cyr. Their decision had everything to do with the subtle deepening they both saw in St. Cyr's eyes when Dru's name was mentioned. Right now, it was not their place to intrude on whatever was going on between those two. Besides, the information had no value in the scheme of things.

It was well into the night when Theron said, "Mind if I turn on my computer? We can look up this Bernat guy."

"By all means," Roopnaraine said eagerly. He had been throwing hungry looks at the laptop from the moment they had sat down. It was the very model he wanted. Sleek. State of the art. Performed as fast as the speed of thought, the TV commercial said. It was available only in Japan, and cost at least eight thousand U.S.

Theron turned to it and logged on. Dalrymple and Roopnaraine rose quickly from their chairs and stood behind him, staring in open-mouthed admiration at the rapid-fire switches of the screen as Theron's fingers flew across the keyboard.

The flight of Theron's fingers finally ended and the screen lingered on the single page of search results for the name "Alejandro Bernat." He clicked on one of the links, bringing up a photo file of the man. There were photographs of him from his youth to the present. Above the pictures, a single no-frills list.

Name: Bernat, Alejandro Samorante.

Place of birth: Caracas, Venezuela.

Date of birth: C. 1945 -

Country of residence: Venezuela.

Occupation: Real estate developer.

Bernat was alone in some of the shots. In others, he was in the company of men and women, many of whom Theron recognized as members of the world's most elite business and social circles.

Theron scrolled down. More of the same. Bernat the international business tycoon. Bernat the globe-trotting socialite. Bernat the gentleman farmer. A slew of innocent, flattering pictures, and captions.

Then there it was. The very last shot. On the very last page.

Simultaneously, the three men gasped.

22

For the first time in his life, Grant Featherhorn knew the dizzying, orgasmic feeling of absolute power. He relished the feeling, as he always knew he would. It even gave him an erection. Power was something he had craved since his early days on the Inner Circle track at Pilgrim Boone, more than two decades ago. He could pinpoint the very day that craving began. It was the day he had witnessed Lawton Pilgrim unleash the full force of his power against his own friend. The friend deserved it.

Friends, Featherhorn had determined then, did not matter. You could not count on their loyalty. Only power was loyal. Therefore, only power mattered.

He stepped jauntily along the deserted hallway, lovingly fingering the rich cherry paneling, the gilded picture frames, the stainless steel nameplates and doorknobs.

"To think, it is I who now reign over this. All of it," he breathed in wonderment.

He recalled his conversation with Pilgrim the day before. For a few gut-twisting moments during that conversation he thought he would lose it all, everything he had set up so carefully these last two years with Bernat.

He had met Bernat on his first trip to Venezuela, at a reception the American Chamber of Commerce in Caracas hosted to introduce the newly appointed president of Pilgrim Boone's Latin America/Caribbean division to the country's movers and shakers. He and Bernat had clicked instantly, and Bernat had aggressively cultivated the relationship since then. He must have seen a kindred spirit, Featherhorn chuckled, remembering how often Bernat had flown him from Caracas in his private helicopter to his ranch.

At first, these visits were purely social. He would party with a few of Bernat's friends, or simply relax quietly for a weekend. On the quiet weekends, Bernat would rarely bother him. He was free to roam the ranch and he did so, drinking in the pure, sweet air and enjoying the magnificent vistas.

Soon, the tone of the visits changed. Certain movers and shakers began to show up at the ranch when he was there. They spent hours discussing business and politics in the region, especially in Brazil, Argentina, Chile, and Colombia. They were joined on these occasions by men from other Latin American countries, all of them well-known industrialists, with an army brass or two in the mix. Every now and then, one or two European businessmen would join them as well. Sometimes, Bernat would fly the whole group in his Sali to neighboring countries to survey his land holdings and farm operations. Once, they even flew to France.

Featherhorn was totally and unashamedly spellbound by Bernat's wealth, his investments, his influence. Truth be told, he was enthralled by the lifestyle of the rich and powerful in Latin America, period. He had seen wealth and high living in the States, but what he had seen was nothing like this. This was feudalism pure and simple. There was no other word for it. What else could you call a system where legions of peons spent their entire lives in bondage to men of unimaginable wealth, men who owned tens of thousands of acres of land? These peons were Indians, poor whites, blacks, mixed breeds—all bound in obsequious servitude in a society where they lacked choices.

Featherhorn was fascinated. Oh, the absolute luxury of it!

It wouldn't last, his gut told him. But while it did, it established order. The president of Pilgrim Boone's Latin America/Caribbean division was not about to rock any boats, not while investors the world over appreciated the status quo, not while Pilgrim Boone's clients appreciated the status quo.

In less than a year, thanks to Bernat's connections, he had pulled in a few prize private-sector accounts for Pilgrim Boone. There were none of the big FIS contracts yet. Those would come later, he was sure. For now, it was enough that Pilgrim Boone was snapping at the heels of its competition in the region, gaining on ground hogged by bigger names.

Lawton Pilgrim was ecstatic.

Featherhorn's annual bonus reached staggering amounts. He was becoming a force, a voice to be reckoned with when it came to Latin American business. At the Caribbean Central American Action's annual conference in Miami, where regional heads of state extolled their countries' investment virtues and aired their grievances about U.S. policies toward their struggling economies even as their delegations quietly pandered to corporate powers, lobbying firms, and consultants, it was Featherhorn's words that the press quoted most.

Featherhorn never made much of his intimacy with Alejandro Bernat in his confidential reports for Pilgrim Boone. In fact, he never mentioned Bernat at all in his reports. Why? He couldn't exactly put his finger on it. Suspicious by nature, it had occurred to him that Bernat either might be setting him up or he might be using their connection as a cover for some personal gain.

It was that knowing look, that exchange of glances, an arched eyebrow, a strained smile, a too-quick closing of a drawer or hanging up of a phone when he appeared unexpectedly—little signs he caught at seemingly ordinary moments at the ranch that told him there was more going on with Bernat and his highly placed contacts than he was being told.

When, after two years, those little signs amounted to naught, he shrugged them off with relief.

Then, in the early stages of the Savoy negotiations, Bernat told him that he had to win the contract for Savoy by any means necessary. *Any* means, Bernat had repeated, staring at him meaningfully.

And he told him why.

At first, Featherhorn was appalled. Then he was offended. Bernat remained quiet, giving him plenty of time to think.

As the ugly implications of Bernat's words sank in, Featherhorn became enraged. He tossed his head angrily. "No!" he shouted. He would sink the deal first, he rasped, striding back and forth across the marble floor of the patio at Bernat's sprawling hacienda, jabbing the air with his index finger for added emphasis.

How could Bernat even think— He stopped abruptly in front of Bernat, gazing at him with a mix of wonder and rage. Who did this man think he was? Was he talking about Pilgrim Boone? *Pilgrim Boone!*

"This isn't about Pilgrim Boone, Grant. It is about you," Alejandro said patiently.

"It's all the same. I want no part of it. Nothing. Nada! That's not my goddamn thing! How dare you think it is!"

"You are saying, then, that you would give up all you have acquired, thanks to me? The life you have grown accustomed to? That delightful villa you bought in the mountains? The jet I allow you to use for your private affairs? The, er, entertainment you enjoy so much? Ah, Grant. It is now that you understand what we truly mean by the expression *gozar de la vida*. Your barbaric English language cannot begin to convey the depth of that expression. It is so much more than your "enjoy life." And you would give it all up?" Bernat tut-tutted and shook his head with feigned disappointment.

Featherhorn did not respond.

Bernat continued, goading Featherhorn with his patronizing voice. "But what am I saying? All those things are so very banal. And you are not a common man. In the end, you can live without those luxuries. But," he paused and swept the air with a meticulously manicured hand adorned with a single, ancient-looking heavy gold ring on the middle finger, "what you absolutely cannot live without is the power you have acquired. You could not stand to lose that, could you, Grant, this new ability of yours to influence so much that goes on in poor countries like ours?"

Bernat sat forward and looked steadily at Featherhorn, a mixture of amusement and disdain in his eyes.

Featherhorn blinked first. When he did, Bernat sat back, smiled, and puffed on his *Cohiba*, the finest of Cuban cigars.

Featherhorn sat down and looked out at the shimmering tropical horizon.

Bernat, too, looked into the distance. Without turning his head, he spoke to Featherhorn. His voice was just above a whisper.

"No. I don't think so, Grant. And you will have even more power and influence and wealth because of your generous participation in this endeavor, the kind of wealth and power for which you carry so much lust in your heart, in your eyes."

"Lawton Pilgrim would never stand for it. I would be out of Pilgrim Boone in a heartbeat," Featherhorn ventured weakly.

"Lawton Pilgrim will never know."

Featherhorn laughed. "Oh, yes, he would. You don't know the length of that man's reach."

"Yes, I do. And mine is longer."

Featherhorn stared at Bernat, amazed, as always, at the arrogance of the man. Bernat shrugged and held up his hand again, this time to stop Featherhorn from speaking.

"I know, I know. You think I am arrogant. Arrogance has nothing to do with it. I am merely stating facts. Lawton Pilgrim will not be a problem. Your integrity will be protected."

Featherhorn did not miss the mockery in Bernat's voice when he said the word "integrity." He buckled, of course. Bernat had read him right. He lusted after the kind of power Bernat spoke of. If he could have that while maintaining an impeccable reputation, why not go for it? Bernat himself was living proof that it could be done.

And now this, Featherhorn laughed to himself as his thoughts returned to the present. Lawton was dying, and soon Pilgrim Boone would be all his, covering him with an iron cloak of propriety.

He could not believe his good fortune.

For a fleeting moment he wondered if he really needed Bernat and his *endeavor*. But he thrust that thought out of his mind immediately. Too late now. He was in too deep. Bernat would kill him for sure if he backed out.

His thoughts turned to Lawton. Did he suspect anything? He didn't like the way he had pressed him about his relationship with Bernat. Lawton was a tricky bastard. You never knew what information he had until he dropped it on you.

But it didn't matter now what information he had, did it? He, Featherhorn, held the upper hand.

Smelling like a rose, he chuckled.

He reached his office, closed the door, and leaned against it. He put his hand on his crotch and fondled his erection. Jesus! He really needed to get laid.

He did a fast mental scroll-through of his address book. At a certain name he stopped, unconsciously pursing his lips as if savoring what was to come. He pulled out his cell phone, punched in a single number, and hit the Dial button.

"I'm waiting," said a voice with music in it.

"Good."

He flipped the phone shut, pocketed it, grabbed his jacket, and bolted from the office.

23

The taxi pulled up at the Park Avenue address.

A liveried doorman stepped briskly from the apartment building and crossed the sidewalk to the curb. He opened the passenger door of the cab and stood aside, stiff-backed, until the passenger had paid the fare.

"Any more luggage, Sir?" he asked as the man emerged grasping the handle of a burnished-leather overnight bag.

"Just one suitcase in the trunk, thank you," the man said.

He had a French accent, the doorman noted. And, judging by the cut and fabric of his clothes, he was *real* French. One who spoke the French of Bonaparte.

That's right, the doorman thought defiantly. *Bonaparte!* All those people who looked at him with their dismissive eyes would never dream that a mere doorman knew about Bonaparte. But history was the one subject this particular doorman had excelled in at high school, thanks, mainly, to the teacher he had had. Mrs. Robinson. She had brought history to life, recounting the stories of men of like Hammurabai, king of Babylon. Darius, king of Persia, and after him, Xerxes. Hannibal, the great military commander of Carthage. And Napoleon Bonaparte, emperor of France. Yes, he knew his history. Just like he knew accents. And he could tell the difference between the French of France and that other stuff that Canadians and Haitians and Africans spoke. After twenty years on the job here, with all those Europeans coming and going, why, he'd even picked up a few words from their various languages: French, Spanish, German, even Swedish. He could give the standard greetings in all of them.

The doorman removed a leather suitcase from the trunk. It matched the overnight bag the man carried, he observed. He slammed the trunk shut and tapped the backside of the car to send the cabbie on his way.

The man, meanwhile, had remained on the sidewalk, looking around and up, craning his neck as if trying to count the floors of the buildings.

"Shall we go in, Sir?" the doorman said when the man brought his eyes back to street level.

The man turned to him with a smile. "Certainly," he said.

The doorman almost stumbled as he caught his first full view of the man's face. *Well, I'll be damned! A black Frenchman!* He recovered quickly, though. At least he hoped he did. It wouldn't do to display emotion in front of the guests. No, it wouldn't do at all. This man could pass for white, but he's definitely got a piece of Africa in him. Can't fool old Oswald when it comes to that. No, sir. Not this Oswald at all.

He smiled back at the man. Nice to see one of *us* coming to stay in this building. Now watch this jet-black doorman blow you for six, young fella, he thought gleefully.

"*Soyez le bienvenu à New York, patron,*" he said in flawless Bonaparte as they moved toward the entrance to the lobby.

The man stopped, turned again to him, and grinned. "*Merci, monsieur—*" He squinted at the doorman's badge. "Oswald. *C'est Oswald, n'est-ce pas? Oui. C'est ça. Merci, Oswald.*"

Oswald inclined his head. "*Après vous, patron,*" he beamed, gesturing to the open door. Bet he thinks I'm a native, he thought, lifting his chest a little higher.

"May I ring someone for you, Sir?" Oswald said in English when they reached the reception desk. He had reached his limit with the French. No need to ruin the impression he had made on the visitor.

"Actually, no. No one is home at this time. But I do have a key. I'll just go up on my own," the man responded easily in English, reaching for his suitcase.

"Oh, I'd be glad to help you with that, Sir," Oswald said quickly, appreciating the man's decency for not pressing on in French. He didn't doubt for a moment that the man knew he had exhausted his vocabulary. That's how you can tell the difference between people with breeding and people who were just rich, he thought for the umpteenth time in his Park Avenue career. *Manners.* True aristocrats, the true nobility, they have the manners.

"Not at all. I can manage," the man said. He gripped the suitcase firmly as he straightened up.

Their eyes met and held for a fraction of a second. Recognition and understanding passed between them. *We're the same.*

Oswald lowered his eyes first. "Would you mind signing in, Sir? House rules, I'm afraid, Sir. It is your first visit here," he said, stating the obvious.

"Indeed, yes. And no, I do not mind signing in at all. I was informed of the rules."

He printed his name, "François Lescault," and signed it with an indecipherable flourish. A real European signature that nobody can imitate, Oswald noted appreciatively. He had seen enough of them in his years on the desk.

"Thank you, Sir. May I know what floor, Sir?"

"Seven. I've already written it next to my signature."

Oswald glanced at the register. "My apologies, Sir. I overlooked it. Thank you, Sir. The elevator is to your left. Have a good day, Sir."

"*Merci*, Oswald."

Oswald studied the register as the man walked toward the elevator. Can't be too careful, he thought. You have to make these strangers tell you what it is they wrote down. See if the two match. Lots of high-class scamps around these days—white, black, and in between.

256

He leaned forward discreetly to get another look at the visitor but the man had already stepped into the elevator. Oswald looked at the register again. Apartment 7B, eh? And he has a key. Black man, too. A Paris man.

He shook his head and sighed. Oh, well. Like I been sayin', Oswald, my boy, times ain't changin', they revoltin'.

"Yep. Times is just plain revoltin'," he said aloud.

Half an hour later, François Lescault emerged from the steaming shower, feeling totally refreshed.

He rubbed himself vigorously with one of the huge Egyptian cotton towels he had found in the bathroom, grunting contentedly at the tingling sensation created by the friction of the towel on his bare skin. Not that the flight from Paris had sapped his energy. He was used to traveling from one continent to another at a moment's notice. The term *jet lag* had no meaning for him; no place in his lexicon. He hit the ground running wherever he landed.

He secured the towel around his waist and went into the kitchen. The owner of the apartment, Natalie Giroux, was a middle-aged, French-born naturalized American citizen who liked his company whenever she returned to France. She had told him he could stay at her place for a few days if ever he was in New York and needed a place to stay, provided she was away—as she now was.

She had stocked the refrigerator with some of the best gourmet French dishes, brought in, no doubt, from some choice restaurant like The Four Seasons. He had traveled first class, but he had not eaten much during the flight and was ravenous. He decided there and then to sample all of the dishes at once.

In no time he had located plates, cutlery, glasses, and wine. He dined formally in the dining room, savoring the food and wine. As he dined, his thoughts drifted to the assignments that had brought him to New York.

"Keep an eye on Grant Featherhorn, a woman named Drucilla Durane, and a man named Theron St. Cyr. St. Cyr is a Frenchman, like you. There's plenty of local talent that you can use. I'll let you know if and when further action is necessary," Bernat had said.

24

Theron plowed through some of the most eclectic and protected databases, automatically filtering out results where "Alejandro" and "Bernat" occurred separately, and entries that were repeats, even if they were housed in different databases.

As far as he knew, he was one of a handful of people in the world who had access to these databases. They had been found and hacked by the genius brother of a young woman who had been abducted at Orly Airport in Paris. The girl had just arrived from Vietnam to begin her first semester as an undergraduate at the Sorbonne. She was the perfect pigeon: alone, eager, careless.

Grief-stricken and enraged, the brother had torn through the dungeons of the Web, a cyber tornado, until he came across Theron's code name and contact information. He had made contact immediately and offered his services to Theron's outfit. He demanded pictures of every suspected kidnapper known to Theron. He came to Theron, he said, because he had no time for the official bureaucracies that lumbered through these cases, and also because he had plans for the animal that had taken his sister, plans no authorities had any business knowing about, he added grimly.

Theron did not hesitate. The memory of Tabatha's mutilated torso was still fresh in his mind. He e-mailed hundreds of pictures to the young man in Vietnam known only to him as "Sanspaix." *Without peace.* Among them were pictures that no intelligence agency had, pictures gleaned from the files of the various underground and underbelly groups that prowled about in cyberspace chasing their respective quarries.

Theron's torment over his own sister's death had led him to the very bowels of Europe's biggest cities, into the lairs of some of these nether-world groups. He and Sanspaix communicated frequently. A month after their first contact, Theron received a happy but gruesome e-mail from Sanspaix.

"My sister is home. She is safe, but not sound. It will take much time for her to heal," the electronic note said. "I am grateful to you. Below are two gifts for you. You will not hear from Sanspaix again. But I will always be here when you need me."

Scrolling down, St. Cyr had come upon a high-resolution picture that made him look away and retch. It was a scene in the middle of what looked like a tropical jungle. It showed the body of a man who had been strung taut between four trees. He had been tied with dried sisal rope and it had cut deeply into his flesh. The photo had been taken from the front and he clearly had been whipped to death with the bloodied length of barbed wire draped across the pulpy, reddish-black mass that his body had become. He had been beaten from head to toe. Caught in the picture were swarms of giant blue flies with tiny rainbow wings feeding along the entire length of his body.

The dead man's eyes, what was left of them, were bulbous and staring. His mouth stretched grotesquely, baring his teeth where blows had stripped away his lips. Theron knew he had had died in excruciating pain, bawling for mercy, or death.

There was no caption. There was no need for one.

When he turned back to the screen again, Theron kept his eyes tightly closed as he scrolled away from the picture. He opened them to a mug shot of a known trafficker of women and girls. It was one of the pictures that he had sent to Sanspaix.

The message was clear. This was the identity of the dead man.

Theron stared at the picture for a long time, wondering if this man had also been one of Tabatha's abductors and killers.

Finally, he shrugged and scrolled down again. "Good riddance, bastard," he said aloud.

He came to a link near the bottom of the e-mail and clicked on it. A blank screen appeared and stayed there. Silent. Empty. He was about to hit "Return" when words began to roll across the screen.

"Brother in pain, the link that brought you here will vanish forever as soon as you close the e-mail so be sure to memorize the addresses and passwords on this page. It is a page that gives you access to some of the most highly classified intelligence databases. Once you end a search, all record of it will vanish. Just like these words. *Pouf!*"

And vanish the words did. Theron accessed one of the databases and a keyword prompt came up instantly. Just for the heck of it, Theron typed in the name Ramajun Musar. The picture and description that came up made him shudder. Ramajun "Ramy" Musar was a sadist whose criminal activities no ordinary human mind could imagine.

Half an hour later he found the reason why Ramy had gone unpunished so long. Buried deep, in fine print, his name was on a list of "Special Intelligence Operatives," or S.I.O.s.

Ramy had been an informant for American, British, French, and Israeli intelligence. Freedom was the price he had exacted from them all. Freedom, and a blind eye to his indulgences.

Theron pounded his fist on the desk for several minutes in utter despair. How many more? he moaned. How many more of him are there?

That very night, he gave up his crusade against the abductors of women and girls. Two days later, he caught a flight to Dominica, a quiet, pristine little island in the eastern Caribbean that few tourists had discovered. He spent a month there taking stock of his life.

On his way back to France he stopped in New York for a few days and engaged a few well-positioned, trusted friends in long discussions on the U.S. and world economic trends, global politics, the state of the black America and the rest of the African diaspora, and business opportunities.

By the time he got back to France he had a plan. Less than a month later, Trans-Global Solutions was in business.

Trans-Global had brought him to Andrew Goodings, Guyana, and the two men who were standing behind him with as much shock on their faces as his.

"It can't be! No way!"

Dalrymple's outburst jarred the others out of the shock caused by the picture on the screen. He moved quickly from behind St. Cyr and leaned into the screen, squinting hard, touching the face of the woman in the picture with his finger.

Still touching her face, he turned to Roopnaraine. His eyes were wide and questioning.

Roopnaraine's mouth was open and his head was moving from side to side. His eyes finally met Dalrymple's and silently confirmed what they both knew. Yes. It was she. The picture was as clear as day. It was Leila.

Dalrymple swung back to the screen. His hand dropped listlessly to his side. He began to speak. His words came out in a pitiful stutter.

"But...but....What is she?... How does she?..."

He broke off and turned to St. Cyr as if he could provide the answers. As if *he* could give a reasonable explanation about what this ordinary Guyanese woman, *his woman*, was doing with the two men in the picture captioned "Alejandro Bernat, Ramajun Musar and unidentified woman."

Theron, meanwhile, had fallen back in the chair and was staring at the picture on the screen. His arms hung limply over the sides of the chair.

Finally, he turned first to Roopnaraine, then to Dalrymple. Dalrymple's eyes opened even wider when he saw the expression on Theron's face.

"You know this woman?" Theron asked in a dull voice.

Dalrymple nodded.

Theron shifted his gaze to Roopnaraine, who also nodded.

"Who is she?"

"Her name is Leila. She's my...she is my...." Dalrymple seemed embarrassed.

"She's supposed to be his mistress," Roopnaraine said gratingly.

"And you know for sure that she's Guyanese." It was more a statement than a question.

"Yes. How can she not be? She's from Pakaraima."

"You've known her long, then." Again an assertion rather than a question.

"About a year."

"That's just about the time the negotiations on the Savoy deal began. How…"

Roopnaraine could stand it no longer. Compton clearly was still in shock. Just look at him, spouting out answers like a blasted machine. He could be implicating himself in God-knows-what without even knowing it. After all, what did they really know about this St. Cyr, with his state-of-the-art computer and search tricks no ordinary person could ever know?

He speared Theron with his eyes and cut him off gruffly. "Mr. St. Cyr, do you know something about this woman?"

Theron returned Roopnaraine's stare through half-closed eyes. Roopnaraine could not help noticing how drawn he was. Three deep lines had suddenly etched themselves into his forehead.

"This woman, Mr. Roopnaraine, is what they call in the European underworld *an operator*. Operators usually are owned by, and operate on behalf of, someone high up in the drug trade or some other criminal activity. They kill, steal, sabotage, you name it. They are deadly but smooth, so smooth they slip in and out of normal, everyday lives, and even in and out of high society, with ease. I have seen this woman's picture before, but I never had cause to investigate her. She was never linked to what I was involved with at the time."

"So she is—Leila is Bernat's buck-girl mistress." Dalrymple's voice was almost a whisper. Before anyone could say anything, he half-staggered to one of the chairs and plopped into it like a deflated sack. Compton Dalrymple was a broken man. And a frightened man.

Theron felt sorry for him. He had already made the connection with the story of the man in Venezuela named Alejandro. Dalrymple had every reason to be afraid. He had been sleeping with the mistress of Alejandro Bernat. Coincidence or strategy?

"And you, Mr. St. Cyr. You know the second man in the picture, don't you?" Roopnaraine's voice was still harsh. He was growing more and more desperate to de-link Compton from the crazy picture Theron St. Cyr was drawing about underworlds and operators and sabotage and murder. This wasn't no flippin' Hollywood. This was Guyana. Leila was a Guyanese woman. Since when did Guyanese women, and a country girl at that, know about that kind of life, much less get mixed up in it? There must be a simple explanation for that picture.

Besides, he didn't like the idea of some Franco-American, or whatever the hell he was with his funny accent, pitying his best friend. Oh, yes, he had seen the look St. Cyr gave him.

Theron sighed and shook his head. He understood Roopnaraine's protectiveness.

"Yes. I know him. He is dead now, thank God. May his soul forever rot in hell. He is from a time and a circumstance I thought I would never have to recall. You do not want to know of these things."

"No, I definitely don't."

The silence between them hung heavy and long. Grudgingly, Roopnaraine pushed his anger aside and conceded that St. Cyr probably knew what he was talking about. He didn't look or sound like a man who would just make up a story like that. He also seemed genuinely shaken by the whole thing.

Roopnaraine spoke first, addressing Theron. "So what's this Ramy doing with Bernat and Leila?"

In response, St. Cyr turned back to his laptop. He aimed the cursor at the picture and clicked. A page of text appeared instantly. Roopnaraine moved closer and the two men read it together. They read silently, for the most part. Every now and then one or the other would mutter a sentence aloud.

The source of the report was one of the anonymous underground groups that fed information to crusaders for "the good of human society, the earth, and the environment." Theron had dealt directly with them before he closed down his Tabatha project.

The report estimated, admittedly on circumstantial evidence only, that

Alejandro Bernat was one of Latin America's biggest drug lords who, so far, had steered clear of every Venezuelan and international law enforcement and intelligence agency. That he had "friends" in these agencies went without question, the report said. How else could he maintain such a squeaky-clean façade? How else could he move so freely in the world of blueblood? So far, however, no one has been able to finger any of these "friends."

The other man in the picture, the report went on to detail, was Ramajun Musar, a trafficker in women, body parts, and every variety of hard drug that exist. He had been stabbed to death, supposedly in a botched delivery of kidnapped teenage girls to the middleman for a slave owner in Amsterdam. He was one of the "brokers" in Bernat's drug empire. Unknown to Bernat, he was also an informant for all the major intelligence agencies. It is said that he was deliberately killed because some of his human-parts retrieval activities had become too demonic even for the agencies that protected him."

Roopnaraine inhaled deeply and exhaled with a sound of disgust.

"Right!" Theron muttered in agreement.

The report went on to estimate that Bernat should be desperate for new transshipment routes since U.S. authorities in their latest assault on drug trafficking were shutting down the known routes. The U.S. now had a new, far more sophisticated electronic arsenal in the form of a closet high school genius who had hacked his way into the labyrinthine global supply chain of illicit drugs while looking for a way to extricate himself and his family from trailer camp poverty.

Since he had no computer of his own, the genius had used one in the school library to run his operation. A fellow genius, suspicious of his rival's sudden, unexplained manifestations of the easy life, followed his electronic footprints on the library computer and snitched to the feds. Instead of locking the genius away, the feds put his talents to use.

"They resemble a bit, Bernat and Musar," Roopnaraine said, gazing at the laptop screen.

"Yes, I noticed that," Theron said slowly. He turned to Roopnaraine. "Tell me, would you be able to find out if this Bernat is in Guyana? Or if he has been here in the last few days?"

"We could try. Why?"

"Just a hunch."

Roopnaraine waited for more, but Theron said nothing further.

"So Bernat must have a connection inside Savoy," Roopnaraine said.

"Or in Pilgrim Boone," Theron said, looking him dead in the eye.

"I was hoping you wouldn't say that."

"Why? Your contract with them means that much to you?"

Roopnaraine smiled and glanced at Dalrymple, who was still slumped in his chair with his eyes closed. Roopnaraine knew he wasn't asleep. Theron, following Roopnaraine's glance, knew it too.

Taking his cue from Roopnaraine, Theron kept his eyes trained on Dalrymple and remained silent.

They waited.

Dalrymple did not disappoint them. He sat up abruptly.

"It damn well doesn't," he exploded, shaking his head from side to side. "As far as I'm concerned, that contract is shredded!"

He took a deep breath and exhaled slowly, as if ridding himself of every attachment to Pilgrim Boone, Savoy, and Leila, whatever role she might be playing.

"Any idea who Bernat could be hooked into at Pilgrim Boone?" he asked, turning to face St. Cyr.

St. Cyr did not hesitate. "Featherhorn. A man named Grant Featherhorn."

Dalrymple shot up from his chair and stood over St. Cyr, looking down at him as if he had taken leave of his senses. "Did you say Grant Featherhorn?"

"You heard me."

Dalrymple threw up his hands up and turned away, rolling his eyes.

"That's highly unlikely, Mr. St. Cyr," Roopnaraine said with amusement. "Grant Featherhorn is Pilgrim Boone's top man in the entire Caribbean and Latin America region. You want to tell me *he's* mixed up in running drugs? Drugs? Like a common criminal? I sincerely doubt that."

"What makes you think he's the one?" Dalrymple said.

"Some things someone said. A gut feeling. But you've both dealt with him. What kind of man is he?"

"Well—" Roopnaraine hesitated. He did not like Featherhorn, although he could not say why. He knew Dalrymple felt the same way about him. They had discussed it on more than one occasion. They even felt guilty about their feelings because Featherhorn had been nothing but professional, even humorous at times, whenever they met.

Maybe their dislike had to do with a coolness they saw—felt, rather—between Dru and him. They couldn't put a finger on it because Featherhorn and Dru were always cordial to each other in public. Still, Dru always seemed to freeze up a bit when he was around. She never got close to him physically either. It was as if she found him repulsive.

For his part, Featherhorn treated Dru with the utmost respect, always soliciting her input and making a big show of giving her ideas careful consideration. And yet...

Roopnaraine looked at Dalrymple helplessly.

"Please, take your time," Theron said with exaggerated patience.

"Well, he's...he's...er...most professional," Dalrymple volunteered. "That much I can say. A very competent man. And democratic. Yes, that's it. Democratic. Everyone's ideas were important to him. He..."

"You both hate his guts, don't you?" Theron interrupted impatiently.

"Well, er, hate might be too strong a word, Mr. St. Cyr. It's more a matter of—"

"How does he treat Dru?" Theron knew he was being rude but he was beyond caring.

"What do you mean 'How does he treat Dru?' "

"He treats her like shit, doesn't he? On the surface, he seems all goody-goody and professional and nice. But she hates him, he hates her, and you two saw that, didn't you?"

"Er—"

"Didn't you!" Theron was shouting now. "Why don't you say it? Why do you want to defend him?"

"Because deep down he's the type of man who would crush you like a mosquito without a second thought, that's why!" Dalrymple snapped before he could stop himself.

They all stared at each other in silence.

"That's it. That's it, Nelson. I never realized it till now," Dalrymple continued, dropping into his chair again. His chin dropped to his chest and he sighed.

"Nelson," he said glumly, without raising his head, "remember that time when Dru was in your office and Featherhorn called her there from New York? Remember how she looked before she picked up the phone? Remember the face she made after she talked to him? We figured it out then, didn't we?"

25

"They're in his room now."

The breathing on the other end of the telephone line changed.

It was a barely perceptible change. More like a deepening. No, a lengthening. A lengthening, ever so slight, in the pull-and-push of each breath.

Leila heard it, nonetheless, because she knew him so well.

"How long?" she heard him ask, his voice empty.

The emptiness did not fool her. That subtle change in his breathing belied the anxiety she knew her news had caused. So! There's much more to this tête-à-tête that Compton and Nelson are having with St. Cyr than I imagined, she mused.

Suddenly, she was filled with trepidation, a rush of foreboding that made her hands grow cold and shake. The feeling stunned her. Hadn't she and fear parted company years ago? Why, then, was it here again? Why was it now violating what she had made herself become?

Maybe it's what I *thought* I had made myself become, she thought with dismay.

Her shoulders slumped. She was not afraid for herself. She had stopped coveting her own life long ago. No, this fear wasn't about her. This fear, she realized with shock, this utterly unwanted sensation of being vulnerable, of possessing something so precious that she couldn't bear to lose it, was all about someone else.

Compton! She was afraid of losing Compton Dalrymple!

The realization was at once startling and damning.

How could she? How could she have allowed herself to become so attached to an assignment?

I want to know everything he and his partner know about the Savoy negotiations. Everything and everyone involved, Alejandro had instructed.

And that was all her seduction of Compton Dalrymple one year ago was supposed to yield.

Information.

Maybe it's because he's a good man, she mused.

Yes. Deep down, beneath the bluster and swagger, Compton Dalrymple was a decent man. And so, for that matter, was his best friend, Nelson Roopnaraine.

Andrew Goodings had been a good man, too. She had never regretted an assignment until this one. The newspapers, over several days, had covered his life story in full. The worst thing you could say about Goodings was that he seemed to think that he loved his country more than anyone else; that he knew more than anyone else what was best for Guyanese.

What is it like to have that kind of love? Leila thought. She suddenly thought of her parents and her stomach felt hollow. She hadn't thought of her parents in years.

Why now? She knew the answer, of course. They were good people. Decent people. *You live like a she-dog,* her father had told her two days before he died.

Still feeling the sting of those words, Leila pushed the memory of her parents out of her mind and turned her attention again to Dalrymple and Roopnaraine. What difference did it make that they sometimes bit off more than they could chew with all those contracts from Americans and Asians and Europeans? So what if they made a ton of money because they were good at marketing themselves? Good at getting others to believe they were the best thing in Guyana since *pepperpot.*

And they *were* good. *Are* good.

They knew all the right words, had the right look, the right connections, made all the right moves. How could anyone resist them? And what they delivered wasn't bad, either. It just wasn't worth the big bucks they asked, and got, for it.

But why should she care? Their clients certainly didn't seem to mind paying up, the way they kept going back to them with more work.

And yet Compton and Nelson were so maddeningly predictable, Leila thought, knitting her brow. They shared the same simple view of the world, a view they loved to hold forth on after they had emptied a bottle of XM rum. The way they saw it, the world was divided into rich and poor. Rich people, poor people. Rich countries, poor countries. Anything in between was transitory, en route either to the rich camp or the poor camp.

They also believed that every human being was born equal in the eyes of the universe. That no one had the right to dominate another human being, to rob another human being of his dignity or his life. Everyone was entitled to wealth and abundance, and it was up to each person to make the effort to acquire that wealth and abundance. Being born poor was no excuse. All it took was a dedicated effort, with proper use of the senses God gave you, discipline to put off immediate gratification and the guts and tenacity to smash any obstacle that tried to hold you back. If you couldn't give it that much, then you deserved whatever you got for the crappy effort you made to pull yourself out of the rat hole.

Most important, Compton or Nelson would add, you had to have morals. Plain, decent morals like you learned in Sunday school. If people lived without morals life would be chaos, and when there is chaos, everybody loses.

"And you have to remember," the other would chime in, raising his index finger and wagging it like a preacher sermonizing, "that the sins of the father will be visited upon you, unto the third and fourth generation. It's true! Just look at ol' man Jarvis. The most dishonest judge ever to warm the bench. Terrorized innocent people all over the country! Now look! His own grandson is keeping the jailhouse warm. And let's not even talk about those Kennedys in America. You know what they said about Joe, his connections and how he made his money? And look at what happened to his sons and grandsons. So you see, de Bible don't lie!"

Leila chuckled. She had been the audience for this philosophical outpouring many times since she started seeing Dalrymple. The poor, sweet, simple fools. Alejandro wouldn't have a second thought asking her to get rid of them.

Her heart lurched. She would do it. If she had to take Compton's life, she would do it. She would never disobey Alejandro. She couldn't. Not after all he had done for her.

Or could she?

Her hand flew to her mouth. Simply posing that question was an act of betrayal. For the first time since she and her family had become involved with Alejandro Bernat—and try as she would, she could not remember her life without Alejandro Bernat in it—she had dared to entertain the thought that she might act against his wishes.

Where did that come from? Had she gone mad?

Furious with herself, she mentally lashed out at the cause of her betrayal. Those two jackasses! Why couldn't they just mind their own business? Why the hell were they getting mixed up with St. Cyr?

"How long, Leila?" Bernat repeated. The ominous quiet in his voice sliced into her thoughts.

"A little over an hour," she said into the phone, keeping her own voice neutral, knowing that he had already sensed and analyzed the lapse in her response. Calmly, she waited out the long silence that followed. As she waited, her thoughts, wayward and reckless, turned again to Dalrymple and Roopnaraine.

What a shock it had been to see them come into the hotel lobby at that hour, especially after Compton had told her that he would be at Nelson's house until late that evening. There were no receptions or parties at the hotel. Hardly anyone was in the restaurants or at the bar. The place was deader than a doornail. Not a thing was going on. That was unusual for the Pegasus.

Normally, at this time of the year, the hotel would be teeming with foreigners—business executives negotiating deals, would-be investors,

Caribbean Community officials with matters to resolve at the secretariat downtown, a few tourists, and groups of party-hearty expatriate Guyanese who had come home for their high school reunion.

Now, however, the business people, investors, and Caricom officials were all in Barbados for a regional trade and investment conference. Because the highly influential *Economist* magazine was the organizer, the conference had attracted just about all of the Caricom heads of state and a long list of top government and private-sector speakers and attendees from Europe, North America, and Asia. The word in the snootier commercial and political circles was that anybody who was anybody with business in the region, anyone interested in doing business in the region, or anyone harboring political ambitions in the region, would be a fool to miss it.

Just this morning, Leila had asked Compton why he and Nelson were not attending. Compton had replied testily that they were catching too much hell with the Pilgrim Boone contract to go anywhere. His tone had irritated her. What was he snarling at *her* for? Was it *her* fault that they were catching hell over another one of their contracts that, for all their talk about morals, didn't do a damn thing for poor people anyway? Compton had simply walked out of the house without another word and she, in turn, had simply shrugged and gone about her business.

As for alumni and tourists, Leila thought as she reflected on the scene in the hotel, most of them had been scared away by all the reports of crime in the media.

Ostensibly, she had been hanging out in the lobby with a couple of girlfriends who had come from London to bury their grandmother when Dalrymple and Roopnaraine arrived. In reality, though, she was watching Theron St. Cyr's movements as Alejandro had instructed her to do.

Dalrymple and Roopnaraine had stopped briefly at Reception. Judging from the coy smile and batting eyelids Sharon—Miss Cat Eyes—lavished on Dalrymple, Leila guessed that "lover boy Compton" had turned on the charm and was really pumping it up.

A few minutes later, he and Roopnaraine had headed for the elevators, looking neither left nor right. As they passed within a few feet of her group, she ducked down, pretending to scratch her ankle, making soft hissing sounds as if in pain and causing her girlfriends to tinkle the ice in their rum-and-Pepsis indignantly and grumble that "mosquitoes shouldn't be biting people in a place like this."

Leila did not raise her head again until she heard the elevator *ping* a second time, signaling that it was on its way up. She watched the floor numbers light up as the elevator made its ascent. It stopped only once, at the floor on which St. Cyr had his room, and then made its way down to the lobby again without stopping.

No one got off when the doors whooshed open.

An hour later, Leila's girlfriends stretched, yawned, and announced they were going to bed. Leila kissed them and watched them walk giggly and unsteadily toward the elevators, each one's arm hooked in the other's for support.

The moment the doors closed behind them, Leila moved to a corner of the lobby that was hidden from the front desk and called Alejandro on her cell phone.

His voice, cold and clinical now, dragged her wandering mind back to their conversation.

"You must find out what they talked about. I want to know by tomorrow."

"You will," she said coolly.

"They still have not come down?"

"I can see the elevator from where I am. They have not come down."

Alejandro clicked his tongue against the roof of his mouth. "As I said, I want to know by tomorrow what they spent all this time talking about."

Leila heard the abrupt disconnect and shuddered. Pursing her lips, she snapped her phone shut and shoved it into her handbag.

She sat for a while longer, staring at nothing in particular, her eyebrows pulled together in a deep frown. Then she stood up and headed for the door, her jaw tight with renewed determination.

She would wait in her car in the parking lot until they came out. If they were alone, she would take the shortcut back to her house—the one behind the cemetery that Nelson avoided—and wait for Compton to show up. If they came out with St. Cyr, she would follow them, see where they went, then return to her house.

One way or the other, before the sun rose she would have the information Alejandro needed.

26

Alejandro Bernat stood on the balcony outside his bedroom, delighting, as he never tired of doing, in the endless moon-washed expanse of land that belonged to him. He half-cocked his ear to the early night symphony—a raucous mix of man, beast, and insect.

Every now and then, a familiar song, usually, that drifted up to the balcony from one of the campfires of his watchmen. The lyrics spoke of unrequited love, of a home far away, of dying.

Bernat closed his eyes and inhaled deeply, savoring the fragrance of his Cohiba. This was the time of day he cherished most. It was at this most private time that he put into perspective any new information he had acquired from the legions of people he dealt with during the day.

He never used cocaine at this time. He needed his mind to be razor sharp as he replayed, in the minutest detail, every conversation, every report, every scene that had come before him. Then, he would mix and match new information with old, until everything fit into a picture that, to him, made the utmost sense. And from that picture, he determined the moves he would make the following day, or at some time in the future, if it was a question of acting later than sooner.

The entire ritual lasted two, sometimes three, hours. It was this ritual, this daily discipline and nothing more, that was truly responsible for the charmed life he was rumored to have. For Alejandro Bernat never made a bad move.

His conversation with Leila was on his mind now. She had hesitated at that one, simple question. She, Leila, who never hesitated, whose responses never required thought before she spoke them because she was so utterly detached, now, after all these years, had broken her pattern.

Bernat looked for broken patterns the way predators scoured the sounds and scents in the air. It was the only way a man like him could survive. A broken pattern meant a situation had been compromised. It meant danger lurked nearby.

Ah, Leila! Leila! Leila!

His heart felt like a ball of lead in his chest. The lines of his jaws hardened. His eyes narrowed with resolve. He balled his hand into a fist and pounded it on the marble ledge of the balcony. Cocaine and marijuana production was booming in the Andes. Growers in Bolivia and Peru had already surpassed those in Colombia. He needed that air corridor through Guyana. Let the locals stick to boats. They're babies in this game. "Small thinkers," Bernat scoffed aloud. "Too excited by the fast money to think big."

Bernat rolled his shoulders back and forth and twisted his head from side to side to work the kinks out of his neck. The movements seemed to give a fresh spark to his thoughts. The big picture appeared in sharp focus.

Yes, Guyana was perfect for a visionary like him. The DEA was all over the Caribbean and Central America. And forget Mexico. Too much heat down there. Those crazies weren't content with just killing their own people. They had declared war on the *yanqui* border.

It was an entirely different ball game on the other side of the world. The Asians were more controlled. He liked that. He was still trying to make a connection in that part of the world. Opium use was climbing in Europe and America and the trade out of Afghanistan had skyrocketed, eating into profits from cocaine and weed. There was more land under opium poppy cultivation in Afghanistan alone than all of the land Latin America had in coca. Add Myanmar and the rest of the golden triangle—

Thailand, Vietnam, and Laos—and the total amount of land devoted to opium was mind-boggling. The Afghan warlords were raking in billions. They probably pray every day to their gods that the Americans never leave, Bernat chuckled. Once the Americans had landed and sent the Taliban packing, that was the end of the ban the Taliban had put on opium.

Bernat sighed. He wondered if the opium poppy could be grown in Latin America. Guyana might be just the place to test the idea. Someday I'll find out, he promised himself. Until then, I'll have to find a way to get a piece of Asia. Too bad Ramy hadn't signed off with the cartel in Kyrgyzstan before he got himself killed. I warned him to stay out of the human trade. Wouldn't listen! Pigheaded and disrespectful like the rest of his generation of Bernat blood. God rest his foolish soul.

Alejandro made the sign of the cross. There was no point in dwelling on the excesses of certain members of his extended family. He already knew how and when to put an end to that. Guyana was the priority now, and things there weren't as wrinkle-free as they were supposed to be. That infuriated him. It would all fall his way eventually, he was sure. The authorities could dick around all they wanted over the death of Andrew Goodings. Sooner or later they would agree to what Savoy was offering. They had no choice. Not after he, Alejandro, had made MacPherson see what the consequences of deciding otherwise would be.

He was close. In spite of the delay, nothing and no one could derail his plans. "Not even you, my sweet Leila," he said into the night.

He took a long pull on his cigar and blew rings at the moon. "No, Leila," he said softly as he watched the ascent of each perfectly formed ring. "I simply will not allow it."

He made the sign of the cross again.

⁓⋇⁓

Minutes after the door closed behind Roopnaraine and Dalrymple, St. Cyr whipped out his cell phone and called Transportation Minister Reginald MacPherson.

Andrew had given him the minister's mobile number and e-mail address, with a strict warning that neither was to be used "unless in the most warranted circumstances."

St. Cyr considered this a most warranted circumstance. He had not contacted the minister before now. In fact, he had never spoken to MacPherson, not even after Andrew died.

"MacPherson is not supposed to know anything about you, Theron," Andrew had said. "Not who you are, how you came to be in Guyana, or what you're doing here."

But Andrew had also assured him that the minister had been sufficiently prepped to know that it would be worth his while to accept a call, if one ever came, from the number that belonged to Theron St. Cyr.

"Good evening, Sir. I'm calling to say that I leave tomorrow for the States," St. Cyr said when the minister answered the phone with a perfunctory "Yes?"

"I see."

No questions. No small talk. No names. Goodings was adamant about that. You just never know who's listening, he had said.

At the time St. Cyr had jokingly accused Goodings of living too long in America and watching too much cloak-and-dagger TV. But here was, carrying out Goodings's last instructions to the letter, he thought wryly.

He said to MacPherson: "I learned much from my brief visit. What I learned will be very useful in my work."

"That is very good to hear. It's always gratifying to know that a small country such as mine can be of help to others. Will you come back to visit us again?" There was a hint of excitement in the minister's voice.

"I will. Very soon."

"Wonderful. Safe passage." The minister's phone went silent.

Theron flipped his mobile shut and stuffed it in his shirt pocket. "You would have been proud of me, Andrew," he said under his breath. In that seemingly empty exchange, he had communicated to MacPherson two important pieces of information. One: Andrew's suspicions were right. If they weren't, he would not have promised to return "very soon." Two: he had a good lead and the trail led back to the States, hence his rapid departure. He knew that MacPherson got both messages. Andrew had worked out the language with both of them.

His thoughts switched to New York. He would call Dru, of course, to let her know he was back, and to make sure that she was okay. He had promised her that he would see her when he got back, but now he wasn't sure he wanted to do so. He feared that by now she would have gotten over whatever it was that had spooked her earlier and made her cry out to him. If that were the case, Dru would have already reverted to the frigid, suspicious woman she had been on the plane and in the lobby of the Pegasus. The bruising he had suffered from his encounter with *that* Dru was still raw.

He got up from the desk. He should start to pack. He was glad to be leaving. He still could not believe all that had happened in such a short time. At times he felt as if he were in a nightmare. He would wake up and everything would be normal again. He would be back in his office in New York, juggling projects and upbraiding himself, as he had done in the two years since he took up permanent residence in America, for not trying to reconnect with Drucilla Durane. He wanted to, but he didn't want to risk subjecting himself to feelings that too often led to pain. He had seen that kind of pain over and over again. In husbands, lovers, fathers, brothers. Men like himself—shattered by the loss, or actions, of a woman who meant the world to them.

Sometimes, after Tabatha died and he formed his vigilante group, he personally had to deliver the news of death to these men.

But it doesn't always have to be painful, Theron.

The woman who had spoken those words had long departed, driven away by his bogeyman. She had tried so hard.

He sighed and turned his thoughts to the reason why Andrew had sent for him. The same reason, he now knew, that had led to Andrew's death. Was there a connection between Alejandro Bernat and Grant Featherhorn? If so, what was it? After reading those reports, it was easy to figure out why a drug mogul like Bernat would want Savoy to win the contract in Guyana. The new infrastructure would provide the alternative route he needed for his illicit trade.

But *Featherhorn!* Where did *he* fit in? And what about Lawson Pilgrim? Was he involved, too?

Theron stood still, the motions of packing suspended as he turned these questions over in his mind.

He was still standing this way, a pair of neatly folded boxer shorts in one hand and two short-sleeved shirts on hangers in the other, when the door to his room burst open and three men strode in.

One of them—a portly man with baby-smooth skin and a boyish, dimpled smile—wore a dark-green military uniform with a chestful of brass, ribbons, and braids. He carried a baton in one hand and kept smacking it against the palm of his other hand.

The other two men, lean and mean looking, wore the same dark-green, but their shirt-jackets were short-sleeved and bore neither brass, braids, nor ribbons. They wore black berets.

They flanked their senior officer and raised their Uzis to take dead aim at Theron's head. Theron's breathing slowed and he stared directly into the officer's eyes. He didn't blink. He didn't move. Not even a muscle twitched.

Show no fear. Force the stranger to show his hand.

The standoff lasted several minutes before the officer abruptly turned his back to Theron and closed the door. He closed it so softly that the others in the room didn't even hear the lock catch. For a few seconds, he remained with this back to the room, as if lost in thought. When he turned around, he was still smiling.

He beamed at Theron and moved toward him, stopping just a few inches away from him. He looked intently into Theron's face, and then appraised him from head to toe.

The lean, mean men kept their guns trained on Theron.

Finally, the officer spoke. "Packing, are we? Don't tell me you're planning to leave our lovely country so soon, Mr. St. Cyr," he said in a surprisingly high-pitched voice. His accent sounded like a battle between Guyanese and British in which neither side was winning.

Theron stared back at him mutely. He had run into such characters before. Renegade officers and soldiers. They appeared benign, but they could be the worst kind of sadists.

He stood as if bolted to the ground, hoping the fear that was beginning to roil in his gut did not show in his face.

The officer hmmphed. He looked past Theron, beyond the window into the black night where the Atlantic frolicked.

The two gunmen scowled and tightened their grips on their guns.

The officer hmmphed again and crossed the room to the window. He stood there for a good minute—Theron mentally counted the seconds—staring out, saying nothing.

Finally, he spoke again. This time there was no swagger in his voice and the Guyanese accent seemed to have overwhelmed its British rival.

"If you must leave, Mr. St. Cyr, you must do so now. We will see that you get to the airport safely." He turned away from the window and Theron swung to face him, a look of confusion on his face. The soldiers quickstepped until their guns were pointing once more at Theron's forehead.

Theron glanced at them warily and opened his mouth to speak, but the officer held up his hand, silencing him.

"At ease, men," the officer said to his men. The men lowered their guns and dropped their shoulders, but they kept their eyes on Theron.

The officer continued speaking. "There's no need to say anything, Mr. St. Cyr. We're here, compliments of Andrew Goodings." He paused and his expression turned sheepish. "Sorry about the dramatic entry. It was a performance for the cameras in the corridor. We stretched it out a bit longer than necessary, I'm afraid."

He paused again, as if waiting for a comment from Theron, but Theron kept his mouth clamped shut. The officer nodded and continued. "Andrew Goodings…" he swallowed hard, then pressed on. "Andrew Goodings was very kind to me a lifetime ago. I am deeply indebted to him for that act of kindness. The only time he collected on that debt was when he asked me to look out for you. That was the day before he died."

27

It was just the three of them in Lawton Pilgrim's office—Dru, Grant Featherhorn, and Lawton himself.

Dru had come in at seven, intending to catch Lawton alone before the usual Monday morning gathering of the Inner Circle. She had spent the entire weekend weighing her options and had finally made up her mind late Sunday night to go straight to Lawton and voice her concerns about Featherhorn.

St. Cyr would disapprove, she knew. He had warned her not to say a word to anyone about Featherhorn, not even to Lawton. But she had argued defiantly to herself that she had no reason not to trust Lawton Pilgrim, her mentor. What right did she have to deprive him of information that could jeopardize the company that was his whole life? The same company, the same man, who had given her the career and the renown she had dreamed of attaining when she was in college.

It would be wrong—traitorous—to deny Lawton the chance to secure the integrity of Pilgrim Boone. Worse, it would be ingratitude on her part. Her mother's words rang in her ears. *Ingratitude is worse than witchcraft.*

In the security of her own home, her own country, she had seen things more clearly, and they were not as frightening as they had seemed in Guyana. She would tell Lawton about Featherhorn. And Lawton, in his inimitable way, would set about unraveling the mystery. *He'll get to the bottom of it and fix it, she told herself. I know him. Theron doesn't have half the resources or connections Lawton has. Neither, for that matter, does the Guyana government.*

I'm only making it easier for Guyana, Dru kept insisting to herself as she rode the subway into Manhattan that morning. Theron would understand eventually.

Sitting in Lawton's office now, the eyes of two of the country's most powerful corporate executives trained on her, she fought hard to hide her agitation. She had been shocked to find Featherhorn there. He had taken off his jacket and rolled up his sleeves almost to his elbows. He slouched comfortably—too comfortably, Dru observed resentfully—in one of Lawton's two antique fireside chairs. He had a steaming cardboard cup of coffee in his hand and a smirk on his face.

Lawton sat on the leather sofa opposite him. He, too, was in shirtsleeves, and he clutched his prized coffee mug. It was a classic ivory-colored mug that bore his initials embossed in gold. A grateful client had had a set of four custom-made for him by the house of Lenox. Beneath the vulgar overbrew of Featherhorn's Starbucks, Dru could discern the earthy bouquet of the black Nepalese tea Lawton favored. Steam wisped languidly from the Lenox mug.

Pilgrim had greeted Dru affectionately, jumping up from his chair and hugging her in an uncharacteristic show of relief.

Featherhorn had approached her genially and pecked her lightly on the cheek. Dru had suppressed a grimace as his lips made contact with her skin. The gesture was typical of Featherhorn when he was in the presence of others, especially Lawton. But she did not miss the look in his eyes that Lawton could not see, nor the quick, derisive smile that told her he not only had anticipated her early arrival, but had deliberately thwarted it by showing up in Lawton's office ahead of her.

She had moved away from him as quickly as she discreetly could and taken a seat in the second antique chair, facing Lawton.

"Before you brief us on Guyana, Dru, there are a couple of things I must clue you in on," Lawton was saying. "I want to do it now, before the day gets going, because I know that you more than anyone else will be affected by these things; these decisions I have made."

A fist-size knot formed in the pit of Dru's stomach. He's moving me out, she thought with alarm. I should have seen it coming. First Jamaica, now Guyana. What else could he do?

She bowed her head and stared at the floor.

"I'm dying, Dru."

Dru's head jerked up. She blinked at Lawton Pilgrim. And blinked again. She smiled, slid to the edge of her chair, and leaned toward him. "I'm sorry, Lawton. I think I misheard you. My ears must be jet-lagged. Would you repeat what you just said?"

"I said I'm dying, Dru. I have cancer. The doctors have given me three months to live," he paused, looked at his wristwatch and added. "Actually, I have about a week less than that now."

Dru's smile fell away. She slammed back in her chair and glared at Lawton. "That's not funny, Lawton. That's not funny at all," she snapped, not caring that she could pay dearly for her impudence.

Abruptly, she shot forward and swung toward Featherhorn. Belligerence blazed in her eyes. "Is this one of your stupid ideas, Grant? Play a joke on Dru? Make her feel lousier than she already feels? Yes, I bet this was your idea, you sick son of a—"

"Stop it Dru! Stop it at once!"

Lawton's command bit into the air. Dru fell back into the chair, her face crumpling, her hands limp in her lap. "I don't believe you, Lawton," she said tremulously. "It's not true."

"Whether you think it's true or not is of no consequence, Dru. I'm telling you the truth. Just accept it." His tone had softened. He seemed relaxed, vaguely insouciant.

His hands told a different story. They shook as they guided the coffee mug to his lips. Dru found her eyes drawn to them. Lawton Pilgrim's hands never trembled.

As if reading her thoughts, Pilgrim abruptly set the mug down on the coffee table. "Moving right along, then," he said briskly. "Understandably, I've been forced to accelerate my succession plans. Are you with me, Dru?"

Dru dragged her eyes up to meet his. Her eyes brimmed with tears. She swallowed hard and nodded.

"Grant will succeed me as CEO of Pilgrim Boone," Lawton said. He held Dru in a firm gaze. "I'll make a formal announcement to the entire staff later today, after I announce it to the Circle."

Dru retched. She clamped both hands over her mouth and doubled over, forcing down the urge to vomit.

Pilgrim jumped up in alarm and patted her back. "Are you okay, Dru? Are you okay?" He had expected her to be shocked, but he wasn't prepared for this. He continued to pat her back until he heard her manage a weak, "I'm okay."

Lawton breathed a sigh of relief and sat down again. Glancing disdainfully at Featherhorn, who was smiling and had not moved an inch, he said to Dru: "I know this is a lot for you to take all at once, Dru, but surely you understand why I had to do it this way. It would have been inconsiderate of me to let you hear this for the first time in front of the others."

Dru lifted her head and her eyes met his. She saw understanding in his. She saw the understanding change to something else. A plea for forgiveness? Impossible. Why would Lawton need her forgiveness?

Only then did it hit her that he knew. Lawton had known all along how Grant had made her life hell. *And he had done nothing about it.*

And now, adding insult to injury, he had given Grant the reins of the company, elevated him to the supreme position, put him in full charge of her future, her very life, with the company.

She drew herself up erect and turned to Grant. He smiled at her. It was a smile she knew well.

28

Something exploded in Dru's head. She had to stop this madness.

Pilgrim Boone must not, could not be put into the hands of Grant Featherhorn. Lawton had to know the truth. Two days ago, as they had driven her to the airport, Dalrymple and Roopnaraine had told her about their visit to Theron and what they had found out about the man named Alejandro Bernat, the one whose name the minister had queried her about.

She sprang to her feet and jabbed an accusing finger at Featherhorn. "You can't, Lawton! You can't make him CEO! He may embroil Pilgrim Boone in a scandal of the worst kind!" she cried.

Lawton stared at her. It was his turn to be shocked. "Dru…," he began.

Dru would not let him continue. She planted herself in front of Featherhorn, who had flattened himself against the back of his chair, eyes agape.

Dru's chest heaved. The torment she had endured from this hateful man welled up and crashed against the walls that had held it in check for so many years. The walls gave way. Any sense of restraint that may have been left in Dru disintegrated.

"Listen to me, Lawton!" Dru shouted. "Your precious Grant may be mixed up with a drug lord in Venezuela, who may be planning to run drugs through Guyana if air transportation really takes off. The man's name is Alejandro Bernat. He's the one who probably had Andrew Goodings killed because Goodings was telling MacPherson to go slow on the deal, to have everything and all the parties involved thoroughly checked out first, and, if anything untoward turned up, to kill the deal entirely. Let Grant tell us what he knows. Ask him, Lawton! Ask him about Bernat!"

A mocking curl of the lips had replaced the surprise on Featherhorn's face during Dru's tirade. He was convinced that Dru was fishing. She had no proof of a relationship between him and Bernat. Someone obviously had fed her information, but that someone had not yet connected all the dots. If they had, Dru would not be using words like "may" and "probably." She would be spilling out the details herself instead of using Lawton to try to extract the information from him. Still, her outburst was unsettling. If Dru knew someone who had come up with information about Bernat and who was curious enough to start digging into Bernat's relationships, it was only a matter of time before that someone made the connection between...

Featherhorn folded his arms and stared at Dru with feigned amusement. He shifted his gaze to Pilgrim and encountered the older man's frigid glare. His heart leapt. For an instant, he was once more the unsophisticated recruit in the awesome presence of the iconic Lawton Pilgrim.

Why, he believes her, the son of a bitch! He knows what she's saying is true even if she has no proof. Why wouldn't he believe her anyway? He's already found out about the meeting with Bernat and queried me about it, hasn't he? All Dru did with that stupid outburst was connect his dots. She'll pay for this. Oh, how she will pay for this.

He kept his face impassive. He would not let Pilgrim see the fear that had begun to twist his stomach into knots.

"Go ahead and ask him, Lawton!" Dru screeched.

Lawton turned slowly away from Featherhorn and looked up at Dru with pained eyes. "Sit down, Dru," he said gently.

Dru was taken aback. This was not happening. This could not be happening. Lawton was not dismissing everything she had said.

She challenged Lawton, dismay making her voice shrill. "Sit down? Lawton, didn't you hear a word I said? Aren't you going to ask him about Bernat? Aren't you going to ask him anything at all?"

"I said sit down, Dru!" Lawton said sharply.

Dru complied. Her eyes, wide with disbelief, remained on Lawton's face. She clasped her hands tight in her lap to stop them from trembling. She felt as if she were falling into an abyss.

"Those are very serious charges, Dru," Lawton said quietly. "If what you are implying is true, then we will have to go to the federal authorities and we will have to provide proof to back up your charges. We will also have to inform Savoy and pull out of the negotiations immediately. Word will get out, of course, and Pilgrim Boone will be ruined. No one will care that we took the high road and reported the whole sordid affair ourselves. On the other hand, if it turns out that none of what you're charging is true, that whoever gave you this information was playing some sort of game to get us out of the negotiations—and I can see some of our rivals stooping that low—irreparable damage will have been done to Pilgrim Boone and to Grant. Grant would probably sue you, and the company, for libel."

He paused to let the full import of his words sink in. He took a deep breath and continued. "So! What proof do you have, Dru, that drug traffickers are conspiring to take over the air routes that Savoy hopes to open in Guyana. Why are you convinced that Grant is mixed up in this heinous conspiracy?"

The tone of his voice, like that of a father to a wayward child, told Dru that it was all over for her. Truth be told, she had known it the moment Lawton had ordered her to sit down. The wagons were circled and she was not in their protective embrace.

She bowed her head. There was a lesson here somewhere. An ugly lesson someone who had been fired from Pilgrim Boone had tried to teach her. It had been early in her career at Pilgrim Boone and she had refused to listen, telling herself it was a case of sour grapes, the facile defense of an underperformer who walked around with a chip on his shoulder. She was ready to listen now.

The man's words came roaring back to her now: "Be careful, Dru. When push comes to shove, the white boys will always side with the white boys."

For the second time since she walked into Lawton Pilgrim's office that morning Dru felt like throwing up. Lawton, whether he believed her or not, was not going to question Grant Featherhorn, at least not in front of her. She had no proof to give him, of course. She had not waited long enough for Theron's case to pan out. It would be useless to argue that her information had come from a reliable source. She could not, would not, bring Theron's name into it for fear she would have to explain how she came to get the information from him. And if she did that, it would look as if she had betrayed Pilgrim Boone, consorted with the enemy, as the TV dramas would have put it.

Dru raised her head and once again met Lawton's eyes, eyes that pleaded with her to understand the position he had taken. She shifted her gaze to his mouth. It was drawn into a reproving line, a show he was putting on for Featherhorn, Dru supposed. But you can't have it both ways, Lawton. You can't have it both ways.

Her eyes remained empty as they traveled slowly back to Lawton's. She stood up. "I have no proof to give you, Lawton," she said in a steady voice. "You'll have my resignation within the hour."

Dru strode toward the door. The antique handwoven Armenian carpet that Lawton had bought at a Christie's auction for two hundred thousand dollars swallowed any sound the defiance of her steps would have made. She didn't deign to look at Featherhorn.

Her heart pounded in the silence that followed her. She was almost at the door and Lawton still had not said a word in response to her offer to resign. She had hoped—foolishly, she told herself—that he would, even under the circumstances. She had not expected Featherhorn to say anything. Frankly, she would not have paid any attention to anything he might have said.

She opened the door with a firm twist of the gleaming brass knob and pulled it shut just as firmly behind her. Isn't that something? she thought with a wry smile. She had figuratively and literally closed the door firmly on her career at Pilgrim Boone.

29

The eyewitness was explaining to the lone TV reporter and a crowd of onlookers that the woman who lay dead in the middle of the road had had no chance at all to save herself.

The eyewitness was taking the fullest advantage of his day on camera, knowing that an opportunity like this would never come his way again. He gave the performance of his life, recreating with his voice and facial expressions and exaggerated gestures the horror he had just witnessed, and his audience rewarded him with sighs and grunts and drawn-out sounds of sucked teeth on perfect cue.

"The BMW was speeding, coming up fast behind the dray cart when it suddenly cut out into the oncoming traffic side of the road. It looked like he just wanted to overtake the dray cart. But he miscalculated bad! There was no way that poor lady could have swerved out of the way in time. Accidents like this happen all the time in Georgetown. It's the law of the jungle on the roads. All this drug business that got people buying these fast fancy cars. This place is getting like the French connection. Money floating around like it falling from trees and every Tom, Dick, and Harry driving around in these BMWs like they on the racetrack. People right to call them Bad Man Wagon because that's exactly who drive them, people who think they're more bad than everybody else. I keep saying we should go back to the old days and give everybody bicycle. Guyana was a safe country when bicycle was kyar. None of this dashing helter-skelter t'rough de streets like life don't mean nothing."

The longer he spoke, the more animated he became and the more his language lapsed into the Guyanese patois. He came up for a quick breath of air and rushed on, fearing the reporter and her cameraman might seize the moment to question someone else, a groundless fear on his part. With a dearth of local production worthy of viewing, nothing captured the TV audience more than "man-in-the-street" commentary. Both the reporter and cameraman knew this.

The eyewitness hit his stride again. "And this lambsy-bambsy government we got ain' doing a damn thing. But you and I know why. Politics is a hell of a thing. And to think, that beast ended this lady's life and he didn't get even a scratch. There he is over there. Watch he. Standing up as cool as cucumber talking to the police. Rich boy. Got party connections. He know he gon' get off. Not a day in jail for he. Life, eh? But God gon' take care of him. Mark my words. God don' sleep nor slumbuh."

The reporter darted in with a question. "Do you know who the lady is, Sir?"

The eyewitness seemed offended. "Do I know who the lady is? I know who the lady is, yes. She live on my street. One of the most beautiful women in Georgetown. Never mind how she look under that sheet, with her head smash in and bloody like that. And never mind what people say 'bout she. How she dis and how she dat. She's a kind lady. Generous. She—"

The reporter dove in again. "Can you tell us her name?"

The eyewitness shook his head and sighed deeply. He kept his eyes downcast as he responded to the reporter. "Her name? Leila. Her name is Leila."

30

Dru slipped the envelope with a check for the month's rent under Mr. Jackson's door and hurried downstairs to meet her brother Lance.

He and Phil were driving to Martha's Vineyard where they jointly owned a house. They had persuaded her to go with them.

It had taken a lot of persuading.

Approaching New York on the way from Washington with Phil, Lance had suddenly decided to visit his parents. The visit extended well into the night and he and Phil slept over. In conversation with his parents, Lance was shocked to learn that Dru not only had quit her job at Pilgrim Boone, but also had virtually cut herself off from family and friends.

"When she called to tell us she had left the firm, she kept saying these strange things about having to stay away from the family for the time being, that she did not want anything to happen to her or to us," his mother explained tearfully.

Not getting any answer on Dru's landline or cell phone, Lance and Phil decided to stop at her apartment the next morning before setting out for Martha's Vineyard. Dru finally opened the door after Lance threatened at the top of his voice that he would call the police if she did not.

He refused to accept her explanation for her behavior.

"Turn off the dribble, Dru! You were doing just fine at Pilgrim Boone and everyone knows it! Besides, you gave Mom and Dad a bunch of crap about your having to stay away from the family in order to protect them. What's that all about? What the hell's going on, Dru? Does this have anything to do with that contract in Guyana you were negotiating, or with that French guy you had me check up on?" he demanded angrily after Dru had prattled on for a good ten minutes about being tired of banging her head against the glass ceiling at Pilgrim Boone.

She had responded—too quickly, Lance told Phil later—that the Frenchman had nothing to do with anything, that she just needed to get away.

"So come with us," Phil had interjected, catching both Dru and Lance off guard because he had remained mute while the two argued.

Phil admitted to himself that he was being utterly selfish. But, he also insisted silently, taking Dru with them was really the best solution. Dru was not going to reveal anything—at least not now—and Lance would keep pushing and prodding until he and Dru started shouting at each other. Eventually, Lance would stomp off in a huff and he and Phil would drive in sour silence all the way to Martha's Vineyard. Once there, Lance would walk around feeling and looking morose and the entire vacation they had planned for all these months would end up a goddamn disaster.

He struck hard while he had their attention. "Pack a few things and come to Martha's Vineyard if you really need to get away, Dru. No one will bother you there, and Lance will know where you are all the time and that you're okay. You can stay at the house as long as you like, too, even after we leave."

Lance nodded vigorously in agreement. He smiled for the first time since he and Phil had arrived at Dru's apartment. "Phil's right, Dru. Go throw a few things together and come with us. The villa is the best place for you right now. I promise I won't pester you about what's going on in your life. You can tell me whatever you want to tell me, but only when you're good and ready."

Dru told only her parents where she was going and she swore them to secrecy. She would be safe, for the time being at least, with Lance and Phil, and could think things through without having to worry about Featherhorn or Bernat's people coming after her and finding her at her apartment. Theron would be looking for her because he had promised to see her when he got back from Guyana, but she was too ashamed to contact him. He had advised her not to say a word to anyone about Bernat or Featherhorn, and she had ignored his advice. Now Featherhorn—and no doubt Bernat by now, if there really was a link between them—knew that someone was connecting the dots.

31

An officious female voice told Theron he would have to be put through to the public relations department for information about Miss Durane.

It sounded ominous. Theron's head began to ache. He had called Dru's home several times since his return to New York, but had gotten no answer. He'd even called late at night when he was sure she would be at home and still there was no answer. He'd left messages each time, of course, but Dru had not returned a single call. Either she was not at home, or she was deliberately avoiding him. He didn't have her mobile number.

He hadn't planned to contact her through Pilgrim Boone. For all he knew, Grant Featherhorn, or someone else, was watching her closely, even listening in on her calls. It would do Dru no good to be caught talking to him. Bernat most likely had spies all over the place. People in his line of business, with his kind of money, could afford to employ an army of peons. Theron was certain Bernat already knew about him and his relationship with Andrew Goodings. And if Bernat had also heard about the scene in the lobby of the Pegasus, he would have apprised Featherhorn of it and warned him to keep an eye on Dru to see if there was any further contact between them.

The more he analyzed the situation, and with no word from or of Dru, the more agitated he became. He finally broke his resolve and called Pilgrim Boone. And now that he had, an anal receptionist was telling him that he had to go through PR. That could mean only one thing: Something was definitely up with Dru. It didn't feel good.

He struggled to keep his voice calm. "I'm sorry, but this seems rather strange. I called Ms. Durane last week at this very number and I was put through to her office directly. I didn't have to go through your public relations department. Is there something wrong?"

The officious voice grew even more officious. "The public relations department would be more than happy to answer your questions, Sir. I'll transfer you now."

Theron heard the abrupt *click* as the receptionist switched the call without waiting for him to answer. He forced himself to keep his mind blank until public relations came on the line.

"Public relations, Dana Waldron speaking."

"Ms. Waldron, I called to speak to Drucilla Durane and I was transferred to you. Is there any reason why I cannot speak with Ms. Durane directly, as I did last week?"

"I'm sorry, Mr.—I'm sorry I did not get your name."

"That is correct. You did not get my name, Ms. Waldron. Will I be allowed to speak to Ms. Durane?"

"Are you a client of Ms. Durane's, Sir?"

Her polite indulgence and that high-pitched American voice were too much for Theron. His voice rose. "What difference does it make if I'm a client or not? May I or may I not speak to Ms. Durane? What is so hard about that?"

"I'm afraid you can't. Ms. Durane no longer works for Pilgrim Boone. However, if you are a client, I can direct you to someone who is handling her portfolios."

Theron was stunned. "She doesn't work there? But that's impossible!"

Dana Waldron did not deign to reply.

Theron pulled himself together. This was not the time to lose it. He needed information that Waldron might have. "Forgive my outburst, Ms.

Waldron. Isn't this rather sudden? Ms. Durane indicated nothing to me that she was leaving when I spoke to her at this office last week."

"And you are?" Ms. Waldron's voice was frosty.

Theron didn't bother to answer. He slammed down the phone, grabbed his wallet, and dashed out of his apartment.

Out on the street he waved frantically at the first cab he saw, once again thanking God that he lived on the West Side of Manhattan where it was easier to find an empty cab than over on the East Side.

He started to give directions to the cab driver before he had even closed the door. "I've got to get to Brooklyn fast! Take Riverside all the way down to Seventy-ninth, get on Eleventh Avenue and take it to Twenty-third Street, get back on the highway to the bridge! That's the fastest way at this time of the day!"

He caught the cabby's offended expression in the rear view mirror and shrugged. "Tough! You're looking at the one who's paying, buddy," he muttered, not caring if the cab driver heard him.

His mind screamed with questions about Dru's whereabouts. He had to get to her apartment. He was bound to find an answer there. At the very least he would find a clue as to where she had gone, or what may have happened to her, *if* anything had happened.

He pulled out his cell phone and dialed Dru's apartment. It rang four times before the answering machine came on. He hung up. No point leaving another message. If only he had her mobile…

He snapped his fingers. Of course! Why didn't he think of it before? He could have Amelia track down her number.

Amelia Barbineau was the receptionist at Trans-Global. She had a bachelor's degree in computer science information systems from New York Institute of Technology, and was working on a master's in the same subject. She was from Guadeloupe and spoke French fluently, a requirement for the receptionist position at Trans-Global. When she had applied for the job, she had written cheekily in her cover letter, in French, that she wanted "a no-brain job, like answering phones and filing paper," while she was in school. Tickled by such outrageous candor, and seeing immense value in her advanced computer skills—not to mention her aptitude in spoken *and* written French—Theron had called her in for an interview. Ten minutes into the interview, he had offered her the job. As he had expected, she had proved to be Trans-Global's best resource for pulling information from the Internet in a hurry.

He dialed the general number for Trans-Global, and Amelia answered on the first ring. Theron cut her off before she finished her standard greeting. "It's me, Amelia, I need the mobile number for Drucilla Durane. She lives in Brooklyn. Look it up and I'll call you back in five minutes," he said agitatedly.

He was about to ring off when Amelia said coolly, "Please stay on the line, Mr. St. Cyr. I'll have the number for you in just a few seconds."

Theron sighed, feeling a little foolish. He pressed the phone to his ear, somewhat calmed by the rapid *tap-tap-tap* of Amelia's fingers as they flew across her keyboard.

True to her word, Amelia was dictating a number to him after no more than ten seconds. Theron memorized the number, thanked her, hung up, and dialed Dru.

The call did not activate.

He clicked off and dialed again.

Still nothing.

"Sometimes you can't get a signal around here," the taxi driver said dryly.

"Yeah, thanks," Theron replied sourly.

The taxi driver shrugged. Theron kept the phone in his hand. He would try again in a minute or so. He contemplated all sorts of scenarios as the cab sped along Riverside Drive, shooting through more amber lights than green. Where could Dru be? Was she okay? Had she been fired? Had she let slip—inadvertently or deliberately—their suspicions about Featherhorn and Bernat? Had Featherhorn threatened her and forced her to resign? Maybe she had left Pilgrim Boone of her own accord, knowing what she knew and afraid for her life. But where *was* she?

Guilt assailed him. If anything happened to Dru, it would be his fault for telling her about Bernat and implicating Featherhorn, just like it had been his fault that Tabatha was kidnapped and killed. It was because of him that she had gone to Germany in the first place. When she was having doubts and wanted to change her mind about the trip, he had laughed and called her a wimp. Insulted, she had made up her mind there and then.

Thoughts of Tabatha and of Dru meeting a similar fate turned his nagging headache into an implacable migraine. He leaned back in the seat and squeezed his eyes shut. He took deep breaths and tried to force the images of both women out of his mind but it was useless. He kept seeing their faces.

Tabatha's and Dru's. Dru's and Tabatha's.

The blast of a car horn made his eyes fly open. He sat up and took in the traffic ahead. The cab had rejoined the West Side Highway and was approaching the Chambers Street turnoff that would take them to the Brooklyn Bridge. Cars in the two left lanes were slowing.

Theron snapped at the driver. "Don't you see the buildup ahead? Go around to the FDR north and take the bridge from there!"

The cab driver wore the turban of a Sikh. His face, reflected in the rearview mirror, was impassive. He spoke politely to Theron in slightly accented English. "I will try that way if you wish, Sir, although I know they are doing roadwork in the tunnel and that could slow us more." Before Theron could respond, he accelerated and made a daring move into the lane to his right.

Theron felt foolish. He said in a conciliatory tone, "Look, I don't mean to be rude. It's just that I am very anxious to get where I am going."

"I don't take any of it personally, Sir. Just give me the exact address of where you are going and I will get you there in no time."

Theron thought fleetingly that the cab driver sounded as officious as the woman he had dealt with at Pilgrim Boone earlier. He gave the driver Dru's address and sat back, staring anxiously at the thickening traffic ahead. His rubbed his temples to help ease the throbbing in his head. He had to get a grip on himself. He had to be ready to face, to deal with, whatever he would find when he got to Dru's.

He dialed her mobile number again.

"Connection failed," the screen said.

Theron clicked off the phone and stuffed it in the inside pocket of his jacket. He folded his arms, threw his head back on the seat, and closed his eyes.

He felt utterly, despairingly, helpless.

32

"If you're looking for the person who lives there you won't find anyone at home."

Mr. Jackson had been sweeping and dusting in the lobby while surreptitiously keeping an eye on the stranger's increasingly aggressive thumb on the buzzer. Theron had been pressing Dru's buzzer off and on for a good five minutes before Mr. Jackson finally spoke up. He had never seen this man before and he was suspicious, especially after Dru's strange behavior. Dru had paid him the rent for the following month, but she hadn't given it to him in person as she usually did. Instead, she had slipped the check under the door in an envelope. Even odder, the rent was nowhere near due. Dru always gave him her rent on the first of the month. That was two weeks away.

Maybe she had had to travel suddenly, he had reasoned. But even that was no explanation. Whenever Dru traveled, no matter what the circumstances, she would drop by with the rent before she left and let him know where she was going and why. And she'd say something about the plants, too. So this check-under-the-door business was very much out of the ordinary.

Mr. Jackson did not like things out of the ordinary. This strange man pressing the devil out of Dru's buzzer was also out of the ordinary. Who was he? And why did he think he would find Dru at home at this time of the day?

Mr. Jackson had had enough time to study the younger man. He didn't look like a salesman, he concluded. Clothes too expensive. For sure he wasn't a lawyer. He wasn't carrying one of those Coach briefcases that those nose-in-the-air professionals who lived in the building walked around with. If only they knew how mindless they looked, like clones of the models in magazines. And the man at the door certainly wasn't family because Mr. Jackson had met all of Dru's family—the ones who were most important to her, she had whispered to him—when she had had that barbecue in the backyard to celebrate her last promotion at her job and this man leaning on the buzzer definitely was not there.

If the stranger really knew Dru, Mr. Jackson decided, he would know that she had a job—and a fancy one on Wall Street at that—which is where she would be at this hour. Or, he would know where she was. True, the stranger looked like a decent man. But he seemed just a bit too anxious to get into Dru's apartment for Mr. Jackson's liking.

Mr. Jackson wondered if Dru was involved in anything untoward. He hoped she was simply running away from this man, who looked like he could be a real pest, the way his finger stayed stuck on that buzzer. Dru was the upright type, no question about that. But you never knew with people these days. Some of the best and brightest were into all sorts of wild things, from what he saw on TV.

Theron took his finger off the buzzer and turned to Mr. Jackson. "I beg your pardon?"

"I said the occupant is not there." Mr. Jackson repeated in a louder voice, deftly wielding a long-handled dust mop around the intricate molding above the fireplace in the lobby.

"Do you have any idea when she will be back?"

So he knows it's a *she* who lives there, Mr. Jackson thought, recalling how relieved he had been when Dru had taken his advice and inscribed only her initials on the buzzer pad. Well, that still doesn't mean a damn thing. Any idiot can get that right when the odds are fifty-fifty.

"'Fraid not," he said to Theron. Abruptly turning his back, he shuffled away from the fireplace and proceeded to sweep the area around a huge potted plant.

Theron would not be put off. He strode across the foyer and planted himself in front of the older man. "Excuse me for being such a bother, sir, but have you seen her at all today or recently?" His tone was polite, but he added what he thought was enough authority to get the man's full attention.

Mr. Jackson slowed his sweeping to a halt, lifted his head, and dragged his gaze up and down St. Cyr's six-foot frame. "That's a mighty lot of questions coming from a total stranger," he said dispassionately, settling his eyes squarely on Theron's.

"Yes, I suppose so," Theron said equably. "But I'm worried about Ms. Durane. I've been trying to reach her by phone but I'm not getting any answer. I finally called her office at Pilgrim Boone and they told me she no longer works there."

He dropped the names deliberately. At any other time he would have appreciated the man's iron silence about one of his tenants, but this was not one of those times. He was worried sick about Dru.

Mr. Jackson didn't flinch. This was the first time he was hearing that Dru no longer worked at Pilgrim Boone but he kept his surprise to himself. He still was not convinced that this man had Dru's best interests at heart. So what if he knows her name and where she works—worked, if what he says is true. *Let's see just how well he knows her.*

"Did you try reaching her family?" He scrutinized Theron's face for muscle twitches and shifting eyeballs, telltale signs of lying.

"I don't know her family."

Mr. Jackson let that hang just long enough to make Theron uncomfortable. Then, with a knowing "uh-huh," he turned his back once again and resumed sweeping. He would protect Dru at all costs. *Buddy, if Dru didn't think you were good enough to meet her family, then you'll be buying ice in hell before you get anything out of me!*

Theron scooted around and stood in front of Mr. Jackson again.

"Look, I know I'm a perfect stranger to you, but I assure you I'm her friend. I really must know where she is. I need to know she's all right. Believe me, I can find her family if I need to but I wouldn't want to alarm them."

Mr. Jackson ignored him and kept on working his broom in the crevice at the base of a stone column. Finally, he said, "You mean she's in some kind of trouble?"

He spoke in the same languid tone, but Theron observed that he was jabbing harder than necessary at the crevice. Theron sighed inwardly with relief. He said, "That's what I'm trying to find out, sir. If Dru is in trouble. Something happened in Guyana."

Something in the way Theron spoke those words rang true with Mr. Jackson and made him relent. He decided to tell Dru's visitor what he knew. He arranged his lanky frame against the stone column and gave Theron his full attention.

"Well, all I know is that she's gone somewhere for a while. She paid me her rent already—that's a good two weeks ahead of time—and she paid it in a way she's never done before."

"How is that?"

"She slipped it under my door."

"That doesn't seem such an unusual thing to do."

Mr. Jackson pursed his lips and looked at Theron sideways. It was a look that made Theron think of Dru's neck roll all those years ago in Marseille.

Theron quickly nodded, conceding that his statement was presumptuous; that he was out of line.

Mr. Jackson acknowledged the gesture by once more looking squarely at Theron. "It's unusual for her," he said. "She always gives me her rent in person, says it gives her a chance to check up on me." He chuckled and added, "She says I remind her of her father, and she doesn't like seeing me alone so much."

"Oh. So Dru's definitely not in her apartment now, correct?"

Mr. Jackson took note of the *Dru*. "Right. I told you before that she wasn't home, didn't I?"

Theron thanked him and turned to leave.

"If I see her, who should I say was asking?"

"Just tell her Theron needs to know she's okay."

"Tay-who?"

"Theron."

Theron walked quickly toward Eastern Parkway, hoping he would soon find a taxi that would take him back into Manhattan. He was furious with Dru and at the same time afraid for her. She had gone into hiding. That much was clear.

Theron suspected that she had done something foolish, like blurting out what she knew to Featherhorn, or saying something to Pilgrim, who might have taken it right back to Featherhorn. He wouldn't put it past Pilgrim to protect Featherhorn, even if he had to hold his nose to do so. In the world where Pilgrim Boone dwelled, who was more important—Drucilla Durane or Grant Featherhorn? Featherhorn, of course. Why should Lawton Pilgrim turn his back on Featherhorn—endangering the reputation of his firm in the process—based on accusations made by an ambitious young woman who was probably on the verge of losing the contract she was negotiating for a valued client? Worse, they were accusations that she couldn't back up with a shred of concrete evidence.

But Dru wouldn't see it that way, Theron fumed. Oh, no! Dru would view it all in terms of right and wrong. She would march into a futile battle against the odious Featherhorn, throwing herself like a shield in front of Lawton Pilgrim and her precious Pilgrim Boone. She was so smart and yet she could not see that the Pilgrim Boone she revered and was so proud to be associated with was not driven by what was right or wrong. She could not see that the man who was her mentor, but who above all else belonged to the tiny elite of a heartless universe, that man had not gotten to the top by virtue of moral stances. Was she really that naïve?

For a moment, Theron wished Dru were beside him so that he could grab her by the shoulders and shake her hard. *What the hell will it take for her to see the light when it comes to Lawton Pilgrim and Pilgrim Boone?* he asked himself.

Theron tried her cell phone again. The call went through this time but it went straight to voicemail. He left a terse message. "Dru, it's Theron St. Cyr. Please call me as soon as you get this message. It's urgent."

He pocketed his phone. He could feel his anxiety mounting despite his anger. He forced himself to remain calm. He had to keep a clear head. He had to think rationally. What if Dru hadn't said anything to anyone? He wrestled with that question, all the while keeping his eye on the traffic for a taxi. If it wasn't something she herself said or did, then something else or someone had spooked her, he reasoned. Why else would she run away? And how long would she be safe where she was hiding?

Theron could think of only one person who could answer his questions: Dru's nemesis, Grant Featherhorn.

Theron glanced at his watch. At this hour he'd be better off taking the subway back uptown if he wanted to confront Featherhorn. It was already close to rush hour. Traffic would be deadly by the time he got to the Brooklyn Bridge in a taxi, and it would be far worse on the FDR Drive or the West Side Highway.

His mind worked nonstop as he rode the Seventh Avenue train uptown. He was certain that Dru was in trouble, certain that Featherhorn had everything to do with that trouble, and that the trouble itself had everything to do with Guyana, Savoy, and Bernat. He had to find a way to talk to Featherhorn without revealing his own connection to Dru, but how should he approach him? What should he say to him? Scenarios came and went in a discordant sequence of mental images, like raw footage in the hands of an editor who had suddenly gone insane.

The tangle of scenarios revived his headache. Questions hammered him mercilessly. Could he get Featherhorn to admit to an involvement with Bernat and at the same time reveal what he knew about Dru's disappearance? Even if he got Featherhorn to talk, he would have to find a way to record their conversation to use as evidence for MacPherson. Would he be able to do so? Could he even risk showing his face to Featherhorn? What if Featherhorn knew of his relationship with Andrew Goodings? What if whoever killed Andrew had seen them together, had photographed them and sent the pictures to Bernat?

And yet, all through his mental tossing and turning, Theron had the strangely comforting feeling that Dru was physically safe, at least for the moment. From what the old man at her apartment building had said, her departure was planned.

The train pulled into the Wall Street station in Manhattan. Suddenly, it began to buck and groan, jolting Theron out of his musing. A few of the passengers who were standing lost their balance and grabbed frantically at the overhead bars or at each other to keep from falling.

Sounds of annoyance flooded the car.

The train finally came to a halt and the doors slid open. Theron watched absently as the few exiting passengers fought their way through the throng on the platform. The people outside were already closing in on the doors. Profanities flew back and forth. Some of them were directed at the Metropolitan Transit Authority for causing yet another rush hour screw-up, but most bounced between the exiting passengers and those waiting to board.

Above the cacophony, a loudspeaker squawked something about a delay in service due to police activity at 14th Street, and then gave the MTA's formulaic apology for any inconvenience caused. This provoked even more profanity, hissing between teeth, and sardonic outbursts of "Yeah, right!"

Theron's thoughts began to drift back to Dru. Suddenly, he sat up straight.

Wall Street.

He sprang from his seat and bolted toward the closing doors. From among the bodies jammed tight against each other, hands with New York subway reflexes shot out and held the doors back, long enough for Theron to squeeze through. On the platform, he turned to wave his thanks to whoever had held the doors, but all he saw were the backs of the subway riders pressed against the doors as the train screeched away.

33

Alone in his office, the door closed, ribbons of vermilion from the late afternoon sun undulating playfully on the walls, Lawton Pilgrim felt oddly at peace.

The world was what it was, crap and all.

He could think of several colleagues who, were they in his position, would be stricken with panic, anger, fear—all of the crippling emotions he had shied away from for as long as he could remember.

At least two of those colleagues—in his mind's eye he saw their faces clearly—would seriously contemplate suicide. One of them might even go all the way. That would be Frank Taubin, CEO of Global Development Advisers, a no-account firm Taubin's father-in-law had set up for him when he married his ugly-as-sin daughter and made her cup run over with happiness.

Pilgrim's lips curled in contempt. Frank had been a jelly belly since high school but he was a crafty son of a bitch. In a situation like this he would kill himself out of sheer fear that his father-in-law would kill him first if he got the chance. But in his final moment of life—Pilgrim could not help chuckling as he thought of it—Frank would glean satisfaction from the misery his death would bring to the old man in the end, for Ari Rosensheim would be left to cope with his hopelessly spoiled, and now inconsolably bereaved, daughter.

Pilgrim himself would have nothing to do with suicide. He had come to terms with the fact that the world into which he was born was no more. The fierce independence with which he had built and sustained Pilgrim Boone mattered little these days. Merger mania was rampaging through the accounting industry, as it was in just about every other industry. The Big Eight had become the Big Six, then the Big Five. The survivors were reptiles with voracious appetites, puffed up with victory in their war against Levitt's campaign to stop them from consulting for their audit clients.

Their victory was no surprise, really. Hadn't they poured tens of millions of dollars into the election campaigns of the politicians they had co-opted to their dastardly cause? Hadn't they hired a pack of bulldogs to further spread their propaganda on Capitol Hill?

And spread it those bulldogs did. The fat cats in that namby-pamby Congress told Levitt that if he didn't cool it they would cut off funding for his SEC. Even the CEOs of some of the Big Five's biggest clients were pressuring Levitt to back off. What could the poor man do under that kind of assault?

Pilgrim uttered a loud sigh. *Oh, well! I won't be around when it all comes crashing down.*

And it was bound to crash, he kept telling himself. Would Pilgrim Boone go down with the whole stinking pile? Could Grant keep the firm from being sucked into the death hole, when Grant himself believed that the new values, that the new way of doing things, was, how did he put it? "Simply wonderful?" Not that the old ways were saintly. Power and profit had always been the great motivators.

But I had my limits. There were lines I would never cross.

Today there were no limits. The pursuit of profit had run amok. Simply besting the competition was no longer enough. You had to control the marketplace. And in order to do that you had to kill the competition. That's really what this merger mania was about: killing off the competition to control the marketplace. And that meant controlling everything that fed the marketplace: resources, and whoever had those resources; the people who you wanted to buy your products or services, by planting the "right" messages in their minds; the lawmakers who made the laws that affected your profits; even control of the way money moved. Business—big business, not the little guys in the neighborhoods—had become a *Reich* of its own, incestuous relationships and all.

It's not fun anymore.

Lawton settled himself more comfortably in the custom-made leather sofa, stretched out his legs, steepled his fingers on his six-pack stomach and closed his eyes. No sounds came from the corridors outside. The telephones, fax machines, his secretary's buzzer—all were silent. It was well after six and the administrative staff was long gone. In fact, as far as he knew, the place was empty. It was the eve of the July Fourth holiday and the staff had begun to bail out at noon.

As was his custom, at 4 P.M. he had walked every floor of the firm to wish whoever was still around a happy holiday. He had encountered less than a handful of his employees and they were packing up to go. If anyone remained on the premises at this hour it would be Grant. Lawton had not bothered to check Grant's office during his rounds. He had no desire to run into the younger man.

His thoughts lingered now on Grant, the newly announced CEO-to-be of Pilgrim Boone. Although he had not shown it then, Lawton had been deeply shaken by Dru's outburst that Grant was consorting with Alejandro Bernat to use Savoy's project in Guyana—if Savoy got the contract—as a cover for a drug trafficking operation. Not for a moment had he doubted Dru. That she had no proof did not matter. He knew Grant, and he was well aware of his clandestine meetings with Bernat. Besides, Grant himself had confirmed Dru's story.

Lawton recalled the events of that day, the day he had undertaken the invidious task of informing Dru that Grant would be his successor. After Dru had left, he and Grant sat in silence for several minutes. He had studiously avoided Grant's eyes, but he could feel Grant's eyes drilling into him, daring him to question, to accuse, as Dru had done. He had done neither. And the silence, stretching out until it had lost its awkwardness and become a declaration of the way things were, was all the proof he needed of Grant's guilt.

He knew from that silence, too, that he no longer had a place at Pilgrim Boone. *Chief executive emeritus*, the industry and the press would politely label him. He could show up every day if he cared to, occupy the same office, make phone calls, give his personal staff this or that to do. But effectively he would be the proverbial fifth wheel and Grant would make sure everyone knew it.

It was then he had begun to see his cancer as a blessing. He would be gone long before the crap hit the fan. His eyes had met Grant's only briefly when they rose in unison from their respective seats, Grant's eyes clearly mocking what must have been the reflection of resignation in his.

"Well, Grant," he recalled saying in a voice that showed he clung stubbornly to his pride, "I guess it's time to make the announcement."

Grant had smiled his cocky smile. "After you, Lawton," he had said grandly, executing a small bow as he allowed Lawton to step ahead of him.

That was the last time he and Grant had been alone in the same room, the last time, in fact, that Grant had come to his office.

Lawton shook his head and sighed. Chief executive *emeritus*. Me. Imagine!

In that moment of absolute aloneness, Lawton realized that he wanted no part of that title. That, in fact, there was nothing more that he wanted of his life. Whatever covenant his being had made with God when it entered this world, well, that covenant had no meaning now. *Expired*, he chuckled, surprising himself.

Yes, he was ready to—how did the young folks say it?—check out.

Theron crossed Broadway and headed toward the East River end of Wall Street.

He moved quickly. He had a plan.

Suddenly, he stood still, causing the clone of a Brooks Brothers magazine ad walking behind him with a cell phone glued to his ear to collide with him. The clone cursed, straightened his jacket with a hump of his shoulders and stepped off to the right. Without making eye contact with Theron, he strode away, lobbing "Asshole!" over his shoulder, the cell phone reglued to his ear.

Theron waved his hand vaguely at the man's back. He was having second thoughts about his plan. The plan had seemed infallible on the train, but now he wasn't so sure it would work. It could backfire. Featherhorn could simply refuse to play ball and admit to nothing. In fact, Featherhorn could have him thrown out and/or arrested for trespassing, breaking and entering, impersonating a federal officer. Featherhorn could bring up any number of charges. If any of that happened, and if Featherhorn subsequently checked his identity with Bernat, his life, and certainly Dru's, would be lost.

Lost in concentration, he moved forward at tortoise's pace, his gaze fixed on a horizon he did not see, his hands plunged deep into his pockets. He chewed his bottom lip absently, oblivious to the rush of pedestrians headed in the opposite direction; oblivious to their querulous stares as they swerved to avoid him.

Think harder, Theron. What's your backup? What are your precautions?

Precautions! He had to take precautions. The way to do that came to him almost immediately. He stopped cold again and looked at his Rolex. No one bumped into him this time. The business day was far from over in California, he realized as he noted the time.

He looked around quickly. He needed to find a quiet place to work. Some of his acquaintances had offices nearby that any one of them would gladly allow him to use. He would have all the privacy he needed. But he could not be sure those offices weren't bugged. He wasn't being paranoid at all. This was Wall Street, the nucleus of high-stakes finance. He knew at least two CEOs who not only recorded everything said in their own offices, but who also had the offices of all their subordinates bugged.

He turned around and headed back to Broadway. He would swing right on Broadway, make a left on Dey to Church, then a right on Church to The Millennium Hilton. The bar in the lobby would be crowded and noisy, but he knew he could find a quiet corner in the coffee shop upstairs.

He quickened his pace. He had to finish what he was going to do in time to get back to Pilgrim Boone before Featherhorn left, if he hadn't already done so. From the profiles he had read while he was in Guyana, he knew that neither Lawton Pilgrim nor Grant Featherhorn left their offices before 7:30 P.M. They devoted most of the late hours to making personal calls to their biggest West Coast clients who were three hours behind New York. But they might break their routine for the holiday weekend. Theron experienced a moment of panic. What if they had made plans to go to their respective getaways: Pilgrim to his private island in the Bahamas; Featherhorn to his bungalow on Fire Island?

Resolutely, Theron pushed the thought away. Featherhorn wasn't going anywhere, not with Guyana on the brink. Not when he was dealing with a man like Bernat. The thought assuaged his fears. He found the quiet spot he was looking for at The Millennium, settled himself in and ordered coffee.

The moment the waiter left, he pulled a PDA from the breast pocket of his jacket and flipped it open. It fit comfortably in the palm of his hand. The device was the ultimate in personal digital assistant technology and spared him the encumbrance of the laptop computer he carried when he traveled to countries whose IT infrastructure did not have the capacity to support PDAs like his. Slim, weighing less than six ounces in a casing of the latest plastic, it provided phone, Internet access, a range of audio/visual functions, including video conferencing, all the functions of a personal computer, and several specialized applications. It was not yet sold in the United States, but it was already in use in Japan. He had procured his a few months earlier in Tokyo, where he had gone to formalize a partnership with a research firm that specialized in business intelligence.

In no time, he was accessing the information he sought, again using the passwords and databases that Sanspaix had created for him. He studied the data on the screen grimly, committing it to memory. He hoped he would not have to use it, but doing so would be the only way to get through to the person he needed to speak to if a secretary or some other gatekeeper gave him a hard time.

He flipped the device shut and saw that the waiter had already placed his coffee on the table. He caught the waiter's eye and nodded appreciatively, thinking that whoever said menial workers did not know the meaning of discretion had never met this particular waiter or the old man in the building where Dru lived.

He looked at his watch. He didn't have much time to make that call.

34

Dru bolted up in the bed and stared into the blackness, mouth agape, eyes wide in horror.

She covered her face and groaned. *What have I done?*

She had gone to bed early, exhausted after a full day playing vacationer with Lance and Phil. It was their third day on the island and it had been a day of sightseeing, socializing, dining on gourmet soul, and a long lazy stroll on the beach in Oak Bluffs, where wealthy blacks owned gorgeous Victorian gingerbread mansions. The villa that Lance and Phil owned was one of the newer, more modest homes. Built of gray stone in the 1990s, it was a picturesque, spacious four-bedroom Cape Cod tucked behind a brace of tall pines at the end of a secluded road, half a mile from Oak Bluffs Town Beach and less than that to downtown Oak Bluffs. There was white wicker furniture with cushions the color of sunshine on the porch. A grill and a wrought iron table that seated six on the huge deck at the back promised pleasant dining experiences. The house was surrounded by a lush green lawn interrupted here and there by dogwood trees and patches of fragrant bushes and low, flowering plants. Inside, it was tastefully furnished for maximum comfort, without succumbing to clutter or froufrou. Dru had sighed with delight when she saw the beach stone hearth in the living room, imagining how cozy it must be when lit in the winter.

Try as she would, however, she could not fall asleep. So she simply lay there, ruminating on the mess her carefully crafted life had become. She felt lonely. For the first time in her under forty, high achiever life she regretted not having a *significant other* to share her troubles with. She had only herself to blame for that, she admitted. Moated in Pilgrim Boone, she had chased away anyone who had shown too much interest. The excuse she always gave was that she just wasn't ready to commit to a serious relationship, that she wanted to devote this period of her life to her career. She made it sound as though she were doing the chasee a favor. *I'm all about me at this point in time. That's selfish, I know. And it's not fair to you. You deserve someone who can give you all of her attention.* She spoke the words in a voice billowing with regret, while her eyes met his with unassailable finality.

She knew now that her aversion to romantic commitment had more to do with her inability to trust the opposite sex than with her career ambitions. And now she no longer had the refuge of the best job she could ever have hoped for and doubted she would ever find a substitute in the same industry again, at least not at the level she'd achieved. Grant Featherhorn would certainly make sure of that. And Lawton Pilgrim, for whatever time he remained in this world, would not utter a word in her defense, she thought bitterly.

She had lost all respect for Lawton. She didn't even feel sorry for him. For all she cared, he could rot to a slow death with his cancer. A man like that, a man who could so easily compromise every shred of honor and integrity just to maintain a façade of propriety—why else would he sacrifice her for Featherhorn?—had no business polluting the community of decent people. As for Featherhorn, her gut told her that he would get his just deserts as long as Theron St. Cyr was around.

Theron!

At the thought of him, the terror that had made her bolt upright seared her body again like a high voltage electric charge. In her foolish attempt to take matters into her own hands, she had put Theron's life in danger. She was certain that Featherhorn had already relayed to Bernat everything she had said in Lawton's office. And she was equally certain that Bernat would not come after her alone. He would go after Theron as well. There was absolutely no way that a character like Bernat, with connections as wide and deep as a Jesuit's, would not know who Theron St. Cyr was, and what he was doing in Guyana. He would put two and two together and ascertain that it was Theron who had fed her the information she had spewed out to Lawton. Hadn't she and Theron been seen together in public? Heading up to her hotel room, no less? A man like Bernat was bound to have spies all over the place. Why else—how else—would Goodings have been killed?

Dru gritted her teeth and squeezed her eyes shut. She shook her head as if to nullify that day in Lawton's office, a day she would remember for the rest of her life. After a while she opened her eyes and stared out at the moonlit blackness beyond the wispy muslin curtains she had drawn across the window. She could hear the gentle wash of the waters.

She sighed and turned to look at the clock beside her bed. The digits glared back at her in rebellious red. Three a.m.

She flopped back on the pillows and stared up at the ceiling. She had no choice now. She had to get in touch with Theron to warn him, to tell him the foolish thing that she had done, even if it meant incurring his wrath or more contempt.

At least he would be alive.

She made up her mind to leave that very morning. It would mean getting up in a couple of hours to catch the first ferry over to the mainland so that she could get on a flight that would land her in New York well before the business day was over. She would dash home, change, and go straight to Theron's office. She would have to look for the exact address, but it shouldn't be hard to find. She had already found his firm on the Internet. Lance would raise the roof when she told him she was leaving, of course, but she knew he would get over it soon enough.

She was right. Lance *did* raise the roof, accusing her outright of chasing like a teenager after a Frenchman who clearly was causing her grief.

"I'm not chasing after anybody, Frenchman or otherwise," she retorted heatedly. "And why do you keep bringing him up, anyway? What makes you think my leaving has anything to do with him?"

"Because that profile you made me look up describes just the kind of person you would be attracted to, Miss World Citizen. Becaaaaause (he dragged out the word with a roll of his eyes) if this was only about your work, you would have been turning New York upside down until you got things going the way you wanted. The last thing you'd be doing was moping around with that godforsaken look on your face. I *know* this is about that Frenchman. Tell me I'm lying. Tell me!" Lance rolled his neck and stood with his hands on his hips, waiting for her to speak.

"You're lying," Dru snapped. But she avoided her brother's piercing gaze.

"You're the one that's lying. And you're doing the sorriest job of it!" Lance flung back.

"You can think what you want. This is a free country. Now will you drive me to the ferry or do I have to call a cab?"

They drove to the ferry in stony silence.

"Well, are you going to stay mad at me?" she asked him sheepishly as he removed her bag from the trunk of his car.

She was standing close beside him. Without warning, he reached for her and held her to him in a long, hard embrace. Before he let her go he begged her not to do anything that would cause her more anguish.

"Look, Sis, you're one of the smartest women I know, but be careful with this guy. You don't know his kind of black folk. He ain't West Indian and for sure he ain't American. I'll be worrying about you, so don't be scarce. Call me. Promise?"

"I promise," she said, easing herself out of his embrace and kissing him on both cheeks.

Lance's words stayed with her all the way to her apartment. "You don't know his kind of black folk."

Even if it were true, couldn't she learn?

⇌⑂⇌

It was midmorning. Dru decided to call Theron's firm. Surely some-one would tell her where he was, whether he was still in Guyana or if he had returned to the States.

She used her computer to find the phone number and street address for Trans-Global Solutions, and jotted down both in the black leather address book she always carried with her. She held her breath as she dialed.

"Theron St. Cyr, please," she said in her most businesslike voice after a female voice announced the name of the firm and wished the caller "good morning" in French, first, then in English.

"May I say who's calling?"

Dru closed her eyes and exhaled softly with relief. The question could only mean one thing: Theron was in his office and he was okay.

"May I say who's calling?" the voice on the other end of the line repeated firmly, but without losing its tone of solicitousness.

On an impulse, Dru hung up. All of a sudden it did not seem a good idea to speak to Theron on the phone. She would go to his office and speak to him in person. It was better, safer, that way.

She changed quickly into one of her "power" dresses, then ran into the bathroom to fix her hair and apply some makeup. She rushed about, grabbing this and that, putting it all down, then picking it all up again. It was as though she were at war with herself, as if she didn't want to give herself time to think. She knew she had to hurry but her movements were more than those of someone in a hurry. Her hands trembled so much that she had to redo her makeup several times.

Finally she walked into her bedroom, sat down on the bed, and stared at the wall. Uttering a sigh, she gave voice to what her heart had already conceded. "Of course, I could! I could learn about his kind of black folks."

There! She'd said it. All of a sudden she had a feeling of lightness, as if her whole being had been locked in a vise and she had managed to free herself. The sensation brought to mind that day, years ago, in college, when she'd figured out why Chalmers Freeman had responded with varying degrees of anger and scorn after she told him that she was going to Europe to study and do some traveling around afterward. She could even hear herself laugh back then, and that made her laugh now, as she savored the feeling of release. She was ready to be her old self, her pre-Pilgrim Boone self, the self that felt a hot thrill when the unknown loomed big and wide before her.

She stood up, walked over to the full-length mirror, and stared into eyes that seemed to be seeing someone who had been absent for a long time. "You're free, Drucilla Durane," she said to those eyes. "You're free. Ready for the next chapter of your life, whatever it is."

She continued to stare at herself. She wanted to stay in this new feeling, this joyful yet frightening buzz.

What will you do if he wants nothing to do with you after you tell him what you did? The question rudely interrupted her buzz. She pondered it, nevertheless, and addressed her reflection defiantly. "It won't matter. Not in the long run it won't because now I know that I can care for someone other than myself. And that kind of caring means I have me (she slapped her chest)… back. Ergo, I'll be just fine." She fell silent as her bravado cooled a fraction.

"Okay. So maybe I won't be fine for a while if he walks out of my life. But in the long run—and no matter how long the run is—I'll be okay."

Minutes later, she was grabbing her handbag and rushing out of her apartment. She felt light again. She was floating. She glanced at her watch. If the trains were running as efficiently as those scalawags at the Transit Authority swore they did, she should be at Theron's office in half an hour, tops.

Just before she dashed through the door, she caught sight of herself in the antique mirror in the foyer and stopped. Staring straight into her eyes, she said out loud, "You know that's a crock, Durane! He'd better not walk away. And if he does, well, you'll just have to make him come back."

※

"I'm afraid he's out of the office, Ms. Durane," the pretty young woman who came out to meet her said apologetically.

Dru's face fell. "Do you expect him back today?"

"Actually, he has not been here at all today. And I really can't say if he'll be here at all, ma'am. He hasn't called in. Something urgent must have come up. I do apologize, Ms. Durane. It's unlike Mr. St. Cyr to miss his appointments." She seemed genuinely contrite.

Dru hastened to correct her. "I'm afraid I don't exactly have an appointment. That is, I—I didn't make one. I know Theron—Mr. St. Cyr would see me. But I was—I guess I should have made one. I've been away, you see," she finished lamely. She felt foolish. When she had called earlier, she had rushed to the conclusion that Theron was at his office when the receptionist, or whoever had answered the phone—it didn't sound like this girl—had merely gone through the proper routine to get the name of the person calling.

The pretty young woman seemed to grow more erect. Her smile morphed into one of practiced indulgence. Behind it, her thoughts were far from benign. *Christ! What is it with these high-class bitches in heat? Do they really expect Mr. St. Cyr to stop his life for them?* She addressed Dru in a voice drenched in honey. "Would you like to make an appointment now? That way no one will be caught off guard. Mr. St. Cyr is always so busy, I'm sure he would appreciate some advance notice of your visit."

The bite underneath her dulcet tone was not lost on Dru. Dru said briskly, "No. It's all right. An appointment is not necessary. I'll catch him another time."

The woman protested. "Mr. St. Cyr is a very busy man, Ms. Durane. I would advise—"

Dru waved her hand impatiently, cutting her short. She said, "When you do see him, please let him know I was here. The name again is Drucilla Durane. Thank you. You've been most kind. Good day." She swung around and strode away.

Outside, she walked quickly away from the building. She had no idea what to do or where to go next. The Pilgrim Boone Dru would have drawn a sizable measure of satisfaction from having put a secretary in her place. *This* Dru did not give the secretary a second thought. She felt utterly deflated. She was so sure that she would find Theron at his office that she had not made any other plans.

I could call him. Her heart quickening, she stopped in front of an apparel boutique in whose window was displayed an up-and-coming designer's latest glorification of bag-lady wear, extracted her cell phone from her purse and turned it on. She had kept the phone off while she was at Lance's and had forgotten to turn it on when she got back to New York. No sooner had she turned it on and clicked the address book icon than she recalled that she did not have Theron's mobile number. She had been so distraught when he left her that last night in Guyana that she hadn't recorded it in her list of contacts.

Damn!

She locked the keyboard and was about to slip the phone back into her purse when she heard the soft *trrring* announcing the arrival of a message. Deftly, she unlocked the keyboard and opened the message file. There was voice mail. She started to call up the log to check the number that the call had come from when she felt herself shoved from behind. She stumbled, uttering a cry of alarm, instinctively flinging her arms out as if to steady herself against an invisible wall and keep from crashing to the sidewalk. Her purse and phone fell to the ground.

Perhaps her outstretched arms were sufficient to counter gravity's pull. Perhaps the involuntary steps she had taken from the force of the shove were enough to abort a fall. However it happened, she managed to regain her balance. Flummoxed nonetheless, she stared in dismay at her belongings on the ground. The contents of her purse had not spilled, but the display screen of the phone was shattered.

A female voice called out, "You okay, Miss? Need help?"

"No, thanks. I'm okay," Dru responded curtly, not bothering to turn to see who had addressed her. *Goddamn crazy people!* she muttered as she stooped to retrieve her things.

Upright again, she glared around to pluck out the individual who had violated her for no apparent reason. No one stood out. Her eyes fell on a thin woman standing a few paces away, frowning at her. The woman seemed to be in her mid-twenties and was well dressed in a navy-blue coatdress, pearl earrings and necklace, and navy-blue-and-white pumps. Dru rolled her neck and whipped her head in the opposite direction. Still no suspect.

She felt the pull of the thin white woman's stare and swung back to face her. The woman had not budged. She seemed frozen as she frowned at Dru, ignoring the quizzical looks of passersby.

What the hell's her problem? Dru thought irritably. She rolled her eyes dismissively at the woman.

The disturbing import of the shoving episode was beginning to sink in. Dru had once described the streets of Manhattan as bipolar in nature—great for walking but depressing and crazy making if you looked beyond the stunning architecture, window displays, and beautiful people. The shoving incident proved her right. Her attacker had already melted into the crowd of pedestrians.

Dru tucked her purse under her arm and began to fiddle with the phone as she moved toward the boutique with the ode-to-derelicts outfit in the window to get out of the way of the pedestrian traffic. The phone was dead, she knew, but she pressed the power button anyway. As she expected, nothing happened.

Dammit!

She removed her purse from under her arm, snapped it open, and dropped the phone into it. I'll have to get a new one soon. Maybe I should do it right away. She needed to do *something*. She couldn't remain standing there, looking as crazy as that skinny-ass woman who was still staring at her.

A thought struck her. Since she was already in Manhattan, why not go to Pilgrim Boone and collect what was left of her things? There were some disks with her most important contacts and some tapes of exchanges with Grant Featherhorn that she had recorded clandestinely. Foolishly, she had left all those behind when she had stalked out. Now would be a good time to get them. Chances are she wouldn't run into anyone in particular, since it was the Friday before a holiday. Most people would have taken the day off to make a long weekend of it. The place would be practically deserted by now. Her ID was still valid for another week, so she could get past security without a problem. Leona had called to tell her that it had not been invalidated because Lawton was giving her time to get her things out, or to change her mind about quitting.

Dru's thoughts settled briefly on Leona. Out of loyalty to Dru, Leona had wanted to resign after Dru left, but Dru had persuaded her to stay, knowing that one of the other partners would grab her up in no time. Besides, with all the downsizing going on in the industry, it would be almost impossible for someone of Leona's age to find a job. And even if she did, it would not offer anywhere near the benefits and salary she was getting at Pilgrim Boone. Dru didn't want *that* on her conscience. Leona and her husband were helping to put two of their grandchildren through college and needed every penny they made.

Dru sighed and began to once again mull over the idea of going to Pilgrim Boone. Even if Grant and Lawton were still there, she could easily slip in and be out of there before they knew she was around. She really needed those files. She could enlist Leona, but what if she were caught? *Without question she'd be let go.*

Dru made up her mind. She would take the chance herself. *Should I take a taxi or the train?*

Still unsettled by the shoving incident and the destruction of her phone, she decided in favor of the comfort and privacy of a taxi. She stepped away from the boutique and started briskly toward the curb. Had she not been so intent on flagging down a cab, chances are she would have paid more attention to the skinny woman who was now following her to the curb.

A squadron of yellow cabs charged down the street. Dru was about to raise her hand when the skinny woman sidled up to her. "I offered you help and you answered me as if I were the one who pushed you. That wasn't nice," the woman tut-tutted, shaking her head.

Dru stiffened. She stared at the woman who, up close, was frighteningly emaciated. The finely tailored coatdress seemed to swallow her. Her blonde hair fell stringy and lifeless to her shoulders. Her eyes were huge and unblinking.

Oh, hell! Not another psycho, Dru thought worriedly. *There's a lot of them wandering around these days. Nuts dressed to the nines. This one must be off her meds.*

The woman edged closer. Suddenly, her hands darted out toward Dru. In a flash, Dru realized that this was the individual who had pushed her. She jumped back, but the woman thrust herself forward, annihilating the space between them.

Dru's mouth tore open as she sucked in air, readying to hurl her most threatening "BACK OFF" at her assailant, but the words never saw life. Dru felt herself falling. The woman was falling, too, on top of her. Dru could not help marveling at the weight of the woman's body. Its heaviness belied her wasted frame. She felt a stinging sensation in her chest. Time slowed. Brilliant white light splintered behind her eyes and pain exploded as her head smashed against the concrete sidewalk.

The world was darkening. Dru welcomed the darkness, so great was the pain in her head. The last thing she heard were faint, frantic words that sounded like "women shot."

⟶⟩⟩⟩

The black Lincoln Town Car glided smoothly toward an intersection, half a block from where the two blood-soaked bodies lay on the ground. The light was green.

Behind the Town car's tinted windows, the man in the backseat placed a silencer and Beretta M9 pistol in the false bottom of a pigskin briefcase, secured the flap that hid the compartment, scattered around several legal-looking documents, then closed the briefcase and scrambled the numbers on the combination lock. He pressed a button and watched as the glass partition that separated him from Tony, his driver, slid up. He nested himself in the soft leather of the seat and closed his eyes, savoring the hot rush of another kill, proud of the initiative he had shown.

He was a handsome, light-complexioned man of indeterminate ethnicity, thirtyish, fashionably bald, with the fastidiously maintained body of the boxing welterweight champion he once was. He had no visible tattoos or scars. Dressed in his favorite designer wear—Perry Ellis casual—he was, ostensibly, the kind of guy a girl could comfortably introduce to her brothers.

He smiled as he reflected on how the kill went down.

Under orders from his downlink—*the guy must have just come off the friggin' French boat! Ain't red-blooded American contractors good enough no more?*—he had been staking out the building where St. Cyr had his of-

326

fice when he spotted the Durane woman. He'd heard talk that she was a mouth to be shut, but she had disappeared. They'd circulated her picture. Then there she was, sashaying out of St. Cyr's building like she was gonna live forever. So he followed her in the limo, waiting for the right moment to take the initiative. That's what everyone kept telling him to do: show *initiative,* if he wanted to move up in the company.

When he saw that fool junkie woman shove Durane, he instructed Tony to pull up across the street and keep the motor running. He watched the whole scene unfold between Durane and the junkie, waiting for *an initiative moment* to present itself. He knew one would. It was the perfect scenario of distraction and confusion.

The two women were at the curb, people avoiding them like the plague. Then Durane jumped back from the junkie, just as the traffic eased. He couldn't believe his luck. He had a clear line to Durane, but he knew it wouldn't hold for long. He ordered Tony to roll out, quick but not too quick, enough to block oncoming traffic. It was a one-way street. And he got off his shot.

It was beautiful.

He looked back in time to see her fall to the ground, a dark red pool already creeping out on the sidewalk where she fell. Too bad about the other woman, whoever she was. She was in the wrong place at the wrong time. Oh, well. Life was a bitch. It played nasty tricks on those who lived it. The woman was a junkie anyway. She was already dead.

The man was soaring on the high of his initiative. Your turn next, *monsoor Sint Sear*, he muttered, his head lolling from side to side. *I'm coming to take you out. Yeah, you stinkin' snail eater. You think you can mess with Bernat? You're in way over your head, buddy. This ain't* Yewrope. *This is America.* My *turf. And nobody keeps it cleaner for Bernat than I do.*

He heard the sirens and opened his eyes dreamily. A grin cut slowly across his salon-pampered face. The sound of the sirens was music to his ears. It was a validation of his skill, the soundtrack to the drama his initiative had created.

The sirens screamed louder. The man closed his eyes again and began to play his game of discerning the ambulances from the police cars in the wailing that filled the air, and determining the number of each of them that were rushing to the scene of the "incident."

His scene.

Louder still the sirens wailed.

Suddenly, the man sat forward. Playtime was over. Something was not right.

Was the limo moving? Surely the limo was moving.

He tilted his head this way and that, focusing his senses on the scene outside the limousine. And then he knew what was different. Behind the wail of the sirens, a horn blared relentlessly. It was the horn of a police car. *How come the driver's leaning on it? Why aren't the sirens enough?*

The man swung his head to look outside and saw the police car as it advanced at full speed. His gut somersaulting, he saw that the Lincoln was in the middle of the intersection *and it wasn't moving.*

The man felt the Lincoln growl as it tried in vain to accelerate. Panicked, he banged on the partition, trying to get Tony's attention. He heard Tony shout a string of curses; saw him let go of the steering wheel and fumble with the door.

The man swung back to the sound of horn and sirens and knew that he was staring at his own death. He saw death rush at him, less than a second before the out-of-control police car slammed into the Lincoln, right where he was sitting, at ninety miles an hour.

Goddamn tricky bitch! he thought bitterly as he died in the only vehicle accident he'd ever been in.

35

Theron pushed through the revolving door and stepped into the yawning marble and steel lobby of the building that housed the headquarters of Pilgrim Boone. He strode purposefully toward the bank of elevators that would take him up to the floors occupied by firm. When he was halfway across the floor, a security guard called out in the rhythmic lilt of an eastern Caribbean accent, "Would you mind stepping this way, suh?"

Theron pretended not to hear the guard and kept on walking. The guard called out again. Gone was the polite request. This time it was a command. "This way, *suh!*"

Theron glanced at him and the guard beckoned with a crooked finger and a jerk of his chin. Without breaking stride, Theron scowled at him and flashed what looked like an FBI badge. The guard immediately held up both hands, palms facing forward, and nodded him on.

At the elevator bank Theron pressed the Up button several times with exaggerated impatience and kept looking at his watch and shifting his weight from one foot to the other. Every now and then he shot a nasty look at the security guard, who seemed determined to keep him in his sights, FBI or not.

An elevator pinged. Its double doors slid apart. Theron stood aside to allow whoever might be inside to get off. Only one man was in the car. He alighted, nodded curtly at Theron, and moved quickly toward the lobby's main exit. Theron stepped forward and was about to enter the elevator when the man's face registered in his brain.

Grant Featherhorn. Theron recognized him from the picture in the electronic file he had read.

This was not in the plan. The confrontation was supposed to take place in the privacy of Featherhorn's office. With no security guards and a lobby full of people around.

Think fast! Where would Featherhorn be going at this hour? Would there be privacy when he got there?

Theron sprang back from the elevator and started after Featherhorn. Hearing the sudden movement, Featherhorn glanced over his shoulder, frowned at Theron, and continued walking toward the revolving doors.

Theron hurried after him. "Grant Featherhorn, isn't it? Just the man I was looking for," he announced with a wide grin as he caught up with him.

Featherhorn stopped abruptly and turned to face Theron, his eyebrows arched expectantly. Still grinning, Theron extended his hand. Featherhorn proffered his, hesitantly. Theron seized it and pumped it eagerly. Featherhorn allowed the assault on his hand to continue as he sized up Theron from shoes to haircut. *Good-looking black man, confident, cultured, well groomed—must be a somebody, or a somebody's son.* Easing his hand gently from Theron's grip, he gathered his face into a champion-of-civil-rights-and-affirmative-action smile. "Well now, young man. You'll have to forgive me. It's been one hell of a day. Remind me who you are," he said genially.

Theron slipped into unaccented American. "Tom Barry is the name. We haven't met before, but you'll get to know me soon enough."

Featherhorn was amused. "Oh? And why is that?" His tone was patronizing.

The young man's generation of job seekers was known to be audacious.

Theron saw the precipice and approached it decisively. "You were heading to your car, weren't you, Grant? Why don't I ride with you? We can discuss our relationship along the way." The smile remained glued to his face, but his voice had gone flat.

Featherhorn's geniality evaporated. *Grant? Ride with me? Our relationship?* This guy was downright insolent. "I seriously doubt that will happen. Now why don't you write me a let…," he began coldly.

"I said let's go to your car, Grant. You really have no choice."

Featherhorn's head jerked back in surprise but he recovered quickly. He raised his voice to attract the attention of the security guard who, he had noticed out of the corner of his eye, was watching them with interest. "Are you threatening me?"

The security guard snapped to attention. Without waiting to hear more, he strode meaningfully toward Featherhorn and Theron, his expression grim.

Theron's smile broadened. "Send him away, Grant," he said between his teeth. And then he leapt off the precipice. "Alejandro would be very unhappy if he found out that *your* actions caused the Savoy deal to fall through."

Featherhorn gaped at him. Theron's eyes glinted above his smile. Inwardly, his stomach churned. Doubt assaulted him once more. Was it the right thing to say? What if Featherhorn wasn't mixed up with Bernat at all? And even if he were, would he fall for what Theron had implied? What if he refused to go along, to admit that he knew who "Alejandro" was? What if—

"Is everything all right heah, Mistah Feathahohn?" The security guard stood at a respectful distance from the two men. He seemed to ignore Theron, but Theron knew that the guard was aware of his slightest move and would act with dispatch if Featherhorn gave him the right signal.

Featherhorn hadn't gotten this far in life without the benefit of a strong perceptual ability. He sensed rather than saw the tension in "Tom Barry." That raised questions: Was Barry really who he implied he was? Did he really know Bernat? Or was he fishing?

But Featherhorn was no fool either. Painfully mindful of the consequences of crossing Bernat, he would never dream of gambling with the man's wishes. But this Tom Barry should know that, yet he was tense. Why?

He let the security guard's question hang in the air for a long moment, his eyes fastened on Theron. *If the tiniest bead of sweat shows up on his face, I'll crucify his ass.*

Theron fought down the churning in his stomach. He looked at his watch, scrunched up his face, and said to Featherhorn, "We're wasting time, Grant. You know how ugly it can get with Mr. B. You really don't have much time to get this show on the road."

There would be no crucifixion. Featherhorn turned to the security guard. "Yes, Jason. All's well. We were just heading to my car. You have a good holiday now."

"Why, thank you, Mistah Feathahohn. And the same to you." Jason touched his hat with a frugal smile, but did not move. He stared after Featherhorn, shaking his head. *Cheap bastahd! I bring myself ovah heah to defend him if need be, FBI or no FBI, and he can't find it in himself to point a lickle somet'ing my way for a holiday drink. Never mind, Jason boy. Poor-people day will come. De Bible say, de las' shall be fus' and de fus' shall be las'.*

⇻⇤⇥

"I want in," Theron said blandly as Featherhorn's Cadillac limousine pulled away from the curb and swung onto Water Street, toward the ramp for the northbound FDR Drive.

The two men sat well away from each other, each in his corner, up against the door. Featherhorn stared straight ahead, his face frigid with disdain. Theron angled himself toward him, regarding him with intensity. He had read that Featherhorn had an aversion to cell phones and never carried one, but Theron wasn't taking any chances. He remained vigilant, watching Featherhorn's hands closely in case he had acquired one and tried to dial Bernat's number surreptitiously. He seriously doubted Featherhorn would try it, but prudence cost nothing. All he needed was fifteen minutes of Featherhorn answering his questions.

The glass partition that separated them from the driver was closed, keeping their conversation private. Theron decided to stick to unaccented

America. His natural French accent might make Featherhorn more un-comfortable than he already was. Americans were *Americans*. They didn't like people with foreign accents telling them what to do or backing them into a corner.

"Want in on what?" Featherhorn said scornfully.

"Don't be cute, Grant. The deal you made with Bernat."

"I'm afraid I don't know what you're talking about."

Theron sighed. "Grant, Grant! You're going to make me lose my patience. We both know that you and Bernat stand to make millions moving drugs through Guyana once Savoy builds the air infrastructure. And we both know that MacPherson is antsy about the whole thing. Andrew Goodings, whom you and Bernat arranged to have killed, put a bug in his ear and he can't seem to shake it loose. In fact, the word is MacPherson's about to thumbs-down the whole thing. Shall I go on, Grant?"

"Suit yourself."

Theron leaned closer to Featherhorn, resting a forearm on the leather divide between them. "What if I told you that I could get MacPherson to okay the contract for Savoy?"

Grant slowly twisted himself to face Theron. "What do you mean you can get MacPherson to okay the contract?"

Theron's eyes twinkled as he drew back from Featherhorn. "Aha! Finally got your attention, didn't I? You'll talk to me now, eh?"

"Cut the games and answer me, Barry! Can you get MacPherson to greenlight the contract for Savoy?"

"I sure can. For the right amount of equity in your part of the enterprise with Alejandro."

Featherhorn's mouth went slack. Theron stared mutely back at him. Featherhorn finally spoke, his voice just above a whisper. "You're not kidding, are you?"

Theron leaned in again. "No."

Featherhorn took quick stock of his options. This Barry, whoever he was, wasn't kidding. And he wasn't fishing either. He knew too much. He clearly had a damn good source of information. Who the source was didn't matter. It could be Alejandro himself. Featherhorn wouldn't put it past

Bernat to try to force his hand this way—get him to turn up the pressure on the Guyanese government. What Barry said was true. MacPherson *was* leaning toward a "No." It was the last bit of intelligence those two pussies Roopnaraine and Dalrymple had given him before they pulled out of their contract with Pilgrim Boone, bleating in their letter about not wanting their reputation to be "sullied by association as the investigation into the sudden demise of Andrew Goodings moves forward." Arrogant sonsabitches. He would deal with them later, once he took over as CEO.

In the meantime, he *had* to get that contract signed for Savoy. He had assured Bernat that it was a done deal, and Bernat had proceeded with his plans accordingly, locking in new distributors in North America in antici-pation of higher export volumes. The Venezuelan had invested so much in a positive outcome for Savoy that he would literally obliterate any threat to that outcome. He'd already proven that point. Twice, in fact. Barry was right again. If Bernat didn't get his way—

Featherhorn shuddered. Failure in the Savoy negotiations simply was not an option. He said to Theron, "What guarantee do I have that you could swing MacPherson to our side?"

"MacPherson happens to be my uncle and he worships the ground I walk on."

Featherhorn snorted. "You expect me to believe that?"

"Take it or leave it."

Featherhorn ruminated on this for a moment. "Let's say I take it," he said finally.

"Spell out what I get in return."

"You get 10 percent of my share."

"Fifty."

Featherhorn laughed mirthlessly. "Look, Barry, there's no fifty-fifty partnership between Bernat and me and there's not going to be one be-tween you and me. Bernat gets the lion's share. For bringing in the route, I get one-fifth of the transshipment profits. That's *profits*. Guys like you only see the gross numbers. You have no idea what it costs to put together an operation of the magnitude we envision *and* keep it going. There's all the equipment to procure to beat the competition and to stay two, three steps ahead of enforcement. Surveillance, testing, marketing, transportation, banking, you name it. State-of-the-art technology's not cheap. Then there's all the bloodsuckers who show up throughout the whole goddamn pipeline," he ended pointedly.

Theron shrugged. "Those are Bernat's problems, not yours. You just collect a paycheck. Fifty percent or I tell my uncle to red-light Savoy."

Featherhorn wasn't gambling. He couldn't afford to. "Fifty," he said sourly.

Theron slid to a different line of questioning. "Is anyone at Savoy in on it?"

Featherhorn looked at him with disgust. "Christ! What do you think this is? A tea party? Come one, come all? No! No one at Savoy is in on it!"

Theron held up his hands in mock surrender. "Just asking. What about the Durane woman?"

"What about her?"

"How much does she know?"

"She doesn't know a damn thing."

"Are you sure?"

"Yes, I'm sure."

"Not even an ounce of suspicion?"

Featherhorn lied. "Not even an ounce. Her fealty to Pilgrim Boone is unassailable. She'd never believe that a Pilgrim Booner would…" Featherhorn's face reddened. Instead of finishing the sentence, he shrugged and faced the window.

The late-day sun hung low over the East River, a shimmering orange-yellow orb that splashed the sky with golden light. The river shimmered back in silver and white. A tugboat, painted red, white, and black and heading south toward Brooklyn, tooted proudly. Earlier in the day, it might have hauled a freight barge far north with containers stacked ten stories high.

Featherhorn's gaze settled on the middle-aged couple sitting close together in a two-seater Audi convertible in the next lane. The top of the convertible was down and Featherhorn could see that the couple wore the easy suburban chic many city professionals donned on the weekends. The man had one hand on the wheel and his free arm was thrown around the woman's shoulders. They were laughing, set free for a few lazy, hazy, crazy summer days in the country. Featherhorn envied them. He, too, was heading into the country. But there would be no laughter in *his* three-day getaway; only worry, thanks to Tom Barry.

Resentment coursed through him as Barry's voice injected itself into his thoughts.

"Where is she now, Grant? In Guyana?"

Featherhorn kept his gaze on the middle-aged lovebirds. "How would I know?"

"She works for you."

"Not anymore."

"How come?"

"Guyana stressed her out, I guess. She quit."

"You mean she left Pilgrim Boone?"

"Yes."

"Just like that? In the middle of negotiating such a big contract? Why?"

"She got too smart for her own good and took the only way out."

"What does that mean?"

Featherhorn's head swiveled away from the window. He rasped, "You ask a lot of goddamn questions."

Theron was silent for a moment, then he repeated, harshly, "So where is she?"

Featherhorn sighed wearily. "You asked me that before. She's wherever she wants to be. I have no idea and I don't care to know."

"Perhaps she said something that scared you and you bumped her off."

"Killing people is not my thing, Mr. Barry. You're confusing me with our Venezuelan friend. He's the one who's watching her. If she's been keeping bad company he'll know it and he'll take appropriate action. But you should know all this if you're so close to him. Anyway, why do you care about Durane?" Featherhorn squinted at Theron.

Careful, Theron. Don't blow it now. "I always care about the liabilities my investment partners carry." He slid away again. "What about Pilgrim?"

"One foot in the grave. Cancer."

Theron shook his head and uttered a sound that conveyed genuine sympathy. He said, "That's too bad. But let's get back to Miss Durane. I want to be clear. She's no longer on the Pilgrim Boone payroll. And as far as you know, she's de-stressing somewhere in blissful ignorance of Mr. B.'s plans."

"As far as I know, yes. She could be at a poolside somewhere, getting a tan." He chuckled at his joke.

Theron ignored it. Abruptly he said, "Okay. We're done here. Tell your driver I'm getting out."

"What?"

"I said tell your driver that I'm getting off here. He can unlock the doors."

"Are you crazy? We're on the highway, for chrissakes! You can get killed."

"And I suppose that would make you sad. Sorry to disappoint. Take a look outside. It's not like we're moving."

Featherhorn glanced out the window. The holiday exodus was in full march. Traffic on the FDR had come to a standstill.

He looked at Theron and shrugged. "Suit yourself. How do I get in touch with you?"

"You don't, Grant. I'll get to you when the time is right." Theron winked at him.

Featherhorn pressed a button beside the partition and spoke into a small microphone. As soon as he had finished speaking, the lock on Theron's door clicked open and Theron got out. He slammed the door and watched the limo inch away before he climbed over the cement divide between the northbound and southbound traffic and skillfully began negotiating his way off the drive. The southbound traffic began to move just then. Horns blared at Theron. He waved at the cars, grinning.

He made it safely to the west side of the drive and climbed into the grounds of an apartment complex. He sat down on the nearest bench to wait for word he hoped would come soon. In his breast pocket, the

PDA had recorded the entire exchange with Featherhorn. Another feature in the PDA had simultaneously converted the voice recording to data, created a file, and transmitted it to the computer on the desk of the CEO of Savoy Aerospace on the West Coast. Arthur Bloomington had been following the conversation all along, in real time. At least, Theron hoped he had.

Theron felt his PDA vibrate. A message was coming in. His hands trembled as he pulled the device from his pocket and read the screen: Got it all. Thank you. Arthur Bloomington.

Theron folded his lips into a tight line and squeezed his eyes shut. He inhaled slowly and deeply, and then expelled the air in a long sigh of relief. Bloomington had kept his word. He had stayed glued to his computer as Theron had instructed him to do when he had made that phone call from The Millennium Hilton. The fate of Grant Featherhorn now rested in Bloomington's hands. Theron wasn't sure what Bloomington would do, but he knew that the CEO would not allow the information to leak out. The press would have a field day. No, Bloomington had his company's reputation—and his own hide—to protect.

Theron's spirit sagged. The more he thought about it, the more it seemed likely that Featherhorn might get away with nothing graver than dismissal, most likely with a platinum parachute to keep him quiet. He had literally blackmailed his way to Bloomington, using information about Bloomington's heroin-addicted son that he had dredged up from Sanspaix's database to get past the CEO's ferocious secretary. He didn't go into details with the secretary. All he'd said to her was, "Please tell Mr. Bloomington that it's an urgent family matter and that I was asked to speak with him directly." He figured, correctly, that Bloomington, knowing the life his son led, would come to the phone. And indeed, he could hear the anxiety in Bloomington's voice when he picked up the phone.

Theron replayed their conversation in his mind.

"This is Arthur Bloomington."

"Mr. Bloomington, forgive me for intruding—"

"Please get to the point."

"It's about your company's negotiations in Guyana. I—"

"You mean this has nothing to do with my family? Who the hell are you?"

"Please let me explain, sir. Savoy is on the verge of losing its bid in Guyana."

"What the hell are you talking about? What do you know about Guyana? That's not public information!"

Theron told him everything: from the phone call from Andrew Goodings to his arrival in Guyana and his conversation with Goodings, Goodings' untimely death hours later, his brief conversation with Minister MacPherson, the visit by Dalrymple and Roopnaraine, Bernat and his background, Bernat's possible connection to Featherhorn. He deliberately did not mention Dru's name.

Bloomington listened, not saying a word. He was so quiet that Theron at times wondered if he were still on the line. Then he would hear a quick intake of breath, or a catch in the throat that told him that Bloomington was still listening.

Seconds of silence ticked by after Theron finished his report. Bloomington broke the silence. He spoke slowly, articulating each word clearly as if addressing someone for whom he felt great pity. "I don't know who you are, Mr. Barry, but what you just described sounds like someone's very bad dream. Sheer fantasy. Moreover, nothing you said links Featherhorn to Bernat. Instead, what you gave me is pure conjecture. You're wasting my time, Mr. Barry. Please do not call me again." And he hung up, a soft click underscoring the finality of the gesture.

Theron's heart sank. He felt physically and mentally drained. He lowered his head into his hands and tried to think of his next move, but his mind refused to cooperate. It had shut down.

He remained on the bench for what seemed an eternity, his shoulders hunched in despair, his spirit cowed. Then his cell phone rang, startling him out of his wretchedness. Fumbling, because his fingers suddenly felt thick and clumsy, he managed to extract the phone from his pocket without letting it fall. He glanced at the number and his heart lurched.

Bloomington!

He raised the phone to his ear. "Yes?" He said it loudly, afraid that the thudding of his heart would drown out his voice.

Bloomington answered, angry and resigned. "I just had a chat with Lawton Pilgrim. What do you want me to do?"

Now, as he tapped on the phone's miniscule keyboard, Theron's fingers trembled with excitement. He had one more critical e-mail to send. He prayed it would go through.

Signing on with his real name—he had programmed a Tom Barry origination for all of his communications with Bloomington—he uploaded the file of his conversation with Featherhorn to MacPherson in Guyana. A full minute later, the words "Message sent" appeared on the screen.

Breathing a sigh of relief, Theron tucked away the PDA and stood up. Featherhorn said Bernat was having Dru followed. He had to find her before Bernat's tail acted.

36

The young woman ran into the building wringing her hands. She rushed into an empty elevator, hit the button for the fifteenth floor, and crushed herself into a corner, shivering. She wrapped her arms around herself, tight, as if to stop the shivering, but to no avail. She continued to tremble violently.

"Oh, my God, oh, my God, oh, my God! It can't be. I talked to her this morning. Just this morning," she moaned.

She stumbled from the elevator as soon as the door opened and ran down the corridor. The carpet erased her frantic steps. She came to a halt at a door with a brass plate marked TRANS-GLOBAL SOLUTIONS in black lettering and jammed her key into the lock. She was trembling so much that it took her several minutes to unlock the door. When she finally got the door open, she plunged into the room and hurled herself into the chair behind the reception desk. The door swung shut and locked itself with a dull *click*.

Still distraught, the young woman covered her face with her hands again and began to rock back and forth, making a keening sound. "She was here. I talked to her. Oh, I'm so sorry I was cold to her. I'm so very, very sorry," she sobbed.

There was no one to hear her; no one to comfort her. She was alone in the office. Everyone had left early.

Through her sobbing, she heard the faint groan of the elevator. She lifted her head and cocked her ear, listening for footsteps. Mr. St. Cyr had called back to say he would be at the office late in the day. She didn't have to wait, he had told her. Go home early and enjoy the long weekend. She had locked up and left.

On her way to the train station, she had come upon a crime scene and stopped, curious. Yellow tape cordoned off a section of the sidewalk, close to the curb. On the ground were the chalk outlines of two bodies. The lines intersected, as if one of the people had fallen across the other. There were bloodstains inside the lines. Two policemen guarded the scene. Timidly, she had approached them and asked what had happened. One of the policemen had turned away, ignoring her. The other one had told her, gruffly, that two women had been shot. She remembered how her hand flew to her mouth and she exclaimed, "How horrible. Did they die?"

"One of them did," the policeman had said.

She had wanted to know if they had caught the killer, but a small crowd had gathered to listen and the policeman got nervous and said, "No more questions. Keep moving."

She had moved away, continuing to walk toward the subway. But as she passed a newsstand further down the block, her eyes fell on the front page of the evening edition of the new, fast-growing tabloid *City News* with an above-the-fold headline in three-inch block letters:

TWO WOMEN SHOT. ONE DEAD.

Beneath the headline was a picture, in full color, of the dead woman on the ground. The body was covered with a white sheet, but one hand was sticking out and it clutched a purse that she recognized instantly. The woman who had come to see Mr. St. Cyr earlier that day had been carrying the same purse. She remembered it because it was the new Hermès design she liked so much.

She'd snatched the paper from its rack and read the article. She remembered how her knees had buckled and she dropped the paper when she read the sentence: "The dead woman was identified as Drucilla Durane." They buckled again as the door opened and Theron walked in. She held on to the reception desk to steady herself.

"You're still here? I thought I told you that you could leave early."

"Oh, Mr. St. Cyr! Oh, Mr. St. Cyr! It's just awful!"

Theron's shoulders slumped. He was exhausted and in no mood to listen to another one of Celine's dramas. Still, she seemed genuinely upset.

"What's awful, Celine?" he said wearily.

"The woman who came here to see you. She had no appointment. She said her name was Drucilla Dur—"

"Dru? Dru was here? Where is she? Why didn't you tell her to wait for me?" Theron crossed the room in three long strides and stood in front of the distraught girl. He wanted to seize her by the shoulders and shake her.

"Yes! Yes! She was here. This morning. I didn't know you were coming in. It was before you called. She left. And now she's dead. Oh, my God, oh, my God, oh, my God! She's dead, Mr. St. Cyr! They said she was shot with another woman. Didn't you see the police and the yellow tape and the blood? They—"

Theron held up a hand to stop her. He didn't want her to continue.

He felt faint. He hauled himself to the chair Celine had vacated and sank into it. He had seen the yellow tape and the policemen shooing away curious pedestrians, but he had been too tired and too anxious about Dru to stop to find out what was going on. He had kept on walking.

"Which hospital?" His voice was a croak.

"What did you say, Mr. St. Cyr?"

"Hospital. Which one? Where did they take the body?"

"I don't know. Oh, Mr. St. Cyr, I'm so sorry. She looked so crestfallen when I told her you weren't here."

It was a mistake, Theron told himself, shaking his head. A cruel mistake. Dru was not dead. She couldn't be.

He stood up, fighting back the tears that had begun to sting his eyes. He would find out where they took the dead woman's body and prove to everyone that it was not Dru.

It wasn't hard for Theron to find out that Dru and the other woman had been taken to St. Vincent's Hospital on Twelfth Street.

He showed his private investigator badge, and a nurse confirmed that two women had been brought in earlier and that one of them had died. The other one was not wounded at all, only a slight concussion. The nurse said it looked like the one who was shot dead fell against her as she went down.

"Is she still here?" Theron asked hopefully.

"No, she's not at the hospital any more. We offered to keep her over-night for observation, but she didn't want to stay. She didn't have any ID on her. Said she'd lost her purse. She didn't want to give us her name. She was anxious to leave, and since we really didn't need any information from her we didn't press her. We're overworked as it is. She slipped out even before the police had a chance to question her. You can see how crazy this place is."

"What about the dead woman?"

"The deceased? Yes, we have her name. The ID she carried said Drucilla Durane."

Theron's bowels sank to his heels. His face turned gray. The nurse caught his hand and steadied him.

"Are you all right, sir? Here, you'd better sit down for a while. Are you related to the deceased? Sir, I really think you should sit for a while."

Theron shook himself free and ran. Outside, he vomited on the sidewalk.

Somehow he made it home.

After that, he was aware only that sometimes it was day and sometimes it was night. He had no knowledge of what he did between the two and he did not care to know. He wanted to feel nothing, to hear nothing, to do nothing, to see no one.

Except Dru.

He wanted to see Dru, but Dru was dead. He didn't want her to be dead, so he put himself in a place where she was alive and he could touch her. And when he touched her, he told her over and over that he would always protect her.

Sometimes Tabatha came to visit him in that place. Tabatha liked Dru. He knew she would. They would talk and laugh and talk some more and laugh some more. They were so happy, the three of them—he, Dru, and Tabatha—in his dream place.

37

At precisely 8:00 A.M., a Savoy Aerospace executive jet touched down at Teterboro Airport in New Jersey, just twelve miles across the Hudson River from midtown Manhattan.

The oldest operating airport in the New York–New Jersey metropolitan area, Teterboro has been the airport of choice for private jets and corporate aircraft wishing to avoid the commercial congestion of JFK, Newark Liberty International, and LaGuardia. Its 827 acres had been in the service of aviation since 1917, when Walter C. Teter, a New York City investment banker, peevishly sold off the property to an aircraft company after New Jersey's Racing Commission rejected his plans to turn it into a racetrack.

An attractive black flight attendant opened the door of the Savoy jet, an action that simultaneously lowered the staircase. Arthur Bloomington, a strikingly tall, trim seventy-two-year-old, ran down the stairs, buttoning his jacket. He was followed closely by two men, both about ten years his junior, carrying bulging, attorney-style briefcases. They were Jack Steiglitz and Myers Pearl, partners at the West Coast law firm that handled the affairs of Savoy. The three men exuded power and wealth. They wore cus-

346

tom-tailored summer-weight wool suits and handmade shoes of Russian reindeer-calf leather.

At the foot of the stairs, Bloomington, Steiglitz, and Pearl shook hands with the pilot and chief flight attendant, murmured their appreciation for a smooth flight, and hurried toward a limousine, where a uniformed driver stood stiffly beside the open rear door. Each gave the driver a perfunctory greeting and climbed in.

At that hour of the morning, on a holiday weekend, the city that never sleeps seemed fast asleep. The limousine arrived at the headquarters of Pilgrim Boone after a soft, twenty-minute purr.

A shockingly shrunken Lawton Pilgrim greeted the West Coast visitors in person at the elevator. No one was at work on the executive floor. The air was solemn, exacerbated by the grim expressions of the men and the low, grave tones in which they spoke. There would be no record that the meeting that was about to begin had taken place.

"He came with his lawyer," Lawton said to Bloomington as they shook hands. "I didn't tell him why we were meeting, but he probably figured that I said something to you and he wants to make sure he's protected, depending on what comes out at the meeting himself."

Bloomington swore. "So he's got a lawyer. We'll nail his ass anyway."

Lawton led the men down the silent hallway into his office, from where he led them through a barely discernible door in the wood paneling that opened into a small, windowless conference room that Lawton reserved for his most private of private meetings. The room smelled like freshly polished mahogany. Grant Featherhorn stood up as Pilgrim and the three visitors walked in. So did the distinguished-looking middle-aged man beside him, whom Bloomington and his attorneys recognized as Chasbert Parker, one of the country's most highly rated criminal defense lawyer.

The lawyers shook hands with each other. Bloomington ignored Featherhorn and nodded to Parker, whose services he had been forced to enlist on more than one occasion in the past. "Let's get this over and done with," he barked as everyone took his seat at the conference table. Bloomington and his attorneys sat directly across from Featherhorn and Parker. Lawton Pilgrim sat at the head of the table.

Bloomington sat forward, planted his elbows on the table, and glared at Featherhorn. "Here's the deal, you sonofabitch. Take my offer, and you stay out of jail. Don't take it, and so help me you'll rot in the crappiest jail this country has. The charges would be murder, drug running, fraud, and anything else my attorneys could come up with. And I don't have to tell you how very capable they are in that regard."

Featherhorn steepled his fingers under his chin and gazed at the ceiling. A small smile played at the corners of his mouth. His lawyer sat forward. "With all due respect, Mr. Bloomington, what offer are we talking about? You have no case against my client. The recording you have is not admissible in any court and you know it," he said coolly.

Bloomington sat back and studied the lawyer, squinting. He shifted his gaze to Featherhorn, whose smile had broadened as Parker spoke, then shifted it back to Parker. Finally he spoke, in a voice that was ominous in its softness. "Chaz, you don't want to go down that road. Your client has fifteen minutes to sign the papers my lawyers are about to give you. My granddaughter is celebrating her thirteenth birthday today back in L.A., and I promised her I'd be at her party. I intend to keep my promise to my granddaughter."

As if on cue, Steiglitz and Pearl snapped open their briefcases and each withdrew a bound file about half an inch thick. Pearl slid his file to Parker. Steiglitz slid his to Lawton. At the same time, Lawton picked up the unmarked black-and-gold folder that sat on the table before him and slid it toward Parker. Bloomington shot Lawton a look of surprise but said nothing. Lawton's folder landed neatly next to Pearl's.

Parker's face was expressionless as he drew the two files closer to him. Silence blanketed the room as he sped-read Pearl's first, and then Lawton's. Vertical lines appeared on his forehead as he read the first document. They sank into a deep furrow as he read the second.

Sensing his lawyer's growing discomfort, Featherhorn brought his gaze down from the ceiling and straightened himself in his chair. A spasmodic twitch attacked one side of his mouth as the silence stretched out. Each time the twitch attacked, it pulled his resolutely smug smile into a Joker's rictus, giving him a visage of utter insanity.

Glancing up from the file Steiglitz had given him, Lawton Pilgrim caught sight of Grant's face, and struggled to suppress a laugh. He coughed and reached for the bottle of water in front of him. The conference table seated six and he had set a bottle at each place when he arrived at seven. Bloomington had been insistent when he ordered the meeting with Grant. "There's to be no coffee, no tea, no fruit, no kumbaya bagels, rolls, Danishes—*nothing!* I will *not* be billed for feeding that bastard. Besides, I plan to be out of there in half an hour at most," he had said.

When Lawton coughed a third time, Bloomington glanced at him with concern. He had been stunned by Lawton's appearance and intended to ask him about his health before he left for California. This was a man he played golf with, a man who, time and again, had shown that he was as strong as an ox. *Where did this skeleton come from?*

Lawton caught Bloomington's worried eye and shook his head and grinned. Bloomington nodded and returned his gaze to Parker.

Parker closed the second file and once again sat back in his chair. He closed his eyes, took a deep breath, opened his eyes again. The creases disappeared from his forehead.

"Five minutes," Bloomington snapped.

Parker seemed not to hear him. He opened both files again, turned to the last page of each one, and placed the two pages, side by side, in front of Featherhorn. His movements were slow, deliberate, his expression fathomless.

He uncapped his 24-carat, gold-plated pen and handed it to Featherhorn, backside first. "Sign!" he commanded.

38

The official announcement to the people of Guyana that their country was going to have a modern air transport system for travel into the interior was broadcast across the nation on radio and television.

President Sankar himself spoke for a full hour, telling the country that the new system would be a major boost to the economy. It would efficiently move Guyanese, foreign tourists, investors, and cargo. "With this air transport infrastructure in place, and with all the wealth of the interior waiting to be exploited, Guyana will soon be on its way to becoming the economic engine of the Caribbean," he said.

Sankar's speech was followed by a five-minute expression of gratitude to the government and people of Guyana from Arthur Bloomington, chairman and CEO of Savoy Aerospace. Bloomington himself had led the delegation from his company for the official signing of the contract. "The agreement I signed today in Georgetown is a covenant between my company and the people of this great country," he declared expansively.

Minister MacPherson, whom some had begun to call upon to resign for "egotistically" delaying a decision on a proposal to truly usher Guyana into the twenty-first-century—at least as far as transportation was concerned, a newspaper columnist had remarked caustically at a press conference—was extolled for his role in exposing the architects of a sinister plan to use Guyana as a transshipment center for illegal drugs.

Sankar also heaped praise upon Nelson Roopnaraine and Compton Dalrymple, calling them "faithful sons of Guyana who turned their back on big money from one of America's most prestigious firms when they discovered that person or persons in that firm were playing fast and loose with the integrity of our beloved country.

"Their expertise and proven loyalty have rightfully earned them their new role as the government's official private-sector liaison with Savoy Aerospace on this important project," Sankar declared.

At a celebratory reception that night at the president's official residence, Bloomington and MacPherson slipped away for a walk in the gardens of the heavily guarded compound.

The night, hot and fragrant with jasmine, was splashed with silvery light from a lopsided moon. The sky was tossed with a riot of stars that sparkled like tiny blue-white diamonds. Night bees sang.

In deference to protocol, Bloomington waited for the minister to speak first.

"I am relieved that this sordid affair with Grant Featherhorn is behind us, as I am sure you are, too, Mr. Bloomington," MacPherson began.

"It was a very close call for all of us, Mr. Minister. I want you to know that I am eternally grateful for the role you played, at great risk and sacrifice, in assuring the successful conclusion to our bid," Bloomington said.

MacPherson heard the sincerity in his voice and was warmed by it. It was not often that these foreign CEOs took time to say thanks to people like him. Most of the time they were too busy running behind the president.

Bloomington continued. "Well-placed individuals in Washington assure me that Alejandro Bernat is under such close scrutiny that no one dares to do business with him. His operation is effectively shut down."

"Ah, yes. But at such great cost. Good, innocent people have died in the process. I lost a very dear friend," MacPherson replied.

"Yes, I know of that, Mr. Minister. And let me hasten to express my deepest condolences on the death of Andrew Goodings." He let a few moments of silence go by out of respect for the minister's grief, and then continued delicately. "But, thanks to the prudence of Mr. Goodings, we now have much to look forward to. Your government's partnership with Savoy Aerospace will bring tremendous progress, as the president himself said in his speech."

MacPherson halted and turned to Bloomington. "Progress for whom, Mr. Bloomington? As defined by whom? I am still not sure that air is the most important transportation concern for us right now. For poor countries like ours, rail makes much more sense. Andrew tried to tell me that long ago. I didn't have the opportunity to tell him that I understood why he was so adamant about it."

"Then may I ask why you recommended the go-ahead for us?"

"I'm a politician, Mr. Bloomington. A politician calculates his best chances of political survival and acts accordingly. The advocates of air, including our biggest merchants and tourism companies, succeeded in garnering support with the power of gale-force winds. So I decided to, as we say in Guyana, hang my mouth where the soup was dropping. I can be a guardian of the people's interest far more effectively if I survive in office, don't you agree, Mr. Bloomington? There's no telling when the next unsavory opportunist will rear his head."

Bloomington grunted in agreement.

They walked on, in ruminative silence. MacPherson was the first to break it.

"What a tragedy for Pilgrim Boone. I imagine it will take years for the firm to rebuild its reputation, if at all that is possible."

"Oh, it's very possible. With Lawton and Featherhorn gone, the remaining partners will change the name of the firm and keep right on doing business. Don't ever cry for us, Mr. Minister. We always find a way to survive."

"Mmmmm. Just like real politicians. Well, then, we understand each other perfectly, don't we?"

"Perfectly," Bloomington replied with contented a smile.

"What will become of Featherhorn?" MacPherson was genuinely curious.

Bloomington shrugged. "Oh, I wouldn't worry about Grant Featherhorn, Mr. Minister. His name will be dirt on the Street for a few years, thanks to certain strategically placed tidbits of information by nameless persons, and he'll lie low and ride it out. He'll surface to publish a sanitized but best-selling memoir for sure, and then proceed to live a quietly comfortable life, wrapped in the family religion, doing good deeds, and appearing on an eclectic lecture circuit for hefty speaking fees. There might even be a movie based on his book, or on someone else's book about him. Americans are fascinated by scoundrels, Mr. Minister, especially publicly penitent ones. Nobody bothers to dig around to see if that penitence is sincere or not. Eventually, the Street will forgive him. Many will turn to him for advice—for a fee, of course—because he's really a very smart man and they could profit from his brains. Nevertheless, the drug enforcement community will keep a permanent watch on him and because of that he'll never be restored to his former glory. But he'll be just fine."

"I see."

Another silence ticked by.

"Well, it's too bad about Lawton Pilgrim. I admired him. He was a man of great vision. Great daring, too. I read his biography," MacPherson said after a while.

Bloomington sighed. "Yes. Cancer does not discriminate."

"No, it doesn't. By the way, Mr. Bloomington, do you know a man named Theron St. Cyr?"

"Never heard of him. Which reminds me, do you know a man named Tom Barry?"

"Never heard of him."

"Ah, well."

⁂

Theron St. Cyr sat on the edge of his bed one morning and decided it was time to live again.

Dru was gone—killed by forces no different from those that had killed Tabatha. He had found life again after Tabatha. He had lived, even loved. He would live again. This time, however, he would be more mindful of himself. Love would not be a part of his life, not the kind of love that had consumed him and left him defenseless, the kind of love that had transported him with rapture and ripped his heart to shreds.

He lifted himself from the bed and stumbled across the room. Standing before the mirror above his dresser, he contemplated the hollow-eyed, gaunt, unkempt image that eyed him back. He turned his head this way and that. Tugged at the knots in his hair. Bared his teeth. Fingered the growth on his chin. Sniffed under his arms, wrinkling his nose. He stank.

The phone rang. He sighed, stumbled back to the bed and sat on the edge again, staring at the phone on the nightstand beside the bed. The ringing stopped. He heard himself give a confident greeting and invite the caller to leave a message and phone number after the beep.

"Goddamnit, Theron! When the hell are you going to join the world again? You're the CEO of a company, partner. We need you here. We need you, man." Faustin sounded more concerned than angry. He paused and took a deep breath. "*Merde!* Pick up the phone, Theron. Please. I know you're there." He paused again. "All right, man. I'll be over in—"

Theron grabbed the phone. "Hey, Faustin," he said dully. He heard Faustin's long, deep sigh of relief.

"Christ, Theron! I've been calling every day. It's good to have you back. It took you long enough, man." Faustin's voice shook with emotion.

"Yeah? How long?"

"A week. A whole week, Theron."

"A week?" Theron still felt numb.

"Seven days. You never answered your phone in all that time. After the first two days I came over and let myself in. When I saw the state you were in I came every day. I listened to your rambling, your goddamn curses. But I bet you don't even know I was there. You were in zombieland, man. Drunk all the time."

"You're right. I don't remember. Sorry I put you through all that, *mon cher.*"

"So are you coming in?"

"Coming in?"

"Yes. Coming in. To the office. Trans-Global Solutions. Remember?"

"Oh, yeah, right. I guess I should clean up myself and head on over. I look like crap. How are things there?"

Faustin's tone became airy and excited. Theron was awake and beginning to sound lucid. "Everything's cool. Lots of calls—a couple from Guyana. Folks want to talk to you, guy. A bunch of new prospects came in, too. Nice work. Some of it is a bit out of our league, but the people who contacted us said they want no one but Trans-Global to do the job. I'm talking to someone who could give us the kind of expertise we would need for that kind of work. Should be coming in to see me today, in fact."

"I was in love with Dru, Faustin," Theron said abruptly.

Faustin sighed. He had wanted to put off dealing with the subject of Dru for as long as possible, hoping to perk Theron up first with all the exciting news at the firm. "I know, man. I know," he said soberly.

"You want to know what I regret the most? That I never got a chance to tell her so. I gave her the impression that I didn't care." Theron's voice cracked.

Faustin decided the best thing to do was to keep him talking. At least it would keep him from drowning himself in liquor. "You think it would have made a difference to her if you had told her? You really think she has the same feelings for you?"

"I don't know, man. All I know is that I loved her but I realized too late that it was important for me to let her know that."

"Nothing is ever too late. Come on in, Theron. It will do you good. You'll see."

"Okay. But don't hold it against me if I get sappy sometimes. I hurt bad, Faustin."

"Take a hot shower and get dressed. I'll bring over breakfast and we'll come back together."

Two hours later, Theron, shaved, combed, suited and fed, was sitting at his desk in his private office, staring at the walls and wondering if he had it in him to get back into the swing of things, or if he really wanted to do so. It still seemed too soon. His hurt was still raw.

Celine had brought him background documents on the new proposals that Faustin had spoken to him about earlier. He should have been reading them, but it was hard to concentrate. He knew he wasn't going to crawl into a hole again. He had made a decision to carry on with his life and he would stick to that decision. But sticking to that decision didn't mean he had stopped hurting, had stopped loving Dru. Stopped missing her. Wanting her. Her face was everywhere. He heard her voice at the oddest moments.

Celine's appearance with a pot of coffee and a new stack of papers and letters pulled his mind away from Dru. He thumbed through the documents absently. From the time he had taken off his jacket and sat down at his desk, Celine had been her usual officious self, reeling off matters he had to attend to, people he had to get in touch with right away. It was strange how she had greeted him—as if he had simply been away on business trip. True, her eyebrows had shot up when she saw how gaunt and drawn he was. But she had said nothing more than a brisk "Welcome back, Mr. St. Cyr." No expression of regret. No hug of sympathy or reassurance. No sad eyes. Nothing. Nothing even slightly reminiscent of the distraught woman who had broken the news to him of Dru's death.

But then, how could Celine know that part of him had died that day with Drucilla Durane? Only Faustin knew how he felt about Dru. He had no idea what Faustin had said to the staff, but he was sure that there had been no discussion of the nature of his relationship with the woman who was shot dead shortly after she had come to see him.

He sighed and tried again to concentrate on the papers before him. Soon, however, he found himself reading the same words over and over again. He shoved the papers aside. It was no use. His mind would not let Dru go. He needed more time.

He pushed himself up from his chair and moved about the office listlessly, touching mementos, picking up framed photographs of himself with various important people and putting them down again, straightening books on the shelves. He pulled out an original copy of *The Negro as a Business Man*, written by J. H. Harmon, Jr., Arnett G. Lindsay, and Carter

G. Woodson and published in 1929. Edited by Woodson, who was the first black man of slave parentage to earn a doctoral degree at Harvard University, the book covered black entrepreneurship in pre–Civil War America, and the historical role of black entrepreneurs in the banking and insurance industries. One of the entrepreneurs covered in the book was Theron's great-great-great-grandfather on his mother's side.

Theron had read the book twice, but he never tired of its rich lessons and always drew inspiration from its pages. As he thumbed through the book, he found himself thinking of Faustin, of his loyalty, his caring. He was the only one who had shown sympathy. Maybe Celine and the rest of the staff resented his leaving so suddenly, with no instructions on how to handle his portfolios. No, that couldn't be it. Celine was adroit enough to know what to do, how to respond to his clients. Besides, Faustin would have handled anything urgent that came up. Then what?

He looked up abruptly. Something Faustin had said. *How* he'd said it.

No, he would not think it. He dared not think it. It would be insane. Still, he had to find out.

He replaced the book and walked across the hall to Faustin's office. The door was ajar, but as was his custom, he knocked twice—two short, sharp raps—before he went in. Faustin was sitting at his desk. "Faustin, what did you mean when you said—" He stopped, realizing that Faustin had a visitor. A woman. She sat facing Faustin, her back to the door.

"I'm sorry. I didn't realize you had company," Theron said. "I'll come back later." He turned to leave.

"Wait, Theron. Don't go. You should speak to my visitor. She is considering joining our firm. Maybe you can persuade her to do so," Faustin said quickly.

He stood up and moved from behind his desk. The woman stood up, too, and turned, slowly, until she faced Theron. Seeing her, Theron felt as if his knees had turned to water. His chest constricted and he thought he would die of suffocation.

The woman spoke. "Hello, Theron."

Theron stared at her. *She looks so much like Dru, sounds so much like her, but Dru is dead.*

He raised his hand and opened his mouth to say something, but the words caught in his throat. His hand fell limply to his side. He saw that the woman was staring back at him. He managed a croak. "Are you her twin?"

"No. I'm Dru."

"But you're…you're dead." His voice came out in a whisper.

"I'm not. I'm here." Her voice was filled with anguish.

Theron eyed her suspiciously. *She's lying.* He was beginning to think that a game was in progress and that he was at the center of it. What was Faustin trying to do? Was this his sick idea of a way to make him feel better? *Set me up with someone who looks like Dru and I'll live happily ever after?* He would play along, see how far Faustin and this Dru look-alike would go.

He whispered again, angling his head toward the woman. "What are you doing here if you're dead?"

"But I'm not dead, Theron. Can't you see?" Her eyes pleaded with him to believe her.

Faustin could stand it no longer. He planted himself between the two and glared at Theron. "Oh, for chrissakes, Theron. It's Dru, you idiot. In the flesh. She didn't die," he snapped. He sucked his teeth loudly and stalked out of the room muttering something that sounded like "seven days of hell" and slammed the door behind him.

The noise seemed to jolt Theron out of his denial. He took a step closer to Dru. "How is it that you're not dead? They told me at the hospital that the dead woman was Drucilla Durane," he said, his voice was thick with emotion. His eyes remained fixed on hers as he waited for her answer.

"I…I. She…the woman…" Dru gave up. Her eyes brimmed. She swallowed hard and bit her lip, trying to stanch the tears. She tried again. "Theron—"

It was enough for Theron. He swallowed the space between them in two giant strides and gathered her to him. "Don't speak. Don't speak," he moaned.

They remained crushed against each other for a long moment. Finally, Dru eased back and pressed her palms against Theron's chest. "There's a simple explanation," she began.

"It can wait," Theron interrupted her. He held her away from him and looked into her eyes searchingly. "Why didn't you come to me? Why didn't Faustin tell me?"

"I went to see you. Once. With Faustin. But you were—how did he put it?—in zombieland. And it looked as though you were going to stay there for a long time. You stared at me and started to yell that I had no right to do what I did. You were so angry. I took that to mean you didn't want me around; that you had found out that I told Lawton everything in front of Grant. It was a foolish thing for me to do. I didn't listen to you. I thought I could handle it myself. It wasn't until later that I realized I had put your life in danger by letting Grant know what I knew. I went to your office to warn you. The same day of…of the shooting."

Dru leaned against Theron and he wrapped his arms around her again. "I didn't mean those things I said, Dru. I don't even remember saying those things. I was angry, yes. I thought I had been cheated again. I believed you had cheated me by dying. I didn't know about you and Lawton and Grant, though I suspected something like that had happened. When they told me you were dead, I hoped desperately they had made a mistake. I prayed it wasn't you."

Dru's voice was muffled against his chest. "The woman was crazy. She grabbed my purse just before the shot was fired. I didn't have a picture ID on me. Just credit cards, my checkbook, other stuff with my name and address on it. My driver's license had expired and I stopped carrying it around. I haven't yet gotten around to renewing it. So naturally they assumed she was me. I've renewed it since then, though."

Her words hung in the air for a while. Abruptly, Theron held her away from him and said, "What did you say about the woman who died?"

"I said she was crazy. Insane. She had just grabbed my purse when the bullet that was meant for me hit her."

"The bullet that was meant for you? So Bernat *did* try to kill you."

"Apparently not. It turns out the man who did the shooting was Bernat's contractor who went rogue. He died in a car accident minutes later, incidentally. The man's driver tried to run but he was badly hurt in the crash and collapsed a few feet from the car. The police checked him out when they found guns in the limo. He had a record. He was a low-level employee of a local crime gang. The police roughed him up and he told them everything he knew."

"So the police eventually found you and fixed the ID mistake. They must have asked you why you were a target. What did you tell them?"

"I told them I had no idea why. I suggested it might be a case of mistaken identity and they left it at that. No way was I going to mention the name Bernat, or anything to do with drugs, Theron. For all I know, Bernat could have members of the police force on his payroll."

"Thank God, it's over," Theron breathed.

"Yes, thank God. The whole thing was a horrible ordeal."

They remained silent for a while, relishing the feeling of utter relief at being together, alive and well. After a while, Theron led her to the sofa Faustin had installed in his office for his afternoon "power-regeneration naps" and they sat down, holding hands.

"So what happens now, Dru? What becomes of us? You and me?"

Dru held his gaze. "I was very mean to you, Theron. I believed the worst about you. All those years. You have no reason to want there to be an 'us.' No reason to forgive me."

"Yes, I do, Dru. I have every reason to," Theron said huskily.

Dru looked away. "What…what is your reason?" Her voice shook.

"Look at me." Dru turned back to him and he continued. "I went to your house. I was worried sick about you. I was going to tell you how I felt about you, but you were gone."

"So tell me now."

"I love you."

"I love you, too."

Theron's face registered surprise.

"What?" Dru asked.

"That's it? 'I love you, too?' Just like that?"

"Yes. Just like that. Let's not complicate things."

Theron sighed happily. "Yes. Let's not. It's been one misunderstanding after another between us. From the moment we met. No more misunderstandings."

For a long time they sat holding each other, saying nothing, savoring everything about this place they had found at the end of the tortured road each had traveled since their meeting in Marseille.

Soon, Theron eased Dru gently away from him, held her at arm's length, and spoke into her eyes. "Let's start over. Let's go back to the very beginning. *Our* beginning," he said.

Dru clung to his gaze and waited for him to continue. But he didn't. He remained silent, watching her.

The silence stretched out.

Dru arched an eyebrow. She rolled her neck and crossed her eyes.

Theron broke into a slow smile. "We'll fly to Paris and take the train to Marseille." he said. "When can you leave?"

"Whenever you want me to, boss." Dru said.

EPILOGUE

Grant Featherhorn sipped his beer casually and focused on the man approaching him. He didn't recognize the man, but he took in his exquisitely tailored seersucker suit and Italian loafers. No tan, which said to Featherhorn that he had just landed from North America or Europe. A reporter?

Featherhorn frowned, took off his sunglasses, and squinted at the man. He wasn't afraid of reporters. It's just that they sometimes disturbed the peace and peace was what he had come to this Caribbean island to find.

The man smiled at him and waved. Featherhorn nodded and continued to sip his beer.

The man drew closer, striding confidently, too confidently, Featherhorn thought.

Panic engulfed him, but only for a moment. He chided himself. *What do I have to fear?* Hadn't he straightened out all that business with Pilgrim Boone and Savoy? And brilliantly, he might add.

Once again he felt very pleased with himself. He felt pleased with himself every time he thought of the way things had turned out. He had hired the best lawyer his millions could buy and had beaten jail with a couple of million in hush money. True, he had had to sign those awful documents that Bloomington and Lawton had shoved at him. Parker could have shown more gumption; could have put up more of a fight on his behalf, he thought bitterly.

He sighed. His sudden resignation from Pilgrim Boone had been enough to raise all kinds of rumors on Wall Street, none of which was flattering. He suspected that it was Bloomington's lawyers who had hinted to the press about certain habits he had, but he couldn't make a fuss about that. Why give life to the rumors? No, when all was said and done, things hadn't turn out too badly. He would make a comeback, he vowed silently, as the man in the seersucker suit approached his table. *I'll make a comeback so big that every last one of them who slighted me like I was pig dung will come groveling.*

He was staying at the luxurious Half Moon Resort in Montego Bay, Jamaica. He had deserved a vacation, he told himself. After all the brouhaha, he needed to get away and regroup, to come up with a plan that would put him back on top. A major publishing house had already approached him to do a book. They had offered him a ghostwriter and a juicy seven figures. Ostensibly, he was in seclusion thinking about the offer, but he had already made up his mind to take it. The book might even be made into a movie, the publishing house had hinted.

"Hello there. May I join you?"

"Please. Have a seat," Featherhorn said with a warm smile, indicating the chair across from him. He was at Seagrape Terrace, one of the resort's top restaurants located on Sunset Beach. Though it was outdoors, his table was shaded from the blazing Caribbean sun by the restaurant's famed buttonwood canopy.

The stranger sat down. "I'm François Lescault," he said, extending his hand to Featherhorn. He had that deep, rich voice that was common among European men.

"And I'm Grant Featherhorn," Featherhorn said, glancing at the man's hand as he grasped it. It was a not-too-soft, professionally manicured hand. It spoke of wealth and pampering, but also of work. This was not a man who idled the days away. He had *an occupation*, Featherhorn surmised. He appraised the stranger again: handsome, trim and fit, in his early forties. Inexplicably, he was relieved that the man's accent was not American.

"Yes, I know who you are," the man said pleasantly as he withdrew his hand.

"You do? But I'm sorry. I'm forgetting my manners. May I offer you a drink?"

"Certainly, thank you. I'll have whatever you are drinking."

Featherhorn signaled a waiter, who came over at once. "A Red Stripe for my guest and one more for me," he told the waiter.

The waiter departed and Featherhorn turned his gaze back to Lescault. He said, "From your accent I take it you're French. And how do you know me, may I ask?"

"Yes, I am French. And you're being modest, Mr. Featherhorn. You are a famous man. Surely you know that your face and your name have been all over the newspapers—and not just in America." Lescault's smile lit up his liquid gray eyes.

Featherhorn nodded deprecatingly. "And what brings you to Jamaica, may I ask? Surely you're not here to get my autograph," he said. He liked the Frenchman, but he wasn't quite at ease with him. There was something unsettling about his—Featherhorn struggled to find the appropriate word—*overconfidence?*

Lescault laughed. "Oh, no. I'm here on much more serious business," he said.

The waiter arrived with their beer. The two men remained silent as he opened the bottles and filled their glasses.

"What kind of business are you in, Mr. Lescault?" Featherhorn asked when the waiter had left.

Lescault didn't answer. He picked up his glass and raised it in a toast. "Here's to life," he said.

Featherhorn touched his glass to Lescault's. "Here's to life," he repeated.

Lescault took a long swig. "Aahhh!" he uttered appreciatively when he finally lowered his glass. "This is a very good beer. It has a seductive texture. It embodies everything that is right about the Caribbean."

"It is one of the best indeed. But you have not answered my question," Featherhorn said.

"Ah, yes. My line of business." Lescault looked straight into Featherhorn's eyes. "I am a contractor, Mr. Featherhorn."

"Construction?"

"No, Mr. Featherhorn. I am a contractor in the employ of a real estate developer in Venezuela," Lescault said quietly.

Featherhorn's face collapsed. The calm in Lescault's voice filled him with dread. His life was in danger. He looked around as if to call for help, but Lescault placed a warning hand on his, gave him a warm smile, and said, "You signed documents pertaining to certain discussions you had with my employer about a pending transaction in Georgetown, Guyana. Because of these documents that you signed, a great deal of attention is being paid to my employer and his various businesses, Mr. Featherhorn. My employer is a very discreet man. His discretion is the key to his success. It is why he has earned the trust and respect of so many around the world. So you see, Mr. Featherhorn, this new and very great attention has caused him tremendous loss of face—and therefore business—among his peers."

Featherhorn's bowels felt loose. He tried to pull his hand away but Lescault held fast to his wrist. His grip was like a steel vise.

Lescault continued in the same calm voice. "Your betrayal is unforgivable, Mr. Featherhorn."

Grant Featherhorn died in his hotel room that night. The local medical examiner ruled the cause of death "an overdose of pure cocaine."

When the news broke in the United States, no one was surprised—not after all the rumors that flooded Wall Street when he resigned from Pilgrim Boone.

ABOUT THE AUTHOR

Rosalind Kilkenny McLymont is the executive editor of *The Network Journal* and CEO of AfricaStrictlyBusiness. com. A former managing editor of *The Journal of Commerce*, a Knight Ridder Corporation and subsequently Economist Group publication, she is the author of the groundbreaking "rebranding Africa" novel *Middle Ground* and of the nonfiction title *Africa Strictly Business: The Steady March to Prosperity*. She migrated to the United States from Guyana in 1965. A graduate of The City College of New York and New York University and a European Union Fellow, she spent several years in Uganda and the Democratic Republic of Congo as a teacher; served as an entrepreneurship development expert for the United Nations Development Program's Africa Bureau; traveled to Russia with the Alliance of Russian and American Women as a citizen ambassador to contribute to the professional development of women; and served two terms on the Sub-Saharan Africa Advisory Committee of the Export-Import Bank of the United States. She lives in New York with her husband.